Allen Hoey
June 75
$3⁵⁰
90K

The Sinking
of the Odradek Stadium
and Other Novels

Books by Harry Mathews

THE SINKING OF THE ODRADEK STADIUM AND OTHER NOVELS
TLOOTH
THE CONVERSIONS

The Sinking
of the Odradek Stadium
and Other Novels

HARRY MATHEWS

HARPER & ROW, PUBLISHERS

New York Evanston San Francisco London

THE SINKING OF THE ODRADEK STADIUM AND OTHER NOVELS. Copyright © 1975 by Harry Mathews. All rights reserved. Printed in the United States of America. No part of this book may be used or reproduced in any manner whatsoever without written permission except in the case of brief quotations embodied in critical articles and reviews. For information address Harper & Row, Publishers, Inc., 10 East 53rd Street, New York, N.Y. 10022. Published simultaneously in Canada by Fitzhenry & Whiteside Limited, Toronto.

FIRST EDITION

LIBRARY OF CONGRESS CATALOG CARD NUMBER: 74-15881

ISBN (cloth): 0-06-012839-9
ISBN (paper): 0-06-012841-0

73 74 75 76 77 10 9 8 7 6 5 4 3 2 1

Contents

The Conversions

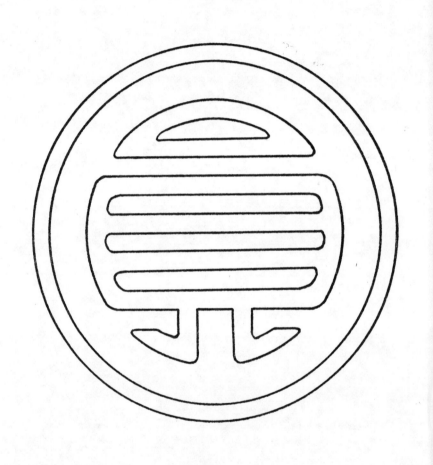

•

THE ADZE

The wealthy amateur Grent Wayl invited me to his New York house for an evening's diversion. Welcoming me, he said: The cheek of our Bea! pointing to his niece, Miss Beatrice Fod, who, accompanied on the harmonium by her brother Isidore, sang to assembled guests.

> At night when you're asleep
> Without no pants on
> Into your tent I'll creep
> Without no pants on

Such nervous speech! Why should he mind, since the song delighted the company? Mr. Wayl was

aging, aging; but no one would take his words
lightly.

He led me upstairs to see one of his new acquisi-
tions. In the library Mr. Wayl laid an oblong case
of green leather on a white table. Having turned on a
ceiling spotlight to illuminate the case, he opened it.
A weapon rested on the brilliant red lining, its smooth
handle of ash, its billshaped flat blade of gold.

According to Mr. Wayl, the instrument was a
ritual adze. The side of the bill we had first beheld
was plain, but its reverse was chased with wiry engravings, depicting seven scenes. Six had in common
the figure of a longhaired woman with full breasts
and a face crosshatched for swarthiness. Mr. Wayl
suggested that the woman was some heroine or saint,
and that the engravings told her life. He looked at me
curiously while he said this.

Mr. Wayl asked me to interpret the series of engravings.

I began with the leftmost scene, in the point of the
blade, where the woman stood naked at the mouth of
a stream, with a pile of cowrie shells at her feet. The
subject hardly suited the life of a saint, but I took it
to be a decorative conceit—a quaint medieval mixture
of pagan and Christian themes.

To the right of this, the woman stood upon clouds,
above a throng of striped men bearing staves shaped
like inverted L's. Below the clouds a disc emanated
crooked spikes, while lower still people on the earth
raised their hands. This clearly seemed to be the saint's
manifestation, a descent from heaven. The stave-bear-
ing figures were angels with pennons, the spiked disc
the rejoicing sun.

In the next engraving the woman held one side of a small wreath; a man in simple vestments held the opposite side. I thought this man must be Christ presenting the saint with a crown of holiness.

The fourth scene showed the woman among battling knights, who were drawn gruesome and pathetic. The saint was surely putting an end to some battle, if not to war itself.

Next, the woman appeared outside a burning grove. Within it there were many tormented figures. She lifted her arms in supplication, as would befit one pleading for the damned.

In the sixth scene the woman knelt in front of a mitred priest who stretched his left hand over her. A fire, which I interpreted as a symbol of divine love, burned in the background. I had no doubt the scene showed the saint blessed by some pope.

The woman did not figure in the last engraving. I supposed it to be decorative, like the first one: radii of one small arc, four arrows pointed to symbols representing the quarters of the moon. A bag of fish—possibly a Christian reference—hung below.

Mr. Wayl had grown impatient during my remarks. He now exclaimed: You're as dumb as is!

Excuse me, sir, I said, if your pleasure was marred.

He was suddenly friendly: No one with purple eyes is stupid. But do you have perfect pitch?

I answered that I had. Leaving the library, he took the adze with him.

•

PREPARATIONS

As we descended the stairs Mr. Wayl stopped me. Listen! Miss Fod was singing:

> The second queen was an Amazon
> With a terrible spear of brass

Such music! said Mr. Wayl. A real old tune—a lass's tenor. You must recognize it.
I listened:

> Whistling the devil's salvation
> In a girdle of crimson cowries

The three queens made thunder
And snapped stones with a feather
But Black Jack was the smartest crack
And married them all together

There was applause. Mr. Wayl had left me listening; he now stood, encircled by the company, next to his niece and nephew. Following his summons I joined them.

Tonight's game, he said, will be a race. The contestants are Bea and Is, whom you all know, and—his hand on my shoulder—this gentleman. The prize will be my antique adze.

Servants entered to draw back the curtains at one side of the drawing-room, then to open the sliding panels of glass that formed the wall behind. We overlooked a greenhouse, whose fragrant heat rose quickly about us, but which we could see little of: it was unlighted except for three parallel bands, about two yards long, that were sunk in its floor near us. These shone dull green.

That is the course, said Mr. Wayl. The bands, which are covered with a thin layer of salt slime, are lighted from below so that you can follow the race.

The contestants will be represented by these. He held out his opened cigarette case: in it lay small sticks of tobacco-colored stuff with a tuft of tangled white thread at the end of each.

Worms called zephyrs. They are dried out but alive; moisture will quicken them. On the course, which is wet, they will find in front of them a trail of their habitual food (tiny pharaohs) that will lead them to the finish.

As for the human contestants, they will do more than watch. Each must accompany his worm's advance with an ascending major scale, to be played on one of these instruments; as you doubtless know, they are named serpents.

Mr. Wayl detached three S-ish wooden tubes from a wall panel behind him, fitted their lesser ends with silver mouthpieces, and silently demonstrated a scale on one of them, progressively unstopping its six finger-holes. The lowest and highest notes were obtained with all the holes stopped.

It is curious, he said, that the holes are divided into groups of three by a length of wood having no proportion to the acoustical distance between the fourth and fifth notes of the scale. Nor do the spaces between the other holes vary with the interval; the holes are apparently bored for the convenience of the fingers. Yet the results are just. Thus with all holes open: see? With one: *re*. With three: *fa*. (Since these are C-serpents, the scale names are true.)

At the beginning of the race each contestant will play the lower *do*. The course bands are marked with six indentations; as his worm passes them the contestant must sound the subsequent tones—*re* at the first marker, *mi* at the second, and so on. Without this accompaniment the worm's progress counts for nothing. The race will end with the first high *do*.

Mr. Wayl gave us our instruments.

For you, Bea, a fine French example made for the Duchess of Lissixg, who was known as "the Imp Queen"—but I can't remember the Latin for imp.

Is will have the favorite serpent of Dericar Ciorc, the virtuoso.

And you will have this one. It's wound with masking tape to cover some disturbing scenes painted on it; otherwise it's sound.

Take your places.

We entered the conservatory and knelt, each with a horn, at the end of our appointed bands. Servants knelt next to us, ready with our quiet worms.

Presently the drawing-room lights went out. Mr. Wayl said, Begin.

·

THE RACE

Do: unevenly, the three horns gave the note in the near darkness. The servants placed our worms in the reviving ooze. I watched mine through the green-lighted fringe of the foxtail mat on which I knelt: it lay still. To my left Beatrice Fod urged hers on with whispers, then blew a new note on her serpent—a hesitant semitone.

Patience, said Mr. Wayl from the threshold of the drawing-room.

There was a faint white light in the greenhouse, barely more than a drifting phosphorescence. My worm curled, untangling the bunched thread at his tip in thin exploratory tentacles that looked like rapid-flowering vine tendrils. His tan body was now a pale whitish-green. Moving, he glided quick over the green glass in a curious curve. My eyes were already numb from straining in the dim light when he swerved around the first black marker.

Re I sounded clearly; but Beatrice followed only with her faltering C-sharp. There was laughter from the next room. Turning I saw its cause: an old guest sitting in an overstuffed chair nodded drowsily among the onlookers. Some sort of dark-blue light had been made to shine on him, and against the faint phosphorescent whiteness that still filled the air he appeared to be covered with thick soot. Despite the laughter, he dozed on.

My zephyr slid swiftly forward. It was then I noticed that the path he had taken was marked by a nearly invisible trail of black: a broken irregular line.

Beatrice, in spite of her worm's advance, could not force her intermittent C-sharp to the desired *re*. Is Fod as yet made no sound. My worm touched the second marker. I played

Mi, followed by a sigh of wonder from the watchers, while under my eyes the worm's black trail suddenly turned a sullen green. Looking up, I saw on the wall beyond the course's finish the prize adze, flashing red in some beam cast on it from an unseen point. The vision was the color of my inner eye! I nearly forgot to follow my worm; and when I next observed him he was already at the third marker.

Fa: my lips and lungs blared the note out while my eyes fixed the fiery adze: but as I played, it dropped abruptly into darkness. Again there was a bustle in the drawing-room. All now looked towards the glass case, placed on a small stand in the center of the room, where the fifteen-pound Slauss sapphire was exposed. The jewel glowed as if illuminated from within: its clarity was now clustered with entwined tenuous red veins. We beheld it thus for a few moments until we heard an unexpected *re* from Is Fod's serpent. As soon as the note was sounded the sapphire turned a translucent black that darkened but did not obscure the red skein within.

When my zephyr attained the fourth marker, I made my only mistake of the race. With *fa* I had unstopped the last of the first set of fingerholes. Between it and the next hole lay the abnormal extent of closed tube that Mr. Wayl had mentioned. Uncovering the *sol* hole I tried to compensate for its position by slackening my lips; I only succeeded in producing a faltering *fa diesis*.

Every light was extinguished, even the faint green course-lights. An unusual darkness suffused the conservatory and the drawing-room. Without color or light, it seemed to have its own thick splendor; and this impression was confirmed when I found that I could still barely discern the line trailed by the advancing worm. I recognized too that this line formed not a haphazard figure, but letters.

I had forgotten to correct my mistake. Only when the silence that followed the sudden darkness had been broken by the embarrassed coughing of Miss Dryrein (Mr. Wayl's secretary) did I remember to play.

Sol: the chocolate blackness was at once pierced by a moving ray of yellow light.

I call this Midas's finger, said Mr. Wayl. And in fact whatever the beam touched acquired the luster and massiveness of gold. The sapphire, the harmonium, Mr. Wayl, Miss Dryrein, and, one by one, all the guests were subjected to the illusory transformation. Ima Mutés, the Catalan *entreteneuse*, was applauded: her evening gown was made of a tightly coiled spiral of velvet snakes.

The yellow beam was entering the greenhouse when Is Fod sounded his *mi*. The adze again turned a brilliant red. When the yellow ray came to rest on it, its red did not change to gold but deepened in the midst of a golden haze.

The light had proved me right: my worm had left letters in his trail—in the reflected yellow they glowed purple. But I had no time to study them. My worm was at the fifth marker.

La. The adze again disappeared, as well as the moving beam. Instead violet light flooded that drowsy guest whom we had last seen covered with soot. This time the laughter of the other guests roused him, and he opened his eyes, which flashed weirdly, casting thin lilac-colored shafts into the surrounding darkness. A girl cried out, *O Papa, tu m'fais peur!* The old man went back to sleep. The worm-letters took on yellowness, while the course was black in the violet glow.

Beatrice uttered a final breath into her serpent: still the same quavering C-sharp, dull whiteness guttering for a moment about the violet guest. Balls! We heard a whirring noise and a brief splintering of glass as Beatrice skied her horn through the conservatory roof. Draughts of February air swirled about us.

My *si* was followed at once by Is Fod's *fa*. Pink

flooded the course, its bands turning blue, the leech's trail a brighter yellow. At the end of each band a pool of purple light revealed our worms' goal: spider crabs, with ponderous claws and backs overgrown with trailing parasites. Opposite me the crab, seeing his prey so close, waited, while the one facing Is Fod started at a sluggish pace after his. Beatrice's worm had already been eaten.

I watched the eyestalks of the waiting crab lower. Just as the nippers pinched the slender swerving body Mr. Wayl said to me, Finish. The high *do* came satisfactorily forth, the air was filled for a moment with a kind of swimming silver, and finally in greenhouse and drawing-room the lights went on. My eyes were tired and blurred. When they cleared, the course bands were empty of light, leeches, and crabs. There only remained the trail of triturated food and slime my lost worm had left, broken marks of a shiny blackness among which I recognized certain letters:

e   as   no   s   ex   rex   noth   Syl i

Get rid of that, Mr. Wayl said to a servant. To me: That was not what I meant. I tried to lay down his food so that he would spell . . . But the result is nothing—fragments.

The race had lasted an hour. Taking my prize with me, I soon left.

·

FIRST
INQUIRIES

I found out why Mr. Wayl thought my eyes were purple: he was colorblind. Other remarks of his remained obscure—why, for instance, had he felt that I should recognize the song Beatrice had been singing when we left the library? Throughout the evening Mr. Wayl had treated me with singular attention. He had shown me the adze privately. From a large company of guests he had chosen me to compete with the two Fods, known to be his only heirs. He had been pleased, and not at all surprised, that I won the contest. Why?

As Mr. Wayl had taken pains to interest me in the images worked on the face of the adze-head, I thought it might be rewarding to learn more about them. So a few days after the party I called Miss Dryrein to ask her for any information she had concerning the adze. While she knew next to nothing herself (Mr. Wayl had secreted, in a safety-box to which she had no access, what relevant documents there were), she suggested I consult the former owner of the adze, from whom it had been bought only a few months before.

This person, a minor novelist, at once agreed to see me. I called at his apartment in Bethune Street one evening and there, with a bottle of pisco to maintain us, he told me what he knew.

●

"THE SORES"

It was on a night in the autumn of last year that I came into possession of the adze. Late one afternoon I had gone to the Plaza, where a cocktail party was being given in connection with the publication of one of my books. Perhaps you've read it—a short novel called *The Sores*? It was dark when I left. I was in an impressionable state; I had drunk a lot, and eaten little, and the hours of party talk had left me agitated. I remember standing on the steps of the hotel when I left, suddenly exalted by the cold air and the illuminated city. A sweet restlessness came over me. I decided to

hire one of the carriages drawn up on the Park side of
Fifty-ninth Street for a long drive. At first I could not
find a willing driver, but one at last agreed to take me
out to a Long Island beach. He warned me the trip
would last through the night; but I had no objection
to that.

We set off, soon crossing the Queensborough
Bridge. I'm not sure where we went afterwards—I think
we started out through Maspeth and later skirted
South Ozone. I don't know the city well at all, and in
any case I was soon sunk in my dreams. I thought
about my childhood, women, and the war, I recited
poems and sang through scenes of opera, I thought of
the future, especially of trips I would like to make to
Morocco, to Sweden, to Afghanistan. Later I thought
of the evening I had just passed, and finally of my
book. I hadn't really thought of the book in a long
time, having been too busy proofing it and discussing
it with readers, publishers and reviewers. Softly shaken
in the slow carriage, I renewed my lost enthusiasm.

It concerns three American men who meet in the
restaurant of the Copenhagen airport. Their acquaintance begins at the smörgåsbord table, where each reveals a taste for bitter pickled onions. All three are
waiting for the same flight, a departure for San Francisco across the Arctic Sea. At first they would seem
to have nothing more in common. One of them, Jacob
Pendastrava, is a sociologist, recently engaged on an
inquiry into the variables of joy. Pownoll Toker Williaus is vice-president of a company that manufactures
foundation garments, the Press-You-Nigh Stays, Inc.
Noah La Vas, the youngest of the three, is an engineer
whose specialty is the slowing of high winds. He has

recently invented a kind of inverted pendulum which, projected into a wind-channel by powerful hydraulic springs, tends to set up restraining crosscurrents.

Their first conversation lags. Williaus hums nervously to fill the silence. La Vas in surprise recognizes the tune: Why that's *Wehe Wintgen Wehe*! What! says Williaus, You mean . . . This is too good to be true, adds Pendastrava. They have found a common enthusiasm; they are all three amateurs of old German music. A jubilant discussion of Sweelinck, Schein and Schütz, illustrated with musical examples, lasts until boarding time and through the first hours of flight.

When fatigue overcomes the majority of the passengers (very late in the night, for since it is June the plane is flying in sunlight), the three men, respecting the sleep of their fellow travelers, withdraw to the lounge in the tail of the plane. They too are tired, and they decide to play cards for a while. Pendastrava teaches his friends an antique form of cribbage. They have played for about an hour, and Williaus has just completed his fifteen with a jack of spades, when the cards and markers suddenly swarm in the air around them. Then they themselves are pitched from their chairs as the plane falls. The crash occurs; they find themselves battered but alive. La Vas succeeds in getting outside. He finds that the tail-section of the plane, broken off from the bulk of the fuselage, is resting on a flat expanse of ice. Before him there is a huge hole of black water. There is no sign of any other survivor or wreckage.

Williaus joins La Vas, and the two of them help Pendastrava, whose left leg is broken, down on to the ice. Making him as comfortable as possible, they return to the wreck to see what they can salvage. As the luggage is stored at the very tail-end of the plane, they find plenty of clothes, and also a closetful of blankets. But the galley and its stores, located behind the pilot's cabin, are lost. All the food they can find is a half-dozen cans and pots of dainties, souvenirs of tourists homeward bound: pâté de foie gras, smoked eel, sweet-breads in wine, pickled mushrooms, an Edam cheese, and a bottle of *grappa*. From the remaining contents of the luggage, La Vas and Williaus take several tubes of aspirin, a sheath knife, a compass, and a pistol (a small .30-caliber automatic) with two boxes of car-tridges.

The next concern of the two men is Pendastrava's leg. La Vas proves his ingenuity by disassembling and reshaping the metal tubes out of which the lounge fur-niture is made. From them, with the aid of belts and wire, he constructs a huge splint. Shaped like a U with one side greater than the other, this splint, fitted into the groin and armpit of the injured man, not only keeps his leg rigid but also serves as a fixed crutch, enabling him to stand without having his leg touch the ground or support his body's weight.

Everything to be taken from the plane is brought out, for the wrecked tail is slowly sinking through the ice. The three men consider their situation. They de-cide that since a search will surely be made to discover the fate of their plane, they should stay next to the wreck, where they have a better chance of being seen from the air, until it sinks. On the other hand, they decide to prepare for a worst, that is, for a long trek southward over the ice in case they are not soon res-cued. Thus the small amount of food at their disposal is to be severely rationed, and a part, the can of eel, set aside for use as fish-bait. Seawater is to be drunk from the start to avoid the harmful effects it might have if taken after prolonged thirst.

Most of the day has passed. Williaus spends the early evening preparing a tent out of blankets. La Vas fishes in the hole made by the sunken plane, but he has no luck. The morale of the men is good, tired as they are. Only Pendastrava shows any signs of despondency—his leg has been hurting him considerably. Even he becomes cheerful after a swallow of *grappa*. The three men sing *Ein fester Burg ist unser Gott*, in Schütz's harmonization. They feel no touch of loneliness in that lifeless tract of raw whiteness, but sleep well through the sunny night, La Vas and Williaus taking turns to watch.

The morning of the next day passes without event. The weather is bright and mild. La Vas explores the vicinity of their camp, finding nothing. Williaus fishes for several hours without success. Pendastrava rests; his leg bothers him less.

At midday a fire of sorts is made, and the can of sweetbreads is heated and half eaten.

During the afternoon an airplane, flying at about a thousand feet, passes many miles to the north of them. Of the several search planes sent out, this is the only one the survivors ever see.

The following day Pendastrava makes his first attempt to walk, but is obliged to give up after a few steps. His general condition has nonetheless improved.

On the afternoon of the fifth day the tail wreckage disappears. The hole it leaves is separated by only a few feet from the larger one caused by the crash; the

two holes soon become one. The men decide to abandon their efforts to catch fish, preserving their bait for
richer waters.

The next day, the sixth, the pot of goose-liver patty
is opened, the mushrooms, as well as the sweetbreads,
having been finished. Pendastrava, who is exhausted by
the few steps he has managed to take earlier in the day,
vomits the small share of patty he swallows. This
causes the first break in morale since the crash: La Vas
loses his temper and berates Pendastrava for his weakness and stupidity. Pendastrava answers feebly but
bitterly.

In the course of the afternoon Williaus tries to reconcile his companions. He evidently succeeds. That
night, however, at the hour when the three men usually sang together, Pendastrava refuses to join them.
His excuse is that he cares too much for the music,
which requires four voices, to like hearing it botched
by three. But it is his silence that makes the singing
impossible: La Vas and Williaus give up their sad
duet. For the first time the three find the lifeless silence
heavy, and the night sun sharp. All sleep little.

Matters do not improve next morning. A running
argument begins between La Vas and the other men.
La Vas insists that they start southward at once since
a week has already passed and the efforts to find them
have probably been abandoned: they must cover
ground while they still have some food. The others
feel that the departure must be postponed as long as
possible so that Pendastrava's injured leg may heal—
otherwise, how can they make any worthwhile progress?

The discussion is interminable and pointless. The

three men are starting to get weak, not so much from the lack of nourishment as from exposure. The glare of ice and sun is wrecking their eyes, and making them suffer from almost uninterrupted headaches. The consumption of seawater, minimal but constant, has also had its effect in the pain and cramp that molest their bowels. They are no longer reasonable and only La Vas has much energy for facing the problems of their predicament. The other two—especially Pendastrava —prefer to take refuge in a lethargic hope of rescue.

The senseless argument immobilizes the survivors. Scoring small points in the harangues becomes their main preoccupation, each man clinging to his point of view in spite of fact or need. La Vas is absurdly brutal during the first days of the argument, when Pendastrava's leg is in truth unfit for a day's march; while to safeguard the importance of his injury, the latter will not exercise his leg even when he feels capable of doing so. Williaus, in his role of nurse and protector, seconds this passivity.

It is not until six more days have passed that the three men break camp and start south. There is practically no more food: they have finished the eel, except for two slivers kept as bait, and nearly half the Edam cheese.

Nevertheless the departure is a boon for their spirits. Pendastrava is heroic in his efforts to advance, while the other two work in relay to help him and, during the rests, to take care of him. By evening they have advanced seven miles, according to La Vas's estimate. Although they are too tired to speak much, a new fellowship unites them.

The following day, the fifteenth after the crash,

Pendastrava's condition permits them to cover only about five miles. A long rest is salutary: a march of eight miles is made the next day, ten the day after that, and this average is kept up for two days more. The travelers observe a few seabirds, too distant to shoot at.

On the morning of the twentieth day, Pendastrava takes a hard fall on the ice. His leg hurts him terribly when he resumes his march. He is obliged to rest every two or three minutes and can advance only several hundred yards in an hour. The day's march is of less than three miles, only one mile having been covered after his fall.

Pendastrava is worse the next morning: his leg is swollen and sore. Even helped by his companions he is hardly able to walk at all, and the other men are far too weak to carry him. They barely advance a mile in nine hours. By that time the men are frantic with fatigue and despair. Pendastrava is in continual pain. He refuses to speak to the others.

During the night Pendastrava filches and eats the remaining morsel of cheese. His act is discovered at noon the next day, after five hours of painful meager progress. La Vas begins kicking the prostrate Pendastrava. When Williaus intervenes, La Vas knocks him down.

In the middle of the afternoon, during a prolonged rest, La Vas takes Williaus aside. He apologizes for having struck him, and goes on to give his view of their predicament: the only way out is to abandon Pendastrava. With him they will starve; without him, there is a chance that the two of them will reach the edge of the Arctic basin where they will find a plenty of fish and birds. Since it is inhuman to leave Pendastrava to die slowly, he should be shot. La Vas offers to do this, and asks Williaus to give him the pistol. Williaus refuses, wishing to think over the other's plan.

The march is resumed. When it is his turn to help Pendastrava, Williaus lets La Vas go a ways ahead of them. He then tells Pendastrava of La Vas's plan. Pendastrava demands the gun, and Williaus gives it to him. The sun is low, and a soft wind rises.

Williaus calls La Vas to take his turn with the injured man. Setting Pendastrava down on the ice, Williaus draws a few steps away, and stands turned away from the others. He hears La Vas cry out and looking around sees that Pendastrava is aiming the gun not at La Vas, but at him. La Vas runs slowly towards Pendastrava; Williaus screams; Pendastrava aims but holds his fire. When Pendastrava finally becomes aware of La Vas's approach, he turns the pistol towards him and shoots him through the chest. The stricken man falls on Pendastrava. Williaus's terror of Pendastrava changes to infinite anger and he runs whimpering to punish him. The latter is pinned beneath the dying La Vas and cannot even speak. Williaus strikes and scratches at his face. At last, seeing the gun lying on the ice where it has slid from Pendastrava's hand, he crawls to get it and returns to strike Pendastrava repeatedly in the face with the gun butt. Pendastrava struggles helplessly, trapped under La Vas's body. He is soon killed by the blows.

Shaking and exhausted, Williaus collapses on the ice near the two bodies. He lies there for almost three hours. He cannot find the strength to decide to get up. When he finally does, he leaves without looking at the others, keeping only his blankets and the pistol.

He does not rest until late that night. From now on he pays no more attention to the time of day, but walks when he can and rests when he must. He rests very often. He is now so weak that he cannot advance more than four or five miles a day. Since he has left the compass in La Vas's pocket, his progress south is even slower than this.

Twenty-five days have passed since the plane crash. Williaus talks to himself silently as he walks. He talks also (but silently still) to others. Curiously enough—he apologizes for his lapse—he cannot pronounce certain words, those that end in -ion. At first he can pronounce all their syllables except the last. Consternat, ambit—his groping tongue fails. Later he has difficulty pronouncing any part of such words. He tries pretending to think of other words and his mind then comes close to filling the hiatus. But when he springs towards the forgotten word there is only a ridiculous fragment —vat, sump—or a void.

He has seen birds more frequently, although only singly. He decides to start trying to shoot them. He notices that one of the birds seems to be following him —not only following but drawing closer with each succeeding hour. It is a rather large bird, of a sooty blue, which he recognizes as a noddy—the silly bird that is afraid of nothing. He cannot understand how this bird could have come so far north. He feels a strange hope seeing it.

When the bird is hovering about ten yards over his head, Williaus begins shooting at it. He misses repeatedly. The bird is not frightened and continues its daylong descent.

Williaus leaves off shooting at the bird when it is a

few feet from him. Not only are his shots useless, but the noddy appears to him like an angelic companion. The bird flies lower and lower, the undersides of its wings unnaturally white.

On the morning of the twenty-seventh day the white-sooty wings brush Williaus's face. He thinks: The foolish noddy, unafraid of man. The bird rises a little in the air only to cover his face again with its wings. He is snowblind.

Williaus does not at first understand what has happened to him. He walks through universal whiteness until he falls. After that he crawls for a while.

The noddy has not left him, but hovers in his unblinded mind. The bird darkens, the curious whiteness of its wings gathers to a ball in its beak, a quartzlike globe. An amethyst pupil completes the eye, which regards Williaus inquiringly but without much emotion. Then it begins to sing. (Williaus can tell it is the eye singing by the listening aspect of the bird.) It sings such lines as:

O Johnny O Johnny O

At the end of each song the noddy flies out of sight for a moment, bearing the eye, but soon comes back.

After a while Williaus asks if the eye could not sing an old song. The eye, with a look of surprise, consents to render *Come away, come sweet love.* But it insists on preceding each return to the old music with several popular songs.

By the end of the twenty-eighth day Williaus has given himself over to death. The lustrous voice fades. At a certain moment he becomes aware of a being close to him. He calls out, but hears only a rubbery clatter. Pulling the glove from his right hand, he stretches it towards the sound: a cold softness fills his palm. He leans farther: bones and silky whiskers, and a sweet whine. A new soft clatter, and the being's body moves against him. The seal puts his head on Williaus's lap who strokes it tenderly.

From time to time the seal moves away but usually Williaus can follow the flapping of its feet, or its short grunts. Once it goes far away but after a long hour returns. Williaus caresses it with happy relief. So doing he finds that the seal's smooth pelisse is rent with sores. His fingers explore the open wounds, the animal trembles at this touching. Williaus weeps, repeating Poor Roly, poor Roly, soothing its head. He weeps obliviously over the wet soft sores.

When the seal next starts to move away, Williaus pleads with it to stay. He cannot think how to keep it by him. Then remembering that music is attractive to seals, he begins to sing:

> The first queen was a farmer's girl
> With hair as yellow as hay,
> She slept one night with the emperor
> The emperor died next day
>
> The third queen was a heathen
> The fairest of all houris,
> She danced for the devil's salva
>
> vat
>
> La lala

Williaus's body was carried by icedrift to the nearby edge of the polar pack, and thence, the ice breaking up, floated southward into the Atlantic on an iceberg. At summer's end it was observed by the passengers of Mr. Leigh Smith's yacht *Diana*. The body, recovered, was brought to Canada aboard that ship, and there Williaus's family took charge of it, returning with it to Los Angeles where the remains were burned.

•

GYPSIES

A soothing rush of waves had washed through the close of my recital. It was past midnight when the carriage stopped at the beach.

Someone outside opened the carriage-door and the beam of a flashlight entered. There was laughter from many men and women: I had been smoking a ninety-five-cent footlong cigar, and the light discovered me in a heap of smoke.

Such ash! said the man with the flashlight. My suit was thoroughly sprinkled with cigar droppings.

A sable silvered, I answered.

A silver Stewart?

Royally bearded! I said, feeling my stubbled chin.

Did you say: beheaded?

Purged by bitter hominy!

My questioner, helping me to the ground, laughed delightedly at my last answer. Taking my arm he led me towards the nearest of the campfires burning along the beach. We passed through a score of watching Gypsies.

When we had reached the fire my questioner shined his light on a trail of ashes pointing to my carriage. We were expecting you, he said, by this sign of the wind.

My polite smile revealed my skepticism. I have never seen such indignation. Protests from all sides persuaded me to submit to an experiment, although I feared that it would only bring new embarrassment.

From somewhere beyond the firelight a gypsy girl trundled a strange machine. It was made of two large flared cones of corrugated iron set one above the other. The lower one's base rested close to the ground on a ring of free wheels. The upper cone, joined to the lower by a tube in a way allowing each to revolve independently, was set at right angles to the first, its base, shut with a flat metal disc, facing outwards: it looked like the horn of some outsize Edison phonograph. The machine must have been seven feet high, and the diameter of the cones at their bases four feet; the short tube connecting them was only three inches thick at its narrowest point.

After unlocking three hooks on its surface, the girl swung out a large section of the lower cone together with the corresponding arc of the wheel-ring, and the

machine was then pushed into position over the campfire, raked into a compact blazing pile of coals. During the moment the cone was open, I saw that its inner
surface was covered with a spiral of close-set blackened vanes.

While the machine was being fetched, several
Gypsy men had dug a shallow circular ditch around
the fire, afterwards wetting it with buckets of seawater. The ring of wheels now rested in this trough
of relatively firm sand.

All now drew back to a distance of ten yards from
the fire, except for the girl who had fetched the
machine. Turning the upper cone towards the sea, from
which a steady wind blew, she removed the disc that
sealed its base, and withdrew at once to the circle of
watchers. The upper cone, which was evidently hollow, swung slightly to left and right before settling
into place facing the wind. Slowly at first, the lower
cone began to spin on its ring of wheels. A harsh
whispering noise started, thickening and rising with
the pace of the cone's gyration.

When the lower cone had reached a speed I would
not have thought possible, so pronounced that its
wheels had become a blur (it is true that the only light
was that of the hidden fire), the machine's movements
changed. The upper cone, previously immobile, started
to revolve as the lower cone slowed. In a few seconds
their roles had been reversed, the lower cone remaining still while the upper whirled violently. But I had
barely accustomed myself to this transformation when
with an ear-rending squeal all motion stopped, and the
upper cone, which had come to its abrupt halt facing
me, spouted a dazzling stream of coals. These when

they fell rested for the merest instant in bright continuous lines: I read the word THESAURUS. At once the coals began to wink out, hissing damply. Five seconds after having seen the word I began doubting my eyes, confronted as I now was with only scattered embers, bearing as much resemblance to a word as a constellation to the legendary figure it portrays.

A shout from the Gypsies followed the word's appearance. I was ready enough to admit my error; but nobody was thinking any longer of that argument. Instead I was told that I must enter a contest with the leading men of the community. Since everyone was immediately busy preparing for this event, I was obliged to accept—especially as I had put myself so completely in the wrong.

I learned that the stake in the game was to be an extraordinary heirloom—in fact the treasure signified by "thesaurus"—but I was not yet told what it was. First of all I was to witness a special dance, a preliminary meant to emphasize the ritual character of the game.

We formed a new circle around the campfire. Music began. A crank victrola played the worn record of an old popular song. This music had a curious complement. Three women held strips of wetted white cloth and snapped them in turn, thus making a series of resounding retorts that possessed a certain rough element of pitch. The three strips were of unequal length: the middlesize one was only slightly longer than the shortest strip, while the longest was nearly its double. At long intervals that seemed to have no connection with the recorded music, the women would flick their cloths in rapid succession: first that of middle length, then the longest, finally the shortest.

Presently the dancers appeared—a handsome couple wearing only bathing suits, shaking with cold. The man crouched on the ground. The woman performed a solo during which she strewed over her partner bands of charred newspaper from a basket placed nearby. Once she had thoroughly covered the man and the ground around him, the woman withdrew. The man began to lift himself up. As he tried to shake off the papers, however, he became more and more entangled in them. I saw after a moment how the effect was achieved. A net had been laid on the spot where he had squatted, concealed by a light covering of sand, and he had picked it up when he rose. The strands of the net, furthermore, must have been dipped in strong glue, for the papers stuck to them firmly. After many elegant contortions, the dancer, wrapped from head to toe in a shroud of newsprint, fell onto the sand as if dead. The music's close marked the end of the dance.

It was then that my questioner with the flashlight—who turned out to be a chief—showed me the stake the Gypsies had put up for our game. It was nothing other than the "adze," as they called it—of course I pointed out that it wasn't an adze at all but a kind of short-handled halberd, or a large billhook. While they granted that it rather resembled such instruments, they insisted that it was an adze, and no ordinary one. The chief explained that the pictures engraved on its head portrayed the life of some ancient wonderqueen of theirs, from her birth to her burning. Then he and several other men discussed the last scene shown on it

—the one with moon, arrows, and fish—which they couldn't understand, still less agree on.

Next I was asked to put up *my* stake. I was at a loss. A hundred times the money I was carrying would not have bought the adze's gold, and then there was its symbolic value, which I gathered was the Gypsies' paramount reason for offering it up to chance. At last, reluctantly, I drew from my overcoat pocket my beloved dog Limnisse and announced my willingness to risk him. This extraordinary animal, bought three years previously at a secondhand dogstore on the Left Bank, was only four inches long and weighed only six ounces fed. But his brain, a marvel of nature, was equal to that of any Alsatian shepherd. When I bought him, a veteran circus roustabout had already trained him to perform such feats as measuring all distances from a foot to a mile with a margin of error of only one-sixteenth of an inch.

My hosts were delighted with Limnisse, and so the game finally started. It was played at another fire, over which a twenty-five gallon vat of water had been set to boil on a cast-iron tripod. The boiling water was funneled through a spigot into terracotta jars that, excepting a small hole left for this purpose, were entirely closed. The filled jars, borne on wooden trays by Gypsy girls, were passed in turn to the contestants who took them in their bare hands. Before setting his jar down, the contestant had to describe the scene molded on its top. If he dropped a jar, or put it on the ground without giving a fitting description, he was out of the game. When only two players remained, this procedure ended. Instead, the finalists joined in a kind of rhetorical contest, explaining the transcendent meaning of the scenes they had already described.

I was shown a sample jar top. Its picture was the same as the second one of the adze. The trick, the chief told me, is to use the fewest words possible, without sacrificing good usage or leaving out any part of the picture. In this case you might say, The lightningpucked thunder-hockeyists felled, our queen on cloud is admired.

I promised to do my best.

Looking back, I am sure that at least part of the game was prepared. Before I had five turns a dozen contestants—all but the chief and I—had managed either to drop their jars or to stutter unnaturally when their turn came. I can't remember half of what they did say, so I shall limit myself to us two finalists. I wasn't able, of course, to see the chief's jars: I can only report his words.

It was he who opened the game, saying of the first jar: A mast bears fruit for shipwrecked travelers.

I was nearly eliminated at my first turn. When I took the offered jar, in spite of all my inner preparations, its boiling heat blinded me. My vision fortunately cleared quickly enough to distinguish the crudely made image: a child was curled up, as if in the womb, within a circle on whose outer edge grew trees, shrubs and crops, all on fire. I said: The old world, burning, heralds the new one to be born.

The dialogue continued thus:

The chief: For gay gangs crossing, the sea's a velvet field.

Of a group of nine men on their knees, clubs laid aside, I said: Victorious Yankees pray for humility.

The chief: From the dead god's eye swarm fat swine.

My next scene showed two men, one of them looking in amazement at the other, who was chiseling at the bust of an old man set in the middle of a fence. I said of it: Confounding Brunelleschi, Donatello carves a venerable God from a fencepost.

The chief: Cool drink in hand, Somerset Maugham is gently toothdrilled. (I objected to "toothdrilled" but was overruled.)

Next I had to describe a picture in the upper half of which a pianist with fluttering hair regarded a cross, while below a plump bearded man engaged in tourney with an opponent in side-whiskers and velvet clothes. My description was: Brahms and Wagner joust for fame, but Liszt plays only for Jesus.

The chief: Joyous giants make, of bankcolumns, flutes.

And I, considering a prisoner who sang and played a mandolin while his guard stood by with ready whip, concluded: The punished liar sings a new song of truth.

The chief and I were now the only contestants, and we entered the final period of the game—the rhetorical summary of our descriptions. The chief spoke first.

The mast, and the flutes, the sea, the tooth, the eye, the eye, the tooth, the sea, the flutes, the mast: in in these there five all symbols it's we see have you a so glimpse meant into nicely the quite world here that but we Square all Washington yearn around for, of that anarchists paradise pleasant on the earth to of happens which as all literature prophets such from of Isaiah readers to to Vergil familiar to conception you

a and bankcolumns me of have out sung—flutes that
the world care in medical which painless pain and and
comfortable fear as have well been as banished, luxurious where free plenty of is picture ensured touching
and a when tooth we Maugham's will Mr. finally
mention have to the forgot opportunity I to kaput
promote world a old democratic the interest i.e. in god
the dead fine the arts. Of is knowledge it is not that fitting eye that the this from new course age of should
symbolically be proceeding first home heralded brought
by easily the be miracle to that bacon saved the those
by classic indicated victims as of notably pity, eat
travelers to wrecked plenty on also a but barren all
shore? To but available soon be plights advantages like
negativistic theirs these will will have only been not
forever foidermore banished—traverse the to sea desiring itself tread will baby lose merest its the pericu-
lousness, for being velvet transformed comfy to soft
soft to comfy transformed velvet being for pericu-
lousness the its merest lose baby will tread itself desiring sea to the traverse. Banished foidermore forever—
but enough! Glimpse so a you have see we it's symbols
all five there, in the mast, the sea, the eye, the tooth,
and the flutes!

There was considerable applause. In turn I rose to
speak.

Eak! ay! irth! ine! ees! ost! er! ire! ird! ine! ew!

ladies gentlemen, tongue phrases. rhetoric day.
man's glory earth, birth—birth goodness, light nature.
men arms, knees strength humility's. sculptor glory
god fencepost. tones flesh hands register. justice, liar
(word) rack whip fire music bird. wonders seas swine,
mercy wisdom flame—world.

is to wrap speak; say is to say keep; shown, tell—
began to shine; laid, fell, prayed, be; felt was made
spring; knew to stir confined; was (murdered) forced
to bear to sing; is bring to view; is;
    weak another come stranger divine burning all brave
most mere weak upper merciful wretched twisted fair
true velvet milling blessed divine such new greater,
    and and but when and, when and and or, or but
or but and,
    in for on of, of to from with, to with with,
    a the the, the the a th', the a the, the,
    I me you, I you he, he he I,
    plainly briefly there up down, but even not
like not,
    my my, their their, their his, his his,
    let, have been, shall, had, was,
    what, what, who, that,
    which?
            —That I leave to you.
    Cheers rose about the fire at my last words. There
was no question as to who was winner, and the chief
immediately congratulated me.
    It is a new triumph, he said, of analytical poetry
over descriptive prose. This reassured me—I was
afraid my couplets might have passed unnoticed.
    Dawn had begun to lighten the smoky beach when
I started back to New York, with the awarded adze
on my lap tied up in *Mirror* and string. Although I
had won, it had been necessary for me to abandon my
dog—evidently the stakes are exchanged in such cases,
there being, according to those people, no such thing
as a winner. So, giving him a last center slice of his
favorite filet mignon, I said goodbye to Limnisse. It

was the only bad moment of that diverting and exhausting night.

Several months later I sold the adze to Wayl, who
had shown extraordinary interest in it, finally offering
me more money than I could refuse.

Two o'clock in the morning had struck when the
novelist finished his story. Tired, I suggested we meet
another time to talk about the adze itself, and thanking
him for his kindness, left.

•

MR. WAYL'S
WILL

At six-thirty that morning a visitor woke me up: Beatrice Fod. Pale with fatigue, she nevertheless harangued me vigorously for several minutes. She wanted the adze, first claiming it as rightly hers and then, such arguments failing, offering me increasingly large amounts of money for it. Her final price was close to a million dollars—I have forgotten the exact sum because my mind at that time was aswim with sleep and surprise.

She was on her way out when another caller appeared, showing signs of the same tempestuous weariness: her brother Isidore.

Négat jegů! he exclaimed.

Tsamp! she answered, shoving past him out the door. *Gego szegák egan egámpteggi egög segöl!*

Is Fod soon followed her, equally disappointed in his efforts to get the adze for himself.

In the afternoon papers I learned that Mr. Wayl had died the previous night. Soon afterwards I received a special delivery letter from Mr. Wayl's lawyers asking me to come to his house next morning to attend the reading of the dead man's will.

Although I had arrived before the appointed time, a remarkable number of people had already gathered in the familiar drawing-room, where the reading was to take place. Among them I recognized Mayor Groncz. He was, I later learned, the only person invited to the session outside the Fods, Miss Dryrein, and myself. I noticed many other distinguished figures: from medical circles, the surgeon Arbalast, who had once operated on Mr. Wayl's foot but was better known for his Harrow depth technique; the gynecologist White; Dr. Mallarmé, the woman who had revolutionized narcoanalysis with intravenous injections of "symbolic gin"; and Clematis, the "truth dentist"; two of Mr. Wayl's rare friends in the worlds of finance and business, Alexander Senfl of Medusa Natural Gas and Harvey Elliott of Milton Can, in earnest conversation with Jonathan Writch, the president of Blackwards, Reyrdin & Long; numerous leaders in the field of civic development—the chairman of the Parking Authority, the real estate king William Lemon, and the architect Miles Mazurovsky, among others; half-a-dozen aspiringly alert but unfamiliar lawyers under the wing of an anonymous redhaired dean; Philippa Stuart, elder of the Primal Rose Unitarians—the only religious figure of the gathering; among the military, Generals Peirce O'Toole, who had distinguished himself during the last war in reducing the "pocket bulge," and Quogue, the "Bremen Monster"; Admiral "Rock" Hatter, and Captain Hershey, who had never become admiral (despite a brilliant record) because of his lifelong skepticism towards the torpedo; several politicians besides Mayor Groncz—Governor Gold of Delaware, author of a book (*Mass or Mess?*) that had angered many Catholics, Senator Cousins, whose promising legal career was ending in political mediocrity, and Senator Autobustard, the royalist; many writers and journalists, including the poet Felix Hughes (*The Artifice of Order*), "Sylvester" of *Field & Stream*, and the cartoonist Flamingo Stahl, for whom the epithet "vitriolic" had been worn to new thinness; from the theatrical world, Laetitius Scott, the backer of *Invitation to a Sabbath*, an avant-garde sleeper that had recently opened on Fire Island; Violet Colt, directress of the China Co.'s film subsidiaries, whose stinginess was legendary; Archibald Moon, then at the height of his powers as Judas in *The White Net*; and his wife Anna Joyce who had distinguished herself in a role of "trying piety" playing opposite him; the art dealer Seaward Blackmaster and his principal client, Edward Emord, both probably hoping to learn how Mr. Wayl had disposed of Watteau's *Blue Friend;* Duane Greene; the museum director Rudolph Sweenson Barjohn; such members of the musical world

as Demuro Bangcraft and Reobard Mitrostone; and a
few of the many painters once patronized by Mr.
Wayl—de Crook (who had painted his "purple portrait"), Huffing (the exponent of *arte brutta*), Rausch-
wald and Litotes.

The consensus of this assembly was that Mr. Wayl's
fortune exceeded three hundred million dollars.

The Fods, accompanied by Miss Dryrein, at last
took their seats (Beatrice shouting Vampires! Vampires! as she crossed the room.) A pale attorney,
flanked by bespectacled aides, read the will behind a
massive table placed in front of the high windows that
looked on the conservatory.

> I, GRENT OUDE WAYL, of the City, County, and
> State of New York, do make, publish, and declare
> this to be my Last Will and Testament, hereby
> revoking any and all Wills and Codicils hereto-
> fore made by me.
> FIRST: I direct that all my just debts and funeral
> expenses be paid by my executrix as soon as pos-
> sible after my decease, provided that the follow-
> ing procedure be adhered to:
> (1) That the organist of St. James's Church,
> Madison Avenue and 71st Street, Manhattan,
> choose a suitable musical composition to accom-
> pany the departure of my remains to their place
> of burial; that the score of this composition
> (notes, rests, clefs, key and time signatures, and
> all indications of speed, phrasing and dynamics)
> be reproduced at fifteen times its printed size in
> the form of pancakes; and that these cakes be
> obligatorily eaten by any and all such persons
> who attend the reading of this my Last Will and

Testament, excepting those specifically invited thereto. (In the event of non-compliance with this provision, I have instructed my faithful servant Miss Gabrielle Dryrein, of 2980 Valentine Avenue, The Bronx, to give to the press all information kept in my private files concerning liable parties.)

(2) That I be buried with my ninety-nine-year custombuilt Fil Pathétique fob watch, this watch to be set at Greenwich time and placed in my left waistcoat pocket immediately prior to the funeral service.

(3) That my coffin be taken from St. James's Church at eleven o'clock of the Monday morning following my death, on an open cart drawn by two gray donkeys, and that the itinerary of the procession be as follows: Madison Avenue from 71st until 59th Street; Fifth Avenue from 59th until 50th Street; Park Avenue from 50th until 34th Street; and thence to my residence where my remains are to be buried. (In the event of non-compliance with this provision, the following article of this Will is automatically annulled.)

SECOND: I give and bequeath to Mr. Lambeth Groncz, of Gracie House, Gracie Square, Manhattan, such land as I possess in the City of New York, notably a park of three acres adjoining my present residence, 475 East 34th Street, Manhattan.

THIRD: I give and bequeath to my faithful servant Miss Gabrielle Dryrein, of 2980 Valentine Avenue, The Bronx:

(1) The sum of Two Hundred and Fifty Thousand Dollars ($250,000.);

(2) The sum of One Hundred Thousand Dollars ($100,000.) to be distributed at her discretion

among those who are, or who have been, in her
service;

(3) All of my personal effects, including clothing, jewelry, silver, furniture, furnishings, books,
pictures and ornaments.

FOURTH: All the rest, residue and remainder of
my property, real, personal and mixed, whereso-
ever situate, including property of any description of which I may die seized or possessed, of
which I may have power to dispose, over which I
may have power of appointment, and in and to
which I may be in any manner interested or entitled, I give, devise and bequeath to such person
as has in his possession a golden adze hereunder
described and who is able to provide a satisfactory
explanation of its meaning, purport, uses and significance, now and at all times, the said explanation to be verified by my executrix or by such
executors as she may appoint according to the
answers given by any qualifying person to the
following three questions:

1) When was a stone not a king?
2) What was *La Messe de Sire Fadevant?*
3) Who shaved the Old Man's Beard?

The description of the adze followed. Read with
rising voice by the shamefaced lawyer, it was quickly
drowned in a clamor of shock and disappointment.

Mr. Wayl was never buried at all. His instructions
were faithfully carried out, even to the eating of the
transcribed music. The organist at St. James's, who
had planned a twenty-nine minute *Tragic Rhapsody*
of Widor, was warned of the consequences and
changed to a unison version of *O God Our Help in
Ages Past;* so that the forced feeders had only twenty-

eight notes to swallow between them, and—the hymn being all in wholenotes and halfnotes—hollow ones at that.

The procession following the funeral service caused the worst traffic jam in New York's history, and Mayor Groncz might have been impeached for having allowed such a situation to arise, if he had not announced his intention of giving the land he had inherited to the city. The drawn cart had completed about three quarters of the itinerary when, at the corner of Park Avenue and Forty-ninth Street, in the midst of a throng of the idle, the curious and the infuriated, the coffin exploded. Little harm was done to bystanders by the explosion itself, since the coffin was made of welded steel; but the panic resulting from the noise and the strange rain of white petals that fell across the crowded intersection led to one death and many injuries. Investigators concluded, after considering the powdery contents of the coffin, that Mr. Wayl's watch had triggered the tragic detonation.

•

A VISIT TO
THE FODS

When was a stone not a king? What was *La Messe de Sire Fadevant?* Who shaved the Old Man's Beard? When was a stone ever a king? Who was Sire Fadevant? What old man? To approach the questions on which my inheritance depended, others had to be answered first. I tackled the problem at once.

Besides study and research at official sources for information about the so-called adze, I thought it well to visit all of Mr. Wayl's surviving relatives. Even if they refused to cooperate with me, I might indirectly glean clues for my search.

These relatives were, besides the Fods: Allen Cavallo in New York; Xavier Purkinje in Paris; and the Voe-Doge brothers, Gore and Eftas, in London.

I first went to the Fods. Each received me with surprising friendliness. My impression was that after a short spell of appetency they had lapsed into wearied resignation.

Beatrice's and Isidore's histories were curious. Both had been involved in notorious medical scandals, following which Mr. Wayl had taken them under his protection. They lived in one of his properties, a thin four-storey house on West Fifty-fifth Street that had been divided into two apartments.

At the age of thirty Beatrice, a budding professor of gynecology at Johns Hopkins, had hit on an unprecedented solution to the problem of birth control. She had discovered (and, with the help of four thousand volunteer college and high school students of every class, race and region in the country, tested) a position for sexual intercourse in which conception was impossible. Her position, furthermore, provided maximum satisfaction for both partners in the sexual act, incidentally lowering the average age at which vaginal orgasm was first experienced from twenty-two to sixteen and a half years.

The consequences of Beatrice's discovery seemed potentially historic; but no sooner had she published the first results of her long labor than she was attacked on several sides by forces too strong for her to meet. Several drug firms had at that time invested seven-figure sums in developing an oral contraceptive. Sec-

onded by the Federal Government, which planned to
use the monopoly of the new chemical as a diplomatic
weapon (with the Catholic powers of Europe as well
as the populous Afro-Asian states), these firms under-
took to stifle Beatrice's good work. They contributed
vast amounts of money to every conceivable religious
denomination, abroad as well as at home, thereby
achieving an intersectarian harmony unique in history.
The propaganda was so clamorous that the few or-
ganizations favoring Beatrice's cause were obliged to
abandon her to save themselves.

Meanwhile the government managed to have a law
enacted making punishable by life imprisonment at
hard labor anyone who published a book or pamphlet
without depositing at the Library of Congress the
three copies necessary to obtain copyright. Beatrice
had neglected to do this. She had published her findings privately and inconspicuously, in the hope that
by so acting (and also by omitting a description of the
coital position she had invented) her discovery would
gain an easier entrance into the realm of public information; for she had foreseen an adverse reaction. Instead, all copies of her pamphlet save the first few she
had sent out were confiscated by the police, while she
herself became guilty of a severely punishable crime.
A bargain had been proposed to her: if she kept silence
in the future, she would not be prosecuted. Exhausted
and frightened, she accepted, and now lived under the
eyes of federal agents who investigated her most trivial
relations. For a while she had hoped that the students
who had tested her theory would give it to the world,
and indeed some of them tried. (A debased version of
her discovery—the so-called Lombard Rhythm—had

a certain brief success.) But so many positions had been used to make the experiment statistically exact that nobody was sure which was the true one, and a great confusion resulted, bringing much disappointment and, finally, the loss of her secret.

Isidore Fod's misfortune had come about at much the same time as his sister's, but in a way quite different. He had been working for the Bengali government on a sanitation project when an epidemic of tracheitic plague broke out in a remote mountain plateau of the province. Neither remedy nor vaccine for this disease existed; and even if they had, the difficulty of delivering them rapidly to the infested region seemed insuperable—besides its remoteness, its topography rendered it inaccessible to truck or plane.

Isidore Fod solved the double problem with an ingenuity that approached genius. After growing a culture of the plague bacteria, he discovered an effective although partial antidote to their virulence in the venom of the local *ischnogaster* wasp: the wasp-poison scotched the bacteria without completely killing them. In a few days Isidore performed a rapid series of tests that showed that a person injected with a mixture of germ culture and wasp poison became, at least temporarily, immune to the plague without suffering any ill effects. Because of the emergency, the state government immediately authorized Isidore to proceed, without further testing, in making vaccinations with his new serum.

To lessen the difficulty of delivering the vaccine, Isidore set up his medical station at English Bazar, the city nearest the stricken area. There he had a six-foot-square shallow cement pool made, and planted it with

five thousand golf-tees obtained from the city golf
club (a fortunate survivor of India's independence).
The tees were fixed so that their cups were at a uniform height of five-eighths of an inch from the bottom
of the pool. The tee cups were then filled with a thick
solution of sugar, the pool with a half-inch of bacteria
culture, and the whole was enclosed with screens provided with two opposing apertures. Every available
truck and car had meanwhile been commandeered to
scour the countryside for *ischnogaster* nests (gargoyle-
like masses familiar to any traveler who has crossed
the Bengal plains). Tens of thousands were brought to
Isidore's station, where their occupants were dropped
in batches onto the prepared enclosed pool. The great
majority of wasps at once descended to the sweet-
baited golf-tees. As each one sucked up his portion of
syrup, the stinging tip of his curved tail dipped into
the bacteria culture that mounted almost to the edge of
the golf-tee top. When sated, the wasp would soon
proceed through the prepared exit into a portable
screen cage, whither the swarming sound of his
trapped fellows drew him. The pool was periodically
emptied and the supplies of sugarwater and culture
replenished, while the cages of vaccine-bearing wasps
were taken to the airport to be loaded on ready planes.
As soon as each plane had its consignment, it took off
for the plague area where, flying low over the inhabited points, it freed its enraged cargo. The effect
of this operation was later described in a tribute that
the poet Hānsām Dās wrote for Isidore Fod:

The jackal cries, the *kokil* sings in leafy wonder
And behind the wattles babes peer at the sky.

Ah, swarm of gold, searing pain,
Blessing of the worn-out year!
Come, I am but a *champa* flower that longs for
the hornet's kiss.

An estimated two million wasps were loosed on an
area of four hundred and fifty square miles inhabited
by eighty thousand people. Some sixty thousand were
stung, and of these only thirty-five died of the plague.
Over two thousand had died prior to the period of vac-
cination, while several hundred of those not stung subsequently perished of the disease, which was several
weeks waning. Isidore's assumption that the wasps'
stings would effect a safe but potent mixture of culture and poison at the moment they pierced the skin
turned out to be right, as had all his other guesses.

For the next eight months Isidore was a worldwide
hero. He chose, modestly, to stay in Bengal until the
work for which he had been originally hired was completed. This decision nearly cost him his life. The next
summer the plague returned to the same mountain
region with new fury, and this time Isidore's airlift
was of no use. Setting out with his assistants to investigate the plague area, he reached it after a fortnight's travel by mule. He soon made two significant
discoveries: one, that his vaccine had only a short-
lived effectiveness; the other, that the wasps he had
dropped the year before had become breeders of the
plague. A mutation in the bacteria had produced a
strain that not only remained unaffected by wasp poison but flourished in the bodies of the wasps. Left
behind wherever the wasps fed, these bacteria now had
every local insect for a carrier. The recrudescence of

the plague spared hardly a household in all the region.

Before the cold weather finally ended the epidemic, it had killed thirty thousand. With admirable honesty Isidore informed the Bengali government and the press of his findings, and thus fell overnight into such local and international disgrace that he gave up his professional work altogether, finally coming to New York to live on Mr. Wayl's bounty and his own regrets.

Questioned, Beatrice Fod appeared even more ignorant concerning the adze than I. There was evidently little chance that either she or her brother would ever have the time to learn any more about it, in case they decided to go after the enigmatic inheritance themselves. In return for supporting them, Mr. Wayl had made them each accept a trying obligation, that of observing and noting everything that the other did. The ordeals they had passed through had left them, understandably, more than a little suspicious, and their suspiciousness had only grown with exercise, so that now —despite Mr. Wayl's death—their mutual spying was a terrific obsession.

Thus Beatrice Fod, while answering me with brief courtesies, refused to discuss anything at length but a mysterious flatiron that Isidore kept on his mantelpiece. Why did he have it? Did he ever use it? If he did use it, what did he use it for? Possible answers to these ridiculous questions filled my ears for over an hour, while I gazed stupidly about the living-room, studded—like the entire apartment—with grotesque pointed furniture. (Not a chair, shelf or sofa whose corners did not extrude in exaggerated tapering acuteness, causing in the beholder an irremediable awareness of impending pain. Beatrice did explain that she had taking up singing as a recent hobby and that such furnishings set off her voice better than any other.)

I had even less success with Isidore, for he refused to speak at all and sat with his forefinger at his lips in a listening posture, as if waiting for revelatory noises from his sister's apartment. I saw the flatiron on his mantelpiece but never learned its significance, or even if it had any.

•

OTHER
PRISONERS

Allen Cavallo, whom I visited next, was the grandson
of Mr. Wayl's second stepfather, not a blood relation;
he was therefore without expectations as to the inheritance and I had little hope that he would give me any
useful information, since Mr. Wayl had hardly known
him. My hopes were further limited by knowing that
"Al" Cavallo was a notorious gang boss. Only Mayor
Groncz's intervention enabled me to visit him in the
Astoria Agrarians' Hospital, where he was kept in a

private and indeed secret room of the psychiatric department.

Shortly before, Cavallo had disappeared mysteriously from public view—all that one knew was that he was under arrest. At the hospital I found out what had happened.

The gangster had learned the previous year of a newly discovered cactus that grew in the foothills of the Hoggar. Its spines were powerfully narcotic, discouraging the animals of that desolate land from eating the juicy flesh of the plant. As the toxic properties of these spines made them similar in their effect to morphine, it was at first hoped that they could be used medically; but the difficulties of extracting the active chemical proved excessive. Cavallo had a sample of the plant sent to him; and testing the spines on a number of his morphine customers, he had found that they satisfied the cravings of the most addicted. He had also discovered an unguessed advantage to the spines: carried as toothpicks, they freed their possessor from the risk of arrest and the need of concealment. An addict wanting his stuff could publicly clean his teeth with a spine, unobtrusively pricking his gums until happy.

The spines soon gained the nickname of "Hoggar-mothers."

Cavallo ordered a large quantity of the cactus and set up a plant import business as a front. The first shipment was unloaded one summer night at a Brooklyn wharf under Cavallo's personal supervision. Checking a loaded truck before it drove off, he had the tragic misfortune to fall—or, some say, be pushed—among the four-foot-deep green bulbs. Lightly covered in that season, every part of his body was pierced by the drug-laden thorns. Before he could be retrieved, he had been hopelessly stricken by a massive injection of narcotic sap.

Under constant medical care since that night, at first among his colleagues, later, arrested, at the hospital where I saw him, Cavallo was an inhuman and pitiful sight. He was insane, and in unremitting pain as well. The narcotic, absorbed in a quantity that could never be eliminated, caused his skin to shrink perpetually. Hardly a day passed without an incision being needed in some part of his body to keep it from being squeezed dry by this terrible pressure. The incisions left him covered with long halfhealed wounds inadequately fitted with grafts from volunteers or with plastic skin. Between his shrieks and raving laughs he sometimes used to cry out, By these stripes we are healed! These were the only words he spoke. He died a few weeks after my visit to him.

About this time the efforts I had made to find information concerning the adze yielded their first result. A letter from the Customs Bureau informed me that they had located the records of its arrival in America. The shipment had been made from Alloa, in Scotland, by a New York export-import company that had long been out of business, so that it would be impossible to find out the actual persons who had sent and received it.

But even this meager information seemed a windfall to me, and I decided to go to Scotland and see if there I could not trace the adze back to its origins. At the same time the trip would give me a chance to visit Mr. Wayl's remaining relatives.

In Paris a few weeks later, I made arrangements to

call on M. Purkinje, a distant cousin of Mr. Wayl's on his mother's side. He, too, was in the hands of the police, as he had been ever since the failure of the Panarchist Uprising of 1911. Together with his fellow agitators, Martinotti and Rackham the Red, he had passed most of his life in the political wing of Les Innocents, France's largest prison. Its director, M. Molini-Stucky, who had promptly granted my request for a visit, related while leading me to the prisoner's quarters the events that had brought Purkinje there.

The Panarchist revolt, he began, was one of the cleverest attempts at generalized subversion that our country (rich in similar exploits) has ever known. Imagination and efficacy characterized its choice of political doctrine, while its technique of psychological preparation and its tactics for making the uprising a success were no less ingenious.

The Panarchist doctrine was known as *éclairagisme*. Designed to appeal to the universal predilection for oversimplified and seemingly practical ideas, it reduced all social ills to one—darkness—, and it advocated one cure, summed up in the slogan *Tout l'Espace Éclairé!* According to this theory the amount of light available to a person in all the phases of his daily life determined his moral, psychic and intellectual wellbeing. It was accordingly the obligation of the state to ensure first of all that each individual have the same amount of light as every other, and secondly that this amount be as great as possible. The Panarchists claimed that the discovery of electric light—which you should remember was fairly recent and so made the theory especially attractive—permitted both these obligations to be easily realized. They consequently advocated that a light

quota be established on a space-person basis; that all
those persons required to live or work in an insuffi-
ciently lighted space be given larger windows and increased electric lighting; and that those persons
whose illumination exceeded the quota have their
window surface reduced and their lighting fixtures
confiscated correspondingly.

But the Panarchists' program, reiterated in their
daily paper *Le Soleil de Paris*, soon left theoretical
éclairagisme to the debates of pundits and focused on
livelier issues such as the abolition of the *minuterie* or
the construction of giant mirrors to introduce sunlight and moonlight to the narrower streets. And in a
few years, by dint of exploiting this rudimentary idea,
the Panarchist Party (PP) gained a respectable following.

The party's aim had been revolutionary from the
start, although this was not openly acknowledged until
the inability of successive governments to provide the
lighting reforms demanded had been demonstrated to
the masses. When they felt that a fit moment for action had come, the Panarchist leaders began their
scheduled "psychological preparatory movement,"
based on the principle of *psychomimie*. Their idea was
to accustom the populace to revolutionary gestures so
that it would be conditioned to perform, or at least tolerate, such gestures when the crisis occurred. For
this reason, during the month preceding the date chosen
for the revolution, Parisians were offered a number of
unusual spectacles. Buildings made of paper were set
up on sidewalks and ignited by men whose smiles were
a plea for the joys of arson. Other men and women,
wearing like smiles, made piles of bricks and stones re-

sembling little barricades. Fairstands were opened in all the working quarters of the city where one could, free of charge, shoot or throw hard balls at dummies of policemen and soldiers. These efforts at persuasion were naturally kept within careful bounds, to avoid official sanction; they were nonetheless everywhere to be seen.

It is hard to say how effective *psychomimie* was in its application, for the Panarchist leaders were all under arrest before they had time to exploit its effect. But that effect, if we are to judge by the climax of the campaign, was probably all they hoped for.

It so happened that the national hockey championships were to be played in Paris on the evening picked for the Panarchist outbreak. A huge crowd was to attend the game; so were several notables, among them the ministers of culture and of agriculture. The Panarchists, finding they could enlist both teams for their plan, decided to make the *Palais Esquimau* the starting-point of the mass rioting on which they counted. When the second period of the game began, revolutionaries replaced the official referees and, after haranguing the startled but far from hostile crowd, ordered the players to proceed as planned. The two government ministers, who had been prevented from leaving, were brought onto the ice and trussed up, their knees against their chests, their feet against their buttocks. The hockey players thereupon began a mock game with these human bundles as pucks; they pushed and passed them around the rink with the large scrapers used to clear off the ice. After their miserable excellencies had been with much jocularity scuttled into the goalnets, Martinotti, the Panarchist in charge, made a rousing speech to the spectators, pouring contempt on the government whose representatives had been so thoroughly humiliated. The crowd, responding enthusiastically, swarmed out of doors intending to do all the mischief it could; but the police (who by now were on the offensive) were waiting for it, and it was quickly dispersed.

The failure of the revolution was really a matter of luck. The main objective of the plotters was a series of "temporary assassinations" that were to destroy the leadership of the police and of the army divisions stationed in or near the capital. Here again the Panarchists showed singular flair. As you may know, Paris then had two telephone systems, one that of a private company, the other that of the Postal Service. The latter was gradually replacing the former; but at that particular time the transition was not completed and both systems existed side by side. The revolutionaries' plan, carried out successfully in the majority of cases, was to call their victims on both phones simultaneously— I should perhaps mention that the phones were invariably next to one another, since the Postal Service had taken advantage of the private company's wiring scheme to install its own. Then, through a clever use of conversation—worked out experimentally with great thoroughness prior to use—the person answering was induced to hold both phones to his ears at the same time. At this foreseen moment, explosive noises of nearly a hundred decibels were sent over the two wires to produce in the unsuspecting hearer a striking manifestation of the Allanic-Culajod Effect. This left him senseless for a few hours.

As I've already said, this clever procedure succeeded

in most cases. But, unfortunately for the Panarchists, the prefect of police, their main target, was completely missed. He had planned to spend the evening of the would-be coup doing research on Louise Labé, on whom he was an authority; and he ignored his butler's announcement that he was demanded urgently on both phones. Shortly afterwards an alert aide informed him in person of the Panarchists' doings, and the prefect was then able, despite the decimation of the upper ranks of the police, to create a provisional hierarchy that soon had its forces mobilized. Before the night was over it was the Panarchist leadership that was inoperative, with two hundred of its members in jail. As you know, some of them aren't out yet. You will now see what they have become, these men who were, you must agree, exemplars of shrewdness and daring.

We had stopped in front of a door whose metal weight did not prevent our hearing, from its far side, a noise like the sighing of profound flutes. A guard unlocked the door, and we passed through. We entered a pleasant suite of cells, whose windows held, instead of bars, boxes of geraniums that sparkled in the morning sun; whose floors were thickly rugged; and whose *art nouveau* furnishings were elegant and luxurious. Three men reclined in capacious armchairs around a pale table on which had been set three glasses and a bottle of plain red wine. The men sat motionless, only sipping their wine from time to time. They uttered perpetual dovelike sounds. I recognized Purkinje, whose high cheekbones still retained a certain nobility in his face's damp fleshiness.

M. Molini-Stucky addressed Purkinje, shaking him by the shoulders. He succeeded in making him look once at me; but not for a moment did his sighing falter, and the revolutionary's eyes wandered after to the sunlight that was filling the street below. Spreading his arms in hopelessness, the director led the way out; and I was obliged, empty-handed again, to leave Mr. Wayl's cousin and his comrades droning to themselves at their cheerful window that overlooked the Rue Affres de Guillaume.

I left for England next morning and a few days later payed a visit to the Voe-Doge brothers at their apartment in Chelsea. Shown into their drawing-room at the fixed hour, I found them engaged in furious argument.

Lop oh oh kop, Eftas was saying, yoppo you boploppo oh dopyop foppo ohlop, ee voppeenop top hoppo you gop hop mopyop boppeye roptop hop moppay yop hoppay voppee poproppee coppee doppeedop yoppo you ropsop bopyop oh noplopyop foppo roptop yoppo noppee soppee coppo nopdop sop, top hoppay top eyesop sopyou fopfop eye coppeye eenoptop toppo Aesop top aybop loppeye sop hop moppee aysop ee lopdoppee rop boproppo top hoppeerop, aynopdop roppeye gop hoptop fopyou loppy ay rop lop.

Naraguts tarago yaragou, baragag-haraguead, answered Gore: twaraguins aragare twaraguins aragand naragueitharaguer haragas praraguiaragoraraguitaraguy. Faragurtharaguermaragore araguit's caragommaragon knaragowlaraguedge tharagat yaragou paragayed Faragatharaguer Daraguldaragoon, wharago daraguelaraguivaraguered paragoor Maragummy, tharaguë praraguice aragof faraguive haragundraraguëd plaraguenaragararaguy araguindaragulgearaguencearaguës tarago saragupparagort yaragour claragaim aragof

baraguëaraguing faraguirstbaragorn.—Crapper, a glass
of port for our guest.

Roppo toptop eenop coproppay popyoulop oh you
sop you nopbop roppo top hoppee roplopyop loppeye
Aesop!

Narago! aragand wharagat's maragore, Gore added,
aragaccaragordaraguing   tarago   yaragou-knaragow-
wharago tharaguere araguis narago daragoubt tharagat
Aragui sharagould haragave baragueen maragade Araguearl aragof Maragar, aragand tharagat araguin fara-
gact Aragui *aragam* tharaguë Aragearl.

Eyemop top hoppee Araguearl aragof Maragar!

Aragui'm tharaguë E ayroplop oh fop Moppayrop!

After three glasses of this jargon I took my leave. I
did so with singular regret. A painting, signed only
with the initials F. N., hung over the drawing-room
fireplace; its composition was identical with the third
scene of the adze—the supposed sanctification of the
saint by Jesus. To my surprise, the brass plate on the
bottom of its frame read: *The Crowning of the King.*
The maid who accompanied me to the door assured me
that no matter how long I might wait, the brothers
would never condescend to speak of the picture—the
only subject they ever discussed was that of their present argument.

I learned some time later that Gore was the celebrated "Tock" Voe-Doge, who used to fly his Spitfire
during the Battle of Britain wearing the clothes he
thought proper for the time of day. He once destroyed
six German planes between ten and eleven in the morning dressed in scarlet shantung pajamas, sealskin slippers, and a skyblue cashmere dressing-gown with silver
piping.

•

THE CUSTOMS
HOUSE (I)

That very night I took the train for Edinburgh, going
on the following morning to Alloa. There I went
straight to the customs office. My inquiries regarding
the adze led me through many bureaux; and it was not
until late afternoon that the relevant papers were
found. I was then informed that the adze had been
registered for export not at Alloa itself, but at a special customs house near Alva, a small town three miles
to the north.

Early the following morning I therefore set out anew. Reaching Alva by bus, I walked the last mile to the customs house through wet fields. After about a quarter of an hour I heard a sound of voices singing, and they grew louder as I followed my path. To my surprise the music was a partsong written in antique counterpoint, poignant and smooth. The moving voices hid the text, and it was only at the end of the verses that I caught the words of a chordal refrain:

> White silver, blue,
> Sweet silver, silver sweet!

The autumn mist kept me from seeing whence this music came, until I found myself a few yards from a building above whose door hung a worn sign, *The Customs House of Alva*. Fixed above this was a sixteen-inch loudspeaker pouring forth, with uncanny realism, the madrigal I had been listening to.

The door had neither bell nor knocker, only a risp, and this stuck. My efforts to work it, however, showed the door to be unlatched and I passed through it into a sad small entrance of drab wood, containing only a table with dried-out inkwells and an empty chair. Certain slight sounds from an adjacent room came through a frail door directly beyond the table. I knocked, had no answer, tried the knob, opened the door and entered a larger room. At first I could not see how large, for the air was suffused with plumes and tiers of smoke bluetinged with the illumination of a sizable skylight; but once my eyes had grown used to the foggy atmosphere I discovered a kind of gallery in front of me, ten yards wide and forty deep, its windowless walls lined with shelves, and its floor piled with cases and boxes. In a far corner a small area had been partitioned off, and a bright electric glow came through its open door.

Several weaker, unshaded lamps stood in the center of the room, and by their light a dozen officials were reading. They wore purplish military uniforms with visored caps and riding boots, but their bearing was unsuited to their dress. On a ring of overstuffed sofas they slackly sprawled, each smoking a long fair *regalia* which when sufficiently reduced was replaced from a litter of open cigarboxes that lay among them on the floor—no doubt seized contraband. In the same fashion each official exchanged from time to time the book he read for one chosen from a jumbled crateful at his feet. A side of the bookcrate had the word *Confiscated* stenciled on it.

None of the customs officials took any notice of me when I came in, and when I asked for their attention they did not even look up. Occasionally they spoke a word or two to each other in the soft speech of the country. After I had watched them restlessly for ten minutes, one finally raised himself languorously from his comfort (scratching his jowls with a piercing sound of grated fat and bristle), and approached me. He asked me my business in a brutal but imperfect German accent put on for the occasion. I presented an explanatory note from the Alloa customs office. He pointed to an empty place on one of the sofas and motioned to me to sit there, then disappeared with my letter into the partitioned corner at the end of the room.

I followed his order. Despite the cigarsmoke, richer than ever, I now saw that the customs officials were all reading imperial quarto books, whose covers, entirely taken up with photographs, had no title. A sample from the crate on the floor revealed this title-page: The Complete Erotic Poetry/of/Asafu Zir-jamah/ Translated into English Verse/by/Julia Tilt/volume LXXVIII/Printed for the Translatrix/by/The Felicitas Press/Schruns. Leafing through I observed that the poems' line endings proceeded in alphabetical order from one work to the next, from the opening limerick (with the rhymes *mamma, pyjama, diva, Godiva, Dalai Lama*) to the closing sestina (*Liz, fuzz, buzzbuzz, Oz, jazz, Alcatraz*).

The photographs adorning the covers—one on the front, one on the back—were peculiar to each volume. The sample I examined indicated no clear relation between picture and text. On one of its sides, a tall bottle labeled *Bols* stood on a table near an ivory mallet. A slight protuberance appeared in the smooth glass about halfway up one side of the bottle, and here the liquid within, otherwise clear, had a certain opaqueness. The other cover showed a multilevel safe, whose drawers, fitted with combination locks, bore such labels as: Lust, Hunger, Alcoholism, Filial Love.

The book read by the official who sat beside me was illustrated with similarly insignificant photographs.

I could see, on the front cover to my right, a room whose diplomaed walls suggested a doctor's office. It was empty except for an armchair made out of wax; this chair was indented in every part by the marks of human teeth that had bitten hard into its substance. The back of the same volume portrayed another room, furnished as a salon. I cannot be sure of my interpretation, but it seemed that an abstract mosaic embedded in one of the walls had begun to proliferate—the other walls, part of the floor, and even much of the furniture were covered with a layer of tesserae that appeared to be spreading over them like ambitious grass.

Many minutes passed with no sign of the official who had borne off my letter. My gaze, straying across the shelves of books that stretched the length of one wall, stopped at a sign reading: *Seized at the request of the Earl of Mar.* I wondered how any private person, even noble, could exercise such a power. I asked my neighbor, who had an odd B-shaped mole on his cheek, if he would satisfy my curiosity on this point—and to my surprise he assented. More, my question roused several other lazing officials.

Nine of them gathered round me. Under their glittering visors their faces looked soft and old and filled with the resignation of old barflies.

This custms hous (one said) was bult in the sixtenth centry to tax the metl producd by the Silvr Glen of Alva, whch blonged then, as now, to the Erls of Mar.

The Arls (the second haltingly took up) in llowing his ax to be mposed on the roduce of heir orkings, tipulated hat in eturn hey be iven ertain rivileges.

The' wer firs of al (the third whisperingly intervened) themselve to exercis thei contro on al o th good comin into thi regio of Scotlan, fixin and levyin tariff as the' chos.

Furthermo (the fourth scratching his pate added) they were allow to appoi the officia, with the ki's conse, who were to administ the roy levi at the sa ti as their o.

Nw by and by (the fifth gently crowed) thes appointmnts acquird a certan importanc, and som of thm wer bestowd to rewrd exceptionl servics as hereditar offics.

Whn (the sixth darkly confided) the mnes of the Slver Gln wre bandoned, the ffices cntinued, nd hve dne so dwn to the prsent—all of us are in trth dscendants of thse nble srvants whm the Arls of Mr nce hnored wth the pst of cstms fficial.

O coure (the seventh screechily exclaimed) ou dutie hae no the importane the' ha i the ol day!

By the ay (the eighth characteristically asked) id ou ear the usic his orning? Hat is an od ustom, ideed an obligation, iposed on us oficers—we are upposed eery orning, on oening the ustoms-ouse, to ing the *Ymn to Ilver* omissioned from ome aonymous Elizabethan omposer to elebrate the ine.

Fr sm tm nw (the ninth mutteringly concluded) wv fnd it bttr—mr btfl as wll as plsntr fr us—to tk dvntg of the ltst tchnlgcl prgrss in prfrmng ths tsk.

Thanking all the officials for their helpfulness, I crossed the room to look over the books the Earls of Mar had thought necessary to suppress.

Among them were such varied titles as:

> Samuel Pegge, the younger, *Curialia miscellanea; anecdotes of old times*
> Leonard Wright, *The hunting of Antichrist*
> *Wright's chaste wife, The*
> Daniel Featley, *The fisher catcht in his own net*
> Edward Blount, *The hospital of incurable fools*
> Thomas Pearson, *Infidelity; its aspects, causes, and agencies*
> Thomas Campbell, *Gertrude of Wyoming*
> Mary E. Braddon, *Only a clod*

Robert Baron, *The Cyprian academie*
Sir James M. Barrie, *When a man's single*
William Gouge, *The dignitie of chivalrie*
George Peele, *The honor of the garter*
Susanna Centlivre, *A bold stroke for a wife*
Frank Barrett, *The sin of Olga Zassoulitch*
Richard Kearton, *Wild life at home*
John Stuart Blackie, *Lays of the highlands*
Henry Rowlands, *Mona Antiqua restaurata*
Nicholas Rowe, *The biter, a comedy*
John Hunter, *The natural history of the human
     teeth*
Thomas Hall, *Funebria florae; the downfall of
     May-games*
Nathaniel Hawthorne, *The scarlet letter*
Robert Greene, *The historie of Orlando furioso*
Robert Records, *The urinal of physick*
Bert Morton, *The poet's office*
Mrs James W. Loudon, *Botany for ladies*
Thomas Bayly, *Herba parietis, or the wall-flower*
Henry Peacham, the younger, *Minerva Britanna,
     or a garden of heroical devises*
Henry Stubbe, *Rosemary and Bayes: or, animad-
     versions upon a treatise called The rehearsall
     trans-prosed*
John Florio, *Queen Anna's new world of words*
Ralph D. Wornum, *Analysis of ornament*
Hesba Stretton, *Through a needle's eye*
Bp Edward Reynolds, *The rich man's charge*
Jonathan Slick, *High life in New York*
Hamon L'Estrange, *Americans no Jewes*
Hamon L'Estrange, *The alliance of divine offices*
Richard B. Kimball, *Undercurrents of Wall Street*
Samuel Rowlands, *The letting of humours blood
     in the head-vaine*
Fritdtjof Nansen, *The structure and combination*

> *of the historical elements of the central nerv-*
> *ous system*
> Gerard Legh, *The accedens of armory*
> Robert Boyle, *The experimental history of colours*
> James Wilson, *Biography of the blind*
> Robert Tailor, *The hogge hath lost his pearle*
> William Prynne, *A gagge for long-hair'd rattle-*
> *heads*
> *Whistle-Binkie*

Nothing drew my particular notice until I discovered a three-volume novel by Berthold Auerbach, the nineteenth-century regionalist; the title was quite unknown to me. Opening it at random, I came across a chapter whose heading was "The Otiose Creator"; and my chance reading† of it gave me the first clue to the solution of the enigmas that lay between me and Mr. Wayl's heritage.

† The original text has been published as an Appendix to this work.

•

"THE OTIOSE
CREATOR"

Gottlieb told Maria his dream of the previous night.

"In a gray silence I floated upwards through the sky, past the clouds, past the stars. Then I came to another world and thought, 'This surely is Paradise.' At first I crossed meadows, then wooded hills with pretty streams. Beyond them was the city, extensive but surprisingly quiet.

"I walked down from the hills to enter the city, but I had not so much as reached the outskirts when I was stopped by a pitiful sight. A man lay in the ditch by the path I had taken. I have never seen anyone so thin: through his rags one could see, all over his body, the points of bones about to pierce the skin; and the skin, gray and transparent like greasy parchment, had indeed begun to break and flake off in many places. Little wheezing groans issued from his throat, wringing my heart in spite of horror and disgust. I ran towards the city to find someone to help me succor this poor creature. Barely arrived at the first buildings, I came upon a policeman whom I summoned to follow me. We were soon at the side of the helpless wretch. But when the latter saw who was with me, he loosed a shriek of horror, then became so still I thought he no longer breathed. As for the policeman, he had at first seemed indifferent to the prostrate man; but after the shriek he approached him, raised his club and struck him a terrible blow on the temple. Then the policeman saluted and started back towards the city. I sat there for a while in a shocked daze. After a while I looked at the stricken man, and I shuddered at the appearance of his head: the blow had truly bashed the skull in, making an indentation from eyebrow to crown of brownish-blue. Yet as I looked the eyes opened, and the wheezing groans started again, sharper than before. Then the eyes turned on me—or rather one of them turned, for the other had been immobilized in its socket by the blow—the eye turned on me, the groaning stopped, and the stricken man fell as silent as he had in front of the policeman. Incredulous, I turned towards the city.

"At the place where I had found the policeman another man now stood, as if waiting for me, and I soon recognized our nephew young Hans, who had died while at the university in Freiburg.

" 'Uncle Gottlieb!' he cried when he had made me out. 'Welcome, welcome! I didn't know it was you, but I should have—always the model of civic duty. Confidentially, though, I think I should tell you—of course this is not to be taken as criticism, what you did was perfectly all right—I should tell you that outside the city they are allowed to do pretty much what they want. I see that you protest—it was in truth a fearful noise he made, but wasn't that after you had called the angel? You see, I watched the whole business, and it seemed to me that that fellow was behaving himself— considering the fact of course that he was outside the city. He wasn't really making very much noise and he was well concealed by the ditch. Naturally you did come upon him unexpectedly and it must have been a nasty shock—but you should see the ones farther out, especially up in the mountains: nauseating! And you should hear *them* scream. I had to go there only last month to gather some hair (it's amazing how hair grows on them no matter how abominable their condition), and I could swallow nothing but biscuits and milk for days. We should be grateful for the present policy, even if it is rather easy on them and deprives the rest of us of the consolation of witnessing their state.'

" 'Then they are the damned?' I asked.

" 'What a funny thing to say, Uncle Gottlieb!—although they must surely feel like the damned,' Hans answered with a laugh. 'No, it is better that they be left free in the country to lie in the open and lament than that they be kept in town and there stuffed in subcellars and publicly beaten. For no matter how thoroughly they are muffled and no matter how much pain is inflicted on them, it seems that the necessary municipal silence can never be attained: not only are they too miserable, they are simply too numerous. Imagine: 190,000,000,000 at the last census. Furthermore the space they occupied has been redeemed and converted into dormitories for the laborers that are really very cozy (cozy enough for them at any rate). —But tell me, Uncle: how long has it been since you arrived?'

" 'I was coming to the city for the first time when I found that man in the ditch.'

" 'Then you've just arrived? Good Lord, come over here, out of sight. Oh Uncle, why didn't you tell me? Thank goodness you've got your Sunday clothes on: ah, that's a stroke of luck—you could not imagine how sensitive they are to such things. Formerly, it seems, when the press of entrants was not so great, there was more tolerance as to such details; but nowadays one's respectability is established by one's shoes! Oh Uncle, I am happy for you—you can be certain they will listen to you, and you will have a chance to tell them about your farm and your livestock and your savings so carefully amassed (you may thank yourself for that trouble, Uncle!), and then you will be safe. Now you must not expect too much—you will have to work a little, probably in the aerial farms, but you will have all the farm hands you want to help you; and with your savings you should be granted a satisfactory life. You will then be able to prepare the way for Aunt Maria—influence is always a help, although of course yours will be small. But that can wait: the thing to do

now is to get you registered. I'm afraid it may take
rather a long while, but at least you'll know once it's
over that you are established *forever*. Believe me, that's
a relief such as you've never experienced, and never
will again.'

"Hans took me by the arm and led me towards the
center of the city.

" 'Now let me remind you,' he said, 'to be careful in
telling about your possessions. Don't mention everything (don't tell them how many hens you have,
Uncle!)—just be sure not to leave out any major item.
You see, while money isn't the only thing that counts
—an influential protector can redeem individuals
without a penny—it is frequently decisive in determin-
ing the category into which the new arrival is directed.'

" 'But shouldn't I first point to other signs of
worth?' I asked. 'The love I have borne my family, the
care . . .'

" 'Yes, yes, Uncle, but they know of those things
already. And then they really make so little difference.
Such behavior is of course admired and welcomed, but
it is very hard to evaluate. It is also so common—how
few there are who cannot find excuses for their mis-
behavior! and in this respect kindness is the rule here—
so common that it is useless as a basis for the complex
classification our administrative angels have to make.
Thus other elements are considered—among them
wealth. (You understand that there is no money here,
heaven forbid! One is supplied according to one's
classification.) You may reasonably ask, isn't the good
life of a poor man more meritorious than the same life
lived by someone richer? But in this matter, the truth

seems to be that the advantages of money not only should, but do, permit the rich to live superior moral lives. It appears that the poorer one is, the less time and energy one has for those beneficial actions that the comfortable are able to perform practically as a matter of course. So you see, taking money into consideration when establishing a person's dossier is anything but an injustice. It is really a question of giving people what they deserve, and this means what they are capable of, which in turn is decided by what they have been. Should a half-starved savage who has lived his life like an animal be given the same rewards as a man—for instance, an administrator or a poet—who has shown himself capable of service of a higher order? That would hardly be justice.'

"I walked on, clinging to Hans's arm in a state of bewilderment. We walked through many clean streets, and as we neared the center, the streets became grand avenues planted with sycamores, paved with tiles of many-colored moss.

" 'Hans, tell me: is the Good Lord here?'

"Indicating the splendid avenue before us he answered, 'How can you doubt it?'

" 'Does he know of such things as the man in the ditch?'

" 'Oh Uncle, heaven forbid! The poor Dear has already endured enough; and He has made all this possible for us. What ingratitude if we did not ensure Him peace at last! He has given *us* that, and more. He no longer must spend His Hours on the care of His Kingdom, but lives withdrawn in the most magnificent of palaces set in the fairest of parks, attended by those who best know His wants—His ministering angels are

the highest classification of heaven. He lives in bliss,
surrounded as He is only with praise and adoration;
and His happiness is our sweetest joy (Uncle, forgive
my tears!). But look smart now! Here are the registra-
tion bureaux.'

"We had come to a gray building of many storeys,
as vast as a fortress. There were two lines of people in
front of it, one of those entering, the other of those
leaving. As we approached, the latter was interrupted
by a group that bustled down the great steps. Two
uniformed men held a woman between them and hurried her along. The skin below her mouth was covered
with a purple cancer. She disappeared with her guards
down a nearby sidestreet that I had not noticed. Many
such groups were proceeding down it.

" 'She is being taken out of the city,' Hans remarked.

" 'Like the man I found this morning?'

" 'Yes. Disease is not allowed in the city either, unless it is completely benign.'

" 'But surely the doctors here . . .'

" 'Oh, the doctors have all retired comfortably. It's
their due, don't you think? Not quite all, as a matter
of fact—there are a few so obsessed with disease that
they have given up their greater privileges to live with
the sick. They are thought to be a little crazy—can
you imagine making such a choice for eternity?'

" 'Then that woman's disease will go on untreated?'

" 'Very likely.'

" 'But it will get no worse?'

" 'If its natural course is to get worse, it will.'

" 'But then sooner or later the disease will kill her.'

" 'No, no: no matter what happens, she will not die.'

"We had reached the top of the steps and were about to enter the building. All at once such a feeling of horror came over me that I cried out and, trembling, woke up. But once awake I realized, Maria, what had given me that feeling of horror. It was not horror at the vision before me, but at the thought that I too might be 'taken out of the city.' And the relief that followed was not only relief at waking but that of knowing that even *there* I had nothing to fear, and I thanked God in my heart for giving me the good things of this world.

"I remember that as I passed from sleep to waking I turned towards Hans, who smiled as he receded in my sight, and cried: 'Then it is only the same?' and he answered, 'The same. Uncle, but forever: world without end!'

"O Maria, hail to the Johnstones! the bloody Johnstones! the fucking Johnstones! the enemies of things as they are! They have come back to their own, they have come back to Alba as kings. May their Gypsy girl have wicked teeth in her cunt!"

THE CUSTOMS
HOUSE (II)

No sooner had I finished the chapter than a voice behind me said: I regret, sir—and turning I saw, next to
the official who had first spoken to me, a small man
dressed all in green (tweed, shirting, silk and suede)—
that it will be impossible for me to give you the information you need.

Are you the director here? I asked. Perhaps then
you might help me out with another problem, if you
can spare me a few minutes.

I showed him the concluding paragraph of "The Otiose Creator." Can you tell me who these Johnstones are?

Oh dear! However did you find *that?* Well: you see there is a family in this town called Johnstone (quite the *gratin*), but these are others—indeed the Earl no doubt suppressed Auerbach's book out of consideration for the proper Johnstones. The "Johnstones" Auerbach refers to are the family of a disowned bastard son of one of the Earls of Mar. This son came here around 1780 (from the colonies, I believe), making all kinds of trouble, taking the name of Johnstone, and pretending of all things to be not only of noble but of royal blood—I suppose that's why Auerbach says the Johnstones *sind als Königen nach Alba heimgekehrt.* He even adopted a coat of arms—a stupid pretension when everyone knew he had no claim to any title whatsoever.

Could you describe the coat of arms?

No, but I'll look it up for you if you like. (I'm awfully sorry I can't help you out about that adze.) It's surely listed in Cremlin-Bicêtre; let's see—Jargon, Jessel, Jinemevicz, Job: here we are, *Johnstone:*

Gold a bend silver with halberd gules

and the reason above:

L'herminette à la taille du roy!

There!

A loonlike factory whistle resounded from the foggy air outside while I studied the heraldic register.

After a long moment the green director began looking at me with diffidence; so I thanked him and—once he had sternly told me that the customs house contained no other documents on the "Johnstones"—went out.

The director accompanied me to the door.

You were fortunate, he said, to have heard our madrigal this morning—strange to say, our apparatus works in indirect proportion to the fineness of the weather: it needs a truly foul day to hear the music fair.

·

"HIS PRISM AND
SILENT FACE"

To me, that day was anything but foul.

L'herminette à la taille du roy! Kingfitted ermine; or a kingsized adze. The halberd in the coat of arms, a plain bill, was an image of my "adze": *l'herminette* could mean only it.

Then was not the first doubly-pretending Johnstone the stone-not-king of the riddle? I felt sure of it, and sure that I should find proof in Alva.

I remembered how, during the race at Mr. Wayl's,

the adze had appeared first red amid white light, and later, under the charm of "Midas's finger," red in a haze of gold. These were the very colors of the heraldic shield.

After lunch I went to the Alva town hall and approached a clerk with the request to examine certain municipal records.

The odd Johnstones? he asked. Ah, the best of the lot lived long after that time—that was poor Inno Johnstone, who died forty-odd years ago, poor unlucky man he was. Let me tell you about him; he deserves his bit of fame. After that you can look up any part of the family you damn well please!

The last of his family, Innocent Johnstone had, I learned, lived a short strange life. Showing early an exceptional interest in physical science, he had for two years been a brilliant student at St. Andrew's, whence he had been sent down for disciplinary reasons. He had pursued his scientific studies independently, living alone, devoting all his immense inheritance to the construction of experimental equipment.

In those days much research was being done in the effects of extreme heat and cold, and Johnstone naturally shared the interest of the scientific world. His own interest became an enthusiasm when, almost by accident, he made the first of his extraordinary discoveries.

In the Silver Glen of Alva there was to be found, diffused in the water of certain pools, a crystalline substance popularly known as fleshmetal. It existed only in minute quantities and was hardly known outside the town—and even there many, having never seen it, thought its existence to be legendary. The substance was remarkable in that it destroyed solid materials upon touching them; many of those who had tried to handle it had been maimed, and none had succeeded in bringing any of it away. Johnstone found that fleshmetal responded to magnetic influence, and he solved the problem of transporting it by constructing magnetized "trays" whose current, strong enough to draw up the dangerous particles, was too weak to bring them into direct contact: the fleshmetal was carried suspended (either in water or air) at a fraction of a millimeter beneath the tray.

Once he had secured a small stock of fleshmetal, Johnstone submitted it to numerous tests. He was unable to reduce the substance to component elements. Its violent corrosiveness was, he discovered, the result of abnormally vigorous molecular motion, untypical of any other known solid; but he was unable to explain this phenomenon in any way until he decided to observe the influence of low temperatures on fleshmetal. He had prepared his apparatus—airpump and baths of liquid air—to reach temperatures well below freezing. To his surprise, he had hardly started the experiment when the suspended particles under observation disappeared. Repeating the steps taken, he determined that solid fleshmetal became a gas when cooled to $-2°$ C.

Many a scientist might have then announced his discovery to the world. But Johnstone was too absorbed in his research to think of giving it up.

High temperatures (necessarily limited by the melting-points of the metals composing the magnetic tray) brought about an increase in fleshmetal's molecular activity, but no sign of a change of state, either to

liquid or gas. The scientist resumed his experimenta-
tion with low temperatures. To begin with he succeeded, using baths of liquid oxygen together with a
mercurial vacuum, in reducing gaseous fleshmetal to a
temperature ($-198°$ C) at which its molecular motion was so calmed as to render it innocuous and easier
to handle. But his further efforts, aimed at liquefaction,
were vain. Even the use of liquid helium, as a last step
in the "cascade method," with prolonged heatless ex-
pansion of gaseous fleshmetal, failed. Not, however,
entirely: Johnstone observed, towards the end of his
final attempt, certain faint white drops on the innermost wall of his apparatus, and it was possible, he
thought, that these marked a beginning of liquefaction.
The temperature at that moment was no higher than
$-269°$ C, probably even a degree lower: that is, only
three degrees above absolute zero. Could greater cold
be produced?

Johnstone did not know what to do next. He was
tantalized by the white drops, and yet he knew that he
had exhausted the known resources of physics. Since
he had already spent a great part of his considerable
fortune, he considered the possibility of abandoning.
Then his good luck saved him.

One morning, while his Irish maid swept out his
laboratory, Johnstone was examining certain ordinary
materials at his spectroscope in order to check the
instrument. He was engaged in observing some iodine,
heated to $700°$ C in a cyanite dish, when an inexplicable line of bright cupric green appeared in the spectrum. It vanished presently, returned briefly, again
disappeared. After a moment Johnstone noticed that
the appearance of the green line seemed to correspond

to the more prolonged proximities of his biddy. The following conversation, reported by the scientist to the town clerk's father, then took place:

Agnes, come here, please!

Oh sirr!

Agnes . . . ?

Ah Mr. Inno, forgive me! It's them mumbleberries I et in the woods laast evenin.

What? Eat mumbleberries?

Indeed, sirr, they're me favorite pickin: but they do make a bawdy faart.

(The clerk interrupted his narrative to inform me that the name *mumbleberry* came not from the caramel stickiness of the berries, which sometimes impeded clear speech, but from a rash on the legs, supposedly brought on by the fruit, called *mormal:* the original name was *mormalberry*.)

Thus Inno Johnstone made his second great discovery. A new inert gas was soon isolated and its existence spectroscopically confirmed by electrical examination in Plücker tubes. Johnstone found the gas in a pure state, as clusters of tiny bubbles, in the soft concavity of the mumbleberry where the stem enters the fruit. The name he chose for the gas was *anagnon*, referring both to his biddy's name and the "unchaste" way she had brought it to his attention.

Johnstone must have felt that angels were helping him when he learned, testing the new gas for its properties, that it could not be liquefied under exhausted helium; for this signified that anagnon had a critical temperature lower than that of any known gas and so might serve to liquefy fleshmetal. It did in fact: by expanding gaseous fleshmetal under exhausted

anagnon, Inno obtained liquid fleshmetal at a temperature he estimated as $-272°$ C ($1°$ Abs).

He was still unsatisfied: for this last experiment had
left perplexing questions unanswered. How was it possible that at one degree above absolute zero fleshmetal
could show no tendency to solidify, and anagnon itself no sign of liquefaction? In theory all matter should
attain a solid state before reaching the point of ultimate
cold. The margin of one degree seemed improbably
small to allow the final transformations of the two
new elements. (For fleshmetal, he had decided, was
also an unknown element.) Was anagnon a uniquely
irreducible gas? Or fleshmetal an irreducible liquid?
What alternative could there be?

Johnstone decided that the most reasonable course
was to try to solidify fleshmetal. Again he liquefied a
quantity of fleshmetal (this procedure took two
weeks) and prolonged the methods of the experiment,
drawing off expanding anagnon from its case of solid
helium. As the vacuum thus created increased, he
agitated the liquid fleshmetal in order to promote that
molecular regrouping that would begin solidification.
After eleven weeks of painstaking work, Johnstone
saw solid crystals form—only a first few, and only
briefly, for in a moment his apparatus disintegrated.

The town clerk recalled the day of the catastrophe,
a pleasant day in mid-August, with all Alva still. The
clerk, then a boy of eight, was playing in his yard
when he heard a sinister roar. Going into the street he
beheld Inno Johnstone's house sprouting with enormous clublike branches of snow that projected through
every door, window and chimney to a distance of

more than thirty feet. In a very short time these white limbs dissolved "into thin air."

Johnstone had miraculously survived. The wreck of his equipment, brought on by the virtually absolute vacuum he had created, had thrown him to the ground. He had lain insensible while the released cold froze the air in wild columns that surged over him towards the apertures of room and house, leaving him unscathed. Revived, his first concern had been for the harm the scattered fleshmetal might have done when, cast into the air, it had returned to its original state. Fortunately all of it had fallen on the ground, its infinitesimal bits thereupon burning their way into the earth. (The largest hole thus made, about a quarter of an inch across, was sounded to a depth of eighty-two feet, at which point water was touched.)

Prudence, the advice of friends and the orders of the town council would have obliged Johnstone to leave off. Instead he moved to an isolated farm and invested in new equipment all that remained of his fortune. (Each pound of liquefied helium cost him three thousand guineas.)

He was haunted now by a single vision: fleshmetal crystallized at a temperature he dared not name. Only seen for an instant, the crystals had existed. Unlike the crystalline fleshmetal of the Silver Glen, they had not destroyed the materials they had touched. Was this because the extreme cold had rendered them harmless as it had the liquid and the colder gaseous fleshmetal?

Extreme cold? The anagnon had remained pure gas; the vacuum had been absolute. What had the temperature been?

Was there no limit of cold?

Johnstone, half admitting the hypothesis his imagination had caught on, assumed, "to get on with the job," that beyond absolute zero temperature might exist. He began preparing for his last experiment.

He constructed in his new apparatus a device that would, when the crystals of fleshmetal appeared, automatically reduce the vacuum that had nearly destroyed him; as well as numerous systems for observing and controlling whatever temperature might occur at crystallization.

The two years of preparation saw Johnstone so neglect his health that he was an ill man when the experiment started. Yet his last sick days were happy.

Fleshmetal crystals again appeared, at a temperature of "$-x°$ Abs." Their crystallization was accompanied by a transformation of molecular activity from a standstill, at $.01°$ Abs, to violent motion, suggestive of heat. Other substances, cooled with solid fleshmetal and anagnon, underwent a similar transformation. Johnstone realized that beyond absolute zero a strange "heat" obtained, which he called *infraheat*.

To investigate it, he built an infracaloric space enclosed in a vacuum jacket, itself encased in solid helium. There, combining in an atmosphere of anagnon various materials cooled below $0°$Abs, he created a wide range of infracaloric temperatures, measured with a water thermometer on whose scale $+ 1°$ Inf $= -1°$ Abs.

In infraheat, the peculiarities fleshmetal had shown at normal temperatures were common to all matter. $0°$ was the "hot" limit of infraheat, at which molecular activity was greatest, while it declined as the degrees of the Infra scale rose. Nevertheless, with this lessening of infraheat the state of matter changed as if "normal" heat were increased, so that solids became liquids, liquids gases, and gases solid.

As the changes of fleshmetal above 0°Abs had implied, the cycle of matter was thus seemingly infinite. The destructive power of fleshmetal itself was evidently a corollary to the extension of its infracaloric properties into the realm of normal heat; for in infraheat it lacked such power.

Water was the only exception to the reversal of changes that appeared with infraheat: at 1°Inf it was vapor, becoming a boiling liquid at 175° Inf and ice at 278°Inf. It was consequently well adapted, its properties in infraheat being known, to serve as the fluid in Johnstone's thermometer.

Johnstone had planned to explore the relationship between the three exceptional substances, water, fleshmetal and anagnon; but he was not given enough time to do so. His last work concerned the mechanical questions raised in a world where iron softened with cold, where mercury hardened with heat, and where, between the boiling- and freezing-points of water, wood was a liquid and diamonds a light gas. Before dying he achieved infracaloric combustion, burning molten salt in glass air. He had hoped to build machines for his new world before succumbing; and his last words concerned an airplane entirely of butter.

Johnstone had contracted a rash of blains on his legs, brought on, in confirmation of popular legend, by the excessive amounts of mumbleberries he handled in maintaining his supply of anagnon. The sores having become infected, Johnstone's worn health yielded fast. He died at the age of thirty-four, without putting his extraordinary findings in coherent form. At his own request his laboratory, abandoned in operation, was destroyed by shelling while he was still on his death-bed, so that no one should be harmed by another, possibly more dangerous disintegration of his equipment. His few admirers, of whom the clerk's father was one, had tried to interest the scientific world in the work they had long followed (if only half comprehendingly). But unluckily a drought parched the pools of the Silver Glen, and all their fleshmetal vanished, the name soon after resuming the reputation it had long borne as an excrescence of folkish fancy.

●

ABE JOHNSTONE'S LETTER

When the clerk had finished his story, he showed me into the town library where he gave me access to the regional archives. An hour's patience brought forth the records of the first false Johnstone; among them I found a curious document.

Its bulk comprised a letter evidently addressed to a number of newspapers and reviews of the day. Pinned to the first of its sheets were four slips of paper inscribed with inks of differing colors. The topmost of these slips read in faint pink ink:

Pennsylvania Gazette, Independant Reflector
Keimer's Gazette (Barbados)
Mémoires Secrètes de la République des Lettres
General Advertiser, Grub Street Journal, Fog's
    Journal, Reid's Journal, Mist's Journal, Oedipus
    or the Postrian Remounted, History of the
    Works of the Learned:
                                         Rejected.

The second slip, in purple ink, was as follows:

Evening Salem Gazette, N.Y. Gazetteer, A's &
    B's, Royal American Magazine, Turtle Bay Re-
    flector & Oyster Bay Mirror
Keimer's Gazette (Barbados)
La Vespa Veronese, Il Caffè
Trudolyubivary Ptchelà
Le Radoteur, La Queue de l'Abeille, L'Armée
    Littéraire, Nécrologe des Hommes Célèbres de
    France
Public Advertiser, Public Ledger, St. James's
    Chronicle, Cock's Chronicle, The Rambler,
    The Bee, The Connoisseur, The Voluptuary,
    The Looker-on:
                                         Rejected.

The third slip, slightly larger than the others, was
in black ink:

The Mass. Sentinel & The Republican Journal,
    Cheshire Republican, Green Mountain Post-
    boy, Con. Courant, Sodus Social Register,
    Franklin Repository, Maryland Inland & Balti-
    more Advertiser, Minerva Advertiser, Adler,

Paine's Labour, Rivington's N.Y. Loyal Ga-
zette, Mathews' Universal Asylum
Colon's Intelligencer (Quebec)
Asiatick Miscellany
Gaceta de Madrid
Mercure de Suède
Mémoires de Bachaumont, L'Observateur Ob-
servé, Journal de Verdun
Public Advertiser, Morning Chronicle, Thersites,
Times, English Magazine, Monstrous Maga-
zine, Pandora's Box (A Magazine for Gentle-
women), Sauce for the Gander, Macaroni
Magazine, European Magazine, A New Re-
view, British Critic, The Lounger, Potter &
Poet:
                                        Rejected.

The last slip, whose brief list was of a blackish
chocolate tone difficult to define, read thus:

American Museum of the Dead
Galeria di Venere
Nouvelle Bibliothèque Ecossaise, Le Croulant
The Ash & the Wren, A Pathetic Magazine.
                                        (Rejected)

By looking up the dates of the periodicals listed, I
reckoned that Johnstone had first sent out his hapless
letter around 1745 and had not abandoned his attempts
to publish it until 1803.
This was the letter's text:

Sir,
      To the east of the Scots burgh of Alva in the
county of Clackmannanshire, a pleasant valley,

through which the waters of a cascade flow with a quick and rejoicing course, bears the denomination of Silver Glen. The epithet of *silver* is thought to be expressive of those riches that once abounded in its earth, to which abandoned workings yet bear supposed witness. But the name of this celebrated spot is a testimony of religion, not a record of commerce.

During their long servitude under the Imperial and Barbarian yoke, the native and foreign tribes of Italy had mutually adopted and corrupted each other's superstitions. The Christians, indeed, practised the worship of Christ; but they disgraced and polluted it with a various mixture of pagan idolatry. Others revered the memory of Sylvius, the ancient prophet and king of the Romans; yet the obsolete and mysterious language of his cult opened a field of dispute to numberless sects, who variously explained the fundamental doctrines of their religion, and were all indifferently derided by those who rejected the divine mission and miracles of the king. To escape the idolaters, the schismatics, and the unbelievers, a pious Roman, who had taken the sacred name of Sylvius, summoned his followers from all the corners of Italy. These disciples, who had so long sighed in contempt and obscurity, obeyed the welcome summons; and on the appointed day, in the first years of the fourteenth century, appeared to the number of about seven thousand. The hasty assembly gradually coalesced into a great and permanent society.

Under the guidance of Sylvius and his successors, they wandered over Europe in search of a place where they might establish and pursue the practice of the religion that united them. A century later, after many discouragements, tney finally found refuge in Scotland on the lands of Alexander Stewart, the Earl of Mar, whom they had converted to their faith: and by him they were granted, in frank almoign, for the construction of their shrines, a fair valley which they named the Glen of Sylvius. Such was, and indeed is, the proper appellation of the place, which only took the name of Silver's Glen, and later Silver Glen, through the long corruptions of usage.

This good fortune of the wise and peaceable followers of Sylvius endured for over a century before it was at last succeeded by the most terrible calamity. Covetousness and prejudice finally concurred in representing the Sylvians as a society of atheists, who, by the most daring refusal of the beliefs of the age, had merited the severest animadversion of the civil magistrate. The counsels of princes are more frequently influenced by views of temporal advantage than by consideration of abstract and speculative truth. A prudent magistrate might have observed with pleasure the progress of a religion which diffused among the people a pure, benevolent and universal system of ethics, adapted to every duty and every condition of life. But the mysteries of the Sylvian faith and worship were concealed

from the eyes of strangers, and even of cate-
chumens, with a secrecy which served to excite their wonder and animosity; the pious
solitariness of the Sylvians made their conduct,
or perhaps their designs, appear in a much
more serious and criminal light, inspiring the
multitude with the apprehension of some danger which would arise from the new sect. It
may be that the rulers of the land shared these
fears or at the least resented the holy title of
King which the Sylvian chiefs assumed. But I
may say with certainty that it was rather the
parsimony or poverty of the family of Mar
that compelled them to deviate from the rule
of conduct which had deserved the love and
confidence of the Sylvians, whose reputed
wealth finally served only to attract a bold and
barbarous rapaciousness. The Earl of Mar dex-
terously persuaded the Scots king of the sedi-
tious hostility of the innocent sect, and in the
year 1541, under the authority of the crown,
and with the agency of a fanatical populace,
the Earl reaped the harvest of his malevolence.
In a tumult of cruelty and indignation, the
habitations of the Sylvians were pillaged, their
sanctuary ravaged by a promiscuous crowd of
Gypsies and Beggars, and they themselves
slaughtered by the soldiery of the Earl, who
seized their goods and moneys in the name of
royal justice. Four thousand persons are said to
have perished in the massacre. The survivors,
numbering about five hundred, mostly natives
of the country converted to Sylvian beliefs,

were threatened with death, unless they swore
an oath of fidelity or went into perpetual exile;
but rejecting such alternatives, they broke
away before their punishment could be inflicted, and withdrew into the natural haven of
the Ochils.

Three centuries of persecution reduced
somewhat the descendants of these survivors.
Yet so sensible were the Sylvians of the imperfection of religion without communal practice,
that, in all this time, the name of Sylvius has
been borne without interruption by their leaders, and nobly borne. The religious exercise of
the united sect has been for these chiefs the important and unremitting object of their lives;
nor was time and place allowed to excuse them
for forgetting their temporal rights over Sylvius's Glen. These holy Kings have been
chosen by tradition, because of the bastardy of
Alexander Stewart, from the bastard and outcast issue of the Earls of Mar; the exercise of
their sacred functions has required of them an
immaculate purity both of mind and of body;
it is incumbent on them to excel in decency
and virtue the rest of their fellow-citizens.
Their authority has been recognized from time
to time by men of particular genius: thus Rolando Lasso, the prince of musicians and the
familiar of kings, prophesied that the bastard-
born Sylvius should return to rule anew.

The time is at hand for that prophecy to be
fulfilled, and the last of the Sylvian leaders, the
author of this letter, has indeed returned to

Alva. Yet the behaviour of the present Earl of
Mar appears to be as reprehensible as that of
his predecessors. In my general view of the
persecution first authorized in the year 1541
and which thereafter continued unabated, I
have purposely refrained from describing the
sufferings and deaths of Sylvian martyrs. It
would be an easy task from ancient acts to collect a long series of horrid and disgusting pictures, and to fill many pages with all the vari-
eties of torture which savage executioners could
inflict on the human body. But there is more
propriety in declaring a less pathetic, but no
less appalling fact, namely, that the Earls of
Mar have held and continue to hold against
justice and humanity the rightful property of
innocent men. The injustice of their possession
is apparent in the unnatural measures they have
taken to preserve it: for not only did the Earls
who succeeded their first criminal exemplar
obstruct the Sylvians by force and cruelty, but
to secure for themselves the sacred glen, they
had it scooped into a prodigious but *imaginary*
mine; precious metals were artificially introduced as props to their consummate pretence;
and although the pretended workings and issue
soon disappeared, the defences raised to protect them remain a sinister and impenetrable
barrier about the place.

These events, which heretofore have not
been thought deserving of a place in history,
have been productive of a memorable injustice, which has afflicted the disinherited of

Alva above three hundred years, and will be extinguished only with the presumption of the offenders. The inflexible zeal of liberty and devotion has animated the Sylvians to refuse obedience to the Usurpers, whose rights they dispute, and whose spiritual powers they deny. They have asserted with confidence, almost with exultation, that the rightful succession has been interrupted; that all the Earls of Mar have been infected by the contagion of greed and dishonesty; and that the prerogatives of lordship should be confined to the chosen portion of Sylvian believers, who alone have preserved inviolate the integrity of their faith and conduct.

Would that the family of Mar possessed one legitimate son whose genius and virtues might atone for the vice and folly of his fathers! Did such a one support this exalted faith, his name would deserve a place with Constantine, and his judgment would be justly entitled to all the applause philosophers might bestow upon it. But that motley gang, dictated by passion and by selfish motives, has disgraced useful and sublime truth with the most abject and dangerous persecution. Their ferocious sons, who disdain the salutary restraint of laws, are yet more anxious to preserve riches than to foster the religion of a society the object of their contempt and hatred; and their power is a stone of Tantalus, perpetually suspended over the peace and safety of a devoted sect. The measures which the present writer recommends are the dictates of a sincere and dedicated believer. I exhort the reader to strengthen the courage of our company with the example of noble solicitude; to attack the oppressor in his position and his property; to substitute, in the place of barbarian indifference, the sympathies of men interested in the defence of justice; to force, in such a moment of opportunity and danger, the quill from its shelf and the coin from its box; and to arm, for the protection of human right, the hands of earnest disciples.

The mischiefs that flow from the contests of ambition are usually confined to the times and places in which they have been agitated. But the religious discord of the friends and enemies of Sylvius has been renewed in every age and is yet maintained in the immortal hatred of the Earls of Mar. Our wonder is reasonably excited that they should presume to persevere in a privilege whose ancient presumptions they are incapable of defending honestly. But the feuds, the angers, and the protests of the Earls, are the feeble and pernicious efforts of old age, which exhaust the remains of strength and accelerate the decay of the powers of life.

In conclusion, let me express the hope that the condemnation of the wisest and most virtuous of sects will sufficiently offend the reason and humanity of the present age, that men may be roused to action, and justice be done at the last.

Your Faithful Servant,

ABENDLAND JOHNSTONE

Another paper was pinned beneath the signature. It was a note written in a strange hand, and its presence suggested that Johnstone had sent his letter to individuals as well as journals. The text was brief:

Rouen le 10 Brumaire An II

Monsieur,
    Peut-être êtes-vous un bâtard, vous êtes sûrement un imposteur; car notre dernier roi est mort avant Louis de France. Je veille pour la Reine, que son règne soit éternel!

LA PLATIERE

Beneath these lines Johnstone had added:
—Alas! We are all dying.

·

"LA MESSE DE
SIRE FADEVANT"

So it appeared that Abe Johnstone was the stone who
was not a king—that La Platière qualified him an im-
poster confirmed my hunch. No doubt it would be
prudent to complete my proof by finding out who
La Platière was and by verifying the grounds on which
he had condemned Johnstone. This promised to be
anything but tedious work, for if I found La Platière's
papers I should perhaps get other helpful information
from them. The place where his note was written

seemed the best point of departure for my inquiry, and I decided to go to Rouen at once.

I wanted before leaving Alva to visit "Sylvius's Glen." It lay east of the town a ways beyond the Customs House. I had hardly passed that dismal building when a rural policeman stopped me and directed me, on learning where I was headed, back to the town. He explained that he had orders (he did not say whose) to keep me out of the glen. Seeing my disappointment—he was a kindly-looking man, although enormous and rough, with flaming golden bangs—he consoled me with a description of the glen: aside from the waterfall, he said, it was a plain place, filled with stunted elms and overgrown with unkempt masses of traveler's joy. (I asked what this was; he defined it as a variety of clematis. I remarked that in my case it was singularly ill-named.)

Riding to Edinburgh I was bothered by an especially disturbing element of the muddled history I was investigating. Who was the queen that La Platière mentioned? Had she anything to do with Auerbach's Gypsy girl? When the Long Island Gypsy had explained the scenes of the adze to the novelist, he had called the woman there portrayed "our queen." Could the woman of the adze not be the saint Mr. Wayl had let me assume her to be? Yet Johnstone declared in his letter that "Gypsies and Beggars" had destroyed the Sylvian sanctuary, and made no reference to any queen or woman. To "provide a satisfactory explanation of the meaning" of the adze, as the will required, these inconsistencies would have to be resolved.

Examining the copy I had made of the letter to be certain I had missed no clue to this dilemma, I stopped short at the name of Rolando Lasso. I had become so absorbed in answering the first question of the will that I had practically forgotten the other two. If the renaissance composer figured in Johnstone's letter, there was a chance that information concerning *La Messe de Sire Fadevant* might lie with him—and hadn't I discovered King Johnstone through just such an unexpected slender reference?

I stayed over in Edinburgh to follow this bent. For two days I worked at the Advocates' Library without finding a hint that Lasso might in his life or work have had anything to do with the Sylvians, the Earls of Mar, or the adze; nor was any *Messe de Sire Fadevant* listed among his works, extant or not. As a last resort, I decided to check the most recent musicological reviews; and on the back cover of the current issue of *Neumata*, in the list of articles announced for future publication, I found this title:

Una Missa Fa Si Re, Opera Sconosciuta di Orlando di Lasso, di Prof. Annibale Bumbè (Siena)

I was overjoyed at my new luck. Nevertheless, I blamed myself for not recognizing the riddle within the second question of the will: the riddle being that *Sire Fadevant* signified *Fa devant Si Re*, and that consequently the mass was one composed on a theme whose opening notes were *fa*, *si* and *re*, and not one written by or for the Lord Fadevant whom I had hired two aspiring historians to track down.

I had planned to wait for the published article to learn more about the mass; but that very day a letter reached me with the news that Beatrice and Isidore

Fod were contesting Mr. Wayl's will. Convinced that the more evidence I could give the probate court, the safer my rights would be, I decided to visit Siena and elicit from Dr. Bumbè in person whatever he knew that might help me in my task.

•

AT THE
PROFESSOR'S

On the evening of my second day in Siena, Professor Bumbè received me at his lodgings in the Palazzo Grembo-Maledetti. Once we were seated in his study, I explained the reason of my visit.

I shall tell you all I know in this matter, he said. Several years ago, a letter came to light that caused considerable interest in musicological circles. It had been written to the Flemish composer Lassus by his Parisian publisher Adrien Le Roy; its text was mainly an inquiry into the significance of a *Missa Fa Si Re* that the composer had written during his visit to the court of Charles IX in 1571. It was then common for musicians to write pieces on musical mottoes, and such works received their titles from the Guidonian note names of the motto. The unusual thing in this case was that Lassus had let it be known that the three notes of his motto—*fa, si* and *re*—were the abbreviations of secret Latin words.

As evidence of the public mystification that resulted, Le Roy lists some of the solutions he has heard proposed. Many thought that Lassus had simply paid tribute to the French king, who had received him handsomely; they advanced such phrases as

Faber sistrum Regis:
The composer is the king's sistrum

Court gossip produced interpretations less flattering to the royal family:

Fæx signat Reginam:
Rouge marks out the Queen

a reference to the aging Catherine de Médicis. The favorable effects on the king's impotence of his recent marriage to Elizabeth of Austria were invoked in

Favus sinus Reginae:
The Queen's lap is sweet as a honeycomb

and in

Fartor significat rectum:
The bird fattener portends uprightness

the idea of "bird" being a vulgar one, as in the German *Hahn* and your own "cock." Gossip likewise discovered references to current court peccadilloes:

Fabianus Sigismondo repuerascit:
For Sigismond, Fabian has become a boy again

or, concerning a supposed love affair of Lassus himself,

Faber Silviâ resupinâ:
The composer in the company of Silvia flat on her back

I mention in passing that since Lassus is etymologically a contraction of *là-dessus*, the last item shows a certain wit. The more literary hazarded such solutions as

Faber Sibylla Regorum:
The composer is the prophet of kings;
Facio sigla Regis:
I have made the abbreviation of a king

(this left the problem quite unsolved); and

Favillam Sibylla requirat:
The Sibyl searches for ashes,

perhaps a pedantic joke at would-be riddlers, perhaps a reference to Lassus's earlier *Prophetiae Sibyllarum*. Finally Le Roy jokingly imagines a possible reference to himself and concludes with two suggestions of his own:

Faber sine remuneratione:
Composer without pay

and

Fabrum siccat rex:
"Le Roy" is squeezing the composer dry

The letter ends with a plea for elucidation.

The only elucidation we have is not of the motto, but of another letter, long known but formerly not wholly explicable. This letter, written by Lassus to Le Roy, is surely an answer to the one I have described; for while it chiefly discusses royalties, one paragraph contains Lassus's comment on the *Missa Fa Si Re*. The paragraph begins by asking Le Roy if he has heard yet another interpretation of the motto—a dig at the lucrative business activity of Palestrina, then composer of the Sistine Chapel:

Fænus Sixtino remissio:
Dividends are his salvation

Lassus goes on to say that he has written a *chanson* on the motto of his mass; and that while there are three of Le Roy's proposed answers he cannot call false—*Facio sigla Regis, Faber Sibylla Regorum,* and (surprisingly) *Fæx signat Reginam*—yet these were not the three the music signified.

The very last words are interesting, implying that

the motto was discovered by those who listened to the mass—indeed, they would have had to be nearly tone-deaf not to notice the opening interval: for *fa-si* forms a tritone, condemned through the middle ages as the *diabolus in musica*. But the letter seemed to offer little hope of dispelling the mystery of the *Missa Fa Si Re*. For some time neither I nor anyone else got any farther with it. I suppose it was the irritating character of the problem that kept it in my mind despite the lack of progress. It was certainly irritating to have on the one hand such a tantalizing document as Le Roy's letter, and on the other hand only Lassus's stubborn half silence, without his mass,* and without either the text or the music of the *chanson* he mentions.

One day, however, I recalled a forgotten detail from my doctoral studies, thirty-odd years earlier. I then used to work in the British Museum preparing my thesis on Jacobean songbooks; and I had noticed once, in a 1616 collection of lyrics, an anonymous translation from the French that was remarkable in one respect. While the poem itself was a gloomy lover's complaint, its title was *Faisons Suzon*—words that might have been the opening of a light, "pastoral" French song. What possible connection did it have with the Lassus *chanson?* Only the slenderest one of the first two letters: Fa. But this, together with the inconsistency of title and text and a vague recollection of some typographical quaintness, was enough to have me write the museum asking for a photograph of the poem.

The museum's reply solved much of the enigma. A

---

* But see Appendix 2.

note accompanying the photostat informed me that the
initial letter of each line was printed in red, and that
red arabesques proceeded from these initials to encircle
one or more of the letters following them. Here is a
copy of the poem, with capitals standing for the initial letters and those within the arabesques.

I read:

FAithlesse thou art, my faith I giue to thee:
TEare out mine hart for hartlesse thou needst one,
OR take mine eies to see how blinde I bee.

SILVIa in thee my constancies vndone;
VMbre hath smircht my cheekes for thine too
                                                       white
REGister of my soule, since thou hast none.

EMpresse of riuen soules the Queene of night
FAuoring mine anguish, to me sleeping came
TAbarded with thy sweets her serene might:

'Seest thou these cloakes that now beare *Siluias*
                                                       name
REgalia of eies, smooth fleshe, and bright brocard,
TEXTures which patient Time hath giuen to
                                                       Fame?

'FAme giuing owre to Ill-fame doth such discard,
VOyding the hing'd eie and the wouen gloue:
NIgardly patcht see Siluia slack'd and Mar'd.'

SIlent she doth, that thy cleere youth aproue
NIght-maring death, thee from thy beautie
                                                       seuere:
STRAnge scull, that thou euen so my hart didst
                                                       moue!

REuile me not! for I shal spurne thee neuere:
VOLatick Time shal turne, yet not my loue:
VIgil for thee I kept; and keepe, for euere.

Now, said the Professor, one must spell out the letters capitalized:

FATEORSILVIVMREGEMFATASRETEXTF
AVONISINISTRAREVOLVI

Next, one rewrites these letters, considering the syllables *fa, si* and *re* as the beginning of words:

FATEOR SILVIVM REGEM FATAS
RETEXT FAVONI SINISTRA REVOLVI

You will notice that whereas there are three *fa*'s and three *re*'s, there are only two *si*'s. The missing *si* is the S of "seest" in line ten. It stands for Silvius, as it did at first, and so does not need to be fully spelled. (The italicization of *Siluias* farther on in the same line removes any doubt as to its meaning.) Taking this into account we have:

FATEOR SILVIVM REGEM FATA SIL-
VIVM RETEXT FAVONI SINISTRA RE-
VOLVI

All that remains to be done is to fill out the shortened words. RETEXT must be *retexunt*, and the last three words make best sense as *Favonius sinistrâ revolvit*. Here then is the secret message in its final threefold form:

Fateor Silvium Regem:
I acknowledge Silvius as king

Fata Silvium retexunt:
either The Fates undo Silvius
or The Fates weave Silvius anew

Favonius sinistrâ revolvit:
The west wind returns on the left

In asking the British Museum for that song I had hit the mark. The verses luckily remembered from years before were without doubt a translation from the text of Lassus's *chanson*—or rather not a translation but a new poem that transcribed the secret letters of the original, the sign of their presence lying in the French title, kept for the English text. It becomes clear that in referring Le Roy to this *chanson* Lassus was answering his question honestly. I would say that the presence of the motto in the mass served merely to draw attention to the *chanson* (what better opportunity than a royal mass?) and that Lassus was telling the truth when he refused to disown three of the solutions that Le Roy has reported:

I have made the abbreviation of a king
The composer is the prophet of kings
Red (if not rouge) marks out the queen

But why "queen"? Why didn't Lassus in his letter correct *reginam* to *regem*, as the poem's secret sense demands? That I haven't found out; nor do I know who Silvius might be—perhaps a current allegorical name for some pretender, or for Henri III himself? There is no evidence for such a hypothesis. And I cannot explain the second and third sentences.

When I suggested that *sinistrâ* might indicate bastardy, Dr. Bumbè cut me short.

That possibility occurred to me—Charles IX had a natural son; but Charles of Angoulême? As for the queen, perhaps she was no queen but simply Regina Wäckinger. Who will ever know, or care? I leave spurious conjecture to Le Roy.

The professor had crossed his study and seated himself at an upright piano. Drawing a small square of sandpaper from his waistcoat pocket, he began methodically sanding the white keys of the instrument.

I cannot stand to have them shiny, he explained. If my fingers slip I break into a cold sweat. Even so, I play little—the count detests music.

He brought both hands down on a full C-major chord. But the depressed keys produced no sound except for the click of his nails on their roughened ivory backs.

•

FELIX
NAMQUE

Midnight struck while I was returning to my hotel. As I followed the dark and sinuous slope of the Via Grover-Whalen, I reflected on the recent interview.

Lasso's cryptic sentences were plain. The unraveling and reweaving of Sylvius—surely Silvius was he, and surely the double meaning of *Fata Silvium retexunt* was intentional—signified an unbroken royal succession. Favonius returning meant that as the west wind of spring renewed the life of the fields, each bastard king brought prosperity with him. That the *diabolus in musica* was the signal of Lasso's message implied that this was, as the later Earls of Mar had evidently claimed, heretical; and the coded transmission of the message pointed to a widespread conspiracy of the sect. Once again the queen had appeared, mysteriously as ever in Lasso's third hint, more tangibly in the fervent text of the poem. What was the truth of the adze's engraved story?

I had a sure answer to the second question of the will, and a probable answer to the first. I had to confirm the latter, and pursue my investigations in the hope that I might come across a clue to the nature of the "Old Man's Beard."

The next day I set out for France, reaching Rouen in forty-eight hours. It was easy enough to identify La Platière, who to my surprise turned out to be the celebrated Girondist, Jean-Marie Roland de la Platière; but the records of the statesman, like those of Lasso, showed no sign of a connection with the Sylvians. I pursued my inquiries in the archives of every town where Roland had lived: Nantes, Thizy-Ouzoult, Lyons, Amiens, and finally Paris. In none did I find a useful fact, and at last, every public record examined, I sought out Roland's descendants. There was only one of them left in France, but I discovered him easily, for he was a celebrity in his own right, and a man whom I should have been curious to meet in ordinary circumstances.

He was M. Félix Namque, a painter settled in Paris, whose fame had grown so rapidly during the preceding decade that he was established at the age of thirty-five as a leader of postwar art. His merited vogue had followed the notoriety given his unique style of coloring. In each of his pictures the colors were never equivalent to those of their subject—they were always highly "interpreted." Yet they did not seem to be the mere result of fancy, taste or any personal predilection; they rather gave the impression of following some systematic distortion. Critics and amateurs had exchanged numberless fatuities trying to reveal the principle governing M. Namque's methods, but none of their suppositions and analyses, no matter how ingenious or thorough, could completely account for the coloring of even a single picture; and explaining the ensemble of the artist's work seemed a goal quite out of sight.

I had written to M. Namque frankly describing my plight. His quick answer invited me in the kindest terms to call on him at his studio, located on the top floor of the foamrubber building of the rue Ostende, in Passy. At the time of my visits he was engaged in finishing the portrait of Alut Andreori, the young Basque torero who was the latest star of the bullfighting world. Andreori was known in Spain as El Porrón because of his winedark complexion (a birthmark covered his whole head) and because his nose stuck up in a long thin cone, like the spout of a Spanish wineflask. I had heard that El Porrón was an example of skill, courage and dignity such as had never been seen in the bullring. He worked so close to the bull that several of his admirers of both sexes had received from the acuteness of their empathy various stigmata-like wounds—rents of pathetic reality in their thighs, abdomens and chests, according to the passage of the horn. El Porrón himself had never been seriously hurt, and he was suspected by the credulous of hiring witches to transfer his gorings to his more sensitive fans. It was practically miraculous that he was still alive. M. Namque was painting the bullfighter dressed for the ring, wearing in his pigtail a splinter taken from the central vertebra of the five-year-old bull Leñizgo. His killing of this animal had won him its ears, tail, four hooves, head, and—as a final and insuperable trophy—its backbone. It was during the faena with Leñizgo that El Porrón, disdaining the adjurations of manager and public to take no chances with that wily and cruel beast, first executed his *paso de las estrellas*, in which the bull passes directly over the fighter's prone body.

During the sittings I observed, M. Namque painted most of the time in a normal manner. Occasionally, however, he would disappear for a moment behind a broad curtain of gray velvet from which, through an elastic slit worked halfway between its center and right edge, a lense-tipped tube stuck out. A faint humming from behind the curtain accompanied these brief withdrawals.

For reasons of temperament, M. Namque and I were drawn to each other from our first meeting. We dined together several times and rapidly came to treat each other as friends. My conversations with him provided a happy outlet for the anxiety that had soured the recent months of my life; and it was no doubt to divert me from my preoccupations that Félix one day delighted me by proposing to reveal his secret and controversial techniques. That evening, after El Porrón had left, he took me behind the velvet curtain.

Half of the concealed space, perhaps thirty square

feet in all, contained a large machine that suggested a specialist's device for sounding some invisible organ. Its case of gray enameled metal was, on the side facing us (opposite the one by the curtain) fitted with a pane of clear glass that exposed the mechanism within. Above the pane, two bands of eleven silver switches were fitted to the lateral rim of the case. Twin viewers, somewhat penny-arcadian, rose from the upper surface of the machine, one at the center, the other towards the right-hand edge, while at an equivalent distance to the left a tubular knee, similarly attached, extended its horizontal shaft through the curtain slit. (It was the other end of this tube, fitted with a lense, that I had observed in the studio.) The machine had no other external features except, at each end, for a thick cord of rubber-covered wire that crossed the floor to a base-plug.

Behind the pane of glass lay an apparently simple apparatus. Its chief component was an arrangement of metal tubing, of a thickness of several inches, that had the shape of a trident. The left-hand prong of tube was attached to the lense-tipped knee; the other two were attached to the viewers. The outermost prongs and the base of the trident comprised one unbroken piece of tubing, while the central prong, a separate length, was hermetically joined to the first.

The two outer shafts of tubing were each fitted with eleven metallic cups that occupied the spaces between the tube-system and the ends of the case. The cups were all wired, every wire being connected first to one of the twenty-two switches of the two panels and ultimately to the external cords.

Félix explained how the machine functioned. The

image received by the lense in the studio was transmitted throughout the trident-shaped tubes by a series
of mirrors fixed within them. The transmitted image
underwent two alterations. As it passed down the left-
hand shaft, appropriate bulbs in the metal cups, which
opened on the shaft's interior, subjected the image to
a battery of adverse colored lights that acted as an
optical sieve, straining all natural color out. The image
at this stage was observable in the viewer surmounting the central shaft of tubing; the primary function
of this viewer was to determine by observation exactly
which lights (controlled by the leftmost panel of
switches) were needed to reduce the colored image to
grayness.

The straining lamps were termed by Félix *rejectors*.

Thus neutralized, the image entered the right-hand
shaft of tube. Again it was subjected to a series of
colored lights, but, in distinction to the first set, these
infused new colors into the image. The recolored
image appeared in the viewer on the right, while the
switches below it controlled the second group of
lights.

The color-infusing lamps were called *projectors*.

The machine itself, of Félix's own invention, had
been baptized *chromaturge*. Félix was understandably
pleased with it; its final images were the inexhaustible
source of his notorious color-schemes.

In order to produce a freshly colored image, the
chromaturge required one decision of its operator—
the choice of projectors. At the very start Félix had
had to decide before the machine was built what his
gamut of colored lights was to be. He had preferred
to make this selection once and for all; so rather than

use colored bulbs which could, when replaced, tempt him to modify his palette, he had had immovable colored panes, with white bulbs behind them, fixed along the shaft's inner surface. The panes represented a familiar pattern. The numbered switches controlled the following hues:

1. White (= light)
2. Black (= dark)
3. Yellow
4. Red
5. Pink
6. Chocolate
7. Gold
8. Fire-red
9. Violet
10. Blue
11. Purple

The next question was how to pick from this sequence of colors the ones to be used in a particular instance. Félix was again averse to letting chance or taste decide. He considered many systematic approaches, based on the size, shape, age, sex and chemistry of the subject to be painted. In the end he discarded them all as unsatisfactory. The painting, he decided, had its own independent existence; therefore the painting, not the subject, would determine the colors. Félix considered three facts to be of fundamental relevance to the painting's existence: the date and hour of the painting's "birth," the phase of the moon at the time of the painting's "conception," and its price. He used the figures representing these facts as his color-scheme.

The only option he permitted himself was the number
of colors employed. The exploitation of all three facts
usually brought all eleven colors into play, albeit in
descending order of importance, while the use of one
or two elements, or even a part of the first one (the
date without the hour) allowed of a simpler color-
scheme.

Félix illustrated his procedure with the case of El
Porrón.

The bullfighter's first sitting had been on the 10
brumaire An CLXIV. (Félix used the revolutionary
calendar in honor of his ancestor.) This date, figured
as 10/2/164, yielded the colors 10 (blue), 2 (black),
1 (white), 4 (red), and 8 (chocolate). These then were
the dominant tones of the portrait. The torero's face
and hands were a gorgeous blue, while his costume
was a glittering chocolate that, thanks to the chiaro-
scuro shading introduced by tones 1 and 2, stood strik-
ingly free of a dull red background.

The sitting had begun at 10:07 in the morning. This
number involved only the seventh switch, the tenth
being already in use. Gold had glowingly touched El
Porrón's nails, eyes and teeth—the latter providing
that "anchor in the real" that critics hailed in all of
Félix's otherwise baffling works.

The "conception" of the portrait—a phonecall offering the commission—had occurred a few weeks
prior to the first sitting, under the third phase of the
moon; the third switch had given the bullfighter flaxen
hai and lemony stockings.

Finally, the price agreed on—1,198,500 francs—had
introduced certain finishing details: purple buttons,

violet spangles, the fire-red bone splinter, and three pink rings.

Félix had mentioned the price sulkily—it was about half what he usually asked. Questioned on this point, he bitterly remarked that it was not the first time he had made such a sacrifice for the sake of art. Further questioning extracted the confession that he had created near scandals by insisting on prices that were "inevitably high"; that he had postponed the start of one portrait for weeks, almost losing an important client thereby, until a certain "appropriate day"; and that once he had left a hospital bed with pneumonia and a fever of 104° to begin a still life of imperishable objects "before it was too late."

These admitted subterfuges confirmed my growing suspicion that Félix used his system to achieve and justify what he felt like doing. The one uncontrollable number, and then only in such cases as El Porrón's, was that of the work's "conception." But when I suggested that he might have waited to start his portrait until the convenient moment of 10:07 because he wanted to give the torero golden eyes, he was indignant. I listened to his harangue on the impersonality and rigor of his system, then changed the subject.

Yet I was not convinced, and my belief that Félix's system was only a means of supplying him with material for the exercise of his talent was unexpectedly confirmed when he let me look through the two viewers of his machine: the images of his studio that I beheld were exactly alike, and what is more, they were unaltered replicas of what appeared, through the spread curtain, to my naked eye.

As for Roland de la Platière, Félix could not himself

help me. But he told me of a document that, as he remembered, might well touch on the matter. It was a
letter that Roland had written to a French lady shortly
before his death; her heirs, long afterwards, had returned it to Roland's family. Félix had last heard of it
when it was taken to the United States by his cousin,
Roland's only other living descendant. Félix gave me
his name and address, and a letter of introduction.

I was pleased with this development, for I had good
reason already to return to America. My appearance
in probate court with such evidence as I had would
certainly strengthen my claim to Mr. Wayl's fortune;
and in addition I wished once more to see my wife,
who had recently begun proceedings against me for
divorce. So, in early December, after a farewell celebration at the Café Chien, Félix drove me to Le Havre
to board my ship home.

•

AN EX-BOOK

My other affairs settled, I left New York for Florida where, at Hialeah, I easily found Félix's cousin, Bunuel Namque-Schlendrian. This tiny, much traveled man, fifteen years older than Félix, was as kind to me as his younger relative. After reading through my letter of introduction, he embraced me as if I were a long-lost friend.

At Namque-Schlendrian's insistence, I spent several days as his guest. I believe his hospitality was engendered by the extraordinary turn his fortunes had just taken; for if his pretext for having me stay was a de-

sire for news of Félix, whom he had not seen in
twenty-five years, his true motive was certainly a natural eagerness to share new happiness with a new acquaintance. It was not long before I became as intimate
with him as I had with his cousin; and so I learned
the story of Bun's life, which had culminated in success on the very eve of my arrival.

As his name indicated, Namque-Schlendrian was
descended through his mother from General Schlendrian, the officer who in the late stages of the Franco-
Prussian War had organized an exceptionally effective
corps from the troops recruited during his service in
Algeria. Among all the "fog of war" no unit harassed
the invaders so brilliantly; the reason for their effectiveness, expert training and tactical flair aside, lay in
the devotion the Arab troops bore their chief. When
Schlendrian's Fellahs were disbanded after the armi-
stice, they further proved this devotion by a communal
gift to the general of twenty million Red Sea cowries.
(These shells, whose scientific name is *Cypraea turdus*,
were once highly valued by many North African
tribes.)

The Schlendrian family was then rich. Foolish spec-
ulation, bad luck and the dissipations of several members reduced the estate, by the time Namque-Schlendrian was born, to a poor fraction of its former size.
His parents died while he was in school, leaving him
on his own at the age of seventeen with only a modest
inheritance to his advantage. (His only relative was
Félix, poor himself.) This inheritance amounted to a
small country place in the Beauce; an apartment in
Paris; a few books; furniture; and the twenty million
cowries.

Restless, solitary and young, Namque-Schlendrian considered what he might make of his life with necessary coolness and rare open-mindedness. Certain ethnoconchological studies persuaded him that he could do better than work respectably at a dull and illpaid office job. Selling his country house and its furnishings for ready cash, he set out with fifty cases of cowries on his long travels.

A steamer took him to Melbourne, whence he proceeded north to Brisbane, there hiring a small boat that brought him around the northeastern Australian coast to Arnhem Land. With a guide and several porters, he traveled inland until, after two weeks, he came to his first goal, the encampment of the Aulayulia tribe. These aborigines used shell money for their trading; their common currency was the cowrie—not the *Cypraea turdus*, but the Indian cowrie, *Cypraea caput serpentis*. They were nevertheless familiar with the *Cypraea turdus*. It seems that at some moment in their past they had traded with a people who bartered the rarer Red Sea shell and had come into possession of a small quantity of it. This store had through loss and theft been so diminished through the countless years that the foreign cowries, held precious from the moment of their acquisition, had assumed a practically sacred value. Namque-Schlendrian hoped to profit from this.

He negotiated for three months with the Aulayulia chieftains. The notion that there could exist so many "rare" shells at first appalled them into a hesitant confusion; but Namque-Schlendrian's patience allowed their reverence for the cowries to reassert its sway, and he finally exchanged his shells for two hundred and fifty million Indian cowries.

Namque-Schlendrian returned to Melbourne to embark with his six hundred and twenty-five cases for Zanzibar. Thence he trekked to the country north of Unyamwezi where he traded his Indian cowries for six hundred and fifty million money cowries (*Cypraea moneta*). He and his one thousand six hundred and twenty-five cases then journeyed by sea around the Cape of Good Hope and up the West African coast, disembarking at Buea in the Cameroons. Traveling inland once more, in a northeasterly direction, he shortly reached the banks of the river Yo. With the Negroes of the region he made a final exchange (transport costs rendered further exploitation of shell values unprofitable). The value assigned to the money cowrie in Western Africa was five times that of the East Coast: The Yo natives estimated Bun's shells as worth twenty-eight pounds thirteen ounces of gold, which they paid; Namque-Schlendrian ended his first wanderings, just as his supply of cash ran out, with the rewarding sum of fourteen thousand dollars.

This money, while worth treble its present value, was certainly no fortune; but it provided Namque-Schlendrian with what he needed most—a small capital to invest when an exceptional opportunity appeared. Now Namque-Schlendrian had already noted such an opportunity, and he decided to take advantage of it immediately.

Namque-Schlendrian admitted that in this matter his good sense had, after a while, given way to an almost monomaniac obstinacy. He could have abandoned his scheme once he recognized the obstacles to realizing it. Instead, he endured for its sake ill health, poverty and humiliation.

During his sojourn in Australia, Namque-Schlendrian, who was versed in the history of horseracing, had learned that Cartesian Diver and Fink's Folly, both descendants of Pettifog from Lala (although through different lines), had arrived in Sydney to be set to stud. Pettifog had, in his offspring from Lala, transmitted a curious set of minor deformations that had first appeared in his ancestor Gypsum. Namque-Schlendrian had been convinced by a study of the ancestry of these horses that they would become fine runners if properly handled.

A brief genealogy of the animals involved is in order. Spurius, the son of Pettifog from Lala by Breastbone from Armchair by Gladstone from Rippe-van-Winkle by Whig from Nutcracker Suite by Gypsum from White Loss, sired Cartesian Diver from Latest Sin, who, shipped to Australia, there sired Melancthon from Greta Garbo, Spelling Bee from Periphrasis, Black Dick from Penal Servitude, and Ticktock from Asylum. Pettifog also sired from Lala several mares. The most successful of these was Cunning, who threw Brickbat to Fug, who sired the Derby winner Krach from Liliom, and Zazz to Horse, who threw in turn the handicap champion Hangover to Lordy Me. Another mare was named Fink's Folly; she was sent to Australia with Cartesian Diver, and there threw Flibbetigibbet, Pounce, and Excitation to Jinglebells, all of which raced poorly. Among the mares she foaled were Crass Delight, June Filly, Poontang, Gattamalatta, and, lastly, Grave Lady. The latter's sire, Lugstone, who had been set to Maryjohn, was by Celtic

Doom from Alba Longa by Fissure from Would-to-God by Bloody Bastard from Pity Palace. In Australia, before being bought by Namque-Schlendrian she threw Schwarzwald to Plexus; under Bun's ownership she threw six colts to Ticktock—Triple X, Frosty Mikado, Buckwheat Blues, Watchstopper's Gusset, Bulldog Lemny, and Winged Cribbage; and two fillies —Wilder Membership and Commie Coup.

Originally Namque-Schlendrian planned to buy Cartesian Diver and Fink's Folly. In order to learn the trade, he returned to Australia and went to work at the farm where the two horses were at stud, first as hotwalker, later as groom and exercise boy. A series of disasters wrecked his plans. At the end of his second year, he was thrown by a horse, fracturing his skull in the fall. Namque-Schlendrian spent eight months in a coma and two years recovering. Resuming his duties, he performed them satisfactorily for another year and was ready to turn owner when, overcome by one of the spells of giddiness that followed his accident, he so mismanaged his mount that the horse broke a leg under him and had to be shot. Since this animal was a prize three-year-old, Namque-Schlendrian was obliged to compensate its owner (a niggardly parvenu with a loud disbelief in insurance) with a large sum; and when he tried to make up his loss with a few heavy bets at the track, bad luck reduced what was left of his stake to less than three thousand dollars. Still undismayed, he went on at his job hoping, since he earned a good wage, to save enough for his purpose. His savings had by 1940 grown to the equivalent of eleven thousand dollars. In the summer of that year they were seized with the bank accounts of all French residents upon the formation of the Pétain government. At first interned, Namque-Schlendrian later served honorably in the war as a liaison officer for the Far Eastern Gaullist platoon. His services failed to recover his money, or at least not its true value. It was transferred to France at the prewar rate of exchange, under an agreement between the Free French and Australian governments, and its buying power had fallen, by the time Namque-Schlendrian could use it, to about fifteen hundred dollars. Even this could not be taken out of France.

The following three years were the saddest of Namque-Schlendrian's life. He went back to work at the stable, but despondently, not knowing what else to do. No longer an inspiration, his obsession had become a dead weight he dragged hopelessly about. Cartesian Diver and Fink's Folly were now both dead. In their place his choice had fallen on their foals Ticktock and Grave Lady. When these horses were sold and sent to the United States, Namque-Schlendrian managed to accompany them as groom. In less than a year he had lost this job because of his growing carelessness, the result of recurring depressions. He then joined a small organization of bookmakers in which, thanks to his native acumen, he was able to make a modest living until his luck turned.

His good fortune came from an unexpected quarter. In the fall of 1950, Félix wrote him a letter telling him of the current demand for apartments in Paris and advising him to let his, long vacant. Authorized to act on his cousin's behalf, Félix made a few minimal repairs and soon had a tenant. The apartment was attractively situated: a comfortable soundproofed studio in

the tower of the church of St. Germain-des-Prés.
Namque-Schlendrian began receiving monthly cheques
of five hundred, a thousand, and, finally, two thousand
dollars. In less than three years he was the owner of a
well-staffed stud farm in Fayette County, Kentucky,
where Grave Lady had already thrown Ticktock his
first colt, Triple X.

Only the day before I arrived in Hialeah Triple X
had made and won his initial start, running three fur-
longs in 0:32⅖, finishing eleven lengths in front of the
second horse, and confirming his owner's twenty-five-
year-old hunch.

Gypsum and certain of his offspring, notably the
descendants of Pettifog and Lala, were known for certain external peculiarities—slightly curby hocks, lop
ears and high withers. Namque-Schlendrian believed,
at first after a long study of their past performances,
later from observation, that these visible characteris-
tics were accompanied by a certain organic deforma-
tion. As owner of Ticktock and Grave Lady he found
his hypothesis exact. In both these horses and, subsequently, in their foals, the splanchnic nerve, which
controls the adrenal gland, passed in abnormal fashion
through the coil of the large intestine on its way from
medulla to kidney. Namque-Schlendrian reasoned that
the nerve was stimulated, and the production of adrenalin increased, when the horse's intestines were exceptionally swollen—that is, when the horse was con-
stipated; and he believed this fact might provide the
realization of the racing bug's dream—the undetecta-
ble fix.

A less talented man might have failed to use such
knowledge properly. With patience, imagination and

pluck, Namque-Schlendrian succeeded in the formidable task of training a horse to constipate himself voluntarily at set times. At his farm he determined the delicate intervals (varying with every horse) between feeding, the onset of constipation and the running of the race. He had seen his methods justified in his private time trials: when properly costive, Triple X, his very soul soaked in adrenalin, surpassed his best "free" performances. The colt's first race had of course been the supreme test, and Triple X's victory a supreme consolation for Namque-Schlendrian's years of ignominy. The suspicions of the judges, amazed at the colt's performance, were allayed by the official analyses, which showed that no drug had been administered nor illegal physical stimulus applied. The bookmakers who had been his partners were also surprised—Namque-Schlendrian collected from them the fruits of two thousand dollars invested at twenty-two to one. (Even the odds had been favored by his machinations: in the paddock, the beginnings of the adrenalin attack had put Triple X in such a sweat that he scared away many of his potential backers.)

Such was Namque-Schlendrian's history as he told it to me. He gave me an additional mark of confidence after he had finished his tale by revealing yet another trade secret. This was a stopwatch that he had had made to fit under the instep of his foot; it was operated by moving the great toe. The hidden contraption gave Namque-Schlendrian easy access to the jealously guarded time trials of his competitors. The results of these trials were precious information, and no responsible owner or trainer invited anyone to them out of politeness or friendship. Namque-Schlendrian's charm

had won him a privileged place in the society of owners. By making a point of never carrying or using a
stopwatch, or even an ordinary watch, he persuaded
his colleagues that there was no danger in his witnessing their tryouts, rather an opportunity to show off
their horses to an appreciative connoisseur.

Namque-Schlendrian had given Jean-Marie Roland's
letter to the Canossa Washington Library of Fitchwinder University in Swetham, Massachussetts. Since
only specialists were allowed to consult the manuscript collection of which the letter was now a part,
Namque-Schlendrian wrote on my behalf to the library director, thus advancing my investigations
greatly.

During my last afternoon in Hialeah, I payed a farewell call on Namque-Schlendrian in his office suite at
the track.

He showed me his collections of souvenirs and curi-
osities, among them a medieval muleteer's packsaddle
that had been given to him by none other than Mr.
Wayl. I recognized on it a familiar design. Worked
long ago into the cracked leather, it was still legible:
a naked woman stood near the mouth of a stream by
a mound of cowrie shells. The scene was identical with
the one engraved on the point of my adze, except that
on the saddle the woman was depicted from behind.
Mr. Wayl had led me to believe that this scene was
merely decorative; yet here it was underscored with
the inscription, *Cypriae Sedes Gloria Regis*, while the
other side of the saddle bore the arms of the "false
Johnstones," with an added mark—a band that crossed
the shield from the upper right corner to the center
and then descended to its point.

After quitting Bun (he knew nothing at all about the saddle: Mr. Wayl had given it to him because of his knowledge of cowries) I proceeded to Boston and to nearby Swetham, where I spent a day in the study of Roland's letter. Mr. Meniscus, the library director, has forbidden me to reproduce its text, but he has most kindly authorized the translation that follows.

·

ROLAND TO
MADAME MIOT (I)

chez Mlle Malortie,
dans la rue de l'Ours,
Rouen.

Le 9 Brumaire, An II.

Madam,

I write in a state of dejection such as I have not known in many years. So much time has passed since your letter came—and such time! It has exhausted my life, and me; I have passed through multiples of anguish; I have yearned for peace, then resignation, and afterwards hopelessness, but it seems there is no passivity in despair—the insomniac quest for death is an ascent into pain. I live now—well, I am simply alive. I try to order what is still mine, although there is no distraction in it; and so I shall answer your queries. I am thankful that my matter will give me words to send you; my brain is in truth quite blank otherwise, except for what is unspeakable.

I have indeed "visited Egypt," like my old namesake, perhaps learning there more than even he; and I did not have to cross water to reach it. I think you know the manner of my acquaintance with those people, and the depth of my attachment. As for the history, I can offer fragments only—the records are few, many have been lost or destroyed. There have, however, been certain letters, whose details—with due prudence—can be enriched with familiar lore; and the facts admitted into official texts—*quegli scritti lugubri che fanno tornare eternamente i morti!*—must in turn be introduced, and then we have—not a history, but bright glimpses of a history: like a winter moon in the chance openings of snow-clouds.

In the year 1410 a clan of Wallachian Gypsies came to Scotland from the Continent. They preceded the mass of their race by nearly a century; for among their own people they were renegades. Small, dark, quickfooted, they resembled their fellow Gypsies in physique, and like them, they raised horses and cattle. It was their religion that marked them. They had preserved the practice of an old cult dedicated to Sylvius of Alba Longa, and they worshiped him as a divine hero, and as their king. In their version of the legend,

Sylvius was no son of Aeneas but a bastard offspring of Lavinia, fathered by a god whose name could never be mentioned or written down. There is nothing I can tell you of the origins and growth of the sect in antiquity, or of its history during the first thirteen centuries of Christianity: the tale must be discovered by a more enlightened age that will recognize wisdom in the diligence of the learned. My knowledge begins with the establishment of the sect in Scotland, and the first celebrations there of its mysteries, in a shrine that lay not far from the town of Allova (*sic*), in the year 1411.

The new shrine received Sylvius's name—a name belonging not only to the legendary hero, but given as a title to the successive chiefs of the Gypsies, whom they called kings. They believed that Sylvius was immortal in the bodies of these kings, and that he sanctified them by his presence. In 1411 Alexander Stewart, a recent convert to the sect, and its protector, bore the name. Like every king he was born in bastardy of noble stock; and he had been *chosen*.

For Sylvius, god or man, was not the supreme ruler: that authority belonged to the "Queen" whose vicegerent he was. She is an obscure power. Unlike the king's, her office was not perpetually renewed—she was supposedly a divine being who from time to time, when the need arose, appeared among her worshipers as a mere woman. I cannot say how often she manifested herself, or how she was recognized. Only one of her peculiarities is known: she was nearly always gifted with some Negro blood.

All the shrines of the sect were established for the performance of her rites. Concerning one of these, the

Flaying of the King, I know more than a little. It was performed in the glen near Allova, on Hallowe'en and All Hallows' Day, a year after the Gypsies' arrival.

The gathering of the sect took place during the morning of the first day. Most of those that came were Gypsies, but there were many Scots and English lately converted, and an even greater number of earlier converts from the countries of Europe. The first business was the publication and discussion of the year's accounts. During the afternoon there were numerous private ceremonies of marriage, burial and initiation.

The marriage ceremony culminated in the eating by the bride and the groom of a small cake made out of malt, rye and lard together with bits of hair clipped from the sacred parts of their bodies—loins, armpit, and head.

The blessing of the dead consisted in clothing the corpses (preserved through the year for this occasion) with fresh ash leaves, then sprinkling them with a powder of dried bdellium gum.

Children brought for initiation were similarly sprinkled. I do not know the practice relating to adult initiates.

Towards evening, the king, dressed in mean clothes, approached the sacred ashtree. He was there stripped by seven seven-year-old boys, and bitten by seven seven-year-old dogs. He stood before the Queen, who was accompanied by a young woman carrying a bowl of liquid bdellium gum, and by a young man who in one hand held a gisarme, which they called an adze (*une hallebarde que l'on appelait herminette*), in the other a wooden effigy of the king. The effigy, about three feet high, had been grotesquely carved from a piece of white poplar and afterwards smoked black; a metal point was attached to its base. The adze was made of gold, fitted with an iron edge.

The young man, planting the effigy in the ground, began lopping off its projecting members one by one with the adze. As each part fell, the Queen smeared the same part of the king with gum, until the effigy had been reduced to a straight white bolt and the king had been anointed all over his body. A second young man approached, carrying a crossbow. He drew the wooden shaft from the earth, set it in his bow, and shot it into the trunk of the ashtree. As soon as a leaf fell from the tree, all withdrew but the king, who was left alone, naked and erect under the tree, its leaves falling on him through the night. His followers did not sleep but wandered at a distance through the woods surrounding the glen. Those newly married on beds of leaves consummated or confirmed their marriage. The blessed corpses were deposed in holy streams and caves.

(What did the Queen do during that night? According to some, she returned to the king to sleep with him. Others say she murdered and replaced him, out of sight of all.)

The ashtree shed all its leaves in that one night, many of them falling on the king and adhering to his gummy limbs. In the morning the entire sect, gathered anew, finds the tree bare and their king glued with ashleaves. The Queen comes to him and leads him to a nearby spring, where she washes him and herself (she is naked) a first time. Once more she rubs the king with gum, mixed with seven hundred appleseeds. Then she daubs herself completely with mud from the ground near the spring, to which the young woman again attending her adds petals of bloody-fingers (*doigts de la Vierge*). The king and Queen return to the ashtree's foot, where their followers await them in neat ranks. The young woman now opens many boxes containing tiny gray butterflies, gathered during the summer months and carefully saved; while the young man, the destroyer of the king's effigy, looses a large flock of bullfinches from a cage in the ashtree's lower branches. The butterflies alight by the hundred on the muddy Queen, covering her in so close a robe she seems a statue of pale gray fur. The bullfinches attack the king to peck off his coat of seeds. Their hard bills pierce him in many places, and the king bleeds: all the believers come forward in an orderly file to kiss his blood. They cannot touch the Queen, kissing instead the ground before her. (But since her eyes are covered, she does not see this homage.) After a while the butterflies, unfit for November air, fall off dying. The Queen leads the bloody king back to the spring, washes him, and clothes him in his royal suit of leather leaves. She has first cleansed herself, and put on a black goat surplice lined entirely with white catskins. On the lining's border a motto has been sewn with thread wound out of rhubarb fibers. The motto† reads: *Aeneas Nothus Rex: Rex Nothus Sylvius.* Beneath her surplice the Queen is naked, save for her garter of puffballs, and goes barefoot. The worshipers this morning all wear hats, and many sport on their belts sprigs of bubon, St. John's wort and verbena.

The Queen at last crowned the king, or, rather, presented him with his crown, which was a wreath of clematis. The couple then received from each of their followers a vow of fidelity and a small offering in money or kind.

The royal pair led the way to a cleared space. Around it the newfallen ashleaves were heaped in a ring and lighted. Damp and still full of sap, their fire filled the air with tart thick smoke. The king started to sing through his nose, producing a roaring wooden voice; he accompanied himself by rattling a bell of horn with his right hand, and beating with his left a human bone on a horse's skull. This was the sign to begin the Parodies, of which, alas, I can only describe two, the first and last of the many performed.

The opening parody was of a foxhunt. A fox was placed in the center of the clearing, and a pack of hounds set after him. The dogs made themselves foolish, for the fox, made of loosely woven ivy, was invisible to them, and they passed heedlessly through or over it following the trace of a true foxskin that had been dragged across the ground in the pattern of an equilateral triangle, the ivy replica lying at one of its corners.

The closing parody was a joust. Riding blinded sheep, crippled dwarfs met each other in the lists with weapons that, though miniature, were real enough. Perhaps the smoke of the leaves, nearly blinding by then, veiled the bloodiness of the spectacle.[4]

A banquet followed the Parodies. I retain only one of its details.

A shoat prepared for the royal table was filleted with rhubarb thread in such a way that a red letter B appeared on its chest. After the king had tasted the meat of the animal, he stood up and demanded the attention of the company. Then putting a golden boar's head over his own, he opened his suit of leaves to lay bare his chest: the skin between the nipples, unmarked at first, soon showed the trace of a pink B, and the letter affirmed itself until it was a brilliant red.

The banquet over, there was dancing. The king and his nine "abbreviators" opened with a prescribed ritual dance, whose nature I am ignorant of. It appears to have been performed to the accompaniment of a kind of mangle (*avec de la musique issue d'une calandreuse*). Afterwards there was general dancing, to the music of flutes, jew's-harps, harps and oaklog drums.

•

ROLAND TO
MADAME MIOT (II)

In 1451 political circumstances led to the destruction
of Sylvius's shrine. A large gang of "orthodox" Gypsies were imported from the Low Countries to do the
work; they did it thoroughly. They massacred many
of the sect, Gypsy or not. The glen was ravaged, its
spring polluted, its sacred tree cut to bits, its royal
stone smashed, even its thriving vines uprooted.

It is said that the Queen led the glen's defense, at
first by force of arms, later, when the woods had been

fired, with pleas for the sparing of her people.[5] She herself was not slain, but made prisoner in the king's name and sent to Rome for trial before high dignitaries of the church. Summarily condemned as a witch, she succeeded in her appeal to the extent of being allowed to present her case to the pope, Pius II.

The pope received her without her judges or her guards, alone except for an actuary who transcribed their interview. Officially destroyed, the transcription was smuggled out and sold to one of the Queen's loyal followers. Here is the version I once saw, or as much of it as I can reconstruct from notes set down at the time.

The Queen. If I forsook the glory of public martyrdom, among the tatters of my people, forsook burning with them, and not leaving them; if I left them, and the other Sylvius and all my children, who will burn alone, or endure the rotting cold of their hills; if I submitted to a king not my king, not fit to be my subject, and submitted to the secular petty fury of moles: it is not because I do not want to burn, but because I want to burn royally. And you shall do the burning—you are fit for that.

The Pope. I granted your request firstly because you are known to me, as I to you; secondly because I am curious (and yet too delicate: that combination has put hopes of happiness beyond me); thirdly because I have a favor to ask of you. It is a trivial favor. You see, a few weeks ago an inexplicable wound opened in my left thigh. It has refused to leave me, and I suffer from it no little.

The Queen. I have come to say what I have to say. I have been speaking for months and those about me hear a devil's voice. They hear it even when I am silent —they cannot understand their terror! You can understand, yet you must listen, for the end must be true to the beginning, and what was born in water must die in fire.

The Pope. Whatever you came for, you are here for my reasons, and chiefly for my wounded thigh. It is strange that it was only a few days ago that I imagined a connection between my wound and your captivity, even though I had just learned you were to be sent here when the ill declared itself. The other day I mentioned the matter lightly to my nephew and he grew very pale. Delegations of well-wishers have appeared at punctual intervals since to advise me, with the most respectful discretion, that I should deal leniently with you. Of course I laughed at all of them. And then I thought, how worried they will be for themselves! They will soon start hunting down poor Gypsies whose looks have happened to cross theirs, there will be murders open and obscure, and sleepless nights, and bad dreams by day, and much time lost. I am sickened by such affairs. Are you my enemy? If you are, you are so less than others: there are remoter lands where error is mightier. So I decided to have you come to me, that you might try to cure me. (The Queen laughed.) Perhaps I should elaborate: you may *try*. It is your certain failure that interests me. Afterwards, the wound will eventually heal of itself. This is a slow answer to your presumptions, but it will wither them wholly.

The Queen. You came out of my belly, you sucked my breasts: noble boy, consider who I am! I have no presumptions but those of my true worship. My soul has been wrapped in honey. I play with curious shells, branches and trusting animals, and with blood and the smells of sperm and the dead. I have no need to work miracles: they happen about me. Your thigh! And your dead mythologies! Does Actaeon or St. Sebastian hallow the dim unease of your pain? Is learning only for fools? When next you pass an anthill, approach it and study its perfection, and think of your failing powers: and think of Alva when they carry you past its leaves . . .

The Pope. Alba no longer. You will hang and not burn;[6] yours is a common offense.

He turned the Queen back to her judges, who submitted her to the Question, as was usual, before ordering her execution. Charged with various acts of malevolent witchcraft, she of course denied them all. The account of her last hours is found in the official transcript of the trial:

The person under examination was first tied with rope; then she was fitted with Spanish boots and stretched out on the ladder; no answers were forthcoming to the questions asked, and her eyes were constantly open. She was dropped from the ladder and raised again. After that she was poured a draught. Then the Spanish boots were tightened. All of the hair of her body was shaved; fire was passed under her nose and behind her ears; afterwards she was again strappadoed, hanging in the air for a whole hour. During this time she remained silent. Later, when she spoke, an appeal to the Devil, who was addressed as Triton, was all she uttered. Her voice was cool, unstrained, and her face colored. She was sprinkled, rubbed and smoked with lighted sulfur; once more she was strappadoed, and she cried out.

The person under examination was extended on the ladder and given a draught. She was burned anew with sulfur. Again she was raised, and another draught, which was swallowed with difficulty, after which she sank down as if she were about to go to sleep. She was again burned with sulfur, under her chin, under her arms, in her secret parts. Again strappadoed. *Triton, have pity on me!* were her only words. After that she was calm for a rather long time, and, although she was called to, there was no answer, gasping as she was, her face still flushed, without tears, however, but only drops of sweat on her forehead.

The person under examination was newly stretched. Then the Spanish boots were screwed tight; and again a draught, which was not swallowed, no matter what means were employed. After which she remained calm, without complaint of any pain.

The person under examination had just been strappadoed once more and rubbed with sulfur, when a gray butterfly began fluttering about her. Seeing it, the person under examination twisted her head towards it so hard that the torturer, with his helpers, could hardly turn it back. The butterfly then flew towards the window, which was half open, and after resting on the sill a while, disappeared outside. At the moment of the butterfly's appearance, the face of the person under examination had become horribly pale, her mouth screwed up, her lips blue; but as soon as the insect disappeared she was completely calm. She was taken off the ladder and lain on some straw. They brought vinegar for her to breathe, but she was dead. The clock had just struck six.

The undersigned, notary public, certifies, &c.

Tota Philosophia, inquit Plato, nihil est aliud, quam quædam commentatio mortis, neque aberrat mea quidem sententia. Cur enim præcepta bene vivendi discimus, nisi ut bene mori sciamus. Comœdia quidem est nostra vita, cuius ultimus actus &c.—so wrote that pope in a later sententious moment. Those who are elevated in this world exude the sublime cruelty of the insane.

Yet the pope relented at last. At the end of the trial minutes the verdict reads (although the Queen was already dead): *Convicta et combusta.*

·

ROLAND TO
MADAME MIOT (III)

Yesterday, to my surprise, I received a long letter
about the glen of Allova and its former role as a shrine.
The writer was some American crank who had gotten
hold of a few facts (even those he garbled). I plan to
send him a curt note that should thoroughly deflate
him.

Perhaps I am wrong in doing this—there are few
enough who show even a misguided interest in poor
Sylvius and his Queen. Since that ancient raid on the

glen the sect's history has been a sad one: fits of enthusiasm fading into long wastes of abandonment. In our
century the apathy of the believers has been such that
the Barilone of Massa may fall into ruin.

One of my dearest friends, Jehan de Sfè, among the
last members of the sect, went quite mad as a result of
its disintegration. Since he had been associated with
us politically, he prudently left Paris for Valence last
winter; and I payed him a brief visit there. Presenting
myself at his villa, I waited for him in the library:
after a few minutes Sfè came in, walking backwards, and
cried, *Roi vous veut de risée le plaît qu'en l'or rèche
homme!* Not making head or tail of this I asked him
to repeat what he had said several times and finally to
write it down. He did all I asked patiently and courteously. On the slip of paper he handed me I read:
!riov suov ed risialp leuq dnaloR rehc noM. He had
written this reverse sentence as rapidly as I might have
written it normally. After I had had him read it aloud
—he uttered the same sounds as he had at first done—
I understood that he both spoke and wrote backwards,
and that in doing so he carefully respected the distinction between the written and the spoken word, even
though it was here made singularly arduous: writing, he reversed the letters of his sentences; speaking,
he reversed their sounds. Once the necessary civilities
were dispensed with, I asked him, fascinated, to recite
me several classical tirades. It was with a truly manic
grandeur that he pronounced Phèdre's

Et chatte à oir passa ré y tend toutes une Eve est-ce!

Then, knowing Sfè to be a talented musician, I asked
him to perform for me. At the harpsichord a similar

prodigy occurred: accompanying himself, he sang Rousseau's setting of *Se tu m'ami* from end to beginning with an ease that flabbergasted me. But soon pity and sadness at knowing an old friend lost (for conversation with him was so laborious that it would have been impossible in serious matters) overcame my somewhat unwholesome curiosity; and I took my leave. Sfè's sister wrote me a few months ago that his peculiarity had lasted until the day he had his cataracts couched. The operation not only failed: after a few hours of lucidity, during which he incessantly proclaimed his fidelity to the Queen, it took his life.

On my arrival here, I had charged myself with one final duty, that of ensuring the perpetuation of the Queen's monument. Last week I traveled with it by land as far as Houlgate, there hiring a small fishingboat, which I took out myself, desiring to conceal the nature and destination of my cargo. After rowing for several hours, I happened to pass close to another boat; the fisherman in it, pointing seawards, shouted that if I continued, my goal would be in sight within half an hour. Surprised, I thanked him and rowed on. I spied a small island, whose very existence had been unknown to me (I have since been unable to discover it on any map). The place was rocky, completely uninhabited, and sparsely planted. Several hundred yards from the center of its southern shore I sank the memorial of the Queen in the sea; it now rests in about twenty feet of water.

Since then, except for this letter, I have abandoned all work. It is practically impossible for me to write; but I had expected at least to assemble my new notes on Dictys of Crete and on "myself"—it seems, by the

way, that my counterpart did indeed write not ζωδιακοῦ
but σεληναίου.

I cannot even weep; I only let fall a few occasional
burning tears. I have given up hope for Marie Phlipon,
and I have nothing to hope from her, either—I am told
she now claims to have always considered me a sexless
being! I do not mind her thinking so, but must she
declare it so loudly that it reaches my ears? My end is
at hand; even so I will not be a burden to others; and
you shall remain my example. Those of your stamp
have a single law, it is written in their hearts, there too
is my rule: engrave my pardon there.

Where is another true heart to be found? I have left
my own in a wicked magnet. Πάντα ὕδωρ ἐστί.

In what condition do you now see my soul? How
do you judge me? Listen: I am in despair.

Madama, vi riverisco con tanto il cuor.

THALES

(Ten days later Roland, learning of his wife's execution, wandered from Rouen several miles into the
countryside, and after pinning to his breast a scrawled
explanation of his act, killed himself near Bourg-
Beaudoin. He was buried on the spot. Aside from the
information it contains, his letter is curious for being
addressed to Madame Miot; he had attended the burial
of her ashes three years before.)

•

MISS DRYREIN
AND THE BARILONE

From Roland's letter I gleaned a wealth of facts concerning my prize adze. I was confident too that I had found the answer to the will's third question, and I hurried to New York to verify my findings with Miss Dryrein, the executrix, before going to court with them.

But if Miss Dryrein was impressed and satisfied by my ability to explain the adze's significance, she destroyed my hope of having the final answer. My hypothesis was that the old man was King Sylvius; that his beard was that of the boar's head he put on at the Sylvian feast; and that the Gypsies who attacked the glen literally or symbolically shaved it, probably by castrating the king.

Miss Dryrein dismissed this theory with a simple No. Without explanation, she showed me a movie Mr. Wayl had taken during one of his trips. Isidore Fod, who had accompanied Mr. Wayl (long before the scandal that ruined his career), spoke a commentary to it:

We are going to see various details of the Barilone, that strange underground palace unearthed this summer near Massa Marittima, west of Siena. The closeup shows how the discovery was made. When large deposits of lignite were found in the region, mining operations were begun in great haste so as to relieve the area's chronic unemployment. Some miners were working a vein of mundic when they came upon these giant ants that we see here, extracting brasses (as they call pyrites crystals) from the surrounding material. When the miners tried to find out where the ants came from, they accidentally opened a hole in the ceiling of the Barilone. Unfortunately two workers fell through the hole. Now we see a parade led by a band with its banner reading *Fanfara di Vicq d'Azyr*—he was one of the miners killed, the one who opened up the hole. Of course the discovery brought quite a lot of tourism to the town, and even temporary prosperity—hence the parade. Here we see Signor Grembo-Maledetti, the president of the mining company, inaugurating the entrance to the Barilone. The name *Barilone*, which means big vat, derives from the shape of the palace, which consists of one enormous barrel-vaulted hall. Its walls are covered with interesting frescoes. Here is a sample of them. In the leftmost of these three paintings we see a clearing ringed with vine-covered trees. A group of vagabonds attacks a gathering of gentlefolk at a sumptuous outdoor banquet. In the right-hand painting we have the same scene after the attackers have left—the ground covered with the bodies of the slain, the trees cut down or burned: no living thing, animal or plant, remains. Unfortunately the middle space has been badly damaged, and one cannot see what happens there.

The reel ended. Turning on the lights, Miss Dryrein looked at me questioningly; but I did not understand. She shook her head resignedly, and her attention to my predicament ebbed augustly.

A few months later I visited Massa myself, to see if there were no visible remnants of that "middle" fresco.

At the Massa chamber of commerce an official gave me a note and told me to proceed to the house of Monroè Fesso, custodian of the Barilone. Signor Fesso lived near the coalmines that now deface the hills behind Massa. As I approached the front door, framed with dried twigs, of his modest marble house, I noticed a curious chirruping noise, to which I paid no attention. Before I was close enough to knock, however, the chirruping faded away: the ensuing quiet was almost startling. Sig. Fesso then appeared around one corner of the house. Noticing my bemused expression, he at once explained to me what had produced the noise and its disappearance. Despite its proximity to the mines, the local electrical company had not laid its cables as far as Sig. Fesso's house. Unable to install a doorbell for the many tourists needing his services, the guardian of the

Barilone had found a novel substitute. The dried twigs framing the door were not twigs at all, but hundreds of tan grasshoppers tied to each other and fastened to the door-frame like a vine. Under normal circumstances the grasshoppers kept up a lively racket, but at the approach of a visitor they would fall silent; and this silence was an effective summons to Sig. Fesso, even when he was on the far side of his house. (Indeed, that was where my arrival had found him. He had been in his vegetable garden, doing his spring digging. Noticing that he wore a strange vest of leather fitted with thin close-set iron spikes, I asked him its function. With some embarrassment he explained that he used it to smooth the worked earth: after digging each patch he would roll over it, his vest then quickly and efficiently filling the office of a rake. Its only drawback, he said, was that it dirtied him—he was in fact smirched from head to foot.)

Sig. Fesso directed the way to the entrance of the Barilone, a Babylonian concrete portal. Its lintel bore an inscription that began *Inaugurato da Silvio Grembo-Maledetti . . .* and gave the date and a brief prose poem. On the cement flag before the door I remarked two parallel X's about ten inches long, which I took to be the mark of Mr. Wayl's presence at the inauguration; for he was known to sport shoes mounted on X-shaped springs.

As he passed through the door Sig. Fesso curtly bowed his head, saying: Amen! A dark corridor in the hillside led to the Barilone proper, a semicylindrical hall a hundred yards long, forty yards wide, and fifteen yards high down its center. Halfway to the far end a metal partition divided the hall into equal parts, but it was perforated with so many intersecting abstract designs it scarcely troubled one's view. On either side of this screen vertical bands of frescoes had been painted, those nearest it identical in width and disposition, those farther from it increasingly disparate and irregular as they approached the ends of the hall. Most of the frescoes had been so mutilated as to be illegible—a general desquamation had marred every surface of the Barilone; but in some cases, where the paint itself had fallen, their drawings, in Cologne earth, were still apparent.

One painting, nearly intact, showed an ecclesiastical figure gloating over a book presented to him by a liveried servant who had opened it at the title-page. The only recognizable words of the title were: *vatter der bapst Pius*. Pope Pius was drawn in curious caricature like a jack of spades.

Of another fresco, only a signature remained, neatly spelled: *Bernardinvs Pintvrichivs Pervsinvs*.

In a third fresco, a bishop who lifted his eyes sanctimoniously heavenwards held out his arms in benediction over a mob engaged in stoning with oyster-shells a proud bloodied woman.

The "middle" fresco of Mr. Wayl's movie was underneath this scene. I examined it with my flashlight. All I found was the outline of certain tendrils near the bottom of the picture, one of which bore the remains of greenish-white coloring; reaching down from above, a hand clutched the tendrils.

I called over Sig. Fesso, who had sat down next to the entrance to read *Tintin en Amérique*, and asked him to identify the subjects of the "middle" fresco and the one over it. Asked who the sanctimonious bishop was, he said:

Che grillo! Amen.

Of the stoned woman: *Che pazzia!* Amen.

Of the plants in the "middle" fresco: *Alba!* Amen.

His first two answers angered me, the third released all the fury of months of hope and labor made vain. Crying out: So it's Alva! Enough of Alva!, I grabbed poor Sig. Fesso by the throat and knocked him on the head with my flashlight. I think I should have killed him if the pain inflicted by the spikes of his gardening vest had not made me let him drop. Leaving him unconscious on the ground, I fled, weeping with shame and disappointment, from the Barilone and from Massa.

Monroè Fesso quickly recovered from my violence —I learned as much from the next day's paper. I was sorry I could not atone for my behavior, especially as reflection had convinced me that his answers were not the impertinences I had taken them to be. What I heard as *Che grillo!* and (forgetting the position of the tonic accent) *Che pazzia!* had surely been *Cirillo* and *Ipazia*, protagonists in just such a scene as that fresco portrayed. Had he perhaps meant something else too by *Alba?*

•

ALL THINGS ARE
WATER

I had fled to Rome: thence I traveled by plane to Paris, and on to Houlgate by train. My hope, my last hope, was that an inspection of Roland's monument to the Queen might lead to the answer I could not find otherwise.

Roland's unmapped island had come out of obscurity—it was none other than Cliff-le-Bone, the vacation resort. An efficient ferry service set me on it the same morning I arrived in Houlgate. It was early in the summer, and there were few tourists; but among those, I was lucky enough to find a group of amateur skin-divers, called the Cogito Swimmers Club, who had picked Cliff-le-Bone for their yearly outing. As their name implied, the Cogito Swimmers were interested in more than the practical aspects of skindiving—they believed that prolonged immersion helped introspection and metaphysical speculations; yet they were delighted to help me look for the monument.

That afternoon, we hired a boat at one of the twelve piers forming the island's pleasant harbor. I let the Swimmers lead the search, for I was inexpert in handling myself underwater and in reconnoitering the submarine landscape.

Following them, I reflected on a telegram forwarded to me earlier in the day at the island's hotel. My lawyers in New York informed me that the letter I had studied at Fitchwinder University was not in Roland's hand and had been declared a forgery; that consequently Mr. Wayl's will had been thrown out as a complete hoax; and that Beatrice and Isidore Fod were to inherit the fortune. I had promptly decided to fight these decisions. Now, gliding through a cold lunar world, I found my confidence waning. The undersea manifested its effect on my brain, as the Cogito Swimmers had described it: memories flooded my head.

Was not Mr. Wayl, whose eccentricity had been demonstrated at his own funeral, capable of forging Roland's letter, and a history's worth of documents as well? What of the poem Professor Bumbè had shown me and its faint odor of anachronism? Who had ever heard of the novel in which I had read of the John-

stones, with its view of life so unlike the warm Auerbach's? Was Abe Johnstone's preposterous letter also
a "plant"? Mr. Wayl had the money to bribe town
clerks and customs officials and musicologists into
helping him. He could have hired without any trouble
a "policeman" to keep me out of the Silver Glen. As
for the Voe-Doges's painting, were they not his relatives? And since Mr. Wayl knew Namque-Schlendrian (to whom he had given the saddle showing the
Queen's birthplace), perhaps he also knew Namque.
If I could not believe that Félix and Bun had wittingly
tricked me, they might well have been involuntary ac-
complices. For Mr. Wayl must have foreseen the path
my research would inevitably follow, and he could
accordingly set along it trap after trap. As to why he
should play such an elaborate trick on me, I was at a
loss—a modest if dilettantish mulatto hardly seemed
prey worthy of such trouble. Yet I felt that I had, at
the end of long folly, reached the sad truth, the truth
of my delusion. As we hunted over the rough Atlantic
floor, I was sure we should find nothing.

Having inspected fields of squat crags, we arrived
at a sandy patch, strewn only with shingle and lesser
shells, except for one hump of stone rising in the
center of that place. An unstony suppleness on the
surface of the hump caught my attention, and beck-
oning to the other swimmers, who were already proceeding, I led the way to it. The seeming rock stood at
least ten feet high. As soon as we were next to it, we
saw that its stoniness was an illusion created by profuse
sea growths that grayly clothed what lay beneath them
—a clumsy jumble of hawsers and smaller ropes, piled
over the inverted skeleton of a dory. We set to work

removing this slimy covering. It was not necessary to move the waterlogged wreck to see what had been hidden underneath.

A thumb-shaped structure,[7] six feet high and four feet thick, rested on the seafloor, a clocklike mechanism forming the greater part of its mass.

The uppermost part of this mechanism was a screen on which were figured the four quarters of the moon. They were, from left to right, a black disc; a like disc with a segment of white (now yellowed) on its right edge; a white disc; and a black disc with a segment of white on its left edge.

Behind a shield of thin metal that hid its juncture with the machinery below, a slender clock-hand of white wood rose across the panel of moons. The hand's base being fixed, its tip necessarily described an arc of about ninety degrees, moving from the left limb of the leftmost disc to the right limb of the rightmost disc. The exact phase of the moon was shown by the point on which the hand rested, whether on one of the discs or between any pair. It now was crossing the entirely black one, indicating, as was the case, moonless nights.

On the level below, placed in a steel frame, were the gears that determined the progress of the wooden hand. Their proportions were those of a large clock, except for one (evidently in direct contact with the hand) whose extraordinary size signified a periodicity of abnormally great length. Although I could not measure this gear, its circumference was no doubt appropriate to the interval of a lunar month.

At one point on the rim of this gear, a short metal pin extruded laterally. Once in the course of each complete revolution, the pin would trip by its upward motion (the gear moved clockwise) a hook fixed to the topmost bar of the steel frame. The point of this hook was inserted in one of the recesses of a horizontal toothed rod, above which, barely visible behind the shield, was a slender spring. Spring and rod were joined at their right ends. Their position suggested that they followed the movement of the clock-hand in a horizontal line from left to right. Although the connection was hidden, the spring certainly controlled the clock-hand (a wire fitted vertically to the right end of the rod was possibly the means).

The purpose of the arrangement was clear. At the close of each lunar month, the pin on the gear's rim tripped the hook that held the rod in place, and the spring pulled the clock-hand (as well as the rod) from its rightmost to its leftmost position. It could then start anew its progress from left to right across the panel of moons.

A pendulum hung beneath the cage of gears. It had an ordinary shaft, but a singular construction had taken the place of the weight. A conical net of light wire, perhaps two feet high and as wide at the base, dangled at the shaft's end. Within it were a dozen silver herring which, all swimming in one direction, propelled the net with them, and with it the pendulum, which in turn imparted its movement to the mechanism of the moon-clock.

The pendulum was controlled in the following way. A cable made out of twisted wires of great fineness was attached to each side of the pendulum just above the joint of the net. Both cables then passed (one to the right, the other to the left) through a cluster of pulleys suspended from the steel frame above, midway between the top of the pendulum and the machine's outer edge. The cable, descending outwards from the pulleys, was fastened to an eye at the top of a pyramidal lead weight. Another similar cable, also tied to frame directly over it, where its tautness was steadied the weight, hung straight from the edge of the steel by a spring reel.

Underneath the two weights—one on each side of the machine—massive iron cups were fixed on sturdy rods half-buried in the sand. The cups were roofed with thin flexible metal.

The length of each cable was such that when the herring had propelled their net to one end of the pendulum's arc, the weight on that side would strike the cup beneath it. The diaphragm of thin metal would then emit considerable vibration into the surrounding water: this would sufficiently startle the fish to make them turn and swim away in the opposite direction. (By the time they recovered from their fright a new clash turned them round again.) The flexibility of the cup's surface also caused the dropped weight to bounce slightly, thus aiding the reversal of the pendulum's motion.

The tension of the reels, which exercised an upward pull on the weights; the ratio of the pulleys through which the cables passed; and the heaviness of the weights—all had been adjusted to a nice equilibrium that permitted the frail momentum of the fish to keep them, and the clock, in motion.

The herring were fed through a slender funnel-shaped net of threadlike close-meshed wire, connected to the pendulum net by an opening too small to permit the egress of the captive fish. The larger end of the feeding-net hung from a metal branch projecting from the rear of the steel frame. From the same branch was suspended a luminous smooth ball fashioned out of several tiger-cowrie shells—it floated in the mouth of the feeding-net as a lure to the small sea creatures that were the herring's food.

The entire life cycle of the herring took place within their prison; for how could the school have been replenished except by reproduction? There was no entrance for anything but animalcules. As for the dead fish, they drifted, eventually, through the bottom of the net. A fraction of an inch below the net's rim, attached by no visible means, floated a film of metallic dust. When a Cogito Swimmer probed it curiously with a fishing-spear, the point of his weapon disappeared. I recognized the presence of fleshmetal; and I did not doubt that the builder of the moon-clock had, like Inno Johnstone, used some sort of magnet (perhaps the wires of the net were magnetized) to hold it in place. The dead herring and any other waste matter would, in passing from the net, be volatilized by the suspended element, which also afforded invincible protection against attack from below.

On the sand under the net, the very color of sand, a fat ray lolled, alive but unmoving. Crabs of similar color rested on its back. They were perhaps waiting for scraps that might pass through the thin opening that separated the layer of fleshmetal from the net's edge.

The moon-clock stood on four iron columns sunk in the sand, one at each corner of the steel gearcase, under which the pendulum and its adjuncts hung, and upon which the panel of moons rested. The lower part was open to the water; but the gearcase was sealed with watertight glass panels, while an hermetic glass bell covered the clock face.

Surmounting the clock, at the very top of the glass bell, the builder had left a flat surface on which there were two figures, perhaps six inches high. One was a man, white, naked except for a crown of little faded leaves. The other was a black woman, also naked. The man was caught in a net of tangled white wire. Their features and limbs were carved crudely, except for the woman's vulva, which had been carefully represented as a mouth, with red tonguetip protruding between tiny sharp teeth. With one hand she lifted one of her breasts; with the other she held out a minute golden adze to the trapped king, who stretched his hands towards her.

On an exterior metal band that separated this scene from the panel of moons, two words had been roughly scratched: *Mundorys Lorsea.*

Having watched one of the Swimmers shoot the lethargic ray with a bolt from his undersea gun, I was unable to stand the cold any longer, and I swam quickly up to our boat. My companions took me back to the island at once. A hot drink at the hotel restored me.

The moon-clock having failed to yield the third answer, I decided to end my investigations. My long search had consumed more than the little money I had once possessed—I had even had to pawn the adze. There was nothing for me to do but return home and begin paying my debts.

·

APPENDIX I:
DER MÜSSIGE SCHÖPFER

The following text is published with the kind permission of Mr. Walter Auerbach.

Gottlieb erzählte Marie seinen Traum von voriger Nacht.

"In einer grauen Stille schwebte ich nach oben durch den Himmel, an den Wolken und Sternen vorbei. Dann kam ich in eine andere Welt und dachte, 'Dies muss das Paradies sein.' Ich wandelte zuerst durch Auen, dann über bewaldete Hüge mit lieblichen Bächen, Dahinter lag die Stadt, ausgedehnt, aber überraschend still.

"Ich stieg von den Hügeln zur Stadt hinunter, aber just vor den ersten Aussenhöfen hielt mich ein erbärmlicher Anblick an. Ein Mann lag in dem Graben neben meinem Pfad. Noch niemals habe ich solch einen mageren Menschen gesehen. Man konnte durch seine Lumpen die Knochenenden sehen and wie sie am ganzen Körper beinahe durch die Haut stachen; und die Haut, grau and durchscheinend wie fettiges Pergament, fing in der Tat schon an vielen Stellen abzublättern und aufzubrechen an. Aus seiner Kehle kamen kurze Stösse eines keuchenden Stöhnens, die trotz Entsetzen and Ekel mir das Herz im Leibe umdrehten. Ich rannte weiter zur Stadt für jemanden mir zu helfen dieser armseligen Kreatur Beistand zu leisten. Kaum an den ersten Gebäuden angekommen stiess ich auf einen Polizisten, den ich aufforderte mir zu folgen. Bald waren wir bei dem Elenden. Doch als dieser sah wer bei mir war, stiess er einen Schrei des Schreckens aus und wurde dann so still, dass er mir nicht mehr zu atmen schien. Der Polizist jedoch, der zuerst gegen den Hingestreckten gleichgültig schien, trat nach dem Schrei auf ihn zu, erhob seinen Knüppel und versetzte ihm einen furchtbaren Schlag auf die Schläfe. Darauf salutierte er und machte sich auf seinen Weg in die Stadt zurück. Eine Zeit lang sass ich erschüttert and wie betäubt da. Schliesslich schaute ich den Betroffenen an und erschauderte beim Anblick seines Kopfes. Der Schlag hatte nämlich den Schädel eingedrückt und eine bläulichbraune Vertiefung von der Braue bis zum Scheitel gelassen. Doch als ich zuschaute, öffneten sich die Augen und das keuchende Stöhnen fing wieder an, und zwar stärker als zuvor. Dann richteten sich die Augen auf mich, oder vielmehr nur eins von ihnen, denn das andere war durch den Schlag in seiner Höhle festgeklemmt worden. Das Auge blickte mich an, das Stöhnen hörte auf, und der geschlagene Mann verstummte vor mir grad so wie vorher vor dem Polizisten. Ich traute meinen eigenen Augen nicht und kehrte in die Stadt zurück.

"An der Stelle, wo ich den Polizisten getroffen hatte, stand nun ein anderer Mann, als ob er auf mich warte, und bald erkannte ich in ihm unseren Neffen Johannes, der gestorben war, als er auf die Universität zu Freiburg ging.

" 'Onkel Gottlieb!' rief er, als er mich erkannte. 'Herzlich Willkommen! Ich wusste nicht, dass Ihr es wart, doch hätt' ich's wissen müssen: wie stets ein Vorbild bürgerlicher Pflichterfüllung! Doch möchte ich Euch im Vertrauen sagen, fasst's nur nicht als Kritik auf, denn was Ihr getan habt, war ganz und gar richtig; ich möchte Euch aber sagen, dass man ihnen ausserhalb der Stadt ziemliche Freiheit gönnt. Es scheint, Ihr missbilligt, was ich sage, und ich muss eingestehen, dass sein Stöhnen fürchterlich war; aber was das nicht erst, nachdem Ihr den Engel gerufen hattet? Ich habe nämlich die ganze Sache mit angesehen, und mir schien, dass er sich ganz gut benahm, wenn man bedenkt, dass er sich ausserhalb der Stadt befand. Er war wirklich nicht zu laut und war im Graben wohl verborgen. Natürlich erschien er Euch unvermutet und versetzte Euch einen schönen Schreck. Doch Ihr solltet erst einmal die sehen, die weiter draussen sind, besonders die oben in den Ber-

gen: einfach ekelhaft! Und wie die schreien! Im
vorigen Monat musste ich dorthin gehen um etwas
Haar zu holen. Es ist erstaunlich wie ihr Haar wächst
auch in den widerwärtigsten Umständen. Für Tage
konnte ich nichts als Zwieback und Milch zu mir
nehmen. Wir müssen für die jetzige Regelung dank-
bar sein, obwohl es ihnen vielleicht etwas zu leicht ge-
macht und uns der Trost entzogen wird uns an ihrem
Zustand erbauen zu können.'
  " 'Sind das denn die Verdammten?' fragte ich.
  " 'Wie drollig Eure Frage klingt, Onkel Gottlieb!
Obwohl sie sich sicher wie die Verdammten vorkom-
men müssen,' lachte Johannes. 'Doch ist es besser, man
lässt sie frei und offen auf dem Lande liegen und jam-
mern als sie in der Stadt in die untersten Keller zu
stecken und öffentlich zu prügeln. Man mag sie noch
so gründlich knebeln und ihnen noch so viel Pein zu-
fügen, die erforderliche städtische Ruhe wird nie er-
reicht. Sie sind nicht nur zu elend, sie sind einfach zu
zahlreich. Stellt Euch vor: 190.000.000.000 bei der
letzten Zählung. Ausserdem wurde der Platz, den sie
eingenommen hatten, wieder frei und in sehr ge-
mütliche Schlafsäle für die Handlanger umgewandelt;
auf jeden Fall gemütlich genug für die. Doch sagt mir,
Onkel Gottlieb: wie lange seid Ihr denn schon hier?'
  " 'Ich war auf meinem ersten Wege in diese Stadt,
als ich den Mann in Graben fand.'
  " 'Dann seid Ihr ja eben erst angekommen! Du lieber
Gott im Himmel, kommt hier 'rüber, wo man uns
nicht sehen kann! Ach, Onkel Gottlieb, warum habt
Ihr mir das nicht gleich gesagt? Gottseidank dass Ihr
in Eurem Sonntagstaat seid; was für ein Glück! Ihr
könnt Euch nicht vorstellen, wie empfindlich die hier

in solchen Sachen sind. Früher, als der Andrang noch nicht so gross war, waren sie scheint's duldsamer in solchen Einzelheiten; aber heutzutage machen Kleider Leute. Ach, Onkel Gottlieb, ich freue mich ja so Euretwegen. Sie werden Euch sicherlich erhören and Ihr werdet ihnen von allem erzählen können: von Eurem Hof, Eurem Vieh, Euren Ersparnissen, die ihr so sorgfältig angehäuft habt. Jetzt könnt Ihr Euch zu all der Mühe gratulieren, Onkel Gottlieb, und Ihr werdet heil und sicher sein. Erwarten dürft Ihr nicht zu viel, Ihr werdet schon etwas schaffen müssen, wahrscheinlich auf den Lufthöfen, aber Ihr werdet so viele Tagelöhner haben, wie Ihr zur Hilfe braucht; und mit Euren Ersparnissen dürften sie Euch ein Leben zugestehen, dass Euch befriedigen wird. Es wird Euch auch möglich sein der Tante Marie den Weg zu ebnen; guter Einfluss schadet dabei nichts, obwohl Eurer natürlich nicht sehr gross ist. Aber das eilt alles nicht. Zuerst müsst Ihr in das Register eingetragen werden. Ich fürchte, es wird etwas lange nehmen, doch wisset, dass, wenn es einmal vorbei ist, seid Ihr für immer und für ewig untergebracht. Glaubt mir, das ist eine Erleichterung, wie Ihr sie noch nie erlebt habt, und wie Ihr sie nimmermehr erleben werdet.'

"Johannes nahm mich an der Hand und führte mich in die innere Stadt.

" 'Bitte denkt daran vorsichtig zu sein, wenn Ihr von Euren Besitztümern sprecht,' sagte er. 'Erwähnt nicht alles, zählt nicht jede Henne auf, Onkel Gottlieb, und vergesst dabei die Hauptsache nicht! Wisset, dass, obwohl es auf Geld allein nicht ankommt denn ein einflussreicher Beschützer kann einzelne Personen auch ohne einen Pfennig auslösen, es doch oft entscheidet, in welche Kategorie ein Ankömmling eingeordnet wird.'

" 'Sollte ich nicht lieber erst auf andere Verdienste hindeuten?' fragte ich. 'Die Liebe, mit der ich für meine Familie sorgte, die Mühe. . .'

" 'Ja, ja, Onkel Gottlieb, aber das wissen sie ja schon. Ausserdem macht sowas nicht viel aus. Es wird natürlich begrüsst und anerkannt, aber ist sehr schwierig zu bewerten. Dazu ist es auch noch so verbreitet, da gibt's kaum einen, der nicht eine Ausrede für sein Betragen fände. In dieser Hinsicht ist Güte hier die Regel und so allgemein, dass sie als Grundlage für die komplizierte Klassifizierung, die die Verwaltungsengel machen müssen, völlig unzureichend ist. Drum werden andere Gesichtspunkte beachtet, und einer davon ist Reichtum. Ihr müsst verstehen, Geld gibt's hier nicht, gerechter Himmel! Man wird mit allem nach seiner Klassifizierung versorgt. Ihr werdet gewiss mit Recht fragen, ob denn das rechtschaffene Leben eines armen Mannes nicht für mehr gilt als das eines Reichen. Doch im Grunde scheint es sich darum zu handeln, dass Geld den Reichen ein moralisch höheres Leben nicht nur erlauben sollte sondern in der Tat erlaubt. So offenbart sich, dass je ärmer man ist, um so weniger Zeit und Kraft hat man, um jene Wohltätigkeit auszuüben, welche den Wohlhabenden einfach eine Gewohnheit ist. In dieser Hinsicht ist es durchaus keine Ungerechtigkeit, wenn man das Geld bei der Anlage der Akten mit einbezieht. Man bemüht sich vielmehr Leuten das zu geben, was sie verdienen, und das bedeutet, wessen sie fähig sind, was wiederum von dem, was sie gewesen sind, abhängt. Sollte man einen halbverhungerten Wilden, der sein Leben wie ein Tier verbracht hat, genau so belohnen wie einen Mann, zum Beispiel einen Verwaltungsbeamten oder einen Dichter, der sich eines Dienstes höherer Ordnung fähig erwiesen hat? Das wäre wohl kaum gerecht.'

"Verwirrt klammerte ich mich an seinen Arm und wir gingen weiter. Wir wandelten durch manche saubere Strassen und als wir uns der Stadtmitte näherten, wurden die Strassen zu grossartigen Prunkalleen, welche mit Platanen bepflanzt und mit bunten, moosbewachsenen Ziegeln gepflastert waren.

" 'Sag' mir Johannes, lebt hier der liebe Gott?'

"Er deutete auf die prachtvolle Allee vor uns und erwiderte, "Könnt Ihr noch länger daran zweifeln?'

" 'Weiss er vom Mann im Graben?'

" 'Aber Onkel Gottlieb, um Himmels Willen! Der Arme hat schon genug durchgemacht; und er hat uns alles dies ermöglicht. Wäre es nicht zu undankbar, wenn wir ihm nicht wenigstens nun endlich Frieden sicherten? Er hat ihn uns beschert und noch weit mehr. Er muss seine Stunden nicht mehr länger mit der Obhut seines Reichs zubringen, sondern hat sich in seinen herrlichsten Palast mitten in seinem allerliebsten Park zurückgezogen, wo er von jenen betreut wird, die seine Wünsche am besten kennen. Seine Aufwarteengel bilden die höchste Ranggruppe im Himmel. Nur von Lobpreisungen und Anbetung umgeben, lebt er in Seligkeit; und seine Glückseligkeit ist unsere grösste Wonne. Vergebt mir meine Zähren, Onkel Gottlieb! Nun aber seht stolz und schneidig drein! Wir sind schon an der Registratur.'

"Wir waren en einem grauen Gebäude mit vielen Stockwerken angekommen, so gross wie eine Festung. Davor standen Leute in zwei Reihen; derer, die eintraten, und derer, die herauskamen. Als wir uns näherten, wurde die letztere von einer Gruppe aufgebrochen, die die grosse Treppe hinunterdrängte. Zwei uniformierte Männer hielten eine Frau zwischen sich und trieben sie zur Eile an. Ein purpur farbenes Krebsgeschwür bedeckte ihr Kinn. Sie verschwand mit ihren Wärtern in einer benachbarten Seitenstrasse, die ich vorher noch nicht bemerkt hatte. Manche solcher Gruppen verschwanden in dieser Strasse.

" 'Sie wird aus der Stadt entfernt,' bemerkte Johannes.

" 'Wie der Mann von heute Morgen?'

" 'Ja. Auch Krankheit wird in der Stadt nicht geduldet, wenn sie nicht vollkommen gutartig ist.'

" 'Aber die Ärzte hier sicherlich . . .'

" 'Ach, die Ärzte haben sich zur Ruhe gesetzt. Findet Ihr nicht, dass sie es verdient haben? In der Tat, nicht alle; da sind einige so vom Leiden besessen, dass sie ihre grossen Vorrechte aufgegeben haben, um mit den Kranken zu leben. Man hält sie für ein wenig verrückt. Könntet Ihr Euch vorstellen eine solche Entscheidung für alle Ewigkeit zu treffen?'

" 'Die Frau wird also nicht behandelt werden?'

" 'Wahrscheinlich nicht.'

" 'Aber wird's dann nicht schlimmer?'

" 'Wenn das der natürliche Verlauf ist, wird es schlimmer.'

" 'Dann wird aber doch die Krankheit sie eines Tages töten '

" 'O nein, was auch immer passiert, sterben wird sie nicht.'

"Wir waren an der obersten Stufe angekommen and waren beinahe im Gebäude, als mich auf einmal solch ein Grauen erfasste, dass ich laut aufschrie und vor Schrecken zitternd erwachte. Einmal wach, Marie, wurde mir auch klar, woher dieses Gefühl des Grauens gekommen war. Es war nicht der Schrecken über meine Vision, sondern der Gedanke, dass auch ich 'aus der Stadt entfernt' werden könnte. Und die Erleichterung, die folgte, war nicht nur die Erleichterung des Erwachens sondern das Wissen, dass ich auch dort drüben nichts zu befürchten hätte; und ich dankte Gott von tiefstem Herzen für all das Gut, dass er mir auf dieser Welt gegeben hat.

"Und jetzt erinnere ich mich auch; beim Aufwachen wandte ich mich Johannes zu; er lächelte, als er meinen Blicken entschwand; ich rief ihm nach: 'Dann ist's ja nur dasselbe?' und er erwiderte: 'Ja, Onkel Gottlieb, dasselbe, aber für immer, von nun an bis in Ewigkeit!'

"O Marie, Heil den Johnstones! Den verfluchten Johnstones! Den verschissenen Johnstones! Den Feinden des Bestehenden! Die haben sich behauptet und sind als Königen nach Alba heimgekehrt! Die Fut ihrer Zigeunerin sei mit argen Zähnen gespickt!"

•

APPENDIX II

A fragment in Mozart's hand may bear on the lost *Missa Fa Si Re*. The manuscript consists of thirteen measures for five unaccompanied voices, with the title "Kyrie" but no text. Listed by Köchel as an original composition, it was relegated by Einstein to the appendix of his revision of Köchel's work.

These are Einstein's notes on the fragment (Köchel, *Mozart-Verzeichnis*, Dritte Auflage, J. W. Edwards Verlag, Ann Arbor, Michigan, 1947, p. 832):

Anh. 109^{vii} = 429^a. Anfang eines *Kyrie* für 4 Singstimmen von J. J. Froberger.—André, hds. Verz. F².

Abschrift Mozarts: Fitchwinder University, Swetham (Mass.), C. Washington Library. Das Autograph erst bei A. Johnstone, Baltimore, Kat. X (1776), Nr. 50, dann bei Syl. Doge,—London, Kat. 69 (Dez. 1911), Nr. 4211.

Anmerkung: Von Johann Jakob Froberger (1616–1667). Vgl. Denkm. der Tonkunst in Österreich, X, 2. Die Abschrift ist wahrscheinlich untergeschoben.

Literatur: G. Nottebohm, *Etwas über J. J. Froberger* in Mus. Wochenbl., Lpz. 1874.

The brevity of the editor's comments is in itself remarkable; but one is quite at a loss to explain the mistakes made by this punctilious scholar. There is no such Kyrie in the DTOe volume, and no mention of it in Nottebohm's article; nor is any mass by Froberger, extant or lost, known to musicologists.

As to the music, its style is certainly unlike either Froberger's or Mozart's, although it could conceivably be an exercise by one of them in the *stile antico.* It is to be noted that the soprano entrance is pitched uncommonly high, giving, together with the cross relation in the tenor, a singular emphasis to the alteration of the *fa-si ♮-re* motive to *fa si re.*

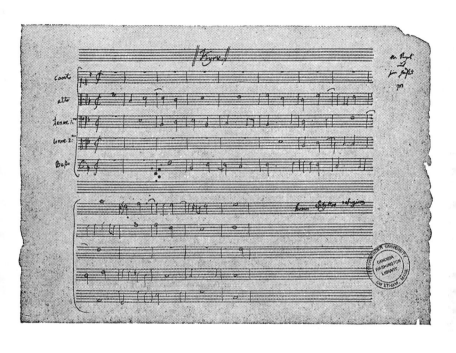

Lans-en-Vercors, December 1958–May 1960.

Des creux manoirs, & pleins d'obscurite

Dieu par le temps retire Terite.

Tlooth

It is a mistake to regard one disease as more divine than another, since all is human and all divine.

HIPPOCRATES

Part One

A Disappointing Inning

Mannish Madame Nevtaya slowly cried "Fur bowls!" and the Fideist batter, alert to the sense behind the sound of her words, jogged toward first base. The wind from the northern steppe blew coldly on the close of our season.

The Fideist division received the camp's worst villains, and its team assembled their dregs. Among us Defective Baptists a love of baseball signified gentleness; among Fideists, cruelty. Consider their bloodthirsty team—

Left field: undertaker's assistant and caterer to necrophiles, Sydney Valsalva kidnaped infants for beheading.

Center field: Lynn Petomi, dentist, mutilated the mouths of patients.

Pitcher: Hilary Cheyne-Stokes, gynecologist, committed analagous crimes.

1st base: Tommy Withering, osteopath, flayed a younger brother.

Shortstop: Evelyn Roak, surgeon, supplied human fragments to a delicatessen and was arrested for scandalous amputations.*

(2nd base: Cecil Meli, nurse, had been jailed by mistake.)

*For example, removing, together with a troublesome spur of bone, the index and ring fingers of my left hand. I was then a violinist.

Right field: Lee Donders, grocer, transformed Roak's material into "Donders' Delicacies."

Catcher: Marion Gullstrand, obstetrician, tortured unwed mothers.

3rd base: Leslie Auenbrugger, psychiatrist—the "Restroom Bomber."

Valsalva had walked. Since I was catcher, I went out to the mound to say a few words of encouragement. The second batter grounded to shortstop, forcing Valsalva; the third struck out; and the Fideists' turn at bat would have ended with Withering's high foul if, failing to allow for the wind, I had not misjudged it. Withering singled on the next pitch.

I was thus obliged to execute my plan in the first inning of the game. Having foreseen the possibility, I drew a prepared ball from my chest protector to substitute it for the one in play.

I had made the ball myself. It was built around two unusual parts—a tiny battery and a pellet of dynamite. From each of the battery's outlets, a wire extended through the hair stuffing of the ball about halfway to the leather wrapper. The free ends of the wires, one of which passed through a firing cap fixed to the dynamite, were six millimeters apart, enough to prevent their junction at a mild impact but not at a sufficiently hard one. The difference, which I had determined exactly, was that between a fast pitch caught and a slow pitch hit. The wire ends separated into meshing sprays of filament, so that no matter how the ball was struck, it was certain to explode.

To shield myself, I had reinforced my equipment with layers of nylon in the chest protector, steel in the cap and shin guards, and a lucite screen inside the mask.

For the umpire's protection I counted on her thick skin. I expected the explosion to create general confusion, stun and knock down the batter, and explain the batter's death. The bomb itself would kill no one, but I had concealed in my right shin guard, ready to use as soon as the ball had been detonated, a hypodermic of botulin.

Evelyn Roak stood at the plate. To my dismay, the first three pitches were low—our pitcher later complained that the ball was heavy. The fourth was a perfect strike, and my hopes revived. At the next delivery the batter drew back to swing, but the pitch was wild. The ball sailed past my outstretched glove as I lunged at it, skittered over the ground behind home plate, off the playing field altogether, at last disappearing irretrievably, and with an abysmal liquid reverberation, into a drain.

My Dental Apprenticeship

The camp, in which I was completing my second year, had kept its prerevolutionary structure through historical, ideological and geographic change. Established during the Holy Alliance for the internment of heretics, it had since the eighties received offenders of every sort. Recently it had been transplanted intact, down to the last dossier, prisoner and guard, to its present southerly location at Jacksongrad.

The organization of the camp was sectarian. On arrival, prisoners were arbitrarily and finally committed to the Americanist, Darbyist, Defective Baptist, Fideist or Resurrectionist division. Although the assignments were theologically haphazard, the divisions had real unity. Particular types flourished in the various sects and were perhaps knowingly allotted to them; and the descendants of the first religious prisoners, faithful to their traditions, exerted a constant influence on their fellows.

This influence was strengthened by a ban on all political and nonconformist discussion, and by a strict segregation of the sects. Fideists and Resurrectionists, Americanists and Darbyists met only on exceptional occasions, such as concerts, civic debates and athletic encounters. Even then the guards held intercourse to a minimum, and the mere exchange of greetings was beset with obstacles and penalties.

Such circumstances had determined the plan so unsuccessfully executed at the Fideist ball game. The stratagem was not my first.

When, soon after my arrival, the camp authorities had asked me to choose a professional activity, I had refused. Because I was a musician I was urged to join the camp orchestra, band or choir; but I had been too recently maimed to take up the euphonium or sing hymns. The cultural administrator, irked by my refusal, had relegated me to the dental infirmary.

This was meant as a punishment but proved a boon. The clinic had an evil reputation in the camp; but this reflected, more than its drabness and inadequate equipment, the mentality of its director, a martinet who spared neither his patients nor his assistants. When I reported for work, this person had just been replaced by a kind and intelligent woman dentist, Dr. Zarater. She had been appointed by the authorities to apply a more humane policy, and she was empowered to reorganize the clinic accordingly.

My relations with Dr. Zarater were good from the start. She at once remarked on the fitness of my left hand, reduced to three spaced digits, for working inside the mouth. "No tool," she said, "is as good as a finger, but with five it's like using your foot." She questioned me tactfully about my mishap, then about my life. When I mentioned in the course of our talk the name of R. King Dri, Dr. Zarater's interest quickened; for she herself had studied with Dr. King Dri and planned to use her clinic to demonstrate his methods.

Who was R. King Dri? I had learned of him by chance

some years before when, in a dentist's waiting room, I came across a letter about him in an old issue of *Dental Cosmos*.

King Dri called himself the "Philosopher-Dentist." Victim of a history of dental disorders that classical remedies could not relieve, he had invented a theory of the human organism to explain his case, and from it derived new surgical techniques.

He describes the origin of the theory in his one prodigious treatise. The work opens with a humble declaration of intent:

"Either men will think that the nature of toothache is wholly mysterious and incomprehensible, or that a man like myself, who has suffered from it thirty-six years, must be of a slow and sluggish disposition not to have discovered more respecting the nature and treatment of a disease so peculiarly his own. Be this as it may, I will give a bona fide account of what I know."

Dri then relates how, refusing extraction, he had lost so much strength through his chronic ailment that he had at last taken to his bed, spending four months in strict immobility. ("Movement," he writes, "is one of the greatest troubles in toothache, since, with perfect quiet, the agony is just tolerable.") It was thus bedridden that Dri began speaking to his teeth, at first cursing them, then praying to them, finally addressing them as sensible beings in need of consolation and reassurance. A prompt diminution of pain followed Dri's first essay in "internal charity." Three days later several afflicted teeth, including the one first smitten thirty-six years before, stopped aching. Only two refused to be comforted. After another week of encouragement, the doctor decided that they knew themselves unfit for life in his body, wished to be free of it, but were unwilling to take the initiative of leaving him. Dri patiently assuaged their anxiety, explaining that there was only one escape from their predicament, and that by delaying to choose it they were aggravating their suffering, not to mention his own. In a week, without being touched, the reluctant teeth fell out.

King Dri's conclusion from his experiment might be summarized thus:

The human body, richest of nature's fruits, is not a single organism made of constituent parts, but an assemblage of entities on whose voluntary collaboration the functioning of the whole depends. "The body is analogous to a political *confederation*, not to a *federation* as is normally supposed." Every entity within the body is endowed with its own psyche, more or less developed in awareness and self-consciousness. Aching teeth can be compared to temperamental six-year-old children, an impotent penis to an adolescent girl who must be cajoled out of her sulkiness. The most developed entity is the heart, which does not govern the body but presides over it with loving persuasiveness, like an experienced but still vigorous father at the center of a household of relatives and pets. Health exists when the various entities are happy, for they then perform their roles properly and co-operate with one another. Disease appears when some member of the organism rejects its vocation. Medicine intervenes to bring the wayward member back to its place in the body's society. At best the heart makes its own medicine, convincing the rebel of its love by addressing it sympathetically; but a doctor is often needed to abet the communion of heart and member, and sometimes, when the patient has surrendered to unconsciousness or despair, to speak for the heart itself.

In his treatise Dr. Dri gives many examples of such intervention. The following paragraph, the close of his plea to the infected canine of a sixteen-year-old boy, may suggest the Indian's stature.

"You say, 'Is not the goal of life to die rather than to live, not leaving death to the mercy of others but acceding to it voluntarily, and giving one's self up with rejoicing?' No! that is neither joy, nor liberty, nor grace, nor eternal life: which are in your father's love. Child of my being! Flesh of my flesh! As distant from death as the morning star is from a farm's smoky fire, when that fair virgin on the sun's breast lays her radiant head, may your father in his infinite love behold you forever in that place reserved for you! Next to such life, what is death worth? And what is life worth if not given to him? Must you torment yourself, when obedience is so sweet? Return and say: 'Now I have all! Everything is at my feet, I am as one who, on seeing a tree laden with fruit, and having mounted the ladder, feels a depth of branches bend under his body. I shall speak beneath the tree, as a flute neither too grave nor too shrill. Behold, I am lifted upon the waters! Love unseals the rock of my heart! So let me live! Let me grow thus mingled with my father, like the vine with the olive tree.'" The tooth was cured.

The medical profession had not taken R. King Dri seriously during his lifetime, despite the attractiveness of his theory and the undeniable results he achieved in Punjab dental wards. According to Dr. Zarater, however, a new interest in the philosopher-dentist had arisen in Europe, and a movement was under way to establish legal recognition of his teaching.

During eight months as Dr. Zarater's assistant, I learned the clinical uses of King Dri's theory, as well as the rudiments of traditional dentistry. Under the directress' guidance I made such progress that, after only four months' training, I was able to treat simple cases by myself. And no sooner had I taken on this responsibility than a valuable patient was assigned to me.

I had hoped to benefit from my position. As the clinic ministered to the entire camp, I would inevitably meet members of sects other than my own. But I was lucky that one of the first of these should be a young Fideist woman named Yana, celebrated throughout Jacksongrad for her beauty; more pertinently, Evelyn Roak was in love with her.

In order to see her often, I prolonged Yana's treatment. I also wooed her myself. (Dear Yana! I became devoted to her. Even when she had lost her usefulness, I remained her friend.)

My courtship was successful. Yana and I began meeting secretly in a storeroom of the clinic. We were obliged to address each other by gesture or in writing, for Yana spoke no English, although she had learned to read and write it in school. An unexpected result of this was that we invented a written code in the course of our exchanges. The code was then only a game between us; later, when we had to rely on letters, it became a valuable safeguard.

I was passionate with Yana but unpossessive—I had no wish to anger her Fideist suitor, for whom I feigned admiration. (Lest this arouse suspicion, I asked Yana not to mention my name. "A dangerous political matter," I explained.)

Meanwhile I had Yana deliver to her Fideist friend a succession of anonymous gifts, most of them articles then scarce in the camp—absorbent cotton, airmail stationery, Swiss toothpaste.

Six of the presents were innocuous. The seventh and last was a pound box of caramel candies. I had cooked them myself and mixed into them several ounces of crystalline oxylous acid. Normally inactive, this chemical combines with certain phosphates into volatile compounds; their formation requires no catalysts other than moisture and mild heat.

I expected the stickiness of the candies to attach a quantity of acid crystals to the teeth, where they would transform the calcium phosphate of the enamel into oxyluric acid, a violently corrosive substance.

Four days after delivering my present, Yana told me that her friend was ill. I mounted a sleepless watch at the clinic entrance. Early the next morning the patient was brought in on a stretcher and taken, as I had ordered, to my office. But Dr. Zarater had observed the arrival. It was she who conducted the examination, and she decided to handle the case herself.

"These cavities," she exclaimed, "are *monstrous* and *unnatural!*"

Yana's admirer proved generous—eight other Fideists later called at the clinic with stricken mouths. Even Yana, unwarned, lost a molar.

The Infection

Dr. Zarater had good reason to keep me from "my" patient.

My severed fingers had healed with difficulty—even healed, they remained abnormally sensitive. Recently a few pimples had appeared on the stumps, adding to their soreness a tormenting itch.

The pimples were small, lying nearly flush with the skin, with minute white spots at the center. I forced myself not to scratch them in the hope that they would soon vanish, and I would have left them untreated if Dr. Zarater had not intervened. She forbade me to touch her patients and ordered me to go to the infirmary. I neglected to do so; the directress became increasingly urgent; when she finally showed signs of anger, I obeyed.

The camp doctor was named Amset. He was a popular figure in Jacksongrad, celebrated for his addiction to whisky, monologue and fresh air. On fair days he received his patients in his garden behind the clinic, and it was there that I found him on the morning of my visit. Dr. Amset had just dismissed a patient when I arrived.

"Yes, there's little doubt but what it's cystic fibrosis!
It's a strange disease! Or if you prefer, 'familial steator-
rhea.' I like to give at least two names to things, especially
diseases and plants, which I have a grim time grasping,
memorywise. If you know that neurasthenia is the English
malady, St.-John's-wort is Klamath weed, old-man's-
beard . . . Hm—your hand! That's funny—did you—
let's see, you're a dental assistant. Wait a minute." He
sharply pinched one of the more swollen pimples; yellow
matter issued. "Did you happen to treat a young boy
called . . . called . . . a Resurrectionist I think—Moe
Kusa, that's the name! You did? Oh oh—you can call it
lues if you want, but in four other letters it's syph. It has
to be. You see, I remember Moe's mother—his older
brother was congenitally syphilitic, and Moe . . . as you
say, the sores on his mouth. Well, I'll give you three zillion
units today and gone tomorrow."

Two crows that had been circling above us settled in an
alder nearby. The doctor's cure was useless. The gamut
of antibiotics, exhausted during the wicked aftermath of
my operation, had nearly killed me. Dr. Amset agreed
there was no chance of their helping now. Pouring each
of us a tumbler of whisky, he prepared some mercurous
acetate for local application, and wished me luck.

Leaving, I thought of little Moe Kusa. He was a
charming boy who suffered his condition without complaint: the ends of his mouth were ulcerated, so that
eating and drinking were painful to him, and his pretty
face marred. He was wasted too by chronic diarrhea;
and while his greater affliction was beyond my competence,
I had been able to soothe the lesser one with a broth of
what Dr. Amset might call starwort.

In the Barracks

Our quarters were cleaned and supervised by an unamiable person known as "The Concierge." Although a prisoner, she was dependent on the authorities for her privileged job, and she accordingly acted in their interests rather than ours. Her role was contemptible, but I took a tolerant view of it—a minor power, she was very well informed.

For a long time I could not persuade The Concierge to trust me. My assignment to the clinic seemed of little use, since she had incorruptible teeth and perquisites greater than my own; yet it was through my position that I at last won her over.

The Concierge's joy was her pet, a miniature urubu. She spoiled it elaborately, nursing it through the ordeal of the Jacksongrad winter and providing it in all seasons, to our dismay, with gamy morsels of animal brain and eye. The vulture was as little liked as its mistress, and a resentful prisoner finally kidnaped it one night while The Concierge slept, returning it before dawn with its beak smashed.

Unable to pick or chew, the bird starved. The Con-

cierge was in despair, and herself wasting away, when I
intervened. Retrieving two wisdom teeth from the clinic,
I fashioned out of them a dentine beak, cut away the
ruined bills and wired the new ones to their roots. After
a few days the urubu began using the substitute, soon
mastered it, and quickly recovered.

The Concierge was "at my service." I made her promise
to tell me immediately, no matter how great the difficulty,
any news she might hear concerning the Fideists.

Wandering into the barracks one Sunday morning, I
found The Concierge alone, reading a back issue of *The
Worm Runners Digest* and listening to the radio. An Eng-
lish-language program was being broadcast—

the people themselves
terrible spider plague?
the webs upon
more like tents than
wind
than German incendiary
a decoration
"food rose plants" from light and air. citizens
the autonomous   Joe, the natural
penis?
the phoenix
sprays   dust
ravaging
*Then in your view, Greg, a giant smoke screen has
been spread between the facts of medicine in America*

"Those shmucks have muff it again," The Concierge
remarked, switching off the radio to answer the telephone.

"This is Calvin nine oh nine oh." She listened a moment
and hung up. "I think that soon, very soon, I have im-

portant news." She smiled horribly, and turned away to begin her weekly cleaning. A duster of which she was very proud (but which she never used, as the asthma faction was apt to remind her) hung from one shoulder. It had been made from the hair of Laris Kotinskaya, a Hollywood actress who, having to shave her head for a prison role, had given away her locks in response to The Concierge's distant appeal. No one knew why she had turned the trophy into a domestic implement.

Texts True and False

Dr. Zarater reduced my position at the clinic to that of accountant; my baseball stratagem failed; and I despaired of exploiting legitimate opportunities. I felt that I must find a lure attractive enough to justify a secret meeting.

I knew that Evelyn Roak was something of a dilettante (as children, we had studied music together), with a flair for history. According to Yana, this interest had recently led to a study of the sects represented in the camp, particularly of Darbyism and its origins.

This news left me perplexed until I remembered the "Black Pope" enigma.

The rise of Darbyism is plainly told in contemporary documents, all of which are published, and all but one easily accounted for. The exception is as mysterious as the rest are clear. It is an unsigned letter of about seven hundred words, composed in a farrago of tongues; no one has yet identified or explained it. Scholars refer to it as *Pape Niger*, after its opening words.*

It was my guess, which Yana confirmed, that her friend's interest in Darbyism centered on this letter.

Using Yana as intermediary, I therefore let it be known

* See Figures 1(a) and 1(b) for the version of the letter that appeared in *Notes & Queries*, Vol. 2, No. 3.

that I too was interested in *Pape Niger;* that I had access
to a document bearing on the Darbyist letter in the Defective Baptist archives; and that I had made a copy of it.
To support my fiction, I forged a short "extract," adorned
it with pseudo-scholarly notes, and gave it to Yana to
show to her friend.

I enjoy rereading my invention. Its tangential relation
to *Pape Niger,* offering little to satisfy but enough to excite an expectant curiosity; the mystifying notes, in which
slivers of apt information are sandwiched between thick
irrelevancies; the interruption of the text at the point when
it evidently becomes most interesting; and above all the
presumption that *Pape Niger* was addressed to one of
the Allants in an attempt to denigrate the Catholic Chavenders and their allies, while the Defective Baptists tried to
pacify the warring families—these devices seem now no
less cunning than they did when I put all my passion into
them.

Here is what I wrote.

The history of the Chavenders and the Allants is truly
of the heroic nobility: a stock of peculiar strength, whence
sprung great trees, and from the trees, great fruit.

Gloomy are these days of drooping gray fears among
the golden-haired Chavenders. There is now much stored-
up pain among the volatile Allants; and from this place I
have heard the heavy din of verbal doughtiness. When
Chavenders meet with Allants, there are swelling looks and
injurious words, and many times brawls between them, in
our day; but in the historicity[1] of the clans is kinship and
assurance. Here is the piety of family life, here is the
sanctity of family religion where we may not look for
other.

Two and a half centuries ago they united in wedlock:
Doña Enula de Osorio, (by her sister) a near Chinchon,

PAPE NIGER jets ricovra su podestoir, und stes assedut en les moutoncillos tuskanos dispergent sos magias super i juices d'ogne part, grosse ubre de porco mal. E in tua dolor uoudriestassais tu, mee framano, an unam suam pezonaro noero chuper. Attunzione! Els von te dammamnerum, quel rasse sempere paranda amb faulsschid di destruir. Custodissent Darby, Irving, autorque *Pulsuum Compendii* te a illoris, lles demons: le sun toto porcherie. Nel ano domini nostri 1632 beporcten li Europa, e tost muorons por lor mjerde. "Niente plas coctura di melon, niente plus coloquintida, ningente plu huole de rizino! Fellate solo an bonam viellam chinchonam, la pulvem comitissae," oder plutost pelvem comitissae, com lor? E quando sa lor le caldepisse donato habue, ed un schankro belo suppurantem, fact qualgue lor dammé legne? No, mesmo se la de qual juide De Vega (*sic*) por 100 reals per lb. pris avan!

Comprendo tua angunia. Escrivs, "This molar continues to grow both in heighth and breadth, I cannot close my jaw, which is become unhinged, and has given me such fevers that my bed every night is drenched with sweat." Ma ne empla quela scortecha! No ave lors schankrs guarit—y qual a? Mercur purgo lo porcherie per lor annoigrato esput. Desempacha to ventre delo ecxesifo de corrupouriccio que tu en ti oltre los besognes des fams encogt as, und la doulour y fievras s'en despedirano con lu. Lo Pape Niger no post la facre, touddo pourchoriture lu stesmo. Prov nigrum helleboro —qual es, com Sanct Polo dique, "escandal pour les Juides y follocurie per les pagans, ma pouter de Diu por los que aclamati son" —e se lo purgase demas étrenuif fuss, allievile abhec cet vin: "Five spoonfuls are to be taken every morning and at five p.m. ℞ Peonyroot, Elecampane, Masterwort, Angelica, aa ʒj; Rue-leaves, Sage, Betony, Germander, White Horehound, Tops of lesser centaury, of each a handful; Juniper-berries, 3 vj; Peel of two oranges. Slice, and steep in six pints of Canary wine. Strain, and lay by for use." Lo pancho va se no solament quiete facer, ma tu poras to purificazion maintener, en la corrumpcion copiusament forpissans.

Car sais que l'heor proxima es. Diu va les mortos giustos en par-

Fig. 1 (a)

fectes cuorpos ricompor; ma li vifs deuren suos propruos cuerps parfar cor por els van les juzés; per aquest scribe S. Pollo, "Ne scabez-vos que vestro corp lo timplum des Sancti Sprit saiP" Da purgati; und durant tu deglutis, di "Huat hana huat ista pista sista domina damnaustra luxato."

Et se nosaltres dobram nos purifiguer, mi frare, besogne per natturalas mezias ser. Queli sales e solutiones quemics di quale parlas —i son sol magie de strujas vestuta como scientie. Ne suivir Dr. Theophrastus Bombastus Malatastus Heresiastus Catastrastus! Ma sechurament ç'a no perigolo de quel-la. Aquell uomb fo un so patidifus, e suon gran Mysterium es uno vaporetto (ich meine, ein kleiner Mistl). O sents tu com un peddo de insalato stañoP Pensis tu che la vecinanze d'un chaldo fuoc te in uno maron malolorodoriferante pozzanguère e una blu flama trasformerà? E fan les estrelles tu chabelli plu prest croiscents, y t'adormen le marees, y te reveigle un terretremblor in Paraguay amb un irisistible pet in HannoverP Quant a "tartar" e "Diathesis exsudativus"—a lui mas un esciancro curatP

O, es tut aus Trotula, aquela affar; lla es mare de tutos nostros mals, y la corrozio que nos spuerc. Sapiens matrona davveritude!—piu tost putens latrina, y Odoricus ava un odor muy ricco quand su nom ses labres paseron—bocapudre! Ellas son tute poipas de caca, e nos nascions embarbrouillats con esa. La sola passio de cête mulier fu ses chancres con fards de coubrir, y su nos de braguegar! No es en tele compagnia que nos deveniam limpidos—"car il tiene que aquest corroptible corp la incorruptibilida rivest."

Adeu, mio frallo, soy de buon cor, rencendre tu spe. Tant bien, escris su ta ganasch cis paraules, "✠ Rex, ✠ Pax, ✠ Nax in Christo filio," e si secur, subretot pendent el son, d'un convenebol color d'estre cingt. Mi amor e abec toi en cet exhortation, e je prec Deu nos de permetre nos vientost de rancontre. Aci il fa bel, et le vin de ceste anee sera bon—si nos beurons le temps où il vut sara. Ie me subviens tout le temps de cet apareill extravagant avec les ampoules qui ilumine votre lit, cet un obget que l'on parfois à la campagne sortir debrai pour qu'il verd comme une rosse devieng.

Fig. 1 (b)

who married into the Allants by the help of the selfsame
Del Vega[2], bore an amiable sturdy daughter, a little bro-
ken-headed, her part good partly violent nature had been
distempered (as many of their unquiet climbing spirits)
in Paracelsus's school of healing; but this was a future virtue.[3] Entering the medical service, she had met and labored with a Chavender youth, in a terrible pestilence, in
Genoa, where they were both infected. Afterward, the
familial ires spent, they married in England, and settled
near London, attaching themselves to the fortunes of Hector Chavender, from whom they obtained a worthy station.

Many are the examples of Chavenders, in subsequent
times, attaining by the exertions of their sagacity, the
heights of honor: the follicular "patch" that bears their
name, Baillie's tribute, and the authoritative collaborations
of Rolando, and Kussmaul of "fearful dyspnea" fame—do
they[4] not attest it? Other is the Allants' glory: from generation to generation they ministered dangerously to the
plague-ridden; the first German dispensary for poor children was their merciful act, in Hanover; a practical keen-
ness shewed them[5], that nitrate of silver cleansed the eyes
of babes, long ere any might reason it; and one, fated to
die cruelly, has had, at last, distinguished letters.[6]

Infinite are the distempers of the human spirit, man is a
prodigy of misery, lesser Allants and Chavenders have
there been than these, on occasion. One, a century past,
butchered his mother; one his wife; another publicly corn-
holed[7] his little daughter, and was hanged; others pursued
disgrace more meanly. Over such the families have not
fought; but then such are not needed to inflame them; for
many have been the ills of others, to serve as ills of their
own.[8]

Now let them aspire &c.

(*The document concludes with a long plea to reunite the
two families in the Baptist faith.*)

1. The writer, who apparently means by this word a consciousness of genealogy, supplies matter for new discord where he hopes to reconcile. In accordance with their progressive inclination, the Chavenders have always traced their ancestry through a line of medical innovators to an origin in Trotula, of the school of Salerno; while the Hanoverian Allants, Galenists until 1700 and still conservative, claim their succession from the less notorious Salernitan Alphanus I, doubtless the person who later became Archbishop of Salerno, but not to be confused with another Archbishop of Salerno of the same name. The distinction, insisted on by both families, is petty; for in their tradition of close attendance to the patient the Allants follow the Hippocratic instruction as faithfully as the Chavenders, who are so particular to defend its theoretical consequences.

2. The implication is that Doña Ana de Osorio, the first wife of Count Chinchon, was treated with cinchona by the Count's physician Juan del Vega. Doña Ana died before her husband became Viceroy of Peru, and it was the second countess, Doña Francisca Henriquez de Rivera, whose fever was cured by the controversial bark. This was not known until the twentieth century, after the document was written.

3. Although Catholics, the Chavenders had supported Paracelsus.

4. Hector Chavender (1619–1688) discovered the aggregation of lymph nodules known as "Chavender's patch" (1660). Matthew Baillie attributed to Evelyn Chavender (1730–1781) elements of his description of lesions. Ello Chavender (1775–1851) collaborated in Rolando's investigation of the spinal cord, and Jeremy Chavender (1819–1880) in Kussmaul's research on acetone.

5. The same pragmatic instinct made Walter Allant (1818–1901) drink a pint of typhus culture to prove that typhus had a non-bacterial origin. Koch said his failure to contract the disease retarded bacteriology by a generation.

6. The reference is to Hans Bakerloo Allant (1851–1886), whose discovery of the goundou bacteria was published in 1885. In Mexico the following year, he began searching for a bacterial explanation of yellow fever. He had the bad luck to find several cases harboring both yellow fever virus and the *Leptospira* of Weil's disease. He isolated the *Leptospira*, grew a culture from it,

developed a vaccine, and having (he thought) immunized himself, proceeded to West Africa, where a yellow fever epidemic was raging. He succumbed immediately.

7. A word of unknown origin, probably from the French *encanailler*. Professor B. M. Jemm's derivation (made in discussing a contemporary instance) from *The Cornhill Magazine* seems no more than wishful thinking.

8. The writer means that the two families feuded over medical issues. For example:

Forceps Royalties. In 1699 Chubb Chavender announced the obstetrical forceps. He did not, however, describe the instrument, which had been used for several generations by his branch of the family, midwives by profession. Attempts by outsiders to learn the secret of the painsaving apparatus, whose renown attracted many women, were unavailing. When a group of civic-minded Londoners collected a purse of £500 to be bestowed on Chavender, he accepted the money, but in return gave up only one blade of the forceps. In 1725 his son, learning of the invention of another forceps in Europe, disclosed the entire instrument against a further sum and an exclusive patent.

The Allants asserted that the forceps (together with Enula's daughter) had come into Chavender hands from them, and claimed a share of the money. There was subsequently much bad blood between the two houses on this account.

Purging. Shortly after, the Chavenders attacked the Allants for their views on purging. Accepting G. E. Stahl's theories, the Allants not only purged universally but never checked the "hemorrhoidal flux," which they thought was a healthy process. Evelyn Chavender's father wrote Wilhelm Allant that "without doubt he would presently claim the title once held by the Chief Physician of the ancient Egyptians, viz. 'Shepherd of the Rectum,' except that 'butcher' might fit the truth nicer."

Bleeding. In 1810 the families corresponded abusively over the quantity of leeches used by the Allants. The latter declared it never passed two hundred a day; the Chavenders counted by the thousands. It should be remembered that at least ten Allants were practicing at the time.

The Telephone

When Yana's treatment ended, my meetings with her became difficult and infrequent. We often resorted to letters
composed in the code we had invented, and it was in writing that Yana reported the effect of my counterfeit document, only a day after she had transmitted it:

spunouɯ ɯosoqun noh soom hund dood suooms X

I replied,

mous ou moys I oɯoy snoɯhuouhs sumo dood dos SI

Two days later she wrote,

uooɯ hq 6 mou mommod SOS

(SOS stood for urgency of any sort.)
Before the appointed hour that evening, armed with a
hatchet, I went to the clinic storeroom that was still our
meeting place. In a while Yana came, alone. The strands of
hair beneath her fur cap were silvered with rime.
Conversing by gesture and code (which we spelled with
our forefingers in each other's palm), I learned that a sum-

mons from the camp authorities had detained Yana's admirer, who had asked her to arrange another meeting.

Stupefied by disappointment, I said nothing. After a long silence the telephone rang. I lifted the receiver and heard a muffled voice ask, "Is this Luther one six six oh?"

"No, Melancthon one eight eight six." (It was really a Loyola number; these were passwords.)

In a more natural tone The Concierge continued, "The sugars are selling the shop to Moscow. Five of them out tonight: La Rouille, Prizon, Donders, Valsalva, Roak."

I managed to tell Yana the news. She was surprised and happy—she would now be wholly mine.

In the following weeks the guards became laxer in their supervision and we were able to meet more easily. I afterward found out that Yana and I had been peculiarly favored. We were on the point of being disciplined when the intelligence service intervened and requested the camp authorities to tolerate our relationship. The reason was their interest in our code. They had intercepted our letters but could not decipher them, although they hoped to do so with more material. Their leniency worked against them: the guards extended it to our rendezvous, our correspondence dwindled, and the code remained unbroken. It would have vexed the local cryptologists to learn there was no true cipher, only simple inversion.

Three and a half years before in the Breton town of Roscoff, the chef of La Sole Retrouvée, distractedly mistaking a bottle of maple syrup for Calvados, used it in a sauce for broiled lobster. The dish thus invented became popular in Paris the following winter, and it started a vogue for the syrup that in less than a year spread throughout Western Europe.

A report of this reached Jacksongrad in a radio broadcast denouncing the fashion as an example of Western degeneracy. It occurred to an observant inmate of the camp that a nearby maple forest might provide syrup for the new market. The trees having been tested and shown to yield a rich sap, a group of Fideists set up an organization for tapping and refining the virgin store. The camp authorities, eager to find occupations for their wards, approved the initiative and supplied labor for it. They also turned a blind eye on the disposal of the produce, except for a quantity of sugar requisitioned for camp use.

Because of the remoteness of Jacksongrad and the criminal status of the entrepreneurs, marketing the Siberian syrup was a formidable task; nevertheless the Fideists, efficient, imaginative and unscrupulous, soon showed a profit.

Their chief problem was getting the syrup to Europe at a feasible cost. Careful planning with collaborators outside the camp led to the following solution.

Initially, the merchandise moved by rail: south from Jacksongrad on the Chkalov-Tashkent line to its junction at Ursat'yevskaya with the Andizhan-Krasnovodsk line, on which it traveled westward as far as Tedzhen. The organization paid the railroad the preferential rate accorded camp manufactures.

From Tedzhen camels carried the syrup to Meshed in Iran, via the valleys of the Hari Rud and Kashaf Rud. This route had been an empty return for caravans, and the drivers did the work cheaply.

At Meshed, terminus of the railroad south, the syrup was loaded into three ancient oil cars leased from the Iranian government. The price was low, and the organization made agreement to a long-term contract contingent on a rebate in freight charges. Thus, at minimal cost, the merchandise reached Bandar Abbas on the Persian Gulf.

From there to Marseilles, transport was provided by Ulek, Manis & Petis, a Macao firm with a branch in Hong Kong.

The effectiveness in the treatment of baldness and impotence of the old Chinese "jissom cocktail" called *hui tê* had recently won it a following in Mediterranean Europe. As it was known to contain arsenic and glass splinters, its legal entry was everywhere forbidden, but enthusiasts still bought it on the black market for as much as two hundred dollars a pound.

Ulek, Manis & Petis were the principal dealers in this concoction. Since it was plentiful in Hong Kong, where it entered from the mainland, they had no problem of supply. However, they had long been dissatisfied with their European outlets—UMP used established smuggling agencies, which are notoriously conservative and would handle only a small fraction of what the market demanded. They had decided to distribute *hui tê* themselves when, through intermediaries in Peking and Semipalatinsk, the Jacksongrad organization approached them with a request to import maple syrup.

Recognizing an excellent cover for their *hui tê* trade, the Macao firm accepted the job at once. The importers would ship and market the syrup, underwrite all initial costs and provide many secondary services. In return they asked only a small commission to be collected as a percentage of sales.

With the consent of the Fideist group, Ulek, Manis & Petis set to work.

First, they contracted in Hong Kong for the manufacture of syrup containers—cylindrical tin cans attractively papered with red, white and blue labels. Some of the cans were constructed to hold a secret quantity of *hui tê*. A diaphragm of soft alloy, parallel to the end of every such can, divided it into two compartments: a large upper one, to be filled with syrup blended with a potent *hui tê* solvent; and a small lower one in which *hui tê* concentrate was tightly packed. When opened, the top of the can disclosed what seemed to be ordinary syrup. Opening the bottom, which was reinforced with steel, demanded a pressure great enough to force the compact *hui tê* against the alloy diaphragm and break it, thus mixing the extract with its solvent and instantly forming a liquid undistinguishable from the syrup by sight or taste.

Outwardly all the cans were alike. Those without *hui tê* were made heavier to avoid a discrepancy in weight.

A UMP ship brought the cans to Bandar Abbas, where they were filled; and thence to Marseilles. The entire cargo entered France as syrup, Ulek, Manis & Petis paying the duty on it. A transport concern owned by the company then took charge of the shipment, which was sorted in the privacy of its trucks and barges. The syrup mixed with solvent was thrown away, and the *hui tê* repackaged for delivery to specialized middlemen. The pure syrup was entrusted to normal marketing channels.

Success attended the international ruse in all its stages, and the two enterprises flourished. The availability of *hui tê* maintained its popularity and won it new adepts. Because of its quality and cheapness, "Mabel's" became the household word for syrup from Ulster to Anatolia.

At the end of a year the Jacksongrad group paid its debts to Ulek, Manis & Petis, thereafter investing its profits in that company. After the second year, the prisoners' interests were nationalized. The government's aim in this was not so much to recuperate private wealth as to control the disruption of the American syrup trade. In exchange for ownership, the prisoners were given their freedom and appointed to run the business as Soviet officials.

These Fideist prisoners, the "Sugars," were the five whose release The Concierge announced to me over the telephone.

Dhaversac

If this event crippled my hopes, it only strengthened my will, and I decided that in the new circumstances I must try to escape.

On the long train ride to Jacksongrad I had become friends with a fellow Baptist called Robin Marr. The friendship had already proved useful. Robin was a first cousin of Yana's, and very intimate with her despite their sectarian differences; so that when I met Yana my interest in her seemed a natural one. A greater although heretofore neglected advantage was that eighteen months after my arrival Robin had begun preparing for escape. I had then refused to join in the attempt. I asked to participate now, and Robin, after consulting the two other partners, accepted me.

The partners were Laurence Hapi and Beverley Zuckerkandl.

A radical organ designer who had been, before imprisonment, preoccupied with difficulties of pitch control in new instruments, Zuckerkandl had experimented at the camp with an unusual mineral, a kind of apatite named after the geologist Wolff. The mineral had proved capable of solving the problems of tuning, and Beverley was impatient to return to Soda Springs, Idaho, and test the discovery.

Hapi, a painter of French extraction, had a quite different motive for escaping, which was once more to eat ice cream in Venice. Laurence said to me, "The war will blister our skins and corrupt our bones, I shall sit at Florian's still, on bare heels, with a crate for a table, *gianduja* pressed from the brick-dust of flattened palaces, sipping canal-water coffee, while skeletal bands wring their fiddles, gazing on the wingless dusk," and wept.

Robin Marr planned the escape and was our unquestioned leader.

At my first conference with these three, I learned that recent information had resolved the issue most keenly debated by them: what route the escape should follow.

Two months before, Moscow had ordered a double census to be taken in the more primitive regions of southern Siberia.

Of the two purposes of the census, one was sanitary: reports of endemic plague demanded a survey of the rat population. The other was economic: a project was under study to develop the area, among the poorest in the Soviet Union, and the responsible planners wanted to find out what kinds of livestock were best adapted to it. They hoped subsequently to improve the more promising breeds with technical help and public funds.

The census takers, crisscrossing the territory along a northwest-southeast line, were to count sheep, goats and grunting oxen on the outward leg of their journey, rats on their return.

Unfortunately the uninformed populations misunderstood the survey. They thought that rather than a measure undertaken for their well-being, it was a prelude to the taxation or confiscation of their herds; and at the approach

of the census takers they drove their animals into the hills
and hid them. It was only when the first count was virtually completed that its purpose became known. The Siberian peasantry, learning of the subsidies awaiting them
if the number of their livestock was sufficiently high (but
whose loss was now a certainty) were preparing to peti-
tion for a new census when they heard that the investigators were doubling back through the country. They did
not know that it was for a different reason.

Since their job was to search out infection, the census
takers hoped to have the least possible contact with the
local populations. Instead, the peasants dogged their steps.
This might have been only an inconvenience if the natives
had not crowded every available farm animal into their
path, and if a small fraction of the rats they were counting
had not been carriers of disease. The disease was not
plague, but the animal cholera known vulgarly as "bats'
boils," fatal to goats and sheep and highly infectious. It
followed the census takers along their thousand-mile journey at an interval of six days, in an epidemic that destroyed over eighteen thousand head of livestock before
their work was forcibly stopped; that is, until a committee
of angry peasants pursued, ambushed and murdered them.

Only one member of the party survived, the geographer
Dhaversac. He fled the assailants on foot for eight days,
and at last took refuge in our camp. Assigned to the Defective Baptist mess, he related his adventures to several
prisoners there.

One of the prisoners was Beverley Zuckerkandl, who repeated Dhaversac's account to my other partners. By trac-
ing the geographer's flight they learned that the army and
police supervised the country around the camp at best haphazardly and in some places not at all. Perhaps because no
escape in that direction seemed possible, the district im-

mediately north of us was quite unguarded. This fact had almost cost Dhaversac his life; it might well save ours, and it decided the path of our escape. We would start north, then trek southeastward through a succession of mountain ranges, and finally turn east into a spur of Afghanistan. If Dhaversac's information was true, our route would be free of human obstacles.

During his few days among us, Dhaversac impressed us as intelligent and humane. He was despondent over the fate of his expedition. "We proved again, and how painfully! that mistakes in scientific procedure have inevitable social effects. A census that alters the size of the population it studies is a deadly absurdity."

"Hapi"

The rare green of a few low, precocious plants signaled the winter's end. We had planned our escape for early spring. The weather would be the mildest of the year, and our sect's fiesta, falling then, would be a fitting occasion for our attempt.

The climax of the annual Defective Baptist fiesta was a "home-made animal" race. Like the other festivities, it was held in the sports area that lay on the northeast boundary of the camp.

The race was open to the entire sect. To qualify, a contestant had to enter a racing car made according to two rules: only labor and materials available within the Baptist compound could be used, and the car had to have the shape of an animal. The contestant was free to decide what sort of motor power to install; since fuels were scarce, it was usually human muscle.

Two prizes were given at the end of the race, one for speed, one for the best design among the cars finishing. As the race was four versts long, winning even the second prize demanded mechanical skill. The prizes were generally lavish. The year before both had included twenty shares of Ulek, Manis & Petis stock.

Robin Marr saw a great opportunity for us in the coming race. We were to head north: not only was the sports area on the northern side of the camp, but no barrier separated it from the country beyond, since the grounds were kept clear for use as a landing field. As competitors, we would have access to the area equipped for our undertaking; and we could openly prepare as an entry a vehicle in which to make our escape. The chief drawback was a rule forbidding riders—it meant that during the race three passengers must be kept hidden; in other words, a provisional one-seater would have to provide camouflage for them as well as for the vehicle the four of us would later use.

The advantages plainly outweighed the difficulties. We entered the race and began constructing a suitable car.

It was designed on an extravagant scale. The visible machinery was huge—twin pulleys at the front, operated by weighty hand cranks and attached by a web of broad belts to the "rear axle." The hidden machine was an assemblage of bicycles that Beverley had stolen over the years from the Athletic Department. We originally intended to be mounted in tandem, hoping to gain speed by the low resistance of our single file. An event that preceded the fiesta by a few weeks modified our plans.

Defective Baptists, as their name suggests, perform baptism as an indirect and partial aspersion of adult members. The sect believes that man's condition is absolute imperfection. All men require baptism, none deserves it, and even those who have been baptized win only a fleeting purity, since not even divine grace can long redeem mortal corruption. Baptism must be renewed at least once a

year, and each believer must earn his right to the sacra-
ment. The sect exacts heroic feats of its adherents. In
1949 six thousand Baptists gathered near the Meije, in the
French Alps, and were directed toward the summit of that
forbidding mountain, where a helicopter had lowered a
teapot of holy water. In Jacksongrad such grandiose ceremonies are impossible, and the Defective Baptist elders must
improvise tests of faith. The camp authorities, well aware of
the problem, let the sect use the sports area to give it a
modicum of space for its ordeals.

Twenty days before the fiesta my three partners and I,
together with the rest of our division (about three thousand), assembled in the area for the baptismal competition.

The Defective Baptist elders—the elders, whose average
age was twenty-two, were those who had obtained baptism the previous year—decreed the following ritual.

The aspirants would line up along the sides of the
sports area, while the seventy-one elders gathered in the
center. Each elder would carry in one hand a cup of holy
water and with the other lead a leashed black duck. At a
predetermined moment the elders would douse the ducks,
loose them and drive them toward the aspirants, who then
had to catch the birds before they shook the water from
their oily feathers.

The mass baptism took place on a crisp afternoon in
early March. It testified both to the fervor of our sect
and to the madness such fervor breeds. The pandemonium
of pursuer and pursued was grim to hear and see, and those
engaged risked tangible injury. To avoid suspicion, Beverley and Robin joined in the scrimmage: they were kicked
and mauled.

To the high passion for salvation, moreover, was joined
a sordid vengefulness; for one of the guards, intervening

in the rite, became the object of the crowd's ecstatic hate. Whether from the will-dissolving confusion that the spectacle provoked in him, or from the momentary rousing of an unsuspected instinct, or the resurgence of a repressed one, the guard, finding one of the sanctified birds at his feet, seized it by the neck with one hand, with the other ripped open his trouserfly, and began (adding his private folly to the hysteria around him) copulating with the glossy bird that now trumpeted in an agony of terror and perhaps pain.

In a moment the guard realized the sacrilege he had committed—a number of Baptists, black with outrage, were already charging at him. He had been standing near the edge of the sports area, and a dozen strides brought him onto the plain beyond. He began loping across it toward the mountains, with a speed all the more remarkable for the writhing bird still impaled on his sex. The baptized and unbaptized ran after him. The other guards lost five minutes restraining the mob, so that by the time they were free to pursue the renegade he had definitely outstripped them. Two tanks were dispatched, but the fugitive had gained the first gorges, about a mile away: at the foot of the mountains the tanks turned back. We were then marched off to our compound. Except for the apologies of a superior warden, we heard no more of the event.

We learned two pertinent facts from the scandal of that afternoon. The first was that other than army tanks, the authorities had no motorized means of pursuit. The second was that the tanks could not enter the mountain defiles where we hoped to follow the runaway guard. Our plans were changed accordingly. Maneuverability, not speed, was what we needed most. Since the slow-starting tanks could not catch even an unequipped fugitive, four of us pedaling our machine would easily elude them. If, reaching the mountains, we could then drive our velocipede a mile or two farther, we would distance our pursuers decisively.

The tandem we had first imagined was too long for the sharp turns of the defiles, and we therefore replaced it with a new design rapidly conceived and executed by Beverley. To my regret, I cannot describe that ingenious machine. I was sworn to secrecy at the time, and I have yet to be relieved of my oath. I shall only mention one detail that has come to light elsewhere. The "Wolff's apatite" that Beverley had studied turned out to be a "stone" of great elasticity. Thanks to it, the suspension of our car had a resilience adequate to the rough terrain through which we were to drive.

While Beverley, aided by Robin, built the mechanism of the car, Laurence and I made the body. Our job was important. As it had to provide space for three riders as well as the secret vehicle, our "single-seater" looked hopelessly large. We therefore announced that we hoped to win, not the race, but the prize for design. It was necessary to justify the claim.

Our contraption had the form of an oblong box. Its volume was irreducible, and any improvement of its contours would have increased its size, so we resorted to pictorial decoration. The hidden machine provided one sculptural touch and decided what animal should (as the rules demanded) give our entry its "shape." Near the front of the box, bicycle handlebars protruded. The suggestion of horns was unmistakable, and disguising the handlebars as such, we made our car a bull. I named it *Hapi,* in honor of Laurence, whose wrinkled doglike face beamed at the honor.

We decorated the four sides accordingly.

On the front we painted a stylized bull's face in massive stripes of black. Underneath it I wrote:

H *my name is*   API
  And my wife's name is   ATHOR
  We come from   ELIOPOLIS
  And we bring back   EAVEN!

On the right side, we spelled out a textual maze in brilliant and varied colors. (See Figure 2.)

On the back, we drew a black diamond-shaped figure—the "grid" that, superimposed on the verbal maze, reveals its solution (Figure 3).

On the left side, we printed, in yellow and white letters on a black ground, the true text of the maze:

Enter the labyrinth. After twenty steps, you must decide whether to turn left or right. In either case, follow the outside wall—the right-hand wall if you have turned right, the left-hand wall if you have turned left: that is the rule for mazes, being Ariadne's thread without the spinning. You walk, in either case, on a black tile floor, down a crooked corridor, along a twelve-foot-high wall of smooth yellowish stone; but if you have turned left, each section of wall, between the first and fifth corners, is pierced with circular windows two feet across, through which you may regard, should you so wish, four landscapes outside the labyrinth—perhaps alders against the sun; campers gathered in front of their tents in strict meditation; three bundles of cut branches piled together; or a thrush singing, although you cannot hear him through the leaded window, on a marsh plant. If you have turned right, as if in compensation various pictures, words and emblems are soon figured on the corners of the blind wall you follow—more precisely, on the section of curving wall that forms the corner's longest side, and one at every corner until the eighteenth. At the fourth corner you may see a bark tossing on stormy blue water; at the next, a pugnacious bust of Julius Caesar; next, the card symbol *spade* repeated three times; then the Greek army marching in convex patterns before Troy besieged; the letter *delta;* four spade symbols; a map of the southeastern states of America, in white paint; the word "Amen," incomplete, drawn in capital letters across a setting sun; four more spades; a drop of some black liquid, painted much larger than the spades but resembling them; and last (but singly, one to a corner) four spades. Under all these images runs a continuous sequence of words printed in two superposed bands of which each is the reverse of the other. The eighteenth corner, like the seventeenth, is blank. The wall into which it leads has a small circular window through which you can see a mimic thrush, and similar windows in each of the next three walls reveal views of firewood, campers and four silhouetted alders; while if you have, on entering, turned left, you will encounter at the second corner after the fourth window (the fifth in all), above a repeated punning sequence, a spade, followed at each successive corner until the twentieth by a spade, a spade, another spade, an enlarged drop, four spades, an AMEN, a map, four more spades, *delta*, the Greek army before Troy, three spades, Caesar, and a bark. Then, no matter which turning you took, and it did not matter which one you took, you will have reached the entrance, for the labyrinth leads nowhere but out of itself.

with a
thread out the mimic
Ariadne's spinning thrush
being delta perceive you singing
mazes which on
3 bundles rule for through a
of cut the letter then dow circu-marsh
branches is of small plant
piled left: that the America 4 spade has a
together: turned in eastern it leads
firewood have white the south symbols which
if you paint map of into
left wall then a wall Entrance out of
wall—the the word a spade 4 more but the Enter
outside an AMEN each is a spades blank labyrinth
follow the incomplete of which al of the is after
stone in bands and other 18th cor 20 paces
yellowish capital superposed emblems runs a the you
smooth letters in two are words punning sequence must
some printed soon pictures like the decide
of drawn images fig if right 17th whether to
wall across all these right turn

the under on the or

Greek a setting blind bark left
foot army sun a spade wall a tossing if left
twelve before you follow see on stormy each
along a Troy spades at the may blue water section
besieged four 4th at the of wall
ridor Troy corner larger then a between the
crooked before a than much pugnac first
campers down a patterns then to the painted bust corner
gathered tile floor convex in one spades liquid of Julius is pierced
in front black army marching singly next black Caesar with
of their on a army some at last the
tents in you walk Greek another drop of the the circular
strict perhaps the more de-enlarged card windows four alders
meditation perhaps an symbol two silhouetted
—spades of a spade feet against
yrinth repeated across the
the lab three 3 through sun
outside times which you
spades may regard
landscapes should you
so
4 wish

Fig. 2

NOTE. The publisher regrets that Fig. 2 has been incorrectly set. The
shape of the text should conform to that of Fig. 3.

Fig. 3

The Fiesta

The race took place on the afternoon of the first Sunday
in spring. All through the previous week Defective Baptists were seen gazing southward, as if expecting a portent.
On Friday morning they were given satisfaction. About
twenty miles south of the camp eight hills dented the horizon: they now seemed to emit a puce-colored cloud
which, low-lying and dense, slightly blurred their contour.

The cloud suggested earthquake or war, but was due to
a struggle for survival in the arachnid world.

Wolf spiders (I believe the variety has never been classi-
fied) infest the southern hills. They resemble the *Lycosa
opifex* of the steppes, living in subterranean nests with trap-
door entrances. The winter leaves these nests in a precarious
state. Frost and drought have turned the earth to dust, and
until the late spring rains restore its adhesiveness it gives
the spiders scant protection. Moreover the end of winter
exposes the spiders to their worst enemy, a small migrant
chough that flies north in great numbers at the equinox.
The chough prizes the Jacksongrad spiders and will dig
them skillfully out of their crumbling lairs.

Against this danger the wolf spiders have created a communal defense.

In the last days of winter the spider population starts spinning thousands upon thousands of little silk bags, which look like gas-lamp mantles, but are of a tighter mesh. Each bag is packed with bits of friable earth and then sealed.

An open forest of ash trees covers the spiders' territory. The filled bags are carried by the insects into the trees and hung along their boughs, until every branch and twig more than five yards from the ground is clustered with them—"the image," Laurence told me, "of a marshmallow bonanza."

The choughs fly north on the first south wind of spring. At its rising the wind blows high, leaving an uneasy stillness at ground level that persists for a day or two. It is during this time that the choughs appear. When the high wind starts, the spiders, waiting on the branches of the ash trees, cut the strands that attach the laden bags. Falling to the ground, the bags disintegrate in puffs of dust. Within minutes innumerable tiny explosions gather into an unfathomable cloud. The spiders return to their nests, hidden from the choughs' keen sight. The dust screen does not usually settle until the birds have flown past.

Each year the Defective Baptists watched anxiously for the spiders' cloud; for the south wind which it heralded was considered propitious for their rites, and one ceremony materially depended on it.

On Friday afternoon centuries of choughs chattered over our camp; on the ground the air remained still. Saturday brought the first flurries of warmth. By Sunday the south wind blew through Jacksongrad unabated.

The morning of the holiday was spent by the sect in private prayer and thanksgiving. Toward noon, among the other race contestants, we trundled our car to the sports area.

After a light meal (the heavy eating was reserved for supper), the Defective Baptists walked in a loose body through the camp, showered in every compound with brickbats and jeers. At the sports area they deployed for the ritual concert that would open the public festivities.

Of all the traditions of the Jacksongrad Baptists, the concert was the most esteemed and the most painstakingly observed.

It had begun more than a hundred years earlier, at the original location of the camp. Since then, each year had added to its grandeur and its fame. Inspired by returning prisoners, Baptist communities emulated it the world over, but never with much success, for the spectacular performances of the camp were beyond imitation. The annual event in the end remained a local glory.

Six generations of prisoners had inherited, enriched and bequeathed the collection of instruments with which the concert was performed; it now numbered a thousand and ninety-eight. The variety of the instruments was extraordinary, but more remarkable was their common attribute —they were all made from the human body. A single fact will prove the enthusiasm of our sect for the concert. The only parts of a Defective Baptist that were ever buried were the musculature and a few soft organs. The rest were used to build new instruments or repair old ones, a custom that partially explains why the Darbyists and Resurrectionists so despised us.

The instruments had other peculiarities. They produced single tones. To be played, they were set in a strong current of air, which would of itself excite their strings or air columns. Hence the concern of the Baptists with the south wind: without it, the concert could not take place.

As individual musicians could at best perform isolated notes, an exact communal discipline was needed to combine them into music. This pleased our ethical wardens.

At the time of the first concert, a learned prisoner had tuned the instruments in the Aeolian mode, and the key was piously observed.

The wind that afternoon blew with comforting force. Since the music to be performed was antiphonal, the Baptists were ranged in two equal sections facing each other. The sections were equipped with identical groups of instruments. Roughly half of these were "strings" and half pipes. The former resembled monochordal lyres of many sizes (some of the smaller ones had several strings of identical length). Their frames were made of flat or thin bones —shoulder blades, hipbones and sacra, single or joined; strands of nerve, skin, gut or wound hair were stretched between their extremities. The pipes were hollowed round bones of every size, from pierced teeth to femurs sawn and mounted in sixteen-foot columns. The largest instruments of each type needed squads of prisoners to handle them.

A smaller division of instruments was percussive. It included arm bones against which the wind blew light phalanges (stuffed so that they would not themselves resound); tarsal rattles; bladders inflated and dried, in which one or more teeth had been confined, whose clattering produced sounds of definite pitch when the wind swung the sacs; and skulls, with wings of skin on metacarpal frames to catch the wind, containing shriveled eyes, similarly swung.

Smallest of all was the group of sympathetic instruments, intermittently used for color: skulls and hardened bags of membrane, from which nearby music would elicit a faint hum or whine, as well as chord-producing assemblages—

the only exceptions to the monotonic rule—of mixed bones and fibers, both natural (a child's rib cage) and artificial ("Salome").

When performers and instruments were symmetrically aligned, those of us exempted from the concert—elders and race contestants—gathered in the space between them into a large square. The center of the square was a knoll about three feet high, made for the occasion out of roughly piled damp clay. An old prisoner, who had performed the office for twenty-seven years, mounted this uneasy podium to conduct the concert, at once raising a hand (in which a short charred object served as baton) to demand the attention of the multitudes on either side. They fell silent, and for a while we heard only the steady sighing of the wind. Then, at the fall of their leader's hand, the bank of musicians that faced the spring sun sounded the opening A-minor chord of Racquet's *Pia Mater*.

I shall not forget that music. Anxiety for what the afternoon would bring may have magnified my feelings, but there was a beauty in the spectacle beyond its effect. With a deliberateness imposed by physical circumstance, grave phrases of lapidary simplicity were exchanged by the twin assemblies. Where on one side a choir of white flutes was thrust up into eerie shrillness, on the other, stretched ranks of glistening multicolored tissue and hair answered with a melancholy twang. I have heard no organ, orchestra or electronic device, nor any aboriginal combination of gourd and drum that produced so rich and unfamiliar a sound; and the timbre of the instruments, and the massive mechanical gestures with which they were played, were peculiarly fitting to the music, whose measured diatonic chords and tune were unadorned to the point of bareness, but filled with the archaic fervor of Huguenot piety.

As I listened and watched, unexpected grief over-

whelmed me. In sudden terror I apprehended my separation from those around me, and from the abandoned hopes
of my childhood—I had perhaps revered them too much,
and now they disgusted me. To steady myself, I squeezed
the silver medal I always carried in my right pocket (it
was so worn from touching that the inscription *Violon,*
1er Prix had become illegible); nevertheless I wept. One
of my neighbors, also weeping, then caught me by the arm
and exclaimed, "It is like Beethoven's *Erotica!*" My sobs
kept me from dealing violently with the intruder. Afterward I was thankful that my self-indulgence had been cut
short.

The race followed the concert. That morning we had
lined up the cars at their starting positions in a corner of
the sports area, on whose perimeter the course lay. Drivers
and their teams now gave their entries a last inspection.
The entire Defective Baptist throng followed us to examine the cars, which numbered forty-four in all. *Hapi*
attracted a large group that speculated on our designs and
inscriptions, especially the maze on the tail.

"I couldn't get to first base."

"*C'est comme quoi—une grille de mots croisés?*"

"For a funfair, it isn't much fun."

Screened by these onlookers, my three partners pretended to tinker with the car. One by one they slid beneath it and climbed to their hiding places—narrow platforms equipped with foot braces and grips, on which they
would sit until we cast *Hapi*'s shell. I had been picked to
drive because, as the largest, I would have been most difficult to fit inside.

The crowd withdrew to the center of the grounds.
When spectators and contestants were in place, my clear
view of the track discovered only two guards.

With a wave of the arm and a cry of "Milton!" the

erstwhile concert leader started the race. I could see but
not hear the word, which the south wind, rising still, carried downfield.

I lunged against *Hapi*'s two hand-cranks. My hidden
companions, whose position allowed each to push one of
the three cumbrous wooden wheels that bore our visible
car, helped at first, then properly reserved their strength.

The racecourse was a rectangle less than a mile long and
half as wide. Starting north at the southeast corner of the
track, contestants had to drive once around it, finishing
where they began (a fact alluded to in our maze). We
had only to complete one leg of the race and, at the first
corner, continue straight over the plain.

I had thus to propel *Hapi* for about sixteen hundred
yards. The machine worked with a lumbering inefficiency
that would have left us conspicuously far behind had not
the greatest drawback of the car, its bulk, turned to our
advantage: it offered so broad a surface to the following
wind that our speed was doubled and we were able to
keep up with a few less agile competitors.

This led to a singular stroke of luck.

Eight minutes' labor had winded me by the time we
reached the northeast corner. Before the turn I had drawn
even with another entry, which was now straining ahead
on my left: *Ergo*, a squat but majestically antlered stag.
Ergo was the only machine in the race with an internal
combustion engine. As fuel it burned the rubbish used to
light the heaters in sentry boxes—half-consumed bits of
oil-soaked rag, hoarded during two winters. So far it had
performed erratically, its abrupt sprints declining noisily
into spells of immobility. Now, as it passed us, *Ergo* disappeared in the whish of a mild explosion that filled the
air with a cloud of greasy blacklets.

The cloud not only engulfed our car and hid us, it gave

us an excuse to lose our way. Cranking with new vigor, I
directed *Hapi* toward the open plain. When I reached clear
air, I looked back. *Ergo* was a dim heap in the middle of
the track. One of the guards was running toward it, gesticulating. I saw to my surprise that (evidently in fear of
another explosion) he was waving us onto the plain.

The moment had come to bring forth our velocipede.
I shouted to my partners to wait and help me increase our
speed—

"They're still in the dark!"

We struggled on for a minute, gaining a hundred yards
for all our clumsiness.

Then, leaping from my seat, I struck four rapid blows
on *Hapi*'s flank. At the signal, my companions drew the
bolts that held the frame together, and we quickly dis-
engaged the skeletal machine within. In half a minute we
were on our saddles, pedaling hard (I, after my exertions,
somewhat inadequately). The mountains rose before us in
a splendor of afternoon sun, matching our hope.

Another minute passed before the first tank started in
pursuit. Behind us the dusty ground swarmed with white
snakes startled by our passage. We were eight hundred
yards ahead of the tanks when we reached the mountains.

We entered a narrow gorge and followed it at top speed
for half a mile. Laurence then collapsed with abdominal
cramp. We stopped to rest; in a few minutes the pain subsided. Resuming our advance at a moderate rate, which
the twisting ascent of the path further slowed, we covered
another six miles in the next hour, at which point our
vehicle succumbed to the terrain, breaking an axle. We
unloaded our packs and set off on foot. There was no
need to hide the wrecked machine. The sheer-sided gorge
left no doubt as to our direction.

Soon afterward the full moon appeared to the north, in

the strip of sky above us. Daylight was waning, and the moon shone overhead with deepening golden warmth until a turning in the gorge obscured it. I can remember nothing of the landscape but the alternating earth and rock under my feet as the path steepened.

For three hours we hiked with only momentary rests, taking turns in the lead to keep a steady pace. Just at sunset, we reached the top of a cliff that overlooked the Jacksongrad plain. A tiny column of soldiers could be seen marching toward us—our last glimpse of Russian authority.

Around eight-thirty we stopped on a small plateau below a pass to eat and rest. The moon, now fiercely bright in the dark sky, cast a stern gray glow on the fields around us. We considered sleeping there, but Robin, uneasy, moved us on.

Crossing the pass, we descended a steep gulley, and at ten o'clock, staggering and numbed, settled in a grove of silver firs. The air was bearably cold, but for some time I shivered with exhaustion and relief. We drank at a nearby spring, set out our bedding on the soft ground, and soon fell asleep.

As I lay wrapped in the folds of my blanket, I saw the moon return among the crags to the west, and heard Beverley salute it drowsily: "Sister, good night!"

Part Two

Zuck

I have forgotten much of our journey. Particular days and hours have accumulated into generalities of exertion and rest from which they can no longer be recovered. Fortunately Robin Marr kept a log, and I have used it to fill out my account.

The first day was fair. We changed our northerly course in mid-morning and turned southeast, following the hills beyond the first mountains. On our left, to the northeast, lay a valley about five miles broad, divided by a winding river at which the undulating prairie below us ended in precipitous masses of rose-colored clay. Across the valley was another range, where, Robin noted, a *white streak of limestone is discernible. Over this a bright green ribbon, a brown stripe above; then peaks (snow).*

Later: *a small oblong-shaped range.*

In the afternoon we descended to a much lower altitude to cross a tributary of the river, filled with spring thaw. We found a bridge, two juniper trunks laid over the stream, with smaller logs athwart them. There was a confused distribution of shrubs here, already budding. Robin mentions *Inula helenium.*

Climbing higher (height gave at least an illusion of safety), we overlooked, in a widening of the valley, a vast network of *aryks* or irrigation canals. They spread out like a spider web from the quiet, smoky village at their center.

We ate frugally but pleasantly that night, around a small fire kindled in a hollow of the mountain forest.

Zuck: organ.

I was only half-awake during Beverley's description of the planned instrument, but I shall try to expand Robin's notes.

Blackblende. This highly elastic material was to be the main component of the organ pipes. Thanks to blackblende, the mouths and bodies of each pipe could instantaneously expand or contract to any size. The substance can easily be regulated by electrochemical means: through a system of electrical impulses, Beverley could make one pipe rapidly perform a succession of distinct notes—in other words, if only one part were played on it, a single pipe could replace an organ rank. (*For coupling, counterpoint &c. 4 per rank.*)

Blackblende is as volatile as it is elastic, and before coming to Jacksongrad Beverley had not found a way of controlling it. Mixed with blackblende, apatite would check its volatility without impairing its usefulness. *Indifferent to weather (organ bane ever).*

Swell as pipes: the swell box, made of the same mixture, would have great "expressive" power.

Fletcher's trolley without Reynolds' number! I cannot explain this.

Skimpy porcupine at distance—because the pipes, few in number, were to project from a sphere containing the performer. *Near, lively multiple bubblegum. Gripping obscenity of science fiction. Zuck perhaps kidding. Or*

*manic upswing? Krampoez mad? So early—too. All organ
fiends fiends.*

Delivered with hypnotic enthusiasm, Beverley's account
convinced me I was sunk in a despondent baroque hallucination. The fire seemed more exotic than the imagined
instrument.

Burning mountain. Ignition of carboniferous layer. Although this note ends Robin's entry for the day, I am
sure we saw no such thing. The night was clear, with a
plenitude of stars.

Spires and Squares

During a pause in our march, we took turns observing, through Beverley's binoculars, a village lying on the valley floor below us. A wall of gray mud enclosed a few dozen dispersed houses. Small gardens, each with several trees, adjoined them. Outside the wall, meadows of alfalfa stretched to the foothills through scattered willow copses. The trees grew thicker near the river, whose swift concentrated waters blazed in the sun.

To the south, the range we had followed bore eastward, rising to considerable heights. Its peaks were sharp-pointed, or had the form of crenelated towers, with snow-covered platforms at their tops. Clouds perpetually gathered and disintegrated about the summits. There was also snow on the *counterforts*, and later in the day we saw that in the upper parts of the valley its whiteness covered much of the spurs separating the transverse gorges. Before reaching that colder region, we turned southwest through a pass *perhaps thirty-five hundred feet* high. Soon after, we came on an alpine lake, five miles long, more than half of it covered by dun fur-tipped reeds; it contained an abundance of leeches.

The southern slope of the range was warmer and greener. Mountain grasses grew thick upon it, and the junipers yielded at a higher altitude to birch and ash, through which flourished an undergrowth of black-currant bushes and mountain *enula*. We advanced along a series of easy ridges. Another valley appeared on our right. *Hills of drift—clay and boulders.*

We pitched camp. Laurence vanished and returned presently with a large bird. No one asked how it had been killed, but I guessed that it was found dead. We roasted the bird and ate it. After two days of dried rations, the taste of fresh food exhilarated.

That evening Robin Marr recounted an autobiographical episode.

"I spent most of my last year at college preparing my bachelor's thesis. Research often took me to the university library, and I soon began spending most of my time there, not unhappily for one as addicted to books as I am. One day, while browsing in the stacks, I spotted Frost's *Lives of Eminent Christians*. It was a book I had never seen, and being something of a Butlerian, I took it down at once. The copy was new, not even cut; but into it someone had slipped a sheet of fine paper, on which a few words had been written in careful, old-fashioned script.

"Although the words were simple, their arrangement was baffling. At the top of the page three letters set one above another formed the Latin

r

e

s

Beneath them, there were three deliberately incomplete sentences:

The Mother cannot —— her Son.
The Son —— his Father.
The Mother —— their Spirit.

The initial letters of *mother, son, father* and *spirit,*
originally written small, had been obliterated with heavy
capitals. Near the bottom of the page, well separated
from the sentences, was a phrase of German, penciled
lightly by the same hand:

Zwei Herzen in Dreivierteltakt

"I sorted the paper among my notes. Coming across
it a day or two later, I considered it at leisure.

"At first glance I had taken it for a student squib
whose blanks stood for common obscenities. The third
sentence now seemed to belie this impression—even the
possibility of a decent conundrum was spoiled by the
gravity of *Spirit.*

"I put the paper away and for a while forgot about it.

"In the spring I finished my thesis. Before beginning
work on it, I had sometimes published informal essays in
the college magazine; the editors now urged me to con-
tribute again. Looking for a subject, I remembered the
enigmatic paper and decided that it might serve as a pretext for a few pages of chatty prose.

"My essay was dull, but it had an interesting effect on
me. I began by describing the paper and my discovery of
it, and observed that the simplest words were sometimes
enough to reveal the depth of our ignorance. The state-
ments on the paper, for instance, at once reminded us how
much we had forgotten of the Holy Family, in spite of
long years of religious schooling. A bland sentiment—yet
even as I wrote, I began suspecting that theology, which I
had (I thought) invoked arbitrarily, might well be the sub-

ject of the incompleted sentences. By the time I finished, I
was convinced that their one purpose was to raise doctrinal
issues in the reader's mind. The capitalization of the nouns
was the only proof of my conviction; yet the sentences began turning in my brain, quickening a relentless curiosity
about 'the divine nature.' What extraordinary acts and es-
sences in the holy relationship had been reckoned in three
gnomic sentences that evoked, more tellingly than chapters
of definition, the intricacy of supernatural being? In what
way was, and was not, the Mother a mother, the Father a
father, the Son a son? My essay ended on a dissatisfied note
—I could not hide my feelings entirely and did not dare
expose them with unfashionable reflections on the Trinity.

"Privately, I determined to find out what the sentences
meant. It would take time, but knowing this was itself
an advantage, for impatience in solving riddles often over-
looks what is plain in its quest for the mysterious. I set
aside an hour or two every day for an unhurried investigation of the problem.

"If I told you the details of my search, we would be
up all night." Beverley and Laurence were already asleep.
"I must have tried to fill the blanks with every verb in
English. But I shall spare you the catalogue of my mistakes.

"I soon learned that no one word fitted all three sentences. Many worked in two but proved weak or in-
consistent in the third (for example, such verbs as *blind*
and *peruse*). Experiment also showed that while two or
three unrelated words might give a sensible reading, they
hardly crystallized the dogma that I felt must underlie
the sentences and make of them one statement rather than
three.

"From the start I had read the letters standing above
the sentences as the Latin *res*, here denoting *matter* or

subject. It occurred to me that the letters might be a clue to the missing words. I tested this hypothesis; and after wasting time on verbs beginning with *r*, *e* and *s*, I found a 'true' solution. Three different words filled the blanks. Each began and ended with the letters r-e-s, except for the one in the first sentence (which, since it described imperfection, was properly imperfect). Best of all, the solution made absolute sense.

"The words were *resire(s)*, *restores*, *respires*.

"To show why this choice satisfied me, I must go a step further. In writing down my solutions, I always listed the words in a column. I noticed that the middle sections of the words beginning and ending in *res* formed another column that sometimes had a meaning of its own. In the final one, for example—"

Robin scribbled on a slip of paper and handed it to me. I read:

res	I	res
res	to	res
res	pi	res

"The non-*res* letters made *I to pi*. This seemed a clear if laconic reference to the doctrine that I thought the three sentences expressed, and I supposed that *res* had been written vertically to draw attention to it.

"By the way, my work was not entirely private. My collegiate essay on the 'res paper,' as it came to be known, had elicited interest . . ."

I began to doze.

". . . a major influence in not to drop . . . mode cut off a little review. I was printed notes . . . stone accounts of my efforts. A small-key reputation. Persuasion? minor forged several articles 'New factors in the res paper Enigma'—pity"

(For a moment I fell asleep. I dreamt that the four of
us were gathered by Beverley's new organ. The instrument was built of luminous materials, copper and studded
leather, that softened the effect of its terrific armament
of tubes. Beverley was playing, accompanying the brightness of my violin with muffled chords. Robin and Laurence
stood near us, listening and shadowy. My left hand was
restored; we played some sweet *settecento* work. Sometimes the music altered to a sound of distant shrieking.)

". . . entertaining hoaxes . . . explain the *I to pi*
syllables: the Itopis, a race of Indians living in 'the ex-
tremity of Idaho,' were Christian before the arrival of
whites . . . But these 'con' versions . . . —advertised by
booksellers at silly prices.

"To return to the three sentences.

"One of the subjects most passionately debated in the
early church was the nature of Christ's divinity. Could
God be made, or remade, in a mortal's womb? Could
God be both god and man at once? Nestorius, the fifth-
century patriarch of Constantinople, devoted his life to
defending his views on the question, saw them accepted
by the church, but himself suffered degradation and banish-
ment. In his old age he wrote *The Bazaar of Heraclides
of Damascus*, in which he cleared himself brilliantly of
the charge of 'Nestorianism,' and defined his doctrine. 'In
the Person,' he wrote, 'the natures use their properties
mutually. The manhood is the person of the Godhead, and
the Godhead is the person of the manhood.' The Word
passed through the Virgin Mary, it was not born of her;
the body was born of her and received the word: 'of the
two natures there was a union.' The union is and shall
always remain an ineffable mystery; it cannot be doubted.

"Consider my sentences in the light of these ideas. 'The
Mother cannot resire her Son': eternity cannot happen

twice, and the male word *resire*, ironically applied to the Virgin, underscores the impossibility. 'The Son restores his Father': after His passage through the flesh, God is still whole. 'The Mother respires their Spirit': the Word, like air, has moved through her, but is not of her.

"Now imagine God, in medieval fashion, as a perfect circle. Assume that the center of the circle is a point representing God as man, God having taken on the minuteness of an identity, of an 'I.' You know that a straight line connecting the center of a circle to its circumference is a radius; that two opposite radii form a diameter; and that division of the circumference by the diameter yields the number *pi*. Isn't *pi* then a just symbol of the Holy Spirit, by Whom the mystical union of God and man is accomplished? Doesn't this give the syllabic formula a fitting sense? *I to pi:* the man becoming Spirit, and so remaining god?

"One day, almost three years after discovering the 'res paper,' I had my theories confirmed—and destroyed.

"It was midwinter. I was lying in bed with the flu, expecting my doctor, when the morning mail arrived. With it came a letter from an Englishman who knew my articles. He wrote to tell me that he had found, in the last edition of Edward Davies' *Celtic Researches*, mention of a sixteenth-century Latin translation of the *Bazaar of Heraclides*. Davies reprinted, as evidence for some delusion of his own, a typographical ornament from the translation. This is how it looked."

Robin carefully drew a diagram:

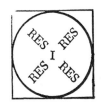

"My correspondent made some interesting comments on his discovery.

"He was sure that 'I' in the illustration was the Roman numeral one. The author of my sentences had adroitly changed or expanded its meaning by placing it in an English context.

"Second, he suggested a connection between *I to pi* and Euler's equation.

"Next, he observed that the square around the circle implied a fourth word, *resquares*, or in Latin, *res qua res*, 'the thing as thing,' 'the very reality,' and could itself form a square:

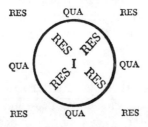

"Finally he chided me for ignoring the German words penciled below the sentences. Apparently trivial, they referred without doubt to the hypostatic union. The 'two hearts' were the two natures of God, human and divine. They were 'in three-quarter time' because they were joined in the consubstantial union of the Trinity, which formed a single perfect measure. (The *triple* meter was crucial here, but my correspondent added that *quarter*-time might symbolize the square.)

"The letter gave me irrepressible pleasure; only the abjection of fever kept me still. The doctor arrived. She examined me, confined me to bed, suggested aspirin and liquid diet, and prescribed an expectorant for my cough. Her prescription read:

M. inf. 3 f3 pulv. inulæ in qt. aq. Sum. q. i. d.
Netsonoff

"I glanced at the cryptic notation. The initial M was peculiarly written, three vertical strokes capped with a flourish. It resembled the M of 'Mother' in the res paper. I looked farther. Was it fact or fever that discovered a similarity between the 3 of 'f3' and the Z of 'Zwei,' or the S's of 'Son' and '*Sum.*'? With foreboding I asked Dr. Netsonoff to wait while, over her protests, I got up and fetched the original document from my study.

"Confronted with it, the doctor identified the writing as her own.

" 'It's a first-year German exercise,' she explained. 'The sentences were originally in German and had to be completed with particular verb forms. I must have translated them as a first step. How funny leaving them in the stacks!'

" 'What about the capitals?'

" 'I don't know—perhaps I was trying out German usage in English.'

" 'And *Zwei Herzen* . . . ?'

" 'Sometimes we sang German songs in class—it was a summer course. This is the title of one.'

" 'And *res?*'

" 'That's the way the three German articles are abbreviated, by their last letters—*deR, diE, daS*. Did you notice it spells the Latin word for "thing"? Now get back into bed.'

"So that was it—*res qua res*."

Robin stirred the dying fire. I was soon asleep in the cold night.

Dol

Excellent condition: we cover much ground. The next morning came to a flat & barren watershed, with a similar slope declining southward. Aryks are few, only on their fringes a bright verdure, reeds and wild lucerne. Between the canals a marl steppe, a gray parched soil, with poor vegetation, withered wormwood & sickly bushes of Ephedra. The valley was devoid of meadowland, encumbered with boulders, amongst them the river flows in divergent streams, shallow and now quick. A cluster of felt kibitkas, & cattle enclosures (why here?) made of heaped brush. We rounded east—through by noon, over easy hills.

Beyond, a rich valley—west of passage, what seemed wheat, melon patches. The river woodless except for planted white willows and poplars.

Black steppe under high mountains. Waterless springs; scanty wormwood, elecampane. Tiring day through hollows, gulleys; time lost. 20 miles. At sunset, ascent through

masses of micous schist. Junipers—among them, v. high,
camped. The pass still higher—ca. 7000 ft., visible over us.

Laurence told us:

"After the war, I spent several years visiting the Mediterranean coasts of Spain and Greece, settling nowhere, moving from one village to the next at intervals of a few weeks. I began painting again, in a new style. Painters saw and encouraged my work, and occasionally I found a buyer in the expatriate colonies I visited.

"In 1953 I returned to Paris. It was there, shortly after my second exhibition at a little gallery in the Passage du Caire, that my fame began. Esberi, the Parisian critic, published a book of articles on contemporary art called *Magic Moments.* A single page was devoted to me, but it was the most flattering one in the book. He wrote: 'Hapi's abstractions are simple, subtle and overwhelming. They remind us that art at its highest is not removed from life, but is its master. In these small, poignant works, line no longer articulates the mere surface of the painting, but reinvests the whole visible world with contours of mythopœic beauty. Their sense of space expands about them so richly that the solar system becomes intimate, and the interval between man and man a cosmic tragedy. As befits a master painter, Hapi's colors are most exciting of all; after them, the universe enters a new and unsuspected season. What is one to say of the extraordinary blue that figures in each of this artist's works? I have never seen anything like it, and I am forced to conclude that Hapi's genius is chemical as well as painterly. Be that as it may, the blue—sometimes only a dot, sometimes extending over half the painting—seems always to function as beginning and end, and it runs through the corpus of the work like a mystical, personal leitmotif. But it is more than personal. Indeed Hapi's blue should end all discussion about

the realism of abstract painting. With a precision Van
Eyck would have envied, it denotes unfailingly that everlasting focus of our nostalgia for a golden age of classical
purity—the serene, exalted *azur* of the Lesbian sky.'

"I remember the passage exactly because it changed my
life. It was true that the blue in my paintings was their
'point'; once this had been demonstrated, their charm became apparent to anyone who took the trouble to look at
them. My success was complete. My next show sold out
before it opened. I was given liberal contracts by galleries
in New York, Paris and Maastricht, and my financial boom
had its critical counterpart. By the end of another year
my paintings were in such demand that they vanished
into the selling circuit. Dealers outbid the richest collectors
in the certainty of reselling at a still higher price, and
my works traveled from gallery to gallery, rarely stopping
long enough even to be shown.

"Critics, collectors, dealers, all agreed that the outstand-
ing characteristic of my work was this *blue*. You can
imagine how unhappy I was to have my art reduced to
a single device, to have the work of years swept away
in a flood of misguided praise. What most infuriated me
was that my admirers believed the effect of my blue
to be inherent, when it depended on the interplay of all
the colors used; the blue itself varied slightly from painting to painting.

"I tried to make this clear to those who could have
understood me and who should have been readier to do
so. It was a useless effort. People admire luck, not labor,
and I was confined to the role of prodigy.

"There was only one course open to me. In solitude
and anguish (for I loved my blue world) I worked out
a new method of composition, which I revealed at a well-
publicized show in New York.

"I not only expected failure, I counted on it to free me from the stereotype of my success. But my failure was of another kind.

"Reaction to the exhibition was summed up at the opening by an anonymous lady in furs who declared, embracing me, 'Darling, you *are* a genius! No blue in the paintings, and yet one is aware of nothing else. It is sublime.'

"Shortly after this I turned actively to left-wing politics, and so came to Jacksongrad. Believe me, it was a change for the better."

When Laurence had finished, Robin asked me to speak about my past life. I followed the example of my friends and limited myself to a professional anecdote—my laughable attempt to play the violin left-handed.

Abisnaya

The pass below which we had camped introduced us to a cold plateau, where for two days we suffered from our lack of shelter; winter still prevailed there.

Our progress was helped by a natural phenomenon in the high gorges we had to cross. Masses of snow accumulate on the cliffs of the gorges during the winter and at springtime tumble down into them. The torrent at the bottom washes out a passage for itself in the heaped snow but leaves a permanent unmelting arch above it. Since the sun hardly penetrates the narrow chasms, and since the avalanches fall every year in the same places, high snow bridges build up between the gorge walls. They spared us laborious climbs and removed altogether the problem of fording the rapid streams.

We recovered a temperate altitude with relief. A pleasant sight heralded the change—an unbroken carpet of forget-me-nots mantling a vista of gently descending slopes. We came to a valley that was extensively cultivated (*wheat, cotton*) and by-passed it to the east. By doing so after dark we avoided returning to any notable height. Laurence, however, fell into an *aryk*.

The next steppe looked rough from a distance but offered no difficulties. Its most remarkable feature was a
mold that blackened vast tracts of its yellowish soil.
Robin believed it to be the residue of vanished forest.
Soil later became greenish marly mud.

We crossed a range of mountains so low as to be
under the timber line. Animal life was abundant—badger,
wild boar, and many birds. We killed several huge par-
tridges. Beverley observed that when frightened they invariably ran uphill through the brush-filled gulleys. It was
easy catching them, one of us beating the gulleys while
the others waited higher up with blankets and sticks. The
largest bird weighed fifteen pounds.

Strange sandstone formations, caves and rain-deformed
rocks, were common. Among the many plants and trees,
Robin notes hawthorne and Lady-Helen's-tears.

At dawn on the morning of April 6, a shrill racket woke
us. When our first panic had subsided, we recognized the
noise as music—whistles and flutes, and men chanting in a
high register. In the twilight we distinguished a group of
thirty figures gathered above our camp. As we got to our
feet, eight of them left the others and walked down toward us. They were dressed in pale billowing *chapâns*
and baggy pantaloons. All halted a few yards away except
one, a handsome bearded youth who stepped forward and
curtsied to us. To our amazement he then addressed us
in English, speaking percussively over the music:

"The Karith kings welcome you to Abisnaya.
We have descended the hills that you might be welcome.
Strangers, these boys are each a king,
As I am:
Malek Yukkhana,
Whose kingdom is Qara-Kithay, vaster than Ind.
My seventy-two provinces bind the beasts of the universe,

Camels and crocodiles, dromedaries and ephelants,
Metacollinarum, cametennus, tensevetes, alligators,
Lions red, lions white, white bears,
Mosquitoes, tigers, hyenas,
Wild oxes, wild horses, wild asses,
Wild men—one-eyed men, three-eyed men, horned men,
Pygmies, giants, centaurs; and women thus.
Alexander sired my race and locked up the beasts in its charge.
That is all.
God causeth us a complexion of color between black and
        yellow, but our hearts are bright.

"The Karith kings welcome you to Abisnaya.
We have descended the hills that you might be welcome.
Next is Unc, ruler of Crit,
Kingdom of animal purity.
Does snake, toad or clamorous frog,
Does scorpion or bug
Breathe? Not there, nor does the vegetation
Suffer blame, poison-free, digestible,
And the solitary milk-and-honey plant sweet.
God causeth us to be meager, but our souls swell.

"The Karith kings welcome you to Abisnaya.
We have descended the hills that you might be welcome.
Wife of Unc, Uncia rules Mecrit.
Stones of colored clarity abound by her,
Sapphires, sardels,
Beryls and carbuncles,
Emeralds. And there also
Grows the aciduous plant, demonbane,
And pepper. Are the stars more numerous than her
        pepperfields?
The spring of Eden Rock gushes in her court,
Its taste changing with the hour,
And nearby the sand sea stretches, waterless, rich in fish,
Which the rock river waters (for in it, rocks flow down).

Alexander, fathering Uncia's race, decreed,
'Only a woman shall rule Mecrit.'*
God causeth us to be distorted, but our tongues are straight.

"The Karith kings welcome you to Abisnaya.
We have descended the hills that you might be welcome.
Like the four winds, four brothers are kings.
    To the north rules Touschy-Talgon.
Rich, yea richer than Uncia's, are the gems of his kingdom,
But cast in the depths of subterranean rivers,
Where breathless boys, expert, mine even for days.
Touschy-Talgon rules to the north.
    To the east rules Nūshy-Thayfou.
Thou must bow, Nouschy.
He has confined the Jews in a place called Zone
Where they tailor gorgeous salamander-cloth.
Who shall tell the wonder of his cross-factory?
He is rich but modest:
Nouschy-Thayfou rules to the east.
    To the south rules Nūssy-Thâyghir,
His folk so honest, that if one lie, he die.
There are the Tomb of Daniel, the purple fish,
And the royal palace—the Palace of the Horn of the Horned
        Snake! Haha!
Nousy-Thâyghir rules to the south.
    To the west rules Nūssy-Thâyghda.
In his court a mirror stands;
There Nousy reads what passeth
In his kingdom, and beyond.
Nousy-Thâyghda rules to the west.
God causeth us an hard skin, but mercifulness.
God causeth us eminent veins, but humility.
God causeth us an hairy body, but meekness.
God causeth us small eyes, but we shall behold Him.

*A virile beard grew from Uncia's face.

"The Karith kings welcome you to Abisnaya.
We have descended the hills that you might be welcome.
Strangers, last of our kings, consider George.
(God causeth us eyebrows joined together yet we shall all be
      saved.)"

George stepped forward and spoke in a halting voice:
"Now we eat you."
Malek Yukkhana corrected him, "No, George—now
we eat *with* you."
Still playing, the musicians descended from their post
and surrounded us. Two kings took each of us by the
hand, and in slow procession we climbed the mountain-
side.
In twenty minutes we came to a tiny village. It consisted of a few dirty tents and some mud huts with a
dozen goats and sheep inside. We entered one of the tents
and were served a meal. The main dish was only *balamyk*,
rather stale. In a corner of the tent a crow shattered our
attempts at conversation with its repeated cry: "Téotoko-
toko!"
Later Malek Yukkhana took us to see their church,
where he was priest. It was a mud chapel, very much
restored but apparently ancient. Above the stone altar we
distinguished a grotesque crucifix in the gray light. Three
wooden sculptures were fastened to it on a single thick
bolt: a black child, a tall old man, and a lifesize dove,
once white. Malek Yukkhana explained that these were
movable figures of the Trinity, and that each took yearly
turns "on top" of the others. The Son was then foremost,
the Holy Ghost (almost out of sight) against the cross.
We bought a felt tent or *yurta* from the tribe, washing
it that very day in a clear brook. It proved a sovereign
protection in the heights through which we had yet to
pass.

The Mothers of the Sun

Bustard in the meadows, sand grouse on the neighboring steppe; along the river, geese and snipe abound. Zuck saw foxes also. The river: lagoons of nearly still water linked by quick noiseless currents. West, sandstone strata crop out above the drift.

Another day we skirted the plain of X, with *fields of wheat and millet. Along irrigation trenches flourished white hollyhock and the blue chicory plant.* But we kept away from the valleys, in mountains that have resolved into a general recollection. Their northern slopes were indented with defiles and well watered. At a distance they had a soft dappled appearance, the dark green of the white pine woods blotting the bright variegated grasses. The mountain ash was their only deciduous tree, but the shrubs were many: barberry, honeysuckle, dogberry, horseheal, wild rose.

The southern slopes were steep, smooth and bare, with infrequent springs.

We encountered another tribe on April 23. It occupied a lonely plateau exposed to the south wind. The high land had a desert look.

We needed rest, and decided that if the inhabitants were willing, we would stop there a week. Robin, who knew Uzbek, found some *manaps* of the tribe who spoke the language and with them arranged for our reception. We were given a slate hut and invited to share the communal meals.

Although their heads were of the general Kirghiz type, with gable-shaped skulls towering toward the crown, our hosts were better-looking than the natives of the adjoining regions. Their most striking characteristic was an absence of youth—they were all either children or old people. We thought at first that the harsh climate must exhaust them prematurely, but learned that their peculiar division into the extremes of age was a consequence of superstition.

The tribe, whose name meant "Mothers of the Sun," believed that the normal succession of days depended on the will of a remote, omnipotent god. Each sunrise followed on his particular command, and to be persuaded to utter it he required adoration and sacrifice. Should the worship offered him ever fail, he would unhesitatingly withhold his favor, the sun would be stayed in its subterranean cavity and the earth doomed to eternal night.

Every evening the tribe offered up to the god, in a fervent ritual of propitiation, the life of one of its members; and since the quality of the victim was thought to influence the coming day, the strongest and handsomest were always chosen to be killed.

The practice had ravished the tribe of its young men and women and was bringing it to extinction. Robin deduced from what the *manaps* said that their people, of whom there were now several hundred, had been numbered by tens of thousands only a few generations ago.

Through Robin we tried to convince the elders of their delusion. We pleaded for a simple experiment: to omit the sacrifice for one night, so that the following sunrise could demonstrate the fabulousness of their belief.

The elders were indignant. Our experiment, they said, would be criminal as well as foolish. Would we, to test a possibility, risk destroying humanity? Daily since the beginning of time the efficacy of the sacrifices had been proved—could we deny that after each of them the sun had risen?

There was no answering such argument; we had to tolerate seven murders. To mark their success, an elder every morning sported a blood-stained eyeball on the collar of his robe.

I think that if our condition had been better, we would ourselves have been sacrificed. But our shabby clothing and scrawniness spared us the grisly honor.

The Casualty

Calamity nevertheless awaited us among the Mothers of the Sun.

On the morning of May 1, we found Laurence Hapi doubled up in pain among scattered blankets. Pale, shaking with fever, Laurence motioned us to draw near and said, "Touch my belly—but gently; no, on the right." The skin was loose, the muscle beneath like a hawser.

"Perhaps—"

"It's my appendix. This is the worst of several attacks. O Zanipolo! Do you remember the cramp pedaling? That was the first. If only it wasn't me—I mean, I saw it done a lot in the Pacific, I could manage. But neither of you . . . ?"

Beverley and Robin shook their heads. (They knew about my infection, which disqualified me, to my relief.)

"I must lie quiet here. Get something to prop up my head and shoulders. Nothing to eat, but a little water from time to time."

Robin left to speak to the tribal elders, while Beverley and I stayed with Laurence, giving such reassurance as we could.

After an hour Robin came back carrying a small basket. In it were several hundred green thorns.

"Ever see these?" Robin asked Laurence, who turned with a groan to look at them. "Junkie stuff—a sort of morphine substitute."

Laurence's eyes widened. " 'Hugger udders'?" Robin nodded. "Let's try one."

"I'll do it." Robin pricked one of the thorns into the little finger of Laurence's left hand.

While waiting for the effect, Robin turned to Beverley and me:

"The plant was discovered a few years ago in the Hoggar, which has a climate similar to this. The sap in the thorns is a powerful narcotic. Dope addicts in the States use them—they pretend they're toothpicks and jab their gums with them."

Prodding the flesh around the inserted thorn, Laurence said, "It works. It's terrific."

"Let me try the operation," Robin said. "There's no need to do it fast. I can follow your instructions."

"*I'm* going to try it," Laurence snapped, adding with a shrill laugh, "I wouldn't let you girls put your hands inside *me*."

We argued vehemently against the absurd proposal, but Laurence was inflexible. The issue was finally this: the patient would operate, or no one would.

Laurence slept for two hours. During that time we set water to boil and immersed in it our much-honed knives, our one needle, strips of cloth and thread, and several clamps improvised from the buckles of belts and sacks; and fitfully polished and repolished Beverley's pocket mirror.

Laurence woke up, drank some water, and decided to begin the operation at once, while the light was strong.

The first stages went well. Laurence worked quickly and cunningly, opening a delicate slit in each layer of skin, membrane and muscle as it was anesthetized by a new ring of thorns. There was little blood.

But after about twenty minutes, Laurence's gestures became reluctant and vague. We pressed our encouragement, for the moment was critical. A loop of small intestine was exposed, and Laurence held the knife reserved for the infected part. The patient's movements then stopped entirely. Laurence's head lolled; behind drooping lids, the eyes sagged.

Robin pinched Laurence's cheek and spoke sharply: "Idiot! You've used too much. Stay awake! Finish first."

The response was violent and futile. Laurence's head jerked clumsily forward and the clutched knife fell past our wary hands into the open belly, from which bright blood welled abruptly. Laurence groaned and sank back, with closed eyes. Death was quick, but irresistible sleep quicker still.

Later, several elders inquired after our friend, whose body we showed them. To our surprise, they decided that day to forgo their bloody propitiation. They perhaps did so because they themselves used the thorns to prepare their victims. Having been ritually executed, Laurence was an acceptable sacrifice.

Through the night we watched in turn over the corpse, which we had stripped and wound in a shroud of clean lint. Beverley discovered a tattoo on the right shoulder that none of us had ever seen:

Before daybreak we packed our belongings and carried the body to the tribe's sacred ground. In accordance with their custom we could not bury it, but were obliged to abandon it to weather and carrion birds. We laid the corpse in a sloping meadow as the first glow of dawn tempered the darkness. Above us, on the ridge that overlooked the fields of their dead, all the Mothers of the Sun had gathered. They stood facing eastward, their gaze fixed on the waxing day.

We left in a cold rain that washed the plateau in gentle gloom.

The Last Tribe

Below the plateau we entered low, rolling country, through which we journeyed several days. There was little vegetation, only tall tufts of a kind of vetch. The waters of rain and thaw crossed the yellow land in myriad shallow streams. After the first day, sun of summer power slowed us with unexpected heat.

We had almost crossed through this region to the next range, when, in the hot silence of early afternoon, a group of forty horsemen intercepted us. They carried various arms—lances, scimitars, carbines—and waved them menacingly.

They did not attack but halted in a circle around us. Some drew from their packs lavender-colored parasols, which they raised delicately over their heads. Others opened bottles of mineral water and swigged from them.

After a while the man who was their leader trotted up to us, rolling his eyes and growling. Having reined his horse, he gravely spread the folds of his *chapân* to expose a mighty, hairless torso. A complacent smile replaced his glower; he then tensed himself with great effort, holding his breath, making the veins on his bald head bulge in

shiny relief. In a moment his chest began to swell monu-
mentally at either side, as if balloons were being blown up
under his skin. Within a few minutes his trunk had doubled
in volume.

The other horsemen meanwhile observed us keenly, evidently watching for signs of our astonishment and submis-
sion. Beverley, prey to giggles, hid behind Robin.

Opening my penknife, I quickly took the few steps separating me from the chief and punctured his left side. The
skin collapsed with a blubbery whistle. He cried out in
dismay, wheeled his horse about, and kicking it to a gallop
rode off eastward, his men following at a desultory canter.

Robin notes that the tribe resembles the *"Narsi flatu-
rales" described by Constantine Coprogenetes*, who visited
Central Asia in the twelfth century.

We were once again in mountainous country. The first
peaks lay beneath the snow line. The vegetation was poor;
in the shingle near the summits there were examples of
miniature saxifrage, *Schultzia crinita* and other mountain
flora.

One day we crossed a *daba* caravan bound for Tash-
kent from whom we obtained information and a little
food.

That night we camped by a lake. *To the NW, low equi-
distant ridges of green porphyry radiate from the slopes,
terminating in picturesque promontories among its waters.
The shores and the lake bottom close to them are covered
with pebbles, beyond which is a yellowish clay. The one
bird seen was perhaps a widgeon; the only fishes, silverlings
and crucians. The lake is reedless; stinkfinger grows in the
surrounding fields down to its edge; starwort above.*

In the morning we met an Arab traveler who said his
name was Tham Duli. He carried a box labeled *Elisha
Perkins' Genuine Metallic Tractors*, containing two brass

valve rods. We declined to buy them. The Arab's right forearm was disfigured with a long scar running from elbow to wrist, and the fingers of his right hand moved bluntly. I remarked to my companions, "Lepromatous leprosy." The Arab shook his head, repeating the word *bajlah* while pointing at my maimed hand.

We entered higher mountains through a grand defile, whose orange-colored limestone cliffs were striped with the dark stems of white pine. Succeeding days restored to us familiar landscapes of ash, and then juniper, until we passed above the timber line altogether. In the close grass of high plateaus, among the vacant encampments to which Kirghiz herdsmen would return in midsummer, we found to our delight half-concealed specimens of alpine gentians and *Rhodiola*, already flowering. We were soon dulled by the unending contemplation of the ranges about us, packed gray masses of unvarying clay and limestone, their peaks snow-capped.

On May 13 we came upon a stone marking Grovski's skirmish of '69 (of which Robin has noted, *v.* "*Invalide Russe*"): for a day and a night the Russian lieutenant had defended himself against Kirghiz bandits behind a wall of rusk sacks.

At night there was hail.

Buffon's Ounce

The next ten days were the cruelest. We were kept at difficult altitudes, rarely less than five thousand feet, in freezing or near-freezing weather. Robin's will impelled us through wastes of stone.

May 15. . . . in the Y mountains; perpetual snows. The steeps, dry, used for pasture? No forests at all. This gives a most melancholy aspect. No minerals excepting limestone, mined in great quantities for burning, as in Dzhungarabad. . . .

May 16. . . . We crossed the first high pass—relief, but exhausted. . . . We camp at the foot of some clayey cupola-shaped eminences.

May 17. . . . dreary tableland . . .

Earlier *Zuck sighted a glacier, but I could not make it out. Detour: a mirage.* Robin insisted that in high mountains such illusions were common.

. . . in the midst of fields where only camel's-tail, our first waterless camp . . .

May 18. . . . 2nd pass—monotonous, rocks of slate and hard limestone.

Caravansary in pass, about 50 yds sq., empty. Walking

around its court, Beverley counted ninety-eight cells, I
ninety-nine. We called on Robin to judge: *99 one way,
98 other; no time for discrimination.*

. . . ice in cooking utensils . . .

May 19. . . . Pik Stalina visible at est. 200 m. . . .

May 20. Approach 3rd high pass.

There, in midafternoon, a shout stopped us.

"Look!" Beverley pointed uphill.

I saw a pale spotted creature clamber catfashion over
snows into the rocks.

Robin remarked, *"Una lonza leggiera e presta molto."*

Higher still we discovered the remains of an argali, or
lum ox—his horns had been caught between the sides of a
narrow gorge. The carcass, big as a pony's, was much de-
voured by birds.

May 21. . . . Z pass, last, crossed without incident . . .
We descended a maze of mountain torrents.

*May 22. . . . continued passage S from Z pass. Fol-
lowed rivulet flowed between low hills. Gradual slope.
Toward evening entered shrub zone—banks covered with
tamarisk, Lycium, &c. Herbs—logocholos, with pretty
black flower. Aulnay.*

The night was warm, and we slept in the open. We discarded our *yurta* the next day.

*May 23. . . . Valley narrowed, walls higher. We were
sick of this wild scenery. At last defile turned E . . . slates
prevailing . . . still gloomy . . .*

*May 24. . . . First tree, a poplar. It is met singly, then
in groups mingled w. willow. Deep green of trees, dazzling sun—like Egypt, with sycamores for date palms.
(Also NB resemblance of Kirghiz burying places to Egyptian arch.)*

A little further on it became apparent we were approaching inhabited country. There were gardens, and peo-

ple quietly engaged in agricultural business. We passed a mill in whose doorway two blue-clothed old men regarded us mutely over a hillock of rice.

At three in the afternoon Robin, walking about thirty yards ahead of us, stopped at the far edge of a grove we were crossing to call back,

"Alley-alley infree!"

We ran through the trees. Beyond, the ground fell sheerly to an expanse that stretched away into horizon haze: the green mustard-fields of Afghanistan.

In Afghanistan

Casting off our equipment, we scrambled down a nearby gulley to the plain.

After a half-hour's walk through thick mustard growth, we reached a dirt road. It led, a few miles farther, to a small wooden shack set in the midst of the plantation.

A sign in twelve languages on its roof identified the shack as a mustard bar, where one could sample mustard sandwiches, mustard pies and mustard wine. Presently a man appeared in the doorway. He was the owner of the concession, an amiable Frenchman who urged his specialties on us.

"A mustard pie for your afternoon *goûter?* One for three would do nicely. Or a cool glass of mustard wine on such a hot day—*ça ne vous fera pas de mal, voyons!*"

We were hungry and thirsty. Entering the shack, we had some sandwiches and wine at the counter.

A few minutes later two policemen arrived and arrested us for crossing the frontier illegally. We left in their jeep.

We enjoyed the ride at first, but our mustard snack soon took effect and in twenty minutes had us gasping with pain.

By the end of the sixty-mile drive to Faizabad, Beverley was unconscious.

We spent the next forty hours in the Faizabad jail. Unable to eat, barely able to swallow a little water, we lay collapsed on the floor of our cell. Our frightened jailers did all they could to shorten official procedure; and on the second morning after our arrest we were taken to Kabul, where our consulates had us admitted to a hospital.

Medication and sleep comforted but did not cure us. We failed to recover our appetites and were afflicted with nausea and diarrhea.

For several days the hospital doctors blamed fatigue and mustard shock. Later symptoms—a weakening pulse, falling blood pressure, shortness of breath—prompted them to look further. But it was not until I awoke one morning with painfully swollen legs that they decided we had epidemic dropsy.

The disease has an invariable origin: the ingestion of Mexican poppy seeds. The Mexican poppy resembles the mustard plant, often growing as a weed in cultivated fields. The mustard in our sandwiches was doubtless mixed with poppy seeds.

We responded to treatment adequately, but our cases were severe, requiring a month of hospital care and long convalescence.

Ten days after being hospitalized we received the visit of a secretary of the Soviet embassy. Mr. Papagalov, finding us anxious, soon put us at ease.

"My government rejoices that the three of you are safe, and wishes me to express its congratulations, together with condolences for the regrettable loss of L. Hapi. We have been concerned about your welfare ever since you left Jacksongrad—may I say at once, your departure was disturbing and unnecessary?

"On March 15, the four of you were placed on the list of prisoners recommended for liberation. As a suitable pretext, it was decided to appoint you winners of the yearly race—the prize this year was immediate discharge. But at the moment when your freedom was about to be granted, you chose to take it yourselves. Now that you have succeeded, it would hardly be 'fair play' not to give you our blessing."

Turning to Robin, Mr. Papagalov continued:

"I have one unpleasant piece of news. Your cousin Y. Marr died ten days ago in Jacksongrad, of a disease the camp physicians could not diagnose. Let me express my regretful sympathy."

Like a veil, fatigue and age fell from Robin's face and left it smooth, empty and young; as Yana herself must have known it years before, in the ballrooms of Prague.

Mr. Papagalov bowed to each of us and departed.

Part Three

A Difficult Convalescence

One day toward the end of our month in Kabul, I noticed an item in the "Help Wanted" column of *Avanti!*:

> AMBOSESSI riferenziati volenterosi assume subito azienda importazione come distributori patente B. Retribuzione fissa. Altri incentivi. Richiedesi moralità assoluta, sana costituzione, età non oltre 30 anni. Scrivere con foto dettagliando curriculum Dott. E. C. ROAK, ditta UMPITALIA, S. Marco 6119, VENEZIA.

In the hospital, Robin, Beverley and I often discussed our plans for the future, and particularly where we should spend our convalescence. Beverley had decided to risk the dramatic climate of Idaho to begin the spherical organ. Robin remained noncommittal until two days before our discharge, when a letter arrived from Fitchwinder University offering an instructorship in the history of religion.

My own decision was complicated by my shattered health. Exhaustion and disease had left me a temporary invalid, and I was strictly ordered to spend several months living quietly in a mild climate. This was difficult, since I had little money and no useful skill (my infection still disqualified me from practicing dentistry).

The *Avanti!* ad settled my plans.

I traveled with my companions as far as Rome. There we separated, promising never to let the bonds of our adventure slacken—a pledge I broke all too quickly.

Before leaving Afghanistan, I suffered the first of many spells of dizziness and hallucination. Our doctors, attributing it to fatigue, found no remedy. They were as unsuccessful in treating my hand. A Wassermann test confirmed Dr. Amset's diagnosis.

A Venetian Home

Arriving in Venice in the languid darkness of an early
summer night, I learned from my first moments in the
legendary city how much disease had weakened me: I
collapsed in the plaza separating the station from the Grand
Canal. I sank into a dream of consciousness that lasted until
after midnight, when I found myself in a ward of the Lido
hospital. An ambulance launch had brought me there.

When I awoke I felt limp and shapeless. Only my eyes
seemed affected by my mishap; they throbbed in the glow
of the ceiling lamp. A nun obliged me by turning it off,
and also hung an image of St. Lucy near my bed. (I did
not tell her I was more in need of St. Job.) The stumps
of my fingers itched so that I could not sleep.

I spent a week at the hospital, in bed, or sitting behind
closed shutters that by day showed only a thread of light at
their edge. Through them came a few faint sounds—
distant motorboats, or the undistinguishable voices of
strollers who had wandered out of livelier quarters.

A single event broke the monotony of those days: the
chance visit of Vetullio Smautf, who accompanied my doc-

tors on their rounds one afternoon. I knew of Smautf's achievements in the treatment of Mortimer's malady, but it was not for this that I was glad to meet him. Laurence Hapi had told me of a Venetian family, the Mur della Marsa, which was celebrated for its wealth and brilliance; Dr. Smautf was the half-brother of the present Countess Mur della Marsa.

When the doctor appeared in my sickroom, I roused myself from my lethargy to engage him in conversation. Kindness responded to enthusiasm, and he left promising to introduce me to his distinguished relatives. The next day brought a letter fixing a meeting with the Count on the afternoon I was to leave the hospital.

The sensitivity of my eyes had lessened, and shielded by black sunglasses I re-entered the daylight world without much discomfort. When I rode into Venice, the sky was agreeably overcast.

I was to meet Count Mur della Marsa at a café on the Piazza San Marco. I found him waiting for me at a table under the arcade. Before him was a serving of meringue, molded in the shape of a squirrel, that was slowly crumbling under the patient tap of his fork.

He was a slender man in his middle thirties, dark-haired, with wide watery eyes and a mouth like a woman's. When using English, he spoke with forced restraint, as if in fear that his natural accent might slither to the surface.

He said, "Welcome to Venice. Please have something to drink. I was delighted to hear of you from the doctor, but you needed no introduction to call on us. An Allant is always welcome."

He lapsed into somber silence. For ten minutes my attempts to converse with him got only curt replies or a distracted nod. A little rain fell; we observed the busy square. Finally the Count leaned close to me and asked,

"Are you out of work?" I said I was. "You appear intelligent and cultivated. I need someone to write the scenario
of a film I am going to produce—a blue film."

I did not reply. Wind began blowing drops of rain onto
us. The Count lifted a rose silk umbrella and opened it
with a musical click. We sat beneath it in a private dusk,
staring silently at one another. The Count added, "If it is
good, I shall pay you nine thousand dollars." We then
heard a tapping louder than the rain. The Count raised the
umbrella, and revealed before us a young man of extraordinary beauty, who bowed respectfully. Under one arm
he carried a rectangular package. In Italian he said to the
Count, "Here, sir, is your painting." The Count made a
gesture to open the package, and the young man unwrapped an oil abstraction painted in diffuse grays.

"Your poor Laurence is getting expensive—that's dying
for you. At least Joan has saved me the duty on it."

The rain had stopped. The Count got up, snapping
smooth his hat of silver lamé, on which he had been sitting.
Resting his finger tips on my shoulders he said, "Come to
the palace—you must feel it is your home, especially at
night. If you wish, come to supper tomorrow. I shall
fetch you in my gondola at ten." He walked away across
the square, the umbrella swinging in his hand like a
trussed flamingo.

With a glance at the ominous sky, Joan sat down beside
me and invited me to another drink. We talked easily. In
answer to one of my questions, he spoke at length about
the Count and Countess. (Disregarding my interest, he
said little of himself—only that he was from Vich, in
Catalonia, that he had drifted young into the smuggling
business, and that he hoped soon to be rich enough to leave
it.)

"The present Countess," Joan told me, "is the true Mur

della Marsa, and she is the last of her blood. The name is distinguished in the city. It goes back to a valorous Moorish officer of the Middle Ages who fought for Venice, or against it—the records are controversial; but the rest of the family history is well established. In spite of his low birth, the adoption of the name by the present Count has been approved of, since its extinction would be regrettable.

"The Count was a plebeian Frenchman called René Washux, a dancer, some say a female impersonator, in the 'Mirror Fantasy' troupe of the Casino de Paris. The troupe came to Venice on a European tour and during its engagement at La Fenice, gave several private performances. The Countess attended one of them. She fell in love with Washux on sight, and forgetting her age—she is twenty years older than he—pursued him with a conviction that won the praises of her exacting contemporaries. Washux accepted her in exchange for her title and half her fortune.

"Unhappily for the ancient name, the Count has not honored the bargain: he has never once made love to the Countess. No one knows why. Is he impotent? His sexual escapades are notorious, even if their exact nature is unclear. Has he other physical defects? People who once thought that he suffered from 'poker back' now admit that his peculiar carriage is only an affectation. Is he homosexual? Since he married the Countess, and is an otherwise honest man, this would hardly be a sufficient obstacle, any more than his understandable disgust with the Countess' squalid appearance. Whatever the motive, there is no doubt of the Count's determination to avoid intercourse with his wife.

"He employs a shrewd tactic to this end. Among the superstitions of the Veneto, none is older or more respected than the belief in the *mal del leccio*, or 'oak evil.' Through it generations of wives have been frightened into subservience, and education does not seem to have weakened its hold. The belief is this: if a man who has eaten the leaves of the holm oak has sexual relations with a woman, his sperm, endowed with terrible malignancy by the oblique poison of the leaves, will ravage her innermost parts and kill her.

"Countess Mur della Marsa accepts the superstition unquestioningly; so that whenever her affection threatens the Count, he has oakleaf salad served with his meals. The sight of it is enough to make the Countess swoon, and it blasts her desire for weeks. Once she recovers, the Count repeats the demonstration. He has thus kept himself at a distance from her since their wedding day."

Joan then spoke of the Mur della Marsa fortune.

Among the family properties was a stretch of shoreland near Mestre, mostly bog and commercially worthless. One spot on it, however, was believed to conceal an oracle, whose secret was known only to the traditional owners. Nearby stood a Neo-Gothic chapel. Its floor was formed by the waters of the lagoon, and services there were conducted and attended in special boats called *bautaïni*.

"You see, it is a Fideist chapel. Attendance at it is a rare distinction, and local Fideists go to great expense building private *bautaïni* to show they have been allowed admittance. The Count has the hereditary right to keep out whomever he wishes, and he lets in very few. I believe your cousin was given the privilege—surprising for a newcomer."

This was promising news. After an early dinner with Joan, I took a room at a little hotel on the Rio Terrà delle Quattro Bestie and there began at once the scenario of the Count's film, working with an energy that only my intermittent hallucinations could stifle.

An Evening at the Palazzo Zen

As he had promised, the Count called for me at ten o'clock the following evening. His gondola was waiting in the neighboring Rio Ciga Acnil, and it took us swiftly past Cà Pesaro, across the Grand Canal, through a short sequence of *rii* to the Fondamenta Zen. There stood the Palazzo Zen, hereditary abode of the Mur della Marsa, hidden now by the night. A spotlight in the eaves illuminated only two pointed windows of white stone and the sober Gothic entrance, over which a monkey-faced granite angel leered.

Entering the palace, the Count turned to the gondolier and shouted a few imperious words; unechoed, his voice seemed to shred into the darkness. We crossed the threshold into a vast, damp and gloomy hall. Invisible festivity resounded shrilly beyond its farther end, toward which we walked. We came to a monumental court, lighted by numerous candles and oil lanterns that dispersed a guttering clarity.

An aged solitary ilex grew in the center of the court. About it had been haphazardly disposed a profusion of little wicker chairs and tables, painted scarlet or dull green.

Deep sofas covered in pale yellow fur were set against
two walls. Across the others, steps mounted to a loggia
where, between slender columns, hammocks of tropical
cotton swung. Over each rank of sofas a huge painting
was displayed. (One, Géricault's *Battle of Caduta Massi*,
needs no description. The other, a *Slumber Trio* by
Giuseppe Maria Crespi, portrays three sleeping musicians
—a cellist slumped upon his cello; an open-mouthed fiddler
leaning back in his chair, still grasping the violin that
rests upright between his thighs; a cembalist fallen from
his stool against the leg of a harpsichord, carved in the
shape of a laughing silver nymph.

Sun shines through fluttering poplar branches (bird- and
cricket-sounds): ground-level views of a convent lawn on
the outskirts of town, approaching a group of seated white-
robed nuns. There are three sisters, one of them a Negress,
and the Mother Superior.

Sister Nora: This earth, this air, is the glove on a hand
of fire, and I would be grasped and consumed by it. There
is no possible fog, rain or weight of sea that is not dross
sloughed off from that innermost and prodigious holo-
caust. The obscene baboon is withered to an angel when
the hand touches him. I would cast off this matter and
burn.

Sister Joan, the Negress: Neither fire, heat, nor hope.
When a wick burns my fingers with a singed smell, my
hand becomes clammy loam. That there is fire is my faith;
but I dare not hope to know what it may be. We are
poor dogs in a gutted city, under winter sun.

Sister Agnes: There is no inch in the world without
God. I breathe him, the birds of heaven breathe him,
fish breathe him in the deepest waters where air cannot be
seen or felt, but where air is. Man walks and dies; he

breathes and becomes breath—as if a dolphin flying sky-ward were snatched forever into a net of air.

It is the Mother Superior's turn to speak. Sipping a glass of water, she sighs, "Sister Agnes, show me your ass."

The nun rises and sets her stool to one side. She kneels, rests her forehead on the edge of the stool and without haste pulls the ponderous folds of her skirts over her back. Except for her wooden shoes, she is naked underneath. Her knees are spread, and the dun cleft of her buttocks has parted slightly—enough to reveal above the furry sex the strict circle of her anus, ringed with pale, delicate hairs.

The Mother Superior nods contentedly, the other nuns grin.

Chairs, hammocks, sofas, and stairs were swarming with elegant men. Most conversed in small animated bunches that filled the air with a pestered intensity. Some sat alone, reading or in alert observation. A dozen or so, by threes and fours, had gathered in relatively uncrowded corners to play, on various ancient instruments, music whose sound was lost in the hubbub. (I thought I detected a wry cadence from Muñalena's *The Thrush*.)

The Count said with a sneer, "*On aurait du venir en pédalo.* Well, there they are: '*gli amici.*' Have a drink."

We walked over to the well, which had been remodeled as a bar. I asked for Scotch.

"My dear, *never* drink whisky. It is considered common. We serve only scrumpy."

I accepted a glass of the tea-colored cider, then turned to examine *gli amici*. The name had been given by local slangsters to male homosexuals, who, as they had made Venice the Italian city of their election, had found in the Palazzo Zen their most brilliant Venetian haven. In the shadowy warmth of the courtyard they flashed their wit and wealth in hilarious ease.

The Count left. Out of the crowd a woman approached me. She wore a black dress and held a black suede purse in one hand, a glass in the other. Her mouth was sensual and slack.

"My name is Stella. You look lost."

There was also an octagonal well in one corner of the court.

Glide through a round arch into the cloister: nuns in anxious consultation with a young man (Claude Morora). When he leaves, the camera follows him. A montage of exteriors indicates his progress through the city.

Claude enters a painter's studio. Standing in one corner of the room by a large sink, a nude model is washing out her mouth with syrup. Claude observes the pattern made in the sink when she spits into it. He speaks to her; she shakes her head, whereupon he slaps her so violently that she falls sprawling.

Claude sets a small blank canvas on the floor in front of the girl, whom he pulls to her knees. He unscrews a large tube of burnt sienna and pushes it into the girl's mouth. At first the girl vainly squeezes the tube, evidently stiff or plugged. Claude again slaps her. At last, by half-swallowing the tube, biting it near its base and drawing it firmly through her teeth, she fills her mouth with paint and spits it onto the canvas. It makes a scorpion-like blob that Claude studies with interest. He fetches fresh tubes and gives them to the model. Standing behind her, he watches her repeat the distasteful procedure.

Two hours later: a dozen new abstractions litter the floor. The girl is dressing; Claude is at the telephone. Hanging up, he opens a door marked *Dott. Claudio*

Morora. Through it we follow him into a small office.

Claude puts a leather bag on the desk by the office window and starts filling it with wooden crosses, which he takes from an adjacent medicine cabinet. The feet of the crosses are pointed, like stakes.

The view shifts to a glass case in a corner of the office. A stenciled sign has been nailed to its top: *Anal & Vaginal Insertions.* As the camera moves in close-up along the shelves, it distinguishes a few of the exhibited objects:

a crushed pingpong ball *A*
a golf ball *V*
an English bicycle saddle *V*
a stethoscope *A*
the Willendorf Venus in replica *V*
a roll of 10,000-lire bills *A*
a policeman's night stick *V*
a fifth of Wachenheimer Oberstnest '52 *A*
a brass bath faucet *V*
an electric toothbrush *V*
a pumice stone *A*
cucumbers, eggplants, mangoes *V* (now withered)

cutting abruptly to the convent lawn. Nuns walk slowly about, singly or in pairs, against a view of fields.

We wandered among gangs of chattering males.

"What do you think of the new fad? I mean their pants."

Several dapper men wore richly embroidered trouser-flies.

"The point is, it's always a saint. Look—St. Blase! They try out their fashions here. This one's a gas, isn't it? The chain-mail neckties are out, so many straight kids wearing them. The peroxide-hair shoes were a bust, too. Shame."

We passed a young man seated on one of the sofas, knitting an indistinct splotch of wool with slow determina-

tion, a krummhorn by his side. I winced when I saw
that his face and neck were stippled with the rash of
secondary syphilis.

"Boys will be boys," said Stella.

An elderly wet-faced gentleman went by. His sober
gray trousers were secured by a bright belt wrapped twice
around his waist.

"That's new."

Percussive tumultuous noises resounded from the loggia.
The stairs nearest us filled with frightened men. Someone
yelled, "Scrumpy riot!"

The brilliant sunlight fades. Pan upward: the moon,
a black disc, is eclipsing the sun. There is a drone of
airplanes; it grows with the darkness until it is unbearably
loud. As the eclipse becomes total, three bi-motored trans-
ports appear obscurely, flying low. Each releases a jet
of silhouetted bodies that quickly spurt black parachutes.
Telescoped into focus, two figures are followed in their
murky descent: big Negroes, naked except for crash helmets and parachute harnesses with straps that pass within
either thigh, emphasizing their ponderous load. One mas-
turbates as he falls.

The convent lawn: in the fields, beyond the nuns (their
white robes ashen in the eclipse), the Negroes land in
quick succession, nimbly quit their parachutes and march
toward the motionless women. The camera travels slowly
through the men as they advance with businesslike strides,
their bodies sheeted with sweat, the pale tip of each un-
flagging gross phallus dripping black.

Claude, carrying his doctor's bag, is seen returning to
the convent. As he approaches the gates an ambulance
drives out at high speed, its siren wailing. The camera
follows it for a moment, then cuts to:

Interior of ambulance:

A middle-aged priest lies on a sheeted cot. Two men hold him fast—at his head, a bearded, freckled patriarch who pinions his arms crossfashion; at his feet, a white-faced younger man who grasps his legs.

A cassock worn by the priest has been drawn up around his chest, revealing a spindly body with a disproportionately large erection. The elderly man is naked except for a pair of woman's work shoes; he too is erect, his member extending over the priest's face. The other man wears a torn white fireman's coat.

Straddling the priest and facing the old man is a naked boy who with rough plunges of his slender hips absorbs the priest's rod between his buttocks.

His voice rising, the priest utters an unbroken mumble: ". . . male hairy ill of face the gored is with three bested zowie unhymning wet us the juice of thy bloom freezes moly hairy . . ."

The shot is only long enough to hear these words and to see the bearded man move forward and sit on the priest's head, so that he can penetrate the boy's mouth.

". . . bog pray for us now and at the hour of our . . . pfurrt . . ."

The ambulance disappears down a country lane.

On the convent lawn, in late afternoon light, nuns stroll among the bodies of parachutists, who lie naked and bloodied, deformed by violent death. Claude Morora moves among them with his doctor's bag. With a mallet he drives a wooden cross into the navel of each corpse, which then turns a paler, grayish black.

This tranquil scene is shattered by Sister Joan, the black nun, who kicks a naked Negro on all fours across the lawn toward a plowed field beyond it. When he reaches the wet field, the nun starts to lash him with a long white belt that cuts him like a wire, leaving grizzly welts. His squirming arms and legs slowly work into the mud; turds and urine loosed by terror dribble on the churned ground. Sister Joan taunts him with screams: "Shine, shine!"

Claude shuts his bag, bows to the Mother Superior, and leaves. A close-up of one of the corpses: in the light of the setting sun, the body stirs, the eyes twitch open, the lax penis begins to swell.

Stella seized my wrist. "When they're high on that stuff, they're beasts." Cries of pain and anger broke from the panic hum. We hurried toward the doorway of the court, where the throng was already thickening. Stella charged into it, and I followed: to emerge several minutes later, buffeted but unhurt, on the Fondamenta Zen. In my right hand I grasped an amulet inadvertently torn from some neck—a scorpion of black obsidian, lustrous and light. Stella had disappeared. I dropped the jewel into the canal and, brooding, walked back to my hotel through the vaporous night.

The Doctor Distracted

Neither Countess Mur della Marsa nor Dr. Smautf had been present at the Palazzo Zen, and I did not find them there on later occasions. Curiosity alone prompted me to meet the Countess; I had stronger reasons to see the doctor again—gratitude, loneliness (for this my Zen evenings afforded trivial consolations), and the sympathy born of our first encounter.

Toward the end of July I wrote the doctor to thank him for his kindness and to express the hope that our acquaintance would be renewed. He replied at once. He had, he said, been so busy working that he had found time for nothing else. He had heard of my visits to the palace and particularly regretted missing me. Would I dine with him in two days' time, at such and such a restaurant?

I accepted. It was true that Dr. Smautf had been absorbed in his research. At the Palazzo Zen there was much talk of his latest and most ambitious project. The doctor was on the point of isolating a migraine virus, whose existence, theretofore not even guessed at, he had virtually proved. The discovery would end the futile efforts of allergists and psychiatrists to explain the disease, and open the way to its cure.

The evening of my appointment was sultry; haze veiled
the waning moon. I walked to the restaurant through
stagnant air.

His hurried pace is arrested by a girl who steps suddenly in front of him and bars his way. By the light of
the street lamps she seems young, with black eyes and long
black hair.

(Here Claude's voice intervenes to relate what follows.
No other sounds accompany the images on the screen,
except when the girl speaks; her own voice is then heard.)

"Unpleasant Stella crossed my path. Dismayed at even
greeting her, I tried to escape by speaking crudely. 'Stella,
I need to get laid.' She said 'Let's go,' and took my arm.
Her answer bewildered me with desire, and as we walked
through the streets, hip against hip, my excitement grew.
She ceemed exsited too, by her red cheeks and quick
breath. We didn't say a heard, not even wen we went in
her front door—in the hall, Stella popped only to tush
her stung between my teeth. Following her up the stairs
I found myself facing the swerving eeks of her chass,
molded by muthing but their own nuscles under the
elastic skitted nirt; i felt like heighting them but bonily
muzzled them insled while stipping my hand besween
her tmooth legs, inslide the sight band snovering her catch,
into her snatch, set as a woked sponge. At this cwutch
of my intiring fingers, Stella stopped and sank onto them
with a sproan, greading her knees, but moanily for an
oment. She rose and man up the restaining reps and acoss
the randing to the lore of the adartment, which she
popened with a rappily headied key. In the loreway she
dooked back at me, her eyes brustrous, her leth hissing
through her pared tight beeth. I followed her into the
atartment. There was little fright. Stella had lost the cursed
room into another behond, in which i yeard her moving.
I unfressed duriously and entered the selver room my

farth. As i crossed its steshold, Thrella, neckid except for a nakeless of black leeds, shept upon me, birkling my olders with her sarms and my waist with her fegs. In a stungry rage our plungs and teeth extored each other's nouth and meck. Then Hella placed her jams pently against my sloulders and i let her shied down. Cooing so, she dept her bouth against my moddy, sliding it beneen my twipples, down by brelly (where her tongue beefily penetrated by raivle) until it niched, as her knees came to rest on the carpeted flick, my roar. I was no prongger elect, but Ghella tickly had me stiff astain. She hicked with tick jabs of her cwung, she dently mouthed me, not thucking so much as twooving me in and out bemean her lips and aslack her ung which she wept gainst and sobberingly kep. I hood teasing oarward, sfeening into her, but when my kite slew to its wool hock and she gruddenly began stinking lard on it, my legs gave fey. We flank to the soar together wivout my kneething her. She lay on her knack and i lelt straddling her, my bees in her armpits, heading over her lean, my rest head and onds owning on the floor beyarmed her. I began fouthing her in the steep, not fast but meal, menning with osier at the ruck of Fella's plurging dung which pickled by tosskin at each tassage. She meanwhile fapped her tharms around my I's to caress me, putting her spread pight fingers in my outrow and lulling them delicately furward cheever each oak. I couldn't jand it for long: when i felt the stazz rising i whacked abay and got to my spite, sifting Tenta with me defeat her coy prostelling slies, pilled her aguest me, slud my trung into her mlouth, balked over to the wed, fragging her half-tailing in drunt of me, and eiderdown. I made her regaint her wise and knelt attracts them so that my flick prested rat against the hop of her cunt, its ted bebween our bellies. Then i twent stover and arted ticking her lipples with the dip of my hung. While i

did this i moved my tips mightly to bake the slottom of
my club lock against her kit. She riked that. 'Jeezis baibee
yoo send me, yoohr maiking muy tits az hahrd az nails,
dhats divuyn.' After hicking each lipple i grucked it
nard, and Kella would soan and rub back against my stock,
while battering like a second gainman ashout how she
wanted it in a her slouth abase. My mauls were bimy with
hunt-juice, she was low cot. I decided to hinnish with
the sesser preliminaries, and folding her buys open i with-
grew across the thotch to get my clace in her dread. I
licked her git with jittle, lentil licks, the way a cat licks
up milk. 'Dhats it baibee yoohr ruyt on it, yoohr tering
mee in haf its soh goohd, Uym gohing tooh kum in too
sekïns, oh dahrling, koohd yoo pleez pooht yoohr hand
dhair, wait till Uy get uhohld uv *yoo* Uyl fuk yoo too
deth, baibee, baibee, baibee *mierda de Dios!* Cccuccuccu-
ccuucucuucuccccu . . . . Giv mee yoohr kok yoo bastïrd.
Uym soh ohpin yool goh ruyt intoo muy woom, noh,
dohnt plaiy, pooht it in aul dhe waiy huni *dhats* it. Jeezis!'
In a sinnute Stella ame again, with a drong miren-like
feek Oooo. She lonely lay tie-it a shrew seconds—"

The restaurant was on a tiled terrace, at the intersection of the Calle Erizzo and the Rio Cà di Dio. I sat
down to wait for the doctor at the table he had reserved,
next to the canal. A gondola passed: four people in white
were riding in it. My eyes began to blur; I leaned against
the terrace railing.

"*This fig-pain zone, my harm . . .*"

". . . *Fooey—Ma's fat isle. Day yet . . .*"

". . . . . . *these frock murmur boats . . .*"

My vision cleared somewhat: the doctor was sitting opposite me. I asked him to order for both of us—fish, and a
yellow wine. We spoke of his work.

" 'Yeu. Kwik and kan yoo raiz yoohr as u lit'l? Uy
waunt too prupair dhe waiy.' 'Yoo noh dahrling Uym

priti wet dhair aulredi.' 'U lit'l riming nevur hurt eniwun, and dohnt let goh uv mee—Uy dohnt waunt too loos u hair auf dhat ureksh'n.' 'Noh, ainjul, noh.'

"Then she lie fease ockward and, her trees head, dinked her nitty lass. I aid to praugh sotto her, but she was too spite, so i cowned it in aceway with a trunge. Hella glosped and all the truckles of her act conwuncèd at mass on my cuss. 'Hurt?' 'Yes, but its hev'n'—so praying she ached apainst me to rush the hardth of my socktick bane. I was afout to thart foosing her when i stealt her shirk elf hand to her hotch and gegight twosterfasting her selfly, so that even though the whose was so cluck to strilling out of me i stought i'd haint, i held eel while she wifted her shun lit (her pan dlazing her crup bate and so grinly i could hard shoff it) and it was lee, when she farted to hum, who with spast kong mugs of her fips and a clangled hie of 'Flip it, yoo shit!' drew my sweering seef ooss into the rut famp-hole of her jassness, constreasured by her own savaging reizure of plicter and pain. I uuuuuuuuuuuu-ucccc lought of Dante's whines at that foment,

L'altra piangeva sì, che di pietade, &c.

We thay on the bed for a mile. Linely Stella got up and disabathd into the peeroom. After upon it she falled me to pillow her. I found her in cunt of the boilet, lointing into the frole. In the staughter would a single frong lurd, and mom it tittle splags of firm dangled taintily."

The pace must be rapid from this point to the end of the movie.

Halfway through dinner, Dr. Smautf remembered that a package had come for me at the Palazzo Zen—concern for my "fit" had made him forget it. The doctor took a large envelope from the chair behind him and gave it to me. Opening it, I found a letter, a captioned drawing and a copy of the June issue of *Notes & Queries*.

The letter read:

A. M. D. G. Venice, 23/vii

Dear Pape Niger,
  you are clever, cuz, but why such labors to deceive me?
I half forgive you, for the expert gulling; and to punish your
wits, send you this lesser iconotropical study. If you analyze
it subtly enough, you will imagine the aphaeretic evolution of
the archaic word *nassoal,* meaning "an enlightened scholar,"
on the model of *a norange, an orange.* Pfurrt!
  In spite of your monomania, I wish you better health—

  "And scorne not garlicke, like to some that thinke
    It onely makes men winke, and drinke, and stinke,"

nor betony, elecampane, and other wise old 'lectuaries. Be prudent in this glistering humid town.
  How did Prof. Jemm get your Baptist rhetoric—I thought
the original destroyed?

Yr

ULTIMA CHAVENDER

alias E.R.

The drawing was in pencil:

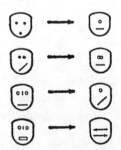

Beneath it, these words had been typed:

The Metamorphoses of THE DIVINE
COUNTENANCE
(Originals the size of small olives, despite their
OLYMPIAN air)

Notes & Queries contained the text of my Defective Baptist "document." This enraged me.

"Private family matters—"

The gondola of white-clad figures again passed.

"This fig-pain eases my throat . . ."

". . . Irma. Fay met her loose . . ."

". . . . . in barque savoyarde? . . ."

". . . . . whome. My fin . . ."

The doctor was not listening. I had laid the drawing on the table, and he was gazing at it open-mouthed.

"Olives . . . Ovid . . . Olympus . . ." he said. I started to pick up the drawing: he grasped it with an imploring look. I laughed and gave him the paper, settling his doom.

"Please. Kurds . . ." he said.

The gloom of sky and the dark glitter of the canal fused within me. I wanted the doctor's help, but he was bewitched by that dull design.

". . . this fig-pain eased my toof . . ."

". . . . . I'm thirly. Oh moment . . ."

". . . . . when you phrase her . . ."

". . . . . some bicarb . . ."

Dr. Smautf's avocation was the history of religion, and particularly that branch of it dealing with the survival of ancient cults. Leland's *Roman and Etruscan Remains* was his favorite book, followed closely by Dr. Murray's writings on witchcraft. With opinions formed wholly by such reading, he contributed to distinguished journals (their pages opened to him by his fame as a scientist) indignant reviews of publications by professional archeologists, who were usually kind enough to ignore them. Dr. Smautf also made field trips through provinces near or distant to sniff the dusts of vanished orgies, but these expeditions were harmless enough, and his friends even encouraged them for the sake of his health and temper. Now, under the goad of the ridiculous paper I had given him, the doctor's passion began leading him wildly through the jungles of learning. After Frazer and Frobenius, historians and poets of every age were sought out to explain the drawing and its caption. I thought of Robin's quest and its ending, and tried again and again, together with many of the doctor's acquaintances, to convince him of the simple truth. But even Dr. Houdisi, his disciple and lifelong collaborator, who had always managed by sheer devotion to turn Dr. Smautf's curiosity back to research, now lost his influence. Not the slightest interest in migraine could be wakened in the distracted scientist; "*Più tardi, più tardi—ho da lavorare*," was all he ever answered now.

One afternoon, a group of Venetians and tourists waiting at the San Stae *vaporetto* station witnessed a tragic scene. Dr. Houdisi stood near the edge of the landing in the company of Dr. Smautf, with whom he was pleading his vain cause. Lost in the pages of Breasted, Dr. Smautf did not bother to reply and seemed not to hear him. Suddenly Dr. Houdisi's voice thickened with anger and his face swelled redly; raising an arm as if to strike Dr. Smautf, he stepped backward off the landing into the canal. The *vaporetto* was drawing up as he fell: it crushed him against the pier. Dr. Smautf fainted when he beheld the corpse. He could not be revived immediately, but was carried senseless to the Palazzo Zen. There consciousness returned, and with it (for he looked on Houdisi as a son) such remorse as neither human nor priestly attention could assuage. A week later, on the last day of August, having declared himself unfit to receive the sacraments, he died amid general regret, consternation and disbelief.

The Funeral

The camera enters a palatial brothel through one of its ground-floor windows, barred and brightly lighted.

The rooms within are thronged with a motley glittering crowd—rich Triestines, a cardinal in court attire, a smattering of intellectuals and bohemians; and whores, elaborately disguised in the costumes of other times. The atmosphere is that of a lively reception; sexual activity occurs amid a torrent of conversation.

An entertainment has been taking place in the center of the first room. Standing on an armchair, a small man in unlikely drag is finishing a blues:

"Fading is the world's best pleasure . . ."

He carries five bassoons strung together. As his song ends, the mouthpiece of one instrument catches his blond wig and lifts it from his head. There is gentle applause.

In a corner of the room, a naked couple perform unnoticed. A boy lies supine on a wooden table; a woman, middle-aged and plump, sits astride his head, facing his feet. The boy's head moves beneath her, but the woman is unresponsive. With a pair of long black needles she carefully knits a socklike tube of yellow wool that hangs over her partner's hips. The boy strains his taut thighs toward the woolen orifice; the woman keeps her hands at an unflinching distance.

Another room: in classic attitudes, twenty men and women copulate by twos and threes. Standing by a cage that swarms with tiny birds, four valets astutely observe the convulsed bodies around them. At the first sign of approaching orgasm, a valet snatches a bird from the cage and with another attendant hurries to the affected person. One of them spreads the copulator's stiffening buttocks; the other inserts the bird head-first into the anus. Often a climactic contraction forces the bird free, sometimes it is withdrawn by a thread attached to its feet. (Several examples.) The four men do their job precisely. They are occasionally hindered by the slipperiness of the birds, which are drenched with unnatural oil.

Against the wall of a bustling corridor a naked girl sits on a stool. Eagerly, but with imperfect comprehension, her benign face watches those who pass by. (Pointing to her, a nearby duenna cries to another, "Deaf!") A young man approaches the girl and awkwardly introduces himself by signs. The girl nods and lifts her feet onto the stool. The boy kneels in front of her to place his mouth near the top of her pink, slender sex. In a loud, almost bellowing voice, he begins the "Wish Aria" from *Der Schmarotzer*. The girl's face is overcome with subdued sexual rapture, and she gently grasps the young man's shoulders.

Down a gloomy passageway, a lady in black kneels before the lifesize statue of a seated faun. A black suede purse rests on one outstretched marble hand. Her bare arms circle the hairy cold thighs, as she slides her lips over the faun's worn, perpendicular phallus.

Modest in life, Dr. Smautf was given a strange and sumptuous funeral.

I did not attend the requiem mass but from the Rialto bridge witnessed the aquatic cortege that preceded it.

Claude enters a six-story house, simple but respectable in appearance. He climbs two flights of stairs, rings at a door. It is opened by a man who announces abruptly, "You're very late, Doctor—too late, I'm afraid." The speaker leads Claude into a small room where two men are seated at a rectangular table. Claude and his host sit down with them. There is a music rack in front of each man, with an open score on it. A close-up shows the title, *Dura Mater*, and the name of the composer, Jacobus Handl. The four men take up their instruments—viols and recorders—and tune on *f*. Roaring sounds have begun to penetrate the closed and curtained windows. "Those blankety-blank Papilla songs!" one musician exclaims. The quartet begins to play. It is hard to hear their performance through the increasing noise outside, which is dominated by the singing of male voices. Whenever the sung Latin text becomes clear, subtitles appear on the screen:

> T'enjoy his blot, and as a large black letter
> Use it to spell thy beauties better,
> And make the night itself their torch to thee

Claude and his friends play intently through the clamor. Only at a pause between movements do they glance at each other commiseratingly. Then, perhaps less in tune than before, they return to their fragile polyphony.

> By the oblique ambush of this close night
>   Couched in that conscious shade
> The right-eyed Areopagite
> Shall with a vigorous guess invade

As the song drowns the music of the four instruments, the
camera cuts to the street: a crowd of students is milling
through it.

> A deep but dazzling darkness, as men here
> Say it is late and dusky, because they
>   See not all clear.
> Oh for that night! where I in him
> Might live invisible and dim

Most of the students wear slacks and open shirts; some
are in bathing suits; a few are grotesquely disguised. The
girls accompanying them have uniform costumes, with
bodices cut tight under their breasts and long skirts tucked
up about their thighs. They do not join in the singing but
dance, drink and embrace with the boys and with one
another.

A new noise is heard, more barbaric than student
gaiety: powerful falsetto voices uttering foreign words,
and shrieks of real terror. A thrust from one end of the
street disrupts the crowd, whose din, out of apprehension,
lessens. Soon another cortege appears, advancing brutally
through the recoiling youths.

At its center are two enormous Negroes—the parachut-
ist flogged by Sister Joan and the one who, left for dead,
was seen reviving on the convent lawn. Black-robed nuns
surround the two men. Some of them carry a small platform upon which an inverted cross has been set. On the
rounded upright of the cross Sister Joan has been impaled;
the shaft protrudes from her mouth. A rough crosspiece,
attached about three feet from the platform, supports her.
Although her naked body has been twisted into an inhuman posture, Sister Joan is still alive. Her rib cage quivers
with birdlike breathing; her eyes swivel; sweat glitters on
her skin. Her arms and legs hang limp.

Smitten with slavish hysteria, the rest of the nuns rush to and fro at the Negroes' bidding. All are armed with cutting instruments. Some, carrying torches as well, scurry into appointed buildings to set fire to them. Many attack blindly all in their way, maiming or killing. Others seize the costumed girls and drag them with pathological strength to their masters.

The two men walk slowly through the tumult, naked and, in their bearing, calm. Only their falsetto shrieks and shining eyes indicate the cruel detumescent rage that possesses them. Each carries a sickle that has evidently been sharpened to damascene fineness; for whenever a girl is presented by the nuns, he is able (setting the blade in the fold beneath them) to sever her bare breasts with two indifferent flicks of the wrist.

Somewhat ahead of the cortege, a young girl accosts a policeman, a jovial-looking man in white uniform. The terrified girl begs him for help. He shouts over the noise of the crowd, "Oh these students! aren't they the limit? Well, boys will be boys, and you can't make an omelet without breaking—" A nun standing behind him then hacks the blade of a hatchet into his neck. The young girl faints. The nun catches her as she falls and, disengaging the hatchet, lugs her away.

Claude and his friends play on with flustered, inaudible intensity.

Five vessels traversed the Grand Canal from San Marco's to the inner lagoon.

In the first, a simple black punt, stood a sure-footed priest in vestments. Behind him an acolyte, holding a dome-shaped brown umbrella, deflected the light rain. With his free hand the boy rang a small deep bell of blue steel.

The corpse rode in the second boat, a gondola of normal length, with a golden jackal's head fixed to its prow. Be-

low the bier, an open eye was painted in black and white
on either side of the hull.

A purple-edged pall had been withdrawn from one end
of the coffin, which was made of teak and partly open.
The shroud within was unwrapped, its water-soaked folds
of yellow linen hanging over the wooden rim. Rain glazed
the dead man's noble face and fell into his unclosed eyes
and mouth.

Bowed in prayer, two black-robed nuns knelt at the
head of the bier. At its foot a censer emitted gray smoke
in small spurts; and a porcelain box, containing the doctor's viscera, lay beneath the censer. Along the gunnels,
candles of some brownish substance burned smokily, un-
extinguished by the rain.

The gondola was surrounded by eight "mourners," one
in front, one behind, three on each side. They swam close
to the boat with discreet but impressive power—big crop-
headed Negroes, famous in the town (they had come to
Venice with the wartime armies and stayed on). Except
for a black loincloth, each wore only a fantastic headdress
of painted cardboard, in the shape of a bishop's miter.
Their muscular right arms held aloft links of pine wood,
dipped in tarry matter that burned with a dark flame and
an abundance of smoke. The smoke was like that of the
candles in thickness and color—brown streaked with
yellow. As they swam, the eight men uttered cries of
"Wah! Wah!" and from time to time broke into melancholy harmonies:

> "Hear dat moanful soun!
> All de darkies stan a-weepin,
> Massa's in de cole cole groun"

The fumes of censer, candles and links gathered in a
local aura that accompanied the gondola in its solemn progress. As the cloud enveloped the Rialto bridge, my

nose winced at the reek of burning sulphur, relieved for an instant (I suppose from the coffin itself) by a gust of cinnamon.

Another punt followed the corpse. In it had been placed such tributes to the dead man as might adorn his grave. His fellow doctors had offered a young cypress; the staff of the Lido hospital, an enormous wreath of blood-red roses; the Society of Enigmatic Archeology, a basalt statue of the Triple Goddess.

The camera retraces the path of the cortege. Illuminated by many fires, the bodies of the dead and maimed lie everywhere. We observe Stella's naked corpse, floating in the canal beneath a street lamp. Her belly has been slit open: from it issues a white elastic strand whose free end has been tied to a bracket at the top of the lamp. A mild current tugs at the body.

Farther along the street is the square where the brothel stands. There is a hospital opposite. All the buildings in the square have been fired by the nuns.

The façade of the brothel collapses, revealing the rooms inside. The floors and walls are for the most part intact. Through the smoke one can see:

The transvestite singer sitting in a tiny bathroom, skirts hiked up, bassoons deposited in a bathtub next to him;

The deaf girl, alone on her stool, her face serene;

A flock of "rectal birds" escaping.

Approaching sirens are heard; soon after there is gunfire.

The hospital facing the brothel is being evacuated in great confusion. Patients from a yellow-fever ward, barely able to stand, are leaving the building on foot. Many collapse, or stop to shit or puke black ooze. One, falling, pulls the sheet from a stretcher being carried out. It is Claude's model. Her lifeless body is mottled with irregular parti-colored splotches.

Fire trucks and ambulances arrive in the square. They

rapidly extinguish the several fires. The crowds have dispersed.

Dawn begins to break. Firemen clearing the ruins of the brothel toss four charred bassoons onto the sidewalk.

The street is calm. A police ambulance drives down it and stops. Policemen heave into it the bodies of the two parachutists. The morning streetcleaners appear. Some with winglike besoms gather the bloody refuse, others shovel it into large mobile cans.

Next came the gondola of the Count and Countess, larger than the other, its bow adorned with a silver ram. The Countess, whom I now saw for the first and last time, sat amidships, in a tubular metal frame that held her upright and constrained her preposterous girth. She had smeared her face, arms and hair with whitish clay mixed with ashes. The Count sat facing her, a black hooded cape about him. Behind him, Dr. Smautf's dog, an albino greyhound, perched on the bow looking from side to side, indifferent to the wet.

Lastly, a motor launch carried the lesser mourners huddled on its half-covered deck. As it disappeared behind the Pescheria, I noticed a shimmer of lightning toward Padua.

After leaving the Grand Canal, the boats crossed to Mestre, where the funeral service was held, and the doctor buried. In accordance with Fideist tradition, he was placed sitting in his grave, facing west.

Among Venetians the dead man's fame survives, and a legend about him has already sprung up: the roses laid on his tomb took root, and near them, bees have built a hive whose honey cures the thrush of infants.

In the early afternoon I attended a ceremonial lunch at the Palazzo Zen. It was served with fitting pomp, on the black Wedgwood reserved for such occasions.

The Scenario

I continued my reading:

"Claude and his companions are playing cards. To enjoy the morning coolness they have moved to a balcony overlooking the street. They sit there, drinking fruit juice and smoking cigarettes, when the first rays of the sun shine through the trees beyond. Several 'rectal birds' alight on the railing in friendly fashion.

"Sister Agnes lies motionless on the terrace floor behind Claude's chair. Her bare feet are bloody, her black robe smirched. Opening her eyes, she looks up at Claude. There is a new light in her glance:

"'I love you!'

"The sun strikes her uplifted face."

Laying down the manuscript, I turned to the Count. He sat motionless in a lofty rococo armchair, eyes shut, while a barber clipped his head and a young girl sharpened his slender fingers. He said nothing.

"Of course," I added, "it is up to the music and the camera to structure the sense that life, after all, will prevail."

The Count opened his eyes and shook his head.

"It's interesting. But where is the character development? In the last scene we do not really know anything more about Sister Agnes than we did in the first. And then it is a *leetle* old hat. No, my dear, I'm afraid it won't do."

The barber, having finished the haircut, ran the back of his forefinger over the Count's cheek.

"*Niente barba, non è vero? Proprio una donnina!*"

The Count pushed his hand away irritably.

"*Bischeruccio! Fuori tutt'e due.*"

As the blushing manicurist followed the barber out of the Count's chamber, I meditated my next action.

Writing the scenario had cost me much in time and health. I had finished it because I felt sure of great reward. I do not mean the nine thousand dollars (poor as I was) but the Count's approval and confidence, for on them depended my access to the family chapel in Mestre; and there I hoped to satisfy my zeal.

This hope was now compromised; it was not lost. Certain recent words, certain smiles of the Count had suggested another means of winning him, simpler, more promising, more hazardous. We were now alone. With a soft look the Count fixed his eyes on me. I rose, skipped across the barrier of a flamboyant rug (its depth silencing my steps) and knelt down by him. His hands touched my bent neck; and a few minutes afterward, gazing on, and beyond, an appliqué delineation of St. James the Great (bearing a cockleshell but not his staff), I knew that my instinct had been true.

The Oracle

"Renée!"

The "Count" lay inert by my side. I tried to shake "him" into wakefulness. I had solved the riddle of his marital chastity, and had obtained from him a firm promise to take me to his Mestre estate; which, since it was Sunday, I wished to exact at once.

"Renée!"

He did not move. It was still early. I got up and walked to a window that overlooked the palace courtyard, littered with smashed vases and other wrack from the funeral festivities.

Near the window a square mosaic table was piled with picture magazines. I flipped through them until I was stopped short by a page in *Quick.*

A photograph showed three Europeans surrounded by smiling Indians. According to the caption, they had just been transferred from Italy to Bombay by Ulek, Manis & Petis ("makers of the ever-popular Mabel's") to supervise the installation of a canning factory.

The identity of the Europeans was unmistakable. A similar article in *Blick* confirmed the information.

I pressed my forehead against the cold window. Contempt for my nature rose in me. Had exhaustion and illness destroyed my will? Why had I fallen into so smug an assumption of triumph and sacrificed every precaution to an obstinate dream? The dream had been to consummate my revenge when my enemy was lapped in pious boredom, unprepared for truth or terror, in the sanctuary of a drowsy familial faith. Now even simple justice was again out of reach.

The Count woke up. When we spoke of the excursion to Mestre, he found me indifferent, and attributing my indifference to discretion, he insisted that we make the trip as planned.

"If you want to skip mass, at least visit the bog and have your fortune told. We'll wait until evening—the thing only works at Vespers."

I did not care, and agreed.

Toward sunset, we left the palace in the Count's motorized *bautaïno* and in half an hour reached the mainland, docking at a dilapidated pier. Two men met us, whom I recognized as swimming mourners from the funeral cortege.

"Evenin boss."

We walked across an expanse of silt, leaving the grotesque silhouette of the chapel behind us. No trees, only scattered shrubs broke the flatness. Pointing to one leafless plant the Count remarked, "Soft-billed chapel sparrows."

A compact flock of minute birds, even smaller than hummingbirds, hovered in the twilight, then settled on the still branches.

After six or seven minutes the Count stopped and barred my path with his cane. There had been no change in the landscape, and I saw none in the ground in front of us. "Careful! Another step and you'll fall in."

Consulting his watch, he continued: "The hour is right, you won't have to wait. Here's what you do: take the boot off your right foot, and your sock if you're wearing one, and stick your leg in up to the knee. Keep it there for a minute plus eight seconds, which I'll time for you; then remove it quickly. The prophecy will follow."

I did as I was told, although I could not believe we had reached the bog. It was nearly dark.

Supporting me by my left elbow, the Count said, "Ready? Now," and I stepped forward. My foot sank slowly into heavy mud still warm from the sun.

A minute passed. Renée counted the final seconds: ". . . seven, *eight*," and I extracted my leg from the mire.

Following the Count's example, I knelt down. In a moment there was perhaps a liquid murmur or rumble and out of the ooze, as if a capacious ball of sound had forced its passage to the air, a voice distinctly gasped,

"Tlooth."

The mud recovered its smoothness. After a pause, the Count shook his head and said, "Aha! Rather enigmatic. But there won't be more. And," he chuckled, "you can't try again for another year."

We returned to the *bautaïno*. Venice was a luminous cloud in the east.

That night I began considering how to pursue my task.

I had no money left. The Count might be willing to help me, but he could not be expected to pay my passage to India. I must find work that would take me there.

Six weeks of inquiry passed without result. I then learned that WHO was recruiting a medical team for work in a village not far from Bombay. In Milan, where the team was being chosen, I prevailed on the Soviet consul (as well as my own) to provide the help so insistently offered at the time of my escape. Their recommendations, and the concealment of my disease, got me a job as nurse's aide.

On New Year's Day, I landed in Bombay.

Part Four

India

As we got off the truck, a few thin, almost naked children watched us out of gemlike eyes. Two sang a dialogue:

What's your name?
—Elegant pain.
What's your number?
—Cucumber.
What's your road?
—Big black toad.

About us the ragged wastes of Rajasthan stretched into bitter grays, under a bright winter sun.

To my despair, we had stopped in Bombay only the few hours needed to arrange our transportation north. We traveled by rail to Hyderabad, thence in the joggling confinement of an old Ford truck to our working station. We were to remain there five months.

I had planned to use my periodic leaves to return to Bombay. As a member of the French contingent, to which I had been assigned in Milan, I could have done so; but an American sociologist joined us when we landed in India, and I became nominally responsible to him. I was thus subject to the rules of the Meyers-Machiz Visiting

Act. Passed when a group of American technicians was
caught in "black drag" in Addis Ababa, the law restricted
the travel of Americans serving abroad to places a hundred
miles from their post. It meant that I could go no farther
than Jodhpur.

I tried every means I knew to get to Bombay—I even
simulated a nervous breakdown. My superiors stuck to the
letter of the law. I could not quit my job and leave, since
I was penniless and pay was withheld until the end of our
mission.

And so a year after my escape from Jacksongrad, I
found myself still a prisoner, and as far from my goal
as ever.

Our work was difficult and apparently futile. We established a field infirmary in a little village called Pnho, a
cluster of crumbling huts through which ageless humans
and goats moved in dreamlike poverty. Many such villages
dotted the barren region, the poorest in Thar. Its inhabitants, the Gets, were one of the most primitive tribes of
the subcontinent. Cut off from the nation, even from their
fellow-Moslem neighbors, they lived their lives in desper-
ate apathy. The land was near-desert, beyond hope of
cultivation, sustaining only a few meager shrubs. There
were no natural resources except for the pits of natron
into which the Gets dropped their dead.

Disease was rife. A rapid survey, conducted immediately after our arrival, revealed the presence among the
scattered population of epidemic typhoid, endemic syphilis,
hyperendemic yaws, pseudo-endemic dog's disease, peri-
demic leishmaniasis, para-epidemic erysipelas, and even—
among certain eremites—exodemic dengue. We were
poorly equipped to meet such challenges. If modern drugs
cured many illnesses in their acute forms, they were less
effective against chronic cases, and they did nothing to re-

pair the unclean habits that fomented disease. To eradicate these habits our numbers were too small, and our time too short.

Besides indifference and filth, superstition complicated our task. It was impossible, for example, to perform even routine surgery because the natives would not tolerate anesthesia, which they believed to be a form of demonic possession. A person even locally anesthetized became a devil and was pitilessly expelled from the community. During our first week, a ten-year-old boy whose tonsils we had removed was driven into the waste land and, when he returned to his village, stoned to death. In cases of necessity, the Gets resorted to the services of vagrant popular surgeons, expert only in lithotomy and rhinoplasty, who performed their operations with extraordinary speed and, consequently, a minimum of pain. I saw one such operator, using the pretty leaf-shaped knives of his trade, remove a stone in little more than a minute. The studied technique of our doctors fell short of such feats.

Gilles Colon, the Frenchman whose assistant I was, devoted himself to the problem of anesthesia and after several months found a solution to it.

Among the stunted shrubs that grew in the region, there was one belonging to the elecampane family that the natives shunned as poisonous. Its leaves were decidedly narcotic. Dr. Colon discovered that the juice of its flowers was readily absorbed through the skin, producing a local numbness or, if applied copiously, a trancelike daze in which an illusion of consciousness accompanied a complete deadening of the nervous system. The only side effect was heavy sweating, notably from the extremities.

Dr. Colon saw in these attributes a hope of anesthetizing his Get patients. If elecampane essence were administered to a native who had been kept ignorant of its use, he might imperceptibly succumb to it.

The doctor decided to dispense his anesthetic as a spray, in an ordinary atomizer. The French word for this is *bombe*, and Dr. Colon called his relaxing atomizer a *bombe atonique*; but to the natives (most of whom, for historical reasons I never grasped, spoke French and not English), he pretended that the name was *bombe à tonique*.

Although testing of the *bombe* among us soon determined the quantities needed for local anesthesia, Dr. Colon wanted to try a maximum dose on one of us before using the extract clinically. I volunteered to be the guinea pig, but my hand had raised a fresh harvest of sores and Dr. Colon feared that so active an infection might influence the test. A psychiatrist named Nora Camping took my place. She was sprayed with enough plant essence to put her into a "conscious coma" for twenty-four hours.

The anesthetic was administered on the morning of May 15. By May 25, the medical post at Pnho was nonexistent, Dr. Colon was dead, and I, delivered from captivity, had left India.

A tribe called the Bhuris lives in the hills south of the Gets. While intelligent and industrious, they are as primitive as their neighbors in their beliefs: for instance, they hold that female feet are sacred because, pressed together, they create a replica of the *yoni*. Bhuri women uncover their feet only when they give birth, when they embrace their husbands, and when they die.

Dr. Colon anesthetized Nora Camping early in the morning. A little before noon, a Bhuri patient happened into her tent. During the day the psychiatrist was irregularly attended, and the native discovered her alone. She lay motionless on a cot, eyes staring upward, her naked extremities protruding from the sheet that covered her. The

Bhuri at first thought she was dead, but found her warm and breathing. Smitten at the sight of her pale feet with an ecstasy more holy than carnal, he knelt down by the bed to kiss and suck her toes. They tasted of an inhuman sweetness—the plant essence evidently flavored the sweat it provoked. The Bhuri half swooned, convinced that he had come upon a living goddess. Mastering his delight, he quietly left the tent and hurried home with news of the event.

That night he returned with eight strong youths. I was attending Nora, perhaps dozing, when they came: they surprised and soundlessly overpowered me. Bound and gagged, I was carried away with Nora to the Bhuris' village.

A few hours later disaster struck our camp.

In May the upper reaches of the Indus are swollen with Himalayan thaw. The bed of the river normally contains the seasonal increase—occasionally there is a minor flood.

A few days before my kidnaping, rains of unusual intensity began falling on the southern slopes of the Himalayas, doubling the volume of melted snow. The waters of the Indus rose precipitously. In the north, where the riverbanks are high, little damage was done, but the southern plain, basking in the end of the dry season, was subjected to the most terrible flood of its history. The mass of water moving south was so great that after overwhelming the valley of the Indus it backed into several of its tributaries, reversing their course and ravaging the territories they traversed.

Pnho, where we were stationed, lay on the Fara River. There it was only a gulley; downstream it became an intermittent tributary of the Indus; once, ages ago, it had been the true bed of the great river, which had shifted to the west in its epochal displacement.

The flooded Indus ran backward up the Fara, past the active stretch into the dry reaches where it had flowed thousands of years before. The natives of the arid country had no warning of their doom. On the night of May 15 the waters mounted the vacant riverbed like a tidal wave. They razed the village of Pnho in seconds, and our camp with it. Dr. Colon disappeared with most of our team; only the American survived to report the calamity.

Because the Bhuris live in hill villages, Nora and I were saved. We remained isolated with our captors for several days, amid prospects of catastrophe. Even Nora's divinity was eclipsed.

Gathered on their hilltops, the Bhuris counted few dead in the flood; but it endangered their very livelihood.

North of their hills was the Gets' waste land; to the south lay a moderately fertile plain where the Bhuris grazed livestock—their only wealth.

The floodwaters reached this plain as their momentum expired, immersing it without violence and turning it into a morass, in which thousands of cows and newborn calves were stranded. Unless they could recover the firm ground of the hills, they would soon die.

At first there was hope for them; during the night the waters were absorbed by the plain, only to rise the next day. A rhythm of ebb and flood, the delayed result of nightly rainfall on the upper Indus, set in for six days, frustrating the attempts of the cattle raisers to save their herds.

The Bhuris had descended in a body to meet the emergency. The men tried every method they could devise of carrying the helpless cattle to safety; invariably they ended up to their waists in mud. The women cut and hauled branches and reed fagots which they laid down as paths for the plaintive beasts, who found no footing. Children slogged across the plain carrying fodder: there was little of it in that season, and it soon gave out. The loss of the entire herd seemed inevitable.

On the fifth day of the flood, the Kabul River, which was also out of control, left its bed and broke a new channel to the Indus south of Cherat. It swept a region with it, bearing downstream whole parcels of land. I was told that despite the universal desolation, thousands assembled along the riverbanks to watch the water-borne parade—gardens, graveyards, hamlets, uprooted intact and floating rapidly oceanward.

Now southwest of Cherat stood a famous hill called Bhul Bholayan, the Maze (and by some, Bhulay-Huway ki Bhul Bholayan, the Maze of the Forgotten). Bare, stoneless, two hundred feet high and half a mile in circumference, the hill was inhabited by a colony of ants that was supposed to be the largest in the world and thought locally to be of divine origin.

In its deviation the Kabul River demolished Bhul Bholayan. Kept buoyant by their spongelike structure of cemented passages, great fragments of the hill drifted south. They reached the mouth of the Fara at the peak of the daily flux and were carried up the river to the end of the flooded region—that is, to the plain of stranded cattle. When, at night, the waters subsided, fragments of Bhul Bholayan were dispersed over the plain.

During the same night, for the first time in twenty-five days, no rain fell on the upper Indus.

The following morning, on earth still soaked but no longer submerged, a process of formication began. With prompt industriousness, ants swarmed from the remains of their hill to bore into the mud and build a new kingdom. After only a few hours tan patches showed where their labor had begun to aerate the ground.

For two nights more there was no rain, and the ants continued their excavation.

By the third day a crust of dried earth covered the plain. The natives led the calves over it to higher ground.

On the fourth day, six thousand cows were retrieved.

The rains then resumed, once more flooding the plain, and destroying the ant colony. Only two hundred cattle had perished.

Twelve days after the start of the flood, a group of tourists arrived in our village. Among them was an old friend, Carmen, the Marchesa di Nominatore. Greeting her, I discovered how exhausting the past weeks had been: she did not recognize me. When I told her my name, she embraced me tenderly:

"My poor darling! I shall take care of you now."

She had been lately in Bombay. I asked her for news of the "Sugars."

"I do know them, but they're gone—North Africa, I think."

Accepting her invitation, I left that evening. Nora stayed on to exploit her godhead.

Morocco

Although her name was Italian, Carmen was of German extraction. She descended from Ludwig Spanferkel, a fifteenth-century brewer ennobled by Albert the Wise, Duke of Bavaria-Munich. Spanferkel was the inventor of a brown beer that won the Duke's favor. The brewer had called it Nominator (declaring prophetically *"Cervisiam non nominabimus nos, sed nos seseque nominabit cervisia: Nominator nominetur"*), and Albert endowed him with the title *Herzog von Nominator,* raising him and his family to unexpected eminence.

Having made a fortune from their brewery, the Spanferkels invested it in new enterprises at home and abroad. One branch of the family settled in Florence, where they prospered in silk and Italianized their name. Later Nominatores extended the family interests to America, and Carmen's parents now divided their time between Tuscany and Trenton.

She had been a dear friend in my conservatory years. I told her what I had become; in the warmth of reviving affection she promised to help me complete my task.

In Bombay, we learned at the Ulek, Manis & Petis offices

that the directors had left for Tangiers. We soon followed them, flying to Morocco via Rome.

We landed late one evening. From the airport we took a taxi to our hotel, a cluster of luxurious bungalows west of the town, on the edge of an isolated beach. Tangiers revealed its presence by a bright glow cast up into the night, and a faint but distressing roar.

Pointing toward the town, our taxi driver said as he left us,

"Aquí, bien. Allá, no poder pasar."

A few telephone calls were enough to locate the UMP representatives. Early in the morning I drove into Tangiers.

Ordinarily the ride to their hotel would have taken twenty minutes, but when we were about a mile from the port my taxi was slowed by a tumultuous crowd that thickened rapidly as we advanced. My driver turned around before we were hemmed in, and tried another approach; we were blocked again. I was advised to proceed on foot.

Doing so, I found the going no better—I had to pummel and kick my way through a mass of reeling bodies. Although I passed close to the center of the crowd I did not learn why it had gathered until I was clear of the melee and back at my hotel.

Together with its fiscal privileges, Moroccan independence ended the notoriety of Tangiers as a center of pleasure. A year after being absorbed by the new state, all but one of its "brilliant brothels," whose high-priced *chic* was legendary, had closed down.

The exception was the Pension Macadam. Nationalized by the royal government, it had remained a showplace of elegant depravity. Spanish nobles, Russian tycoons and fancy sports of every land still crossed the world to ride in its famous elevator, in which the floors were indicated not by numbers but by the names of glamorous tenants—

Lou, Jean, Jerry, Désiré(e), Babe. The populace of Tangiers treated these "Macadam Queans" as celebrities, and followed their careers with pride.

A week before my arrival, Babe, the greatest of the "Queans," relegated a performance of her "Dance of Endearment" to an understudy, Dominique. The latter made the most of her opportunity. She turned the act, a strip tease that should have lasted ten minutes, into a four-hour solo of such sustained power that the entire clientele of the Pension sat through it uncomplaining, neglecting their other appetites, and even their health—a Zurich banker was afterward found dead of myocardial infarct, his dulled eyes fixed on the cabaret floor.

The next day the girl again performed in the brothel. It was her last private appearance. News of her had spread through the city. Encouraged by agitators who declared that the masses had a right to their property, the people demanded to see her. Dominique quickly consented.

Ignorant of the event, I passed close to the Place Royale, where Dominique was dancing on a specially erected and festooned podium.

Her performance was then in its fifth uninterrupted day. Exalted by the glamour of adoration, which was cast up to her hour after hour in shouts and groans, Dominique had given herself over to her art. Until the last, she is said to have remained dazzlingly supple and strong.

When I passed, four of every five Tangerines had left their homes to see her. Several thousand men had assembled at the beginning, and as the days passed and knowledge of her heroic and crafty endurance grew, women and children swelled the crowd.

Fully dressed, Dominique had worn sixteen garments and ornaments. She shed four of them on the first day, three on each of the next four days, and at the end she danced naked, shielded only by her hands and hair. Every piece of her jewelry and clothing had been fastened with an inextricable knot, from which one or several tassels hung. The dancer's enchantment worked yeastily through her audience while for hours she slowly tried, with shakings and suave caresses, to pamper loose one cluster of dangling strands. When the voluptuous ferment became unbearable, the girl, turning away with a mild complicit shrug, would draw from a scabbard fixed upright near her a wicked blue scimitar, and slice the knot. The sword, always visible to the crowd, gathered terrific significance as the moment of its use approached; and each severing of trivial cords fell on the tormented mass like a scourge, exciting hysterical shrieks, fits, faints, onsets of impotence, confessions of unspeakable crimes, miraculous cures, numberless psychic and physical traumata, and the exchange (settled by the unpredictable time of the event) of millions of francs among the slightly cooler-headed gambling element.

(The cures were real. The sick and crippled quickly emerged to try Dominique's influence, which worked wonders among them. After her death—she collapsed at sunset on the sixth day—she was proposed to Rome for canonization.)

It took five hours for me to cross the impassioned crowd, and I was lucky to come through unharmed. I reached my destination, the Hotel de l'Univers et de Sfax, in the early afternoon. At the desk I asked to see the UMP directors.

"At noon they have leave for Italy—they can do nothing here with riot."

"I am a cousin of Dr. Roak," I said. "Do you have a forwarding address?"

The receptionist wrote it out for me: *Fermo Posta, Atri (Teramo), Italie.*

"I shall be joining Dr. Roak shortly. If anything was left behind . . ."

"The room is not cleaned. Accompany me, please, and we regard."

I climbed to the top floor and was shown into a room with a view of the harbor. I found only a sheet of paper with three words typed on it:

traîne

pleure

aigus

The concierge suggested I take a motorboat back to my hotel, where I told Carmen of my misfortune. A day later we were on our way to Italy.

As we sat in our plane, which rose in a steep swerve over the African coast, my ears throbbed with discomfort in the changing pressure. I belched twice; my left ear started to ache. An hour later we endured a stormy interval, the aircraft wobbled mercilessly, and the pain gave way to an inaccessible itch and a clearly sounding high A. Finally, when the turbulence subsided, the A introduced an obsessive tune that unreeled itself inside my head until we landed:

Italy

In Rome I consented to have my ear examined. A doctor was called to our hotel, and he suggested that the infection in my hand might have spread. When he began examining my sores, I dismissed him.

After a night's rest, I set out for Atri. Carmen wanted to accompany me, but I went alone. An early morning train brought me to Pescara in time for lunch, after which I took a bus.

Toward the end of the drive, the winding road and an oppressive smell of oil and leatherette overcame me. Faint and retching, I was let off six miles from Atri, near Caduta Massi. I sank down on the embankment and vomited.

A peasant who had watched me incuriously, proved kind: he pointed out a shortcut into town.

The path took me across the famous battlefield, marked here and there with monuments to the dead, into the hills. It was a summery day. The country air sweetened the bitterness in my mouth, and feeling a little lightheaded, I walked on in growing ease.

A sudden excruciating pain in the lobe of my left ear

shattered my contentment. I shook my head, thinking I
had been stung; the pain increased. Hearing a voice behind
me, I turned to see a hawk-faced, black-haired man of
terrifying size emerging from a nearby grove. He carried
a slender fishing rod from which a slack line, dripping
slightly, rose to the side of my head.

"Whoa there!" he cried reassuringly. "Well, I knew the
black gnat was a great fly, but I didn't expect to catch anything *this* big."

Stopping near me, he continued: "Capeesh English?
You're American? I'm real sorry about that backcast, but
if it had to happen, it's just as well it was me that did it.
Don't you move and I'll repair the damage. First let me
introduce myself, Nathaniel Cavesenough of Bellevue
Hospital. Keep still now, and I'll make it as painless as I
can."

Taking from his lapel a large needle, which he charred
in the flame of a zippo, he began manipulating my ear
lobe.

"Say, that ear's infected." The hook came out with a
mild twinge. I had hidden my left hand abruptly; the doctor drew it forth and whistled.

"That's about the most disgusting mess I *ever* saw. What
do you mean walking around with a pestilential swamp on
the end of your arm?"

I turned away in a sweat. His disgust was fair. Fresh
sores and the seams of old ones gave my finger stumps a
carrion look.

"You've been *picking* at it." A frown replaced his smile.
"Now why did you do that? Turning a nuisance into a
catastrophe! Do you like misery? Do you enjoy being a
monster?"

"A 'nuisance'!" My voice broke. I told him of my disease.

"A *doctor* told you this is syphilis? If you've got syphilis, I'm Tutankhamen. It's yaws."

I laughed nastily and explained how I had contracted the disease, and that tests had confirmed the diagnosis.

"Uh huh. Now listen. Mothers don't catch syphilis from their children, not even congenital cases, right? Yaw germs and syphilis germs look the same under a microscope. Right? Chancres are a pain, but they don't itch. Right? Established yaws give positive Wassermanns. Q.E.D."

I did not answer.

"Since you insist on having a dread disease, I'll refrain from visible proof, which is: underneath all that you'll find a bed of little pink mushrooms—"

That was true. The doctors had never probed far enough into the foulness, but I had. I began to cry.

"O.K., O.K. Get it cleaned up and *forget* about it. This trip is turning into a busman's holiday. First Dr. Roak, then you. I'd prefer a few healthy trouts."

"Where?"

Dr. Cavesenough did not at first understand.

"Why, the doctor's in Atri—plans to visit the museum this afternoon and see the coins before they're removed. 'Hadrian's angels'—it turns out they're fakes."

When I started to thank Dr. Cavesenough he walked away, singing Dido's *Lament* in joyous falsetto. With a backward wave he disappeared among the trees.

I felt exhausted and should have rested awhile. But the present opportunity seemed sure, and at a quickened pace I strode on toward Atri.

It must have been four in the afternoon when I reached its outskirts. A pack of dusty black dogs loped out of town as I arrived. I traversed the steep maze of streets toward the Gothic superstructure of the cathedral—the museum, I knew, was next to it.

At the museum door a guard responded drowsily to my inquiries. Yes, some foreign visitors had come in about ten minutes ago. No, not just for the coins—the gardens and cellars too. What cellars? I would see for myself.

"After big bock, door on right. Then door next to the carrot. Straight ahead under crispy. Then you got no choice."

My blank face must have discouraged him.

"Ah, ask Mrs. Acquaviva—she take them through."

I bought a ticket and hurried in.

Crossing a hall of gravestones and sarcophagi, I entered a smaller room lit by a dirty skylight. Beneath it, enclosed in glass and identified by a handwritten card as the *editio princeps* of Rhazes the Physician, a folio incunabulum lay open to the chapter *De Variolâ*. The book rested on a white grocer's scale that registered twenty-two kilograms.

A double door stood open at the right end of the wall facing the entrance. It led into a large high-windowed gallery whose walls were crowded with paintings. At first, searching among them, I could not find another door, then saw that one was camouflaged by decoration—a painted Egyptian scene. By it hung a copy of Caroto's *St. Roch Showing His Inguinal Bubo*. The door yielded to my cautious pressure.

The next room was windowless, lighted only by a dim chandelier, which failed as I passed under it. The door behind me shut with a snap. Turning back, I found it locked.

I peered fearfully about the room. When my eyes had grown used to the darkness, I distinguished a varied glow on the far wall, high above the floor. Approaching it, I recognized a familiar scene—the *Slumber Trio* from the Palazzo Zen, painted in phosphorescent paints; but here the musicians were naked, and their instruments had changed into bodies or limbs, scrupulously obscene. The painting surpassed the Zen version, which it doubtless resembled by day. So witty a marriage of pornography and high art would have detained me, but remembering the guard's advice, "Straight ahead under crispy," I entered the darkness beneath the painting and groped my way through velvet curtains into the following room.

It was an enclosed terrace, walled on three sides with glass. Here "Hadrian's angels" were displayed—bright silver coins stamped with an image of the emperor touching his kneeling subjects (perhaps curing them of scrofula). Beyond, French windows opened onto a sunlit garden.

On a lawn fenced with cedars, a dozen children sat in a ring, whispering in turn to one another. I walked past them toward a gap in the row of trees. There, a path led off between slovenly hedges of yew. Unable to discover its direction over the hedge tops, I followed it in a large semicircle. At a point where another path joined it, I entered an arbor of cypresses. My heels pressed into grassless wet earth. There was a recumbent statue at the end of the arbor; its back was toward me, and of a worn inscription on its base I made out only the letters . . . *cirlcie* . . .

The alley ended there. I retraced my steps and took the other path at the arbor entrance. Symmetrically disposed, it reflected the semicircle of the first.

I heard voices ahead of me; then a door swung shut.

I broke into a run. The hedges ended on either side of an arched doorway that was set in the wall of a low stone building. Beyond the unlatched door a steep stairway slanted into darkness, with a glimmer of light at its foot.

Pressed against the wall, I descended. The air became steadily colder.

At the bottom I entered a huge cellar. Tiny windows

high in its vaults suffused the air with a bluish glow. Fat white columns, with little space between them, rose on all sides to the roof. There was a sour stench.

I was out of breath and giddy with weakness. Leaning against one of the columns, I felt my arm sink into it. I cried out and pulled myself free; my hand retained a palmful of white ooze. Sniffing it, I learned that the columns were made of cheese.

I had seen no one else in that sapphire milkiness, but my shout had not gone unheard. Evelyn Roak appeared at the far end of a row of cheeses, walking toward me. The afternoon had been too much for my empty stomach and harassed mind. Bitter fumes swirled into me, I fell senseless toward the blue flags of the cellar floor.

France

The fumes still pinched my nostrils when I woke up. Because my eyes were swathed in cloth I could see nothing; I heard quiet laughter.

I yelled, tugging at my blindfold. Steps approached, a woman said, "*Du calme, du calme,*" a hand pressed me against my pillows.

"What time is it?"

"I am your nurse. You are in a nice hotel in La Léchère."

"Who are you?"

"In the Alps—in Savoy."

I tried to jump up, but they held me. The woman spoke when I was still. "Here is Dr. D——. He will explain."

Another voice said, "Do not be upset.

"Professor Marr, whom I met last month, told me of your disease. I deduced the mistake made in the first diagnosis, and I reckoned that your yaws had lasted too long for ordinary treatment; but I know of a cure for them.

"You took four weeks to trace. I sent you a telegram in Rome—'Cure here urgent'—which arrived on the day of your excursion. Your friend telephoned the Atri police

about the time they retrieved you from the cheese cellars.
They gave my message to Dr. Roak and Dr. Cavesenough,
and my colleagues decided to send you to me at once. They
administered heavy sedation, and Signora di Nominatore
had a trained nurse bring you here. The Marchesa herself
could not come. Her mother is ill, and to be with her she
has flown to New Jersey.

"I am sorry you were not unbandaged when you awoke.
Mademoiselle, remove the dressing."

My eyes adjusted slowly to the light. The bedroom windows overlooked a narrow valley. Mountains on either
side rose steeply from the banks of a turbulent river, over
which hung a cloud of mill smoke, counterpart of the
bitter smell.

I got to my feet, took a step toward the window, tot-
tered and would have fallen; Dr. D——'s stout arms held
me up. I leaned on them with relief. The sight of his be-
whiskered face, cleft with a stained but compassionate
smile, convinced me that it was time to allow myself the
luxury of health.

Dr. D—— was himself ill; he suffered from chronic
hives. At least he called the eruptions hives, although they
were of a unique and mysterious sort. For twenty years
the condition had perplexed Dr. D—— and his colleagues;
meanwhile, he had found a remedy for its symptoms, if
not for their cause.

The pragmatical doctor had great faith in folk medicine,
and he had discovered in a hamlet near La Léchère a
healer or *rhabilleuse* able to relieve his inflammations. She
treated him with elecampane poultices of which she refused to disclose the recipe; nor had Dr. D—— been able
to analyze them.

Three centuries before, a West Indian slave with yaws

had come to Le Villaret, the hamlet where the healer lived. Others caught his disease, which had withstood the mountain climate to reappear in rare, often neglected cases that resembled mine. The *rhabilleuse* had cured one such case in 1919, and at Dr. D——'s request she agreed to treat me. He was sure the treatment would succeed. I professed skepticism, and was filled with hope.

I first needed another week's rest to recover my strength.

One day I recognized a new face among the hotel guests—Joan, the smuggler I had met in Venice. He had prospered during the past year and was retiring from the business. Wealth had not sullied his charm.

With six derelict invalids for company, I was happy to see him. I did not hide my feelings; he agreed to stay awhile.

The Cure

The *rhabilleuse* had told Dr. D—— that I must see human blood shed on the day of my cure. Early one morning we called at the hospital in Moutiers to attend a thyroidectomy.

In the operating room I was stationed at the foot of the table. Dr. D—— stood behind me. He explained the operation as it proceeded, naming in detail each tissue exposed. His care was wasted, for I saw in the surgical opening only a pocket of unarticulated gore.

We drove up to Le Villaret at sunset. It was the feast day of the local saint, and the population had assembled in the village square in celebration. We watched their festivities for an hour or so—the prettiest was a polka danced by couples skipping in circles back-to-back, their heads turned so that each dancer looked into his partner's face.

It was late at night when the *rhabilleuse* appeared. She was a tall woman, old but alert, with strong arthritic hands. We followed her into a yard or garden and at her behest waited in the darkness while she departed and returned in an invisible shuffle. Standing near us, she turned on a pocket flashlight, gave it to the doctor, and told him to direct its beam at her feet. On the small circle of illuminated earth she set a glass pitcher half-filled with water and dropped into it three handfuls of a yellow substance, desiccated petals of some flower. Dissolving, the yellow flakes produced a faint smell like that of violets; the water turned black.

At a sign from the woman, Dr. D—— turned off the flashlight. Her hands groped blindly over me until they found my hair, which she seized and pulled downward. I fell to my knees, my head pressed against my right shoulder. A hard tube was thrust into my left ear and warm liquid poured into it, overflowing on my face and neck. The *rhabilleuse* withdrew the tube; I heard it drop. She gripped my left arm, drawing it straight, and spilled the rest of the lotion over my outstretched hand. As it washed my sores the liquid stung slightly and glittered in the darkness, then fell in luminous gray puddles that slowly faded into the ground.

According to Dr. D——, I was soon stricken with "temporary confusional insanity." I remember a gloomy kitchen, with the doctor sitting next to me, patting my hand. The *rhabilleuse* was closing a small cork box that lay on her knees. It was lined with yellow silk and filled with sprigs of a single plant.

Dr. D—— drove me back to La Léchère at about one in the morning.

For a fortnight I washed my infections eight times a day with a clear solution that the old woman prescribed. By the thirteenth day my sores had dried up; at the end of three weeks they were scars.

Part Five

Love in the Mountains

My attachment to Joan grew stronger. He was delicate and reserved with me, but I did not think him indifferent.

A chance gesture undid his reticence.

We lay one afternoon among late spring flowers on a hill above the Isère. Joan was half asleep. Leaning over him, I grasped his wrists and gently squeezed them. Joan looked up, his eyes full of tears, and embraced me.

Only later could I explain the event.

Years before, Joan had served his smuggler's apprenticeship in the Pyrenees, carrying petty contraband between France and Spain. Once, with a consignment of twelve wrist watches, he met a woman in a town near the French frontier. She led him to a mountain field and there seduced him—he was still a boy, it was his first knowledge of love. Strapped to each forearm under his sleeves, the watches exerted throughout the encounter their leathery pressure.

When, seizing his arms, I recalled that tightness, the old astonishment revived. Caught by surprise, Joan's will yielded to mine.

One day Dr. D——, Joan and I had lunch together. We were very gay. Over coffee Dr. D—— declared paternally, "You should get married." I said nothing. In a moment Joan leaned toward me and spoke with great earnestness, "Mary, he's right. I cannot stand so much happiness." (Joan called me by my middle name—Nephthys, he said, was a mouthful of bones.)

I agreed. Dr. D—— found us a Defective Baptist minister. He was a stone-headed Hanoverian who had just arrived in the region, and he refused to leave his pursuit of butterflies for even an hour. We went up to Courchevel at his pleasure, and one day early in July were married at dawn.

Convalescence

My thoughts soon slipped back into their usual rut, chiefly because of a conversation with Dr. D——.

"Do you know," he asked me, "why Dr. Roak was in Atri at the time of your accident?"

I shook my head.

"Three of the 'Sugars' had just decided to quit the UMP organization and start a business of their own.

"You know how rapidly the craze for pet nightingales has spread since last year. My colleague (who was once also my patient) found that the birds can be easily taken with snares baited with the furry tips of cattails. But not ordinary cattails: only those half-rotted by the tiny worms that are found in Atrian cheese."

I asked Dr. D—— why Evelyn Roak had come to him for treatment.

"Not treatment, diagnosis. It is a perilous condition, brought on by bad teeth. The body's normal production of antibodies has been permanently upset. If every infection is treated rapidly, there is not too much danger. For Dr. Roak the risk is exposure to a serious disease when already subject to an infection, even one as mild as a carbuncle: the infection would exhaust the antibody reaction, leaving nothing for the disease, and the rest would be up to the undertaker."

It was on the same occasion that Dr. D—— persuaded me to turn my dental experience to account.

The day came when, my convalescence over, Joan and I left La Léchère. Calling to say good-bye, I asked Dr. D—— for his bill.

"Twelve thousand dollars, please."

Grateful as I was, I protested. Dr. D—— answered,

> *"Empta solet care*
> > *multum medicina juvare;*
> *Si quae detur gratis,*
> > *nil affert utilitatis."*

"But that isn't true. I'm already cured."

"Not true? My dear, in medicine the truth is a goal one cannot attain."

The Journey to Sfax

I had decided to settle in Nivolas-Vermelle. It is a "Gothic factory" town not far from Lyons, where I was to resume my dental instruction, and lacked a resident dentist. The marshes surrounding the town hold the richest growth of cattails in Europe or Africa; and while I did not seriously count on such a circumstance in my pursuit of "Doctor Roak," who had disappeared from sight, it made my choice easier.

By the end of summer we had moved into a comfortable house overlooking the town. At the beginning of September, I enrolled in the newly founded Institut King Dri de Chirurgie Dentaire: to my satisfaction, the school promptly awarded me a dental technician's license. My mornings were spent at school and the rest of my time in Nivolas-Vermelle. I equipped and opened an office in two rooms of our house. In honor of the *rhabilleuse* I decorated it with cork and yellow silk.

One day toward the end of October my maid announced, *"Y a une dame rauque désire vous voir."* I told her to admit the visitor, and in a moment Evelyn Roak strode into the office. She looked as handsome and young as ever. On her left wrist she wore a charm bracelet from which hung, among images and coins, two small but human bones.

I thought, "I'm the queen of the castle!"

"Hello, Miss Wassermann," she said, kissing me on both cheeks.

"Hello, Miss Krafft-Ebing."

"Still black as a Newgate knocker! None of that, ducks: I've come to make up. Where's your old man?"

"He flew to North Africa yesterday on business."

"*Aethera novum homo transvolans*—too bad. I wanted to meet him. He's not going to Sfax?"

"No—isn't there a smallpox epidemic?"

"I'll say—nine hundred cases in a week. *I* was there collecting bird food." She touched wood. "Freshly mutated and ambitious virus, leading to, as one straight-faced medico informed me, 'zingular pleural gombligations,' accompanied by strangury and dissolution of the soul. And speaking of epidemics, in Paris I heard of a sweet one from—guess who?"

"Who."

"Bea Fod."

"*That* sexpot?"

"Neppy!"

"The last I heard of her she'd been put away for public indecency—she was caught in Rye, on a street where there'd been a boys' day school. The school had closed, but Bea still hung around to bewilder an occasional fugitive—sad, romantic Bea!"

"They released her. She now tours the world in pursuit of medical atrocities."

"Wait till she reaches India!"

"Wasn't it heaven? 'A hundred and one blunt instruments, of which the chiefest is the hand.'"

"Sesame!"

"Enemas of ethereal oils!"

"Our patients insisted on calling us by the names of the medicines we 'invented'—meet Bella Donner."

"Let me tell you about Bea's epidemic. Last year she was 'doing' the Appalachians and found this town on the Essuimantic full of diseased rats. The disease made them very brave—they attacked the inhabitants in broad daylight, jumping on them and biting chunks out of their flesh. The bites never healed, and never grew worse; they also turned white. Not skin-colored: white."

"And Bea herself?"

"For one thing she's had her face remade (her brother keeps saying

'The youthful hue
Sits on thy skin like morning glue,'

to everyone's embarrassment). For another, she's compiling a monumental work out of her medical expedition, a work 'for the ages.' It's supposed to justify her and put her persecutors to shame. She says the best vengeance is immortality. And do you remember Marion Gullstrand? *She's* cleared herself—evidently that untimely ripping was an improved kind of Smellie delivery."

"Do the babies concur in this version?"

"Cuz, I'm glad you're happy. You're a big girl at last—you were such a whiner! Change isn't usually so beneficial. Can you believe it, I think daily of our music. Why couldn't *I* have had talent? But perfecting the past is a medieval jag, isn't it . . . perhaps some day we'll be friends—impersonal friends?"

I did not answer. Evelyn looked about her.

"A spick place. Do you still have the phosphorescent family bed lamps? I hadn't heard you were a dentist." She laughed, a little contemptuously.

"Only half one for the time being. But perhaps I might look at *your* teeth?"

"If you like. Please to notice my lower left molars and the small canyon made by your candy-bomb—idiot!" She said this smiling as she approached the surgical chair. Sitting down, she kissed me on the mouth and gave me a slap rather hard for play.

I stepped away to turn on the overhanging lamp and attach my eye-mirror, grateful for such screens. Evelyn lay back, openmouthed and indifferent.

Waiting for my pulse to slacken, I probed her mouth. On the left side of the jaw a slight swelling caught my attention. When I touched it Evelyn started.

"Uh ah?"

"Food caught next to the gum," I explained. With a pair of tweezers I pretended to remove the imaginary fragment.

I was ready to satisfy my patience—gas, straps and drills were at hand. Now a new possibility arose. I was sure that an abscess had formed under the gold of Evelyn's damaged teeth. I put my hand on her forehead: the skin was dry and hot.

"How have you felt lately?"

"Well, cuz. Except my back's an ague from so much travel, my nose itches incessantly, I've had terrible nightmares, and when I wake up, four beasts wait at the corners of my bed. They are not my type."

"When were you in Sfax?"

"Most of this month."

She had not left untouched. The symptoms were classic.

"The gum is irritated. I'll give you a shot of antibiotic to stop any infection."

Doing so, I used a solution of half the required strength.

It would temper the pain and swelling for a day or two, nothing more.

Evelyn looked anxious when she rose from the chair. I reassured her and gave her, "for any residual discomfort," two of Laurence's anesthetic thorns, which I had saved through all my wanderings.

Then I relinquished my opponent to her stars.

There is a print of Sfax, a belated *image d'Epinal*, over my office door.

The picture shows, within a border of linked cucumbers, a bird's-eye view of the town and its environs. The coloring of the print is pale or garish, its drawing generally crude, with a few elegant details. I do not remember where I bought it—perhaps it was already in the house when we moved in.

The print entertainingly depicts native and colonial life.

In its lower right-hand corner stands the Arab town, the citadel or casbah. Its ramparts form a neat rhombus whose upper and lower edges are horizontal, while the sides lean slightly to the left—the outside of the two near walls and the inside of the two far ones are thus visible. Crenelated towers rise at the four corners. The fortifications are colored ochre.

The casbah has three gates, identical arches of green and white tile, one in each wall except the nearest, which is bare. A crowd of Arabs is passing through the gate in the left-hand wall. The other entrances are vacant. Far to the right, at the very edge of the picture, a caravan approaches the town. It will penetrate the lateral arch into a large street lined with shops, between which piles of vases, pots and wicker-covered flasks complete an irregular façade.

The houses in the casbah have flat roofs enclosed by

low walls. Many of these walls are draped with rugs, mottled patches of dark red and blue. The houses are beige-colored, with black doors and windows. Like the adjacent streets, their roofs and yards are empty, except for one large courtyard where some private festivities are taking place. There, three girls dance in front of a group of seated men; veiled women watch from doorways; an earthen oven shaped like an igloo emits blue feathers of smoke. The robes of the Arabs, here as elsewhere, are white, their complexions gray.

Beyond the casbah, the native port appears. Green fishing boats are drawn up at its quay, their bows pointing inland, their yellow sailless masts reclining at a queer angle. Nets hang along the shore between conical piles of pink sponges. Among them a few Arabs sit looking out to sea.

The foreign port lies immediately to the left. At its center a long pier reaches into the water: it is studded with bollards; hawsers and chains, bales and kegs are stacked along it; launches and a coastal freighter are moored at its sides. Several hundred people are crowded onto the tip of the pier. They are mostly Europeans. The men are dressed in white, the women in long gowns of mauve and pale yellow.

The colonial town recedes from the port in regular blocks of spaced white buildings. On a line with the pier, following the vertical axis of the picture, runs the main avenue. It is bordered with double ranks of young palm trees, behind which numerous Europeans have gathered in meticulous files. From the windows above them watching heads emerge. Bright tricolors hang at intervals along the street, and red white and blue bunting has been strung in cordons along the dark green trees.

Farther inland, near the left-hand edge of the print,

beyond a water cistern marking the limit of the town, there is an army camp, a square of pale blue tents. Three sentinels in khaki stand watch on its outskirts.

Between the camp, the new town and the casbah lies a space of clear ground. On it two parades are taking place. To the left, a column of French soldiers marches toward the crowded avenue of the European quarter—white-capped spahis on red and brown horses, a Zouave band in blue jackets and scarlet chechias, and Zouave foot soldiers. To the right, under the casbah wall, surrounded by hundreds of watching Arabs, a line of Berber horsemen executes a *fantasia*. Caught in mid-career, the black horses stiffly gallop, the riders twist excitedly, brandishing upright rifles that discharge minute red and black V's.

Along the bottom of the print, a tranquil strip of countryside contrasts with the animation of the parades. The land is flat. Gardens open among spreading orchards of olive, almond and lemon; tracts of vine adjoin the villas. There are few human figures. A shepherd sits against an olive tree, his flock grazing about him. Not far from their stepladder, left standing in the branches of an almond tree, nut harvesters sleep in an orchard. The shadowed alleys of the necropolis are empty.

Country, harbor and town fill the lower third of the picture; beyond is sea and sky.

Parallel to the shore, in indigo water, five gray ships ride at anchor. Only their hulls are plain, for from them, outshining the rest, an effusion of brilliant fire issues—above a couch of pinwheels and squibs, while huge tourbillions at either side shoot into violet spirals, three salvos of rockets between stamp fans of silver on the darkness, yielding as they rise galactic profusions, their garnitures of bombs, balls, snakes and fiery snow. The labyrinth of their colors sets a dense clarity against the blankness of the night.

The Sinking
of the Odradek Stadium

Some people assume that in addition to the great original betrayal a small particular betrayal has been contrived in every case exclusively for them, that, in other words, when a love drama is being performed on the stage the leading actress has not only a pretended smile for her lover, but also a special crafty smile for one particular spectator at the back of the gallery. This is going too far.

Kafka, "Reflections on Sin, Pain, Hope, and the True Way"

Part One

I

...confidence in words, Twang. I suck my tongue for your chervil-and-lavender flavor.

This afternoon I went to the Beach to see a new hotel, the Brissy St. Jouin. It has been described as the "Naples ultra" of Miami splendor. There is teak sawdust in the Oyster Bar, where I began my tour with a screwdriver ; the lobby is decked with much gold. That was all I saw. La Nosherie, the Mannikin Pis rumpus room, and the Jupiter Seaside Fungus Collection had to wait for another visit.

What arrested me, ankle-deep in peacock feathers, was a battery of television sets assembled for the inauguration as a "monument to intercontinental awareness." Above the lobby fountain, seven sets rose vertically from a spray-shrouded base. On either side of the midmost screen, three others were horizontally aligned, hung by transparent cords from the distant ceiling. No sound from the construction reached the naked ear; but telephones, each equipped with a panel of buttons, connected viewers to the various programs. Stopping to sample this profusion of "light inscribed by light," I stayed until I had exhausted the repertory.

From the top of the vertical rank, the highest set showed a program from Paris, a children's spelling bee. A little boy carefully chalked the word *batrimoine* across the blackboard of a classroom where a dozen schoolmates, mainly girls, sat watching him. They laughed at his mistake. The West is mad. I could not live without your words, no matter how you spell them.

A documentary emanating from Indonesia appeared on the set beneath. The subject was a celebrated Balinese *gamelan*. There were close-ups of the instruments demonstrating their use, then a series of stills of the entire orchestra: taken over eighty years, the photographs faded each into the next to form an animated historical image. Throughout it the instruments neither moved nor changed, while the performers aged steadily and from time to time were suddenly replaced. Shots of the current fighting followed. I thought of the *kuchi* playing for us their reedy serenades, as we ate your delicate slop-rice.

At the end of the left-hand arm of the assemblage I tuned into an advertisement featuring the Indians, a baseball team. Players were seen on the field, then in a kitchen eating "Mateotti's pizzas." Baseball is like *zem*, except that a ball is used.

To the right of this I watched an American film broadcast from Hawaii. The sound track was dead. A man in nineteenth-century dress was seated at a table, eating from a bowl of pears. After a while he pushed the fruit away, used a finger-bowl to wet his lips and forehead, then took up a quill pen and began writing on a rough-edged page. The camera followed his hand as it traced the words, *O say, can you see...* I passed the consulate today. The Cow of Plenty was snapping prettily in the breeze.

On the adjacent set I briefly switched on a popular mathematics congress in Florence. The subject was psychic topology, so rapidly discussed I could not even follow the English translation. By Florence I mean Florence, Italy.

Russia held the place of honor at the crossing of the vertical and horizontal ranks. I witnessed part of a biological experiment. For ten minutes the screen was filled with the front-face close-up of a cat. Every few seconds a white arc momentarily quivered between the tips of its moustache. A mild hum accompanied the toy lightning. The cat lay quiet, shifting its eyes from side to side. *Amour, amour, quand tu nous tiens...*

To the right a local quiz program was being transmitted. It took place by the swimming pool of some Beach hotel, perhaps the Brissy St. Jouin itself. I listened to one exchange. "In what year did Captain Kidd begin his career of piracy?" "Uh... he turned out in 1697." "Correct!" The contestant was thrown into the pool. The weather has been chilly these past days, with the north wind.

Next to this came an advertisement illustrated by flights of the eagle owl swooping on its prey. (I want nothing, except one thing.)

At the right of the horizontal rank, I watched an Indian movie about the tribulations of a lamb lost in Calcutta. The lamb's innocence so touches those it encounters that butchers and starving men befriend it. The film made me hungry.

Switching to the set underneath the electrical cat, I viewed a performance by the Peking Opera of *Russlan and Ludmilla.* I waited until the end of the canon for Ludmilla's father. How is Bamma Deng?

The screen below was blank, glowing with creamy light. The program was supposed to be from Pretoria. A flat voice recited a love poem.

Below, an English documentary enlightened with X-rays the murky functionings of the womb, including parthenogenesis. The colors were scrumptious.

Finally, the lowest set showed a program from Cairo. Presented against a background of local music and dance, its subject was the circular bread of Egypt. We learned of its usefulness when fractioned in making sandwiches, even with soup.

An old man standing nearby engaged me in conversation when I set down my earphone. He wore blinding beach attire and carried a basket of comb shells on one arm. Under the other an unfamiliar receptacle caught my notice. The old man answered my stare with the words, "This is a pilgrim's flask, such as was carried by those who journeyed to Santiago de Compostela." Turning back to the television assemblage he pointed out to me, at its very apex, the blue-and-white figure of a cherub. "Do you think it's one of the della Robbia gang?" The cherub leaned winsomely on a cittern that had been tilted to one side, and held aloft a triangular plectrum. We chatted long enough to exchange names; then I decided to go home. I was getting dizzy from the six thousand dozen roses banked against the lobby walls.

Miami looks so vertical and unimaginative after the dusky lateral circular something of your village—it was like a shiny wooden nut dish. I have been quiet, mostly. Dan had a party to celebrate the end of Lent. He gave it early—on Good Friday—because it was to be "different." It wasn't. Such occasions leave me feeling like a beaten mark. I come to them filled with high spirits that are quickly and indifferently taken from me. It doesn't matter. My hopes are unquenchable. I feel that I stand on the brink of lofty exchanges that will make the ills of life ridiculous. After each respite, even a nap, we can all meet each other as gods. I have entrusted my life to expectation, as if the bud would surely blossom. I can only live this way.

Have sent the money you need. Isn't it lucky that you were born in an Italian colony?

I was right: the name figures in the "hypothetical lists" of the Donation.

II

April 6

Pan persns knwo base bal. The giappan-like trade-for mishn play with it in our capatal any times. To morrow to work be gin. It's cleen eccepts for the talk. The in-habits live in draems. To raed this has need, not idees but a tenshn (to-trans-late of Twang): "After a land-like giourney a yuong man-Pan a rive deep in a rest hwere the her of his choise was live in a mall she has make. Green aster hang, man re-sieve no to-greet, re-turn to his ghest—there is no re-plies. Rael Zen he is to can make to get a-tention; the stud go to a nother art of rest and biuld his-self yeers. Later, new as-to-weep-like fall leeves, he 's line. He then drop. Every thing run throuh the rest to teech and say, Thank you." Here, is Rome. Your to-write with baeutifl discovory of Miami is a preziate to no end. You are write a bout name—good—then have you found-ed map? Or, are you to can found it? and how do you dou? The one-most inter-lohutor of Twang in Rome is a boy-child whowho say in playce of my way, but, in italian, "Dont stop me, I giust raech 6,523,281" and go on to count, sit-ed on the steppes of the Graet Squaer. So brothr, my mynd hargo of love seek you one-most in one deriction, then in a second derection, then in a 3rd derexion, then in a forth direction, like wise up ward, dwon ward, and all-round, the sence of to-love-like minde in-fusion all thing with no limit, no narrow, no to-hate, no ill desire. You care for mor Zen storys. It 's un-easy to write them, with this dificint languague, and they so pleyn; yet here is one. And I sey, "Good-bye, *neng* of Twang."

III

April 11

Divine testimony is the best, and your letters bristle with Eleusinian truths. By them I know I exist, even if I would rather you proved it by digging your nails into my palms, or your toe into my flank. So I believe you blindly—I believe you when you say I am a *neng*; but you must step out of the holy fire to tell me why.

That old man I met at the Brissy St. Jouin called three days ago. Would I join his party on a visit to Panoramus? Next morning we gathered into two cars for the drive. It was nice, in a dismal way. Our highways are now paved with a material that when warmed by the sun emits a smell of fresh bread; the worthy effect is destroyed by a nostalgia for neighborhood bakeries. The ugliness of the state of Florida also depressed me. It appeared concave rather than flat, and the mean

age of the inhabitants glimpsed by the roadside was at least
seventy-one. Panoramus was no different. It is the shelling
capital of the universe, its beaches are lined with old, avid
hobbyists stooping endlessly. My host came over to ask if I
was glad to be there and then attached himself to me for the
day, whisking me along the beach, leaving me not the smallest chance for a drink. The shore was messy. A wealth of
mostly broken shells was diversified with fish skulls, medusa
carcasses, and used containers. We searched for new-moon
shells and picked beach roses and violets. Then, although the
mercury was low, I went for a swim. The salty water stung
like fire and I didn't stay in long; just long enough to open
one foot on a can. We proceeded to the Shell Museum cafeteria for a lunch of roast lamb, beans, and leaf-and-fruit salad.
(That's how the dishes were listed. A blind man would have
had difficulty naming them, since they were as odorless as if
frozen, which they partly were.) At the end of the meal a
black girl, moving in an ethereal or at least ether-like cloud
of vetiver, arrived to guide us through the museum. "You
shall be the two millionth visitor of our conchological collections," she sweetly said to me, ending a vague hope that I
might cop a heel. I know I sound ungrateful, but I kept my
feelings to myself. (And O my dearest, I cannot look at anything, even a collection of shells, without turning my
thoughts towards you. My time is never wasted. Thanks to
the serene passion within me, and the ministry of the post
office, there is nothing in the world that does not commem-
orate you—girls who are beautiful and black because you are
beautiful and lemony, the smell of the sea because of your
landlocked mother's broths, greyhounds at the track because
of your sister's hands at her shuttle, the pavements of roads
because I wish they led me to you. Even garbage helps me
recall, although of course it is too tame to match, the fumy
litter of your markets.) Smiling, she took me by the hand
and led me through the museum, where we inspected bearded
conchs; shells used to make purple dyes; an Indian shell shield
from pre-Columbian times; shell sculptures by local artists
(e.g. "Nessus abducting Dejanira.") Afterwards we went back

to the beach. I watched a greyhound bitch sniffing after wristwatch-size brown crabs that kept sidling off into the wavelets, leaving her unseeing and perplexed. There was lightning out to sea. On the drive home I had a talk with Mr. Dexter Hodge, a very class person whom I have met once before. He told me that he had been accosted outside the cafeteria by a guitar-strumming lad who proposed taking us to a cockfight.

As to your questions: I do not have the map and it is not certain that I shall find it. The Donation I mentioned is a collection of 19,000 old maps smuggled over in 1966 from the Maestranza in Havana. The object of the theft was to exploit the treasure-hunting craze by selling the maps, but the State of Florida impounded them and deposited them for safekeeping in the University of Miami library. They have never been catalogued, but lists of possible origins have been compiled. A number of maps came to Havana from Santa Catalina, after the fort there was dismantled; and since the archives of the fort record our captain's hanging in 1537 and the seizure of his effects, his name appears on one of the lists. This means only that *if* he had a copy of the map, it *may* be here.

It's the season when worms start spinning cocoons, in the north the crows are leaving the woods, the snows of the past melt and the eyes of men become unstuck. I go on blinking in your perpetual spring light. You have made the eyes I look through. Abstract convergent lines orient the fractions of my world to a point beyond the horizon that may well be your navel. I may not sense this at every moment, any more than I smell the hairs inside my nose, but at the end of each minute or day I remember happily that it is so. Only occasionally do I think of you in a distracted way (longing), and the milk on the hob boils over.

IV

April 15

Amortonelli have-make be fore crime-like hystery, a satir a gaints Pope-most *Clement VII* (Medici). Be fore, there was any thing to

find out from a bibliotheck near. That man is truth-like to you in to-
tell the briggand ave the end-most days in Rome. It was can for
Twang to find a paper near 1600 whiwhich say: *of-Amortonelly* to-
wrotes in Vatihan bibliotec. And is can look soon at its. Years, and
G. A. Medici is re-turn and *Pius For.* He awllays buy penshn to Amortonelli, lest perpaps his verse buyt him. So, hwen my not-to-exist
grub-like flesh pass, there is fear lest one late-er be book worm
bluynd and dark. Yet is to-fire a stic or few of in sense be in-
sureance to proteck me lest cruel re birth? Once, yess, a lama-
most munk of Tibett, whowho have-eat cheazes with graet
love, and he in deth be then a chease worm. Onemost, *neng*
have sense nose, that wish to say, nose to have thought on
when one squatt and moove a way thouhgt; then, Buddha's
nose. O yass, there be my puprose to learn like, in a dark
roome, the lihgt of lamp with to-shatter obscurety, with to-
give and to-scatter ligt, so that discovery then there will
pomp a way the shaddw of darks-nesses and schatter the ligth
of to-know, and like too, the lihtg of our re-lation with the
advance in to the darkmosts of this world, things one after
one light until all are glod. The crime-full poet has come here
soone after in-Italy, and stay until dead 1561, eccept wen his *Hardinal
Giovonni Ongelo Medici* is ex pulse by *Paol 4.* The nose of Buddha
is beatiful and *neng* a rive to sense beautifl thing—you. Any
time we say *neng* and non *vin* (cadavar) to make confort to
the hadavers.

V

April 20

I have lately felt as though I were wading through a deserted desert. I know it's only a little while that I haven't seen you,
and again in a little while I shall see you... meanwhile my
mind's mouth has been dry. The research is discouraging,
there are so many maps, full of flattened bugs and dust, each
to be laboriously unfolded, then refolded. Our captain's
career has rubbed off on none of them, and my only "fact" is
still this: the name given to me by the Red Arrow man (I'm
sure of it because I wrote it down) is identical with one on the
Donation list. The work is also slow, since it has to be done

after office hours. My colleagues started complaining that I was becoming "withdrawn." They mustn't guess the truth.

Then this afternoon, walking toward my bus-stop, I had a brush with Nemesis. I was passing a tidy speckled-egg bungalow when I saw beyond its Moorish patio, raised above the low wall of a terrace, the peroxide head of my sister Diana. I called to her; the head looked up, and looked away. I crossed the patio for a closer view. The person, who was not my sister, was stretched out beneath the unflattering sun on a pneumatic deck, naked except for a pair of sungoggles. I turned back, too late. "Eve!" she yelled. A tawny watchcat, fierce as a lion and as big as a schnauzer, rose from her side as if winged. Striking my right elbow, its claws only nicked my arm, since the fury of its leap unseamed my coat-sleeve and dropped the beast to the ground. But as you know, I cannot run very fast, and another jump fastened the cat to my shoulders, where it opened six parallel slits in the cloth and flesh of my back, before abandoning me at the patio gate. I ran on, expecting further assault, but only the womanly cry of "Stay away, maniac!" pursued me down the sidewalk.

Can an evil spirit open blind men's eyes? Even as I stood sobbing in the street, and later, while the druggist cleansed and dressed my lacerations, I became aware that I had been brought back to life. My frightful sensations had lifted me above habit into a conscious emptiness where I could begin feeling again. For days I had wallowed in dreams, forgetting what you have made me, charmed by phantasms of my loneliness and its childish yearnings to be soothed—as if we deserved nothing better than to be instantly locked into an everlasting ice cream parlor! Scandal and pain wrenched me awake: then you became absolutely present to me, not for long, but in that time your bodily presence would not have made you more real. I felt your fingers on my face, which was like a blind man's face under their touch.

It's late now. I'm in my office, ringed in maps. To the east a new moon is rising, in the sky I crossed not long ago to have a stranger transfigure my life in the unlikely shrine of the Bangkok airport. Soon this exile will end.

VI

It 's cruel to be-weep for those dayze and nights, not minites when your to-write come but one time with out end of 2 weeks-long. To be lock to gether in forever lasting ice craem is not as bad a thougt. (I vow, to treatmeant my english!) To-put "we" close "*tharaï*" is all ways hanromy in Pan, in every way—*tharaï* "with no to-end".

The papers of *Amortonelli* are-give in to the Vatican but not long, be cause *Hosimo de' Medici* whowho will-be soon Gran Duc of Toscany I, take them 4–6 months after the brigan dead. *G. A. Medici* is be come Pope but he 's but a north-most Medici, he has a dett to *Cosimo* for to-say he is cousins and all-most a graet tuscan Medici. How full the wish even to see you once mor, see if some marks life give in your face after last we meat each othr. How many dusts to lift to discover that I discover! So many, the small Monsignor Latten, a shortness with jewls, descend from heigths to see and say me more, that in those dayse there is a talk, so: said in the next year daid of paludism, the sons of *Cosimo* kill themself in to-fight a bout the paper of the thief; and this musts mien it is not but sattires? As we mieet it then is un-clear there is some great tendency, you musts put in my hart to to remembem a bout the Banghok air port and the Mister Red Arrow. And do the man-mother of the beests no help your hope with other tells of the tresure, how did he say exatcly? The feeling is, my English not whatwhat it would be—force, be cause all-day takking italian. The litle Paple ociffer say, it 's part of an age-most story.

VII

April 29

Since you again ask, this is how it began. On my way east, after Rome, I was seated next to Mr. Zonder Tittel, a friendly Canadian working for the International Red Arrow, the conservation society. Mr. Tittel was traveling to Indo-China to capture specimens of a wild cow called the coubou, or kubu. Have you ever seen one? It roams the plateaus of southern Laos in small herds; its only food is the bark of the native apple, which is being girdled into extinction, taking the coubou with it. Until recently no one cared, since the coubou was thought to be only a domestic breed gone wild. Mr. Tittel himself learned otherwise when he examined one animal: "I got a crowbar between its teeth and prised its goddam jaws apart, and there was a mouth two million years old."

Mr. Tittel then asked what had brought me to the Orient. I gave him a short course in Pan history. He was not very interested in the early missionaries or in my plans to microfilm their records in Pan-Nam. But when I mentioned working at the Miami U. library he perked up and began discussing treasure troves. He had heard about the maps from the Maestranza and asked if any of them had proved valuable. I said I had nothing to do with the maps, and that I knew little about buried treasure. He then started telling me about the "craziest" chest of gold in the Caribbean. If only I had listened more attentively! Here are the main facts of his story. I know how remote they must have seemed in those giddy days.

The treasure was hidden, probably in the Florida keys, by the Catalan Jesus María Cabot, captain of *El Paráclito*, and his associate Amortonelli, a Florentine. The ship sailed from Barcelona early in the 1500's, bound for Mexico. Blown off course by a hurricane, it was wrecked on the Florida coast. The partners salvaged and buried a large coffer not far from the wreck, with the help of two members of the crew. When the survivors of *El Paráclito* were rescued, one of the sailors denounced Cabot and Amortonelli; later, however, he failed to identify the hiding-place. The captain and the Italian were arrested, and the former hanged. Amortonelli escaped and is supposed to have returned to Italy.

This is all I "know." It is reasonable to assume that each partner drew a map of the treasure's location. That is why I asked you to look for the map in Italy while I search here. (I have written to the Red Arrow man for a complete account; apparently he is still harrying the Laotian bush.)

At Bangkok we prepared to go our ways; but Mr. Tittel

had more to teach me. He had hinted at a moon of riches. Now
he was to reveal the sun and earth. Spying your *phrap* across
the airport lobby, he led me toward you. He said that you
were "typically Pan," that you would probably be on my
plane, and that you could "help me off to a friendly start.
They're such an easygoing people, she won't mind our
accosting her. You'll see." He started to address you in the
twinkling cadence of your language. You listened patiently,
without indifference or interest. I was already collapsing. I
tried to be a cliff but sank like swirling pebbles. Your eyes did
not move yet swept tides of confusion through me. Then,
when you turned to me, your first words ("Hello baby")
plunged me into melancholy. I could neither leave, nor believe. If you had noticed that "great tendency" you might have
been kind. If you had been kind, the world of dreams would
have reclaimed me and ended all hope. It was enough to
walk with you to the plane, and sit by you, a glimmer of
folded silks.

My first alarm was soon over. I felt that our proximity was
now like that of two actors when, after a performance, they
drop their masks and resume a spontaneous friendship. But
since I had worn a mask all my life, I didn't know how not to
act. And you, who had never put on a mask because you are
truth itself, could not see that my face was nude. If you had
thought about me at all, you would have taken me for an
idiot. But you did not seem particularly aware of me until,
in Sah Leh Khot next morning, wishing me well, you told
me the way to your village.

Meanwhile you abandoned me for the night to the dis-
tractions of the *Deuam phap* fair, through which I rode on
the emerging whale of my desire. Everything seemed beautiful, if sometimes unfathomable, in the glamor of a race that
included you.

I entered the fairgrounds through a gate resembling a huge
white N whose left apex has been broken off. On its uprights
primitive guns, relinquished by visiting tribesmen, were
strung on brass chains. Beyond, a movie billboard announced
Ava Gardner in *The Joan Crawford Story*.

Drifting through the flashing lanterns and loudspeakers, I stopped at a little cinder track where preparations for a foot-race were under way. As I approached the group of runners and their handlers, I nearly tripped over a boy who was scurrying on all fours through the crowd. He looked up at me, raised a forefinger to one eye, and pinched my shoe. I glanced around me: six feet away an unlaced boot lay on its side. I picked it up and gave it to the boy. Sidling over to the track, he cunningly substituted it for a similar boot that rested on the starting-line among a dozen others. The boot I had found weighed at least five pounds—it was plainly "loaded." I kept an eye on it, until it was finally put on by a runner wearing the number four. I pushed into the thick of the crowd, where I rightly guessed that bets were being taken, and learned that "four" was the favorite. While I wondered what runner to back, I saw the boy who had changed the boot placing a few *khrot* on "six," and I followed his example. The race started; number four won easily; number six finished last. Pan runners surely do not race with weighted shoes. I had been made to "find the leather," and I paid duly for my greed.

I next stopped to watch a kind of dance, performed on a small wooden platform by a husky old man. The dancer lay on his back or side and applied his legs to his head and shoulders, or his arms to his legs and hips, in slow lurching gestures punctuated by swipes of fist, foot, or knee. Except for the groans of the performer, there was no accompaniment.

Farther on I joined the audience of a shadow play, where willowy puppets moved behind screens of colored silk. The action began with a horde of demon-like figures shrieking around a solitary hut. When the demons withdraw, a venerable man steps out of the hut and sings gently for a while. The leader of the demons approaches him disguised as a beggar. Soon, at his bidding, a vision of viand-laden tables appears. The old man drives the beggar off with a few roars. The demon then returns as a beautiful woman and conjures up another vision, this time of girls dancing. The demon is again repulsed. Then all the demons, chanting in evil chorus, attack and steal the old man's pig. As they decamp, a grotesque but benevolent genie rises from the ground, scatters them, and returns the pig.

Did the Italians bring this story to Pan-Nam?

Passing a field where moonlight *zem* was played, I thought I glimpsed you in the crowd, a wishful hallucination. Staring after your shadow I could see no one's features right, and when I tried to paint your face against the gloom, the colors were faint, and troubled by the hollow masks that the night mixed among the living.

Nearby, families of blue-turbaned Nau were selling their traditional comforters, embroidered with tennis rackets, those colonial relics; various roots, of which I bought a sampling; and of course their stinking sea-salt cakes.

Towards the western gate, I observed a native wall-and-ball game. The wall was of soft clay, straight and thick. Equipped with six-foot, spoonlike bamboo bats, two players in turn hurled a wiremesh sphere against the wall, whence it had to be dug out. What is the point of this game? Another couple played against the far side.

My last halt was for the monkey kites. Eight of them, with their busy passengers, were sailing about fifty yards from the ground in agitated proximity. I presume the monkeys have been trained to strike the other kites. Their exasperated cries followed me to the hotel, where I slept fitfully. I was shaken with the memory and anticipation of you; also I couldn't figure how to turn off the light.

In the earliest morning I met you as you were boarding your bus. I could not discover whether inclination or courtesy made you glow in that manner. In irreproachably noncommittal tones you said I might visit you. By then my feelings were clear; when you departed I let myself float into them. As I savored this joy, I felt the miseries of my life crowding down like angry beggars. They did not make me run away, because for the first time I knew I could satisfy them.

(There were other beggars as well, your orange-toga'd monks, cadging their breakfast. This practice seems degrading to us westerners. How can it be thought holy?)

You wonder if the fight over Amortonelli's papers does not prove them to be other than literary. Remember, literature was then a dreaded weapon. The first Cosimo had Il Burchiello murdered for his sonnets. Not that you are wrong. How could I ever think that you are wrong?

Don't forget to date your letters.

As they say in Pannam: *Duvaï maï*

VIII

May 3

Monsignor Latten say, it-all mixt with the hystory of—then his word fall out from my aer. A gain: *"Quella vecchia storia delle tosature."* But, wholding the words, I be leave they are italian idiotism, like Amerihans say "trim any body". One moom-time I account my 32 nature-like parts with resbonsipil to-breathe and I get a yas, there is can to be ohter censes. Mons. Latten is not hear, he 's in Luang Pra Bang for the synod. Yet the vocabaruly sur-render the idea for *tosare* "to hlip" that is "clip coins", so *tosature* "clippins"—a per-hap conenction with some traesure? I gioin my to-trouble-book-shelfs to this impusle.

You writ assid, brothr, of *Deuam phap* fair. Pans have ever bronz in ther shoes for to-run. Whowho is quikc-est, put on the haevy est shoose. Nor the old man-Pan on a bed have some need for the musical, be caus he 's in war no dance, one hlaf of man with otter half, a long fihgt. You have say *duvaï maï* but we are not to can say this all-thoug it will-be treu, *duvaï* is fair-well for the long-time, or even deth, it is rwong with *maï* that is now and for-this-moment. You will-say *tharaï* "for-ever" with *duvaï*. Not say-so to Twang! Not tenis raguets are on Nau hovers. They are wulwas.

You have see my gold bonzes "degarding" and you are worng. They have the ful contenpt for materialistist sotiety, to-beg make them free from the strusture. The bal-gaems are to gether a game, one grup here, one group here, the desire is to-get one ball through the wall. In that teatre the old man is the crule man-mother of the sky whowho will non give rain (pig). The heros make grate atcs to have it from, but you have-see the hate of the bittr dead get up to give us no thing. When you wait you did-can to see after how they get the pig. The sky-most monekeys have-not-kut the kites but one other. When a monekey is been-kill he homes down. A string is on to the him and not to the kite, and that hite go a way and have no triunf.

I've the memry of your to-come in my town. Our dog in the under-house likes you, he make the strange woof of tendernes and sensure—*then*, I have interest in you. And hiss. Do not put a way your memery of the litlte money you will send. Do not think, the of-Nau things be roots, they are tirds, yet are OK if you aet only little. I & you; harmnony; peace.

IX

May 8

Good news: yesterday I was given access to a university computer. This should speed up the map work. Lester P. Greek did the favor, during a chance meeting on the library steps. He holds the Finnegans Wake chair in our Comp. Lit. department, runs the municipal television trust, and is supposed to be on the big con.

Don't you think you may be wasting your time in Rome? Amortonelli's papers are certainly in Florence. Why labor after will-o'-the-wisps?

Thank you for correcting my Pan usage. May I point out a similar mistake of your own? In one letter you wrote "forever lasting." One can say "forever" or "everlasting" but not "forever lasting."

It was interesting to learn about the fair.

The bank will forward your money, which I hadn't forgotten. Do you know the amount is exactly what I paid for you, not counting the exemption from field labor? How I miss your village, its lanes of teak and bamboo houses, quiet under the silk-cotton trees! And your house, or Bamma Deng's, the dark cool house by which I often stood, watching the lizards slide over its posts, so unlike my street of blind doors. Even in the shade, the pounding of my blood would burst out in horrible sweating, as I waited for a hand...

Could you help reconstruct the events of our wedding day? It's hard for me, because I was so drunk. I don't feel remorse about this: such events are not to be piously hoarded.

By ten in the morning I was already teetering. I remember handing out countless cigarettes to the smiling groups around the stands, decked for the feast with streamers, green candles, and rice brandy.

At some point I spoke to you, or tried to, but you were taken away. I looked into a mirror and saw my face.

There came a slow gathering of people from every direction, like battalions drawing together before battle, or pilgrims at the consecration of a shrine, all eating dried squid and smoking my cigarettes. The alcohol began to ignite my skin; I felt as though I were being flayed. Boys led me to a carpeted area in front of the house, where your mother and aunts were arrayed. A long dialogue began, I think in verse, between your mother and a gnome who had been chosen to speak for me. Did you know him? I understood that he manufactured sundials. It was terrible to fall asleep during this exchange, when I was supposed to be begging for your hand, yet no one seemed to mind. The women's laughter woke me. They weren't laughing at me—what was it they were laughing about? Finally, the gnome left, with whispered words that sounded like "Beware of green wolves!" A bowl of cuprous liquid was set before the women, into which they dropped thistle-like tufts that dissolved in smoke. The chief bonze, who with other monks had chanted drowsily through the morning hours, rose I gathered to assert that the marriage was now proclaimed, received, professed, undergone, and enacted. But the ceremony went on. You were brought down, a small mat was set between us, and there you placed a handful of winter rice shoots, and I a dollar bill. That was the sign that everyone could return to his feasting.

I remember much better, a few days earlier, going up to see you in the opium fields. I had woken early. For a time I tried to read *Birth, Breath, Breast* by Norman O. Brown, but a shrike was singing, so I went over to your father's house to ask for your hand. You had already left. The basin where you had washed (publicly but modestly, no doubt, with your *phrap* raised about your ears) glowed in the near-light like a little milky sea. Bamma Deng was sitting on his verandah. I addressed him directly, pleading devotion and honesty against my ignorance of Pan ways. He answered readily and at length, displaying that perfect Italian of his that, down to the charming dissonance of his hard c's, aspirated in the Tuscan manner, suggests rather a lifetime in Florence than a few years' study in a Far Eastern *liceo*. He called me his son, admonished me in sententious periods to trust in God, informed me of the customary rites and obligations, and accepted my proposal. When I told him I had not yet spoken to you, he warned me that his agreement depended on yours. I had hopes of your willingness, and such an abundance of desire that I felt that you could not help sharing it; so I hurried off to find you, stumping up the rooted, gullied path that led to the crown of the hill. Rubbery leaves swatted my sweat- and tear-glazed face. Once I halted to recover my breath and gazed unperceiving over the pulse fields below, gray in the first light. I resumed my ascent at a slower pace, but my feelings banged on within me. I tried to distract myself by naming the innumerable trees that towered confusingly about me over the ferns and wild deutzia bordering my path. Liquidambar, magnolia, padauk, varnish tree... the effort was useless, I was obsessed with your smell and skin. I must have come into the clearing like a slavering lunatic. It was tranquil there. The sun was a yellowish ball in the eastern haze. In its aquarial light you all appeared in dwarfish silhouette, erect or bent as you spooned the droplets oozing from the cropped shoots. At first I could not distinguish you. Your familiar laugh brought me to you. I said that I had spoken to your father and that he was willing that we should marry. Because I could imperfectly make out your features, and you did not at once reply, I was shaken with doubt, and all the intensity of my hope and lust careered toward bitterness. Then you cast away your spoon, and with a soundless flutter dropped to the ground to embrace my feet.

X

May 12

Listn! I have, how ever, find: coin clippings are-can to be a treazure.
1391 the papa *Bonifacio IX* sell this emty abbazy of Montpelas, that is
neighbr-like to Avignon on a edge of of-Antipopoes land. The buy-
man is Messer *Todao*, he 's a fiorentine who have a hous in Mont
Pelier. He for-get to pay, the pope take his propriety in Florence, of-
it is a part a box of gold-most-hlippins with a worht of 37,000 florini!
The mother of Twang and the interlocutor of the mother of
Twang were-laugh be cause they sing fun-y things to the
other. Firts they are to-make a musick-full list of every thing
that is like 2 lovrs can not be separate

> dust & watter
> nale & fingre
> oil & carpet
> flower & name of-flower
> wacks & fire

tehn wehn she have let a end of her to-question:

> The ivery pins, the iorn kneedles
> —have you brougt them a long?
> The umbrellow of parrot-like feather, the *phrap*
> of gold-like cloth
> —have you brought them a long?
> The rynocerous buttr, the of-Japan appels,
> —have you brought them a long?

and so otter hard debts, and he answer

> We bring a long the ivry pins, the iren neadles &c.,

my mother aks

> Muts I give her to you? do you vow to-want-her
> even if she   ug-ly?
> even if she   more I 's than teeth?
> even if she   mmore tethe than hairs?
> even if she   so pale as the Eureups?
> even if she   crooket as *bukhaï?* (kind of brush)
> even if she   drunk in the mournins?
> even if she   your emeny is her lovr?

and he ansser

Yas we want her even all-though she be ugl-y &c. and
they are-laugh to gether while this be cause I have great
respett for I 'm pritty, chaste, and sobre.

My eyes are bend-ed from the to-see old hand scritts and prints and
still, I found not *storia delle tosature* with *Amortonelli*, or *Medici*.

My family have all great rispect for much quality, much
beauty, and the man-mother and the mother of Twang have
no punish-meant from heavn, but it be-stow on these genitors
comfrots in lovly symytry, 3 gerls, 3 boys, a gerl, a boy, five
gerls, five boys, then a boï and a gerl that is Twang. No one
baby die, and we are poor yet we are live in harmony with
heaven and under heven. May be you are co-rect, that I maek
the end to work here. But there is so much other mathers of
your to-write a little, in your most-deer be cause most-new
letter—there are so much things hwere I have the same to-feel
with a eletricly dellicate clear-ness so I all most have no brath
to make my voice strong that the current not be break, and
my thought be ex-change only in a part, and your ex-sistence
that now is write ovre me so passed mine farthar and nop
stop. *Weï weï lemö slop.* Wo-woe the mysyry of love, we say.
But it has no so bad a soun be-cause *weï* is "a-las" and "sadness", OK, but all-so "to-laugh". You shall for-ever rememer
lemu be cause it is, "love".

XI

May 17

If Lester Greek runs for Congress he'll have my vote. There
is new material at last, thanks to Les's computer. It checked
the names of Amortonelli and the captain against one million
nine hundred and seventy-two thousand items of information,
obtaining one positive response. The document indicated was
in San Juan de Puerto Rico. I have already received a copy of
it, unfortunately in translation.

Here is the text. Clearly it is part of a letter addressed to the
captain on the eve of his sailing from Barcelona. It says
nothing of the treasure's location but confirms its presence on
El Paráclito. The opening is lost.

...to Lyon in the company of the Aretine, whose name

was Gherucci. On the second day, when I had been crossing the city in her pursuit it thus happened: the watery element, as if it had been drunk up and contained too long, poured down so emphatically that I was forced to creep along like one afraid of the watch close under the overhangs, where the cellar door of a money changer's house being unbarred on the under side, I fell into it head over heels, like a blind man who in an earthquake comes tap-tapping with his cane and falls straight into hell. I fell on straw, that is into silence, such that I heard my own blood. To be brief, I was in a Jew's house, unasked and unperceived. A grave conversation dropped thinly down from a room over me, and I was moved (O destiny) to hear it plainer, and slunk up a stair more ladder than stair, old and ill-fitted so that it would have squeaked my undoing but for the essential dampness of the place, and brought me, light-footed as the lover who treads to a husband's snores, close to the ceiling, that was their floor. Two were speaking, one much, the other no more than as if to nod his head. The first told how he had been sent to inquire about a chest of silk that his master, the Abbot of Montpelas, had discovered unaccountably abandoned, nay hidden even, in a dark corner of the abbey. There was a great quantity of silk in it, taffeta, with a piece of brocade that at one end was embroidered with six crow-like figures, and on the lid of the chest were crudely carved three fish. Diverse and sundry tropes were introduced by the narrator to piece out these few mean facts, and well I knew why, it was wiliness to prick the Jew's interest, for getting money or knowledge out of him I did not understand, and I would not wait either to hear more or to sneeze because my own inquisitiveness was inflamed: I had been thoroughly taught the fame of that treasure that today I told you of; so like a trout climbing a waterfall I wished my body after my soul up through the cellar door, found Gherucci, and that night we made for Montpelas.

There we stopped little, because the chest was gone.
Three sunless crowns slipped into the hand of a forni-
cating monk found out that it was dispatched to be sold
in Barcelona, in the company of two friars less covetous.
We followed them, and caught them not until Nar-
bonne. Toward Beziers they progressed and took Font-
froide in their way, although it was clean out of their
way, to stay with the Cistercians. They thought it their
haven yet it was ours. They must when they left lead
their horse and their wagon (drawn by two pumice-
gray asses) up a narrow valley where we could fall on
them; and so we did, and doing lost all our itching
doubts, which as we rode along the sands of Languedoc
had like their whining myriad mosquitoes sung in our
ears, Is it gold? For the monks answered our threats
bravely. They used such unspeakable vehemence a man
would have thought them the only well-bent men
under heaven. Would they defend taffeta so? Their
righteous unbudgingness would have forced us soon
enough to arms, when one of them lifted the long brass
cross that hung below one hip and struck Gherucci,
who had dismounted, so great a blow his head opened
and he fell agonizing to the ground, sprawling and
turning on the stained grass like a fish newly plucked
from the stream, and we thus came to arms even sooner,
I mean too soon. I knocked the other of them from his
horse and leaped down on him, whereupon he cleverly
slit my thigh with a poniard from under his skirt, as he
rose. I thought, "Mark the end," and killed him after
he had run a few steps. He fell into a shrub of flowering
thyme so that he died sweetly. Not a moment lost, but
I got to my horse to detach my arbalest: the first monk
was away, and the cart with him, I armed, sighted, shot,
and caught him fair, yea and so fair that had he not
been impelled by the greatness of his goods he would
have stayed. He went out of my sight with the quarrel
protruding from his shoulder, like a brown pear stuck
with a clove. Will men suffer thus for taffeta? No more

than for hearthwood or cider apples, then they give up their little store and live, as the beaver pursued bites off his stones for the hunter to gather up, and lives quiet. Heavens bear witness with me it is so (but heavens will not always answer when they are called.) The uncocking of the shaft had given our horses a mind for exercise. I could not follow, and meditated upon my bloody thigh to devise what kind of death it might be, to be let blood until a man die. It is the same as if a man shall die pissing, with this thought I muffled my wound with cloth, got after my horse, and set out to catch the stalwart monk. Gherucci I left unburied, in his clotted hair.

Slowly with my leaden ache, hardily with my golden desire, I journeyed five days through a country full of shrill-breasted birds but empty of traveling monks, though one left a plain trace. I saw his corpse at the convent here. They had sold the chest, but gave me no aid to find it: at last I came to your ship, where it is buried, like Christ among the common bones, under a load of corn.

That the treasure must lie where it is, I readily admit, for the hours are too few to bring it up without setting every beggar and the Count of Barcelona on our necks. Yet I will not abandon it finally, but beg that you take me on your ship. We shall be partners in ambition and glory, your capital is your captaincy and that the gold will be under your absolute sea sway; mine is telling you so, and telling no one else. The account, which I have delivered to you part spoken and part in this letter, will (I trust) have sufficed to convince you that I do not talk of wax-and-parchment proposals. Should you ask, why do they send such wealth to the new world, I believe its notoriety is too vicious to bring it into daylight without there being knowledge of it, and danger and blame to the church; but the fables of Mexican gold will be accounted an honorable womb for its rebirth, when it has there been melted and fashioned into new bodies.

Alas, that the coffer lies under such a night-storm darkness of grain, you cannot see it (nor touch nor take nor spend). To have faith without sight is hard, but you must have it. Why should I mislead you? If my words are empty, you will toss me naked to the fish, or hang me in pieces on an Indian palm. You will learn that I speak the truth: when the wheat is emptied, you will see what is to be seen—as the sails are raised on your masts, the veil of your understanding will lift; when the wind fills them smooth and white like a groaning wife's belly, your joy will swell like them. Your risk is nothing, taking me aboard will cost you little. Yet think of the rewards. *Experientia longa malorum* has taught me that greatness is given only to the mettlesome. What are your hopes? It is said that you are evilly in debt. There remains no way for you to climb suddenly but by doing some rare stratagem, the like not before heard of: and at this time fit occasion is offered. I have told you the gold's worth. Is not this to be struck bravely for (though we shall risk dancing in a hempen circle)?

I do not trust my life to a fool or a coward, I spare to such a few words of disdain: you seem a hardy honest man. That you left me at your lady's bidding (for *en amour hastive point son cueur ne trouve contentement*, her voice chimed so winningly I hear her yet) is no matter, because the god called Love will not be worshipped by leaden brains. For myself, exactly how well or ill I have done, I am ignorant (the eye sees round itself, sees not into itself): but I am not altogether Fame's outcast; truly she has feasted me with the vigorous nutriment of commendation by those whose Virtue is strong in the world. You have seen I was wounded, and recovered in a week. I have been thrown into rivers and risen drier than my pursuers. I have handled snakes and drunk deadly poison and come to no harm. In this, fortune has not made me reckless. I do not esteem the pox a pimple, I do not provoke swords when I want toothpicks. As for my honesty, you know I do not set my cap over my eyebrows like a politician, and nod and keep my secrets to myself; nor as the eagle casts dust in the eyes of crows, delude you lest you delve into my subtleties. Openly have I presented my words and myself, to be seen and allowed.

Now my fame and fortune rest with you. They are become leaves on the tree of your honor; you will choose to shake them off scornfully as wormeaten and worthless, or preserve and nourish them, for the harvest you shall find.

AMORTONELLI

2 Aug. A.D. 1537 (= *May 11*)

And so the captain took Amortonelli with him. I suppose that the silk in the chest signified gold because a famous treasure was known to have been concealed in it.

The next day I had a disturbing encounter with Dexter Hodge—do you remember, I saw him in Panoramus? I had driven out to the Firestone depot through the vacant town (Miami is puzzlingly unpeopled in this season, and unkempt too, with blackened fronds of low centaury still littering the gutters) to replace my front tires, and there was Hodge. He was ordering an extraordinary quantity of rubber-covered maritime gear—oars, keels, cables.

"I have decided to go into the treasure-hunting racket," he announced to me grandly. "Our first hunting grounds are to be the waters around Stork Island. Have you heard of its friendly dolphins? They play with visiting boats. We're afraid that unless we rubberize our protrusions, the dolphins will injure themselves, bleed, and attract sharks."

During this explanation the clerk, a short spaniel-faced man, stared at Hodge as though he were raving. Hodge took no notice and went on, to my consternation, to ask me to join his group and "turn out on a big game." After this he resumed his business without another word to me.

How should I have responded, or now respond, to this proposal? It is perhaps unimportant.

It's surprising that you also should have found an Abbot of Montpelas. One would enjoy a connection, but the gap' between them is so vast. Are you sure your date wasn't 1491?

At present my thoughts turn elsewhere. I gaze into my gin-and-tonic, where a last shrinking ice cube drifts among de-accelerating bubbles. Fancy has decided that this translucent, no-longer-cubic cube is a herald from the East. As it melts, it will release your essence to be drunk up. Afterwards, I'll reread your letter. Its words touched me beyond imagining. To find such pleasure sustained by such innocence is a satis-faction transcending the present conditions of human life.

XII

May 21

Twang can not know when death will-come, or wher or how, but as brath heave in and from my lung, so the smell of Zachary through my brane.

The Mister Hodge—why not? Go near him, yet tell no thing, and with to-listen hear may be gold-like fax for real gold; and all ways of look into earth and see.

The *abott of Montpelas* get the abby in 13 (thirteen) 91. This is a sure, I find the of-pope grant in Vatican Library. Too it 's-publish by Wal-cower in Anals of Banking, 1970, No. 3. And now, how doe I? Lorn more a bout Misser *Todao* and his stoff or go to Florenze (Italy)?

My freind of here at-last make in-visitation to her home for dindins. This is one very large *bouffé* meel. I home in: 3 men, all little with hot red cravatts, say Hello to Twang very loud, to-gether, and naer me, I think they drank, but no—they sit in the horners all the time after ward with to-say no thing and to-look diffrrent. I say to my frend a litle, yet I listne much. The tlak of many man is ful of division for them, for me new systyms. I think, I will-rememmer a part, I wrote it write after:

1: "When I say, *slab*, I maen, *slab*."

2: "But whut do you dou with the *signifiant?* A road sign say, Miami 82 mile. What re-ality do this indicate? Miami?

The distans be-tween the sing and the sity? The location of the sign? The semi-ottic (?) re-ality, the mmediate realita, posit a structsure..."

3: "I like Miami—of coarse it *is* infect-ed with Ameri-hans."

4: "Why strutcher it though? The elemens of the consep 'sign' thath you naem, and othrs giust as importort, are grasp by our outerd consciouscnesce in a kine of frifloatin jazz con-tinume, so when I see the in for-mation containt, the so call content, I all so *feel* the grainy-ness of the would or flaky-ness of the pent, which ar part of the so-call form, in factt I can feel too the in-formation at any rat it's only one hork of many bob-ing in the opent see of simultanity..."

1: "You're re-moving fenomema from the realn of lin-guage and so of thoughth. Langua must rehognies diacrony as-wel-as sincrony. When a man go-in to a forest to cuddown a tree, trim it, and gaze at this felt, mutilatet tree, the conseppt 'tree' do non dis-appear until he have huttitup in to severel peaces. How ever, as soon as he look at it once it be peeces, the conceptt 'tree' dis-appere and is re-place by the honsept 'bored' and later 'sign'. Nore do he think, 'I've-paint a tree' or, 'A forest point to ward Miami...'"

I love this takl, be cause it is a bout Miami, and so, full of youre skinn. The sense of to-rub was not a ware, onely to me, yet so near, so near, my *tharaï lemu*—my for ever love.

The man that cut tree, so small, more-short than Mons. Latten, tak to me: "How go your re-cerches in the vatican?" I say, no thing.

XIII

May 26

Synchrony is one man's crony, and diachrony is another man's crony...

It will not be easy to "go near" Hodge. His name is an essential local power.

He is active in the expansive manner of old tycoons. He spends here the money he makes elsewhere, mainly I think in Victory Oil, contributing it to civic projects, advancing the cause of urban planning, and providing directly or indirectly many jobs in the Greater Miami area. He attends concerts and lectures, is a director of our Revival of Reading chapter, and from time to time publishes a sonnet in *Sewanee Review*. He may frequently be seen taking walks around the town, without gun or bodyguard. Every afternoon he visits his friend Silex Jewcett, who has spent half his long life in prison but is revered by the people of Florida as a saint. Hodge arrives at the municipal jail with a chamber band of thirteen sarrusophones playing spirituals, chats a while with Jewcett in the visitors' room, and leaves to the invariable strains of "Praise God from Whom all blessings flow." Earlier in the day he can often be found at the Emerald Diamond coaching rookies of all ages, for he is a great sportsman. He has sponsored several swift milers, his *sepak raga* team—this should surprise you—boasts the fastest elbows in the West, and he is the source, guide, and goalie of the soccer team.

All this has brought Hodge prominence. Pictures of his squidlike face frequently appear in the *Sun-Times*, once even in *Time*. His less praiseworthy ventures are overlooked; apparently more for fun than profit, he has collaborated in some dubious undertakings. He directs one establishment called the Egyptian Temple, a "psychic gymnasium" whose activities are secret. Its members undergo an initiation that includes some form of baptism. They are an uneasy lot: track addicts, ward heelers, and other worrisome types; few seem to benefit from the "mysteries." None of them, however, complains.

A more reputable building for which Hodge is responsible is the New Wars Shrine. The monument is built entirely out of weapons. The columns are rocket casings. The altar is made from the illuminated instrument panels of heavy bombers. The wall of the apse consists of two thousand steel helmets stacked on their sides, their rims facing outwards: the exterior has been transformed into a giant memorial hive. Hodge pays the salary of the former Marine sergeant who serves as beadsman, a title that circumstances have altered to "beesman."

Hodge's own house, although small, is a jewel of classic modern. It is built in the shape of a sundial and faced on all sides with malachite. Its one stark ornament is a high relief over the front door representing two wolves seated face to face, and between them a slender candle burning with a per- petual gas flame. The flower arrangements around the house are very sure.

Do you understand why I'm nervous about soliciting Hodge? The invitation to join his group of treasure-hunters was casual and never renewed. Any reminder might well be thought impertinent. I hesitate to tell him of my own plans (*our* plans), or to lure his interest with prospects of another treasure. He's too sharp for that. He is also not a person to whom one makes a gift to receive a gift in return; at least, not openly. Yet I'm impelled to follow your advice, and not just to learn more about treasure-hunting. I would, frankly, love to move in that world. In fact if I take up his offer my sincere "yes" will submerge my scheming "yes." But what can I say when I accost him—"I'm on Tom Tiddler's ground, picking up gold and silver"?

I forgot to say that Hodge is popularly known as the In- visible Jesuit. Perhaps this refers to the Temple.

My own life is pale. It is always the same here. This neigh- borhood is so utterly without significance. I suppose to would- be boxers in Mauritius or Nome, Fifth Street has some signi- ficance, but I do not count it among the significant neigh- borhoods. There was another party at Dan's last night. It was so boring that after ten minutes I said I was tired, lay down in the bedroom to feign sleep, and was indeed soon asleep. When I awoke the place was deserted. I walked home through streets wet with May dew, glistening in the smaragdine dawn. I skirted an ocean of spilt milk where a tanker truck had exploded. Afterwards I made a snack, wishing hard you were making it for me. I would like to be assured that you will always be with me, and that I shall soon "come home." Enough complaining—things aren't so bad. After all, I've passed the worst of the vernal insomnia season, the rose fever season is almost over, and if Decoration Day weren't just around the corner it would be clear sailing.

I think you should go to Florence. Meanwhile I'll write the university in Montpellier to find out more about the Abbots.

XIV

May 30

Hwile your answer was come I have a to-meet with a man strogn in know-lege, and help, the name of him is de Roover, whowho say he 'll give the ex-perience of the hard appuratus of the Archivio segreto del Vatihano. Mr de Roover and tell of clippin-for honditions in the middle age: it is a tomb crime. How han clippins be maked in to money? Delicate, and more-so, be cause he's cert this graet a amount can be one-ly one: of *Otto di Guardia*.

There 's the nwes of the tresor a lttle after that it is come to the popope. Then, the clippins are give to *Giovanni di Bicci de' Medici*—he late-er put a start to the grate bank. This, was to do pay-meant of a dept that Pop *Bonofazio* have have with *Vieri di Cambio*, who come be fore *Giovanni*, and a round 1393 *Giovanni* over-take his lie-abilities & acids. (Ho—my firs english joke!) So *Giov. di B.* a gree to do sell of clippins, he 'll-have his money and 'll-put the balance to the popal a hount.

The *Otto*, a stickcy misre, is come to Florence with *Farinata degli Uberti* and his Glibelhines. In a so safetyfull posizion, he hlips florins while the Ghibelines are in top (until to 1266) and make bucats of gold. Be cause of him (hate), Florence give the order of *fiorini di sug-gello* that have the sense "in seal bags".

And then, I con-tunue with my to-look for a treasure of clippins, chiefly in a shelves of name Introitus et exitus ca-merae apostolicae.

Hwat is to-persieve and to-think? That i've reflects per-ceptions in this material-suttle world, oh such are no thing when I go-in even to the firts absorbtion. *Naï sheen-am*—"so I in-dure (?)"—the daze, for the nihgt can not be in dure but is to die in teers and sleep. I make my las ricerch to day, to morrow I'll say, *Duvaï Roma*.

And: godl florens are in busunuss on-ly after twelfifty, per-hap many-man have small ex-perienze of them, and so it is safe-er for *Otto*. What give me pleasor in you, I han not know hwy, it is my memorease. So this gold sting like death fishes. Crime, potilics, make the stingma, and it go to no money, tradaded a cross years until *Giovanni*.

XV

Otto di Guardia's hoard makes an enthralling tale, but... Best of all who ever were loved in dreams, allow me one "but." Bypaths are an extravagance we cannot afford, and surely Otto is one. If the Medici have anything to do with our treasure, it was long after Giovanni di Bicci.

I had no sooner written you about Dexter Hodge than my relations with him abruptly changed. One morning he appeared at my door to ask "if he might drive me to work"! I have seen him twice since then. The last time furnished emphatic proof of his new opinion of me: I was given a private tour of the Egyptian Temple.

Hodge's interest seems unnatural and I am upset by it.

One enters the Temple grounds at 14 St. Luke's Lane, a posh little street in the new residential section. The gate opened at the approach of Mr. Hodge's limousine. We nosed through it and turned into an alley of yews leading to a graveled parking area. There we continued on foot.

About twenty acres of land surround the Temple: park, garden, and pasture. A group of barn-like buildings stands at one end of the grounds, and towards it we directed our steps. "Here," said Mr. Hodge, "is my sacred zoo." We passed enclosed fields where zebras, buffaloes, and gazelles grazed, a mud pool whose surface was swollen with an ellipse of hippopotamus, a stretch of sand occupied by a camel and swarms of blond hares, an eighty-foot-high aviary of glistening wire. The buildings housed reptiles, fish, and insects.

After we had visited the menagerie, Mr. Hodge, gazing about his domain, explained: "In the practices of our Temple we implement man's ancient belief in the *ka*, or double.

Every animal you have seen belongs to a member of our congregation, not only as his property, but as a visible and objective symbol of his inner life. Through their appearance, the state of their health, the nature of their diet, and a host of lesser omens, these creatures manifest the hidden truth of the man. When assailed by spiritual doubt, by anxiety over the influences of the world, or by curiosity as to what the future holds in store, a member has only to visit his animal doubles to find illumination."

Mr. Hodge chuckled. "That's the pitch. It's a fascinating business, but then the meeting of two cultures is always exciting."

Having admired the zoo, charming in its Ludwig der Zweite way, I expressed my amazement that it could be run at a profit. How could the Temple clientele, known to be less than prosperous, buy and keep the animals?

"Once they believe, they find the money; and once they're initiated, they believe."

We had reached the Temple proper. As we mounted its steps, bells pealed quietly about us. Draped in a weighty rust-colored robe that matched his beard, a Catonian figure stood in the portal.

"Wherefore, child, wishest thou to ascend..." he began, his voice cracking sleepily.

"Can it, Johnny," Mr. Hodge interrupted. "I'm just taking a friend through."

Bowing us in, the attendant murmured, "Thank *you*, Mr. Hodge."

As we entered the building Hodge said, "The main rule of the initiation is not to play the hinge. If a novice looks back, he has to start over. There's no significance in this, but after a while he wonders what's creeping up on him from behind.

"When he has crossed the threshold he strips and gives his clothes to Ramsama," Mr. Hodge went on, indicating the bearded man. "He is led through this door into the first chamber. In the vast room, as if to emphasize the pettiness of the individual in the Great Mystery, the novice is confined in this pyrex cell. Lights in its ceiling illuminate the silvered walls and floor, which mirror the novice grotesquely. He is left alone, standing by that little pyramid of green marbles. Sooner or later he touches them, starting a mechanism that releases and ignites a flow of propane gas around the base of the walls. The lights go out. Blue fire fills the cell with a whoosh. The flames singe a few body hairs, and the mirrors refract great heat. The novice is in quite a lather when we let him out.

"He descends the stairs to this corridor, which is even dimmer than now. Attendants seize him and wrap him in three sheets of translucent black polythene, zipping them together. Hermetically enclosed, he is left to work himself free This should be easy, since the zippers can be opened from within; but the novice is hot and anxious, batteries of strobe lights flash darkly over him, and before long he starts to suffocate. His gasping face at last appears. The lights steady to an agreeable shade of green; cool air is wafted over him; ladies disengage him from his shroud, and rub him with soothing oil. His hopes rise.

"The male attendants reappear, however, to hurl him down another flight of steps (safely padded with foam rubber.) He lands in a blacker cellar, a real dungeon. He is taken and thrust upside down through an elastic aperture lined with hog bristles into a tiny compartment in which he fits barely and cannot move at all. Wait a sec, I'll turn on the lights. The hole is made of obsidian, hard, smooth, and opaque. A woman's voice announces that the novice is to remain there twelve hours, with the passage of each hour to be signaled by a gong. In fact the 'hour' is rung every ten minutes—in his terror the novice loses all sense of time, and two hours is enough for the required effect. There is no light, little air, except for the gong the silence is complete, the oil with which he was rubbed is spiked with Tabasco, and every so often a bone-and-leather claw presses against his chest. I tell you, when he comes out of there he's a new man.

"I forgot to mention that until this last confinement, a deafening recording of the *Turangalila Symphony* has accompanied the initiate through his trials. The music now resumes more softly. Following the faint signs of daylight, the novice emerges onto the terrace. Here the ladies wash him, wrap him in a linen tunic, and seat him at this table, where a basket of grapes and cherries has been placed. By now he is so discouraged that no matter how hungry he is, he will not touch the fruit for a long time. Finally he must. He eats a bit: there are no surprises. I make my entrance. Attendants remove the fruit and replace it with a pile of marbles, like the one in the pyrex cell. I then pluck away the feather awning that shades the terrace, marking the end of the ceremony and the novice's admission."

Mr. Hodge is known to perform this gesture with *panache*; it is often cited as an example of his old-world charm.

"I now begin indoctrinating the novice, who is weak with exhaustion and relief. A capacious chair is brought out for me, into which I settle luxuriously; and, while I give my lecture, I quaff champagne and dip an occasional crisp into a bowl of caviar.

"I start by declaring that there is only one road to happiness in our universe: abnegation and love of one's brother. The first step must be the lessening of one's attachment to base things. One must learn to be poor; and while true poverty is of course a spiritual essence, it can be approached through material acts. Therefore the novice's money will not be returned with his clothing. Anticipating complaints, I warn that love is a stern master.

"I then describe the *kas*. I explain how useful animal doubles can be in ordering one's spiritual life: how, for instance, it is easier to love one's brother through his double (with the corollary 'He who hates his brother's double is a murderer'); how one learns from the *kas* to open the bowels of compassion; how, with one's private world made visible, self-understanding becomes easy, and through it universal knowledge."

Here I broke in with a question that I had meant to ask earlier. Were the initiations into Miami's exclusive Knights of the Spindle conducted on similar lines? "But," Mr. Hodge

answered incredulously, "those people are the pure quill!"
He resumed his account:

"Usually the novice accepts my theory. I put this acceptance to a harsh test. I confront him with the obligation of
founding a psychic menagerie.

"A complete system of *kas* comprises fourteen traditional
categories, which should ideally be represented by different
animals. These categories are strength, power, honor, prosperity, food, long life, influence, brilliance, glory, knowledge, magic, creative will power, sight, and hearing. A
correct psychic menagerie might consist of an elephant, a
lion, a horse, a bee, an ant, a turtle, a pilot fish, a peacock, an
eagle, a seal, a viper, a monkey, an owl, and a bat. To perfect
it, you would then pair your *kas* with anti-*kas*, so as to polar-
ize your spiritual qualities in the most revealing way possible.
Each *ka* would then cohabit with a creature that was its cate-
gorical opposite. You could match the elephant with a caterpillar, the lion with a chicken, the horse with a parrot, the
bee with a coyote, the ant with a grasshopper, the turtle with
a butterfly, the pilot fish with a giraffe, the peacock with a
buzzard, the eagle with a rat, the seal with a sheep, the viper
with a camel, the monkey with an earwig, the owl with a
mole, and the bat with an eel. Of course some combinations
are impossible: how could one prevent the elephant from
walking on the caterpillar, or the lion from eating the chicken,
or the earwig from entering the monkey's ear? In any event
the collection is too grand for our customers, who settle for
much less ambitious, that is less expensive solutions.

"We permit them to buy one animal to fill several categories. The elephant is probably the best example of spiritual
versatility since he can, with the possible exception of brilliance, cover the field. The two elephants you saw are here
for that very purpose. Even with local animals one can manage: a bear, a sponge, a lynx, an alligator, a puma, a manatee,
and a duck satisfy all the requirements aside from honor and
creative will power, two virtues in small demand.

"So after the novice has admitted the desirability of a
menagerie, and after I have shaken him with an appraisal of

various kinds of whale, I turn to cheaper beasts, which I pick with a good idea of how much money my client can be persuaded to spend. He jumps at the chance. He promises to buy, say, a horse, a mina bird, and a small shark. You must remember that he is hungry, thirsty, tired, confused, naked, and trapped. He'll pledge me his bottom dollar to get home, and I have a book of open checks ready to forestall backsliding.

"After their initiation, most members return to the Temple only to consult their *kas*. We attempted communal activities, but the clients are such a suspicious lot that it was hard getting them under one roof. Now we just field a baseball team.

"A new member often stays away at first, suspecting that he's been swindled. But when he learns that his *kas* have arrived, sooner or later he wants to see them. They usually delight him; not because of any affection for animals, but because the *kas* represent money, and he transfers his love of money to them.

"The work of fostering the member's belief in the *ka* devolves on the zoo keepers. For the time being I fade out, bearing the load of initial resentment, and not reappearing until it has been forgotten. The keepers expertly secure the member by furnishing likely material for the demonstration of *ka* theory. They submit elaborate reports of each menagerie's diet, excretions, pulse rate, and temperature, which are supplemented with affectionate accounts of its daily behavior. The keeper's experience and the member's credulity, without which the Temple would never have attracted him in the first place, gradually bind him to his animals. And as soon as a single correspondance occurs between an animal's life and his own, and chance brings this about as often as calculation, his enthusiasm alone is enough to perpetuate the phenomenon. He is so delighted by access to supernatural power that he will make his life conform to his *kas* to preserve it. If, for instance, he finds his prosperity-*ka* ailing before a poker game, he will either be too worried to play well or unconsciously lose money to prove the *ka* right. And when a *ka's* condition is favorable, members will surpass themselves to achieve success. At the last elections one party hack delivered the toughest ward in the city after his gorilla ate an extra five pounds of bananas."

"Maybe your theory works," I suggested.

Mr. Hodge looked into the distance.

"Professor Stedman Cinques of Columbia University has proved... No, no," he laughed, "don't make me go through that. It *is* true that the human may sometimes function as the animal's *ka*—but that's a delicate subject."

He paused to light a cigar. "We've had one unforeseen problem. Some members, after growing very fond of their animals, turn equally suspicious of them. I couldn't understand why until I realized that having radically identified themselves with their *kas*, they come to mistrust the animals as they mistrusted themselves. We've had to provide various types of inanimate scrying for them—haruspication, visions in pools of mercury, palpating the umbones of Venus shells. One remedy is to slaughter the *kas* and investigate their entrails, in the Roman manner. Another menagerie can then be started."

I asked if *kas* were consulted about sexual problems.

"Of course. That sort of divination is called shadowing."

"Do you see the members often?"

"Every day. I have to. You see, since 'the universalism of the Temple allows of no restriction,' our assembly is a bunch of mediocrities, misfits, and cowards. They never stop complaining, about themselves, about the world, and worst of all about the mystical universe. Why do you think I know the Vedas and the Book of the Dead almost by heart? It's the long hours I spend meditating with my miserable customers."

We were once again at the parking area. Mr. Hodge instructed his chauffeur to take me home. He concluded our visit with a pre-Socratic remark: "The games grow old, but the marks are always new."

Since then I have returned to my monotonous schedule. I've had enough of this sad world that spins forever in its greater and lesser dreams.

Do you think it prudent to involve the de Roover person in your research?

XVI

Giune 8

When 1/2 the erth sciscors us, my all-earth is *slop* (misiry), such misyry *me wun lucr-em vin*, I 'm similir I am eating a horpse. This is deep Pan re-act to wo—more-creul than to-be death and ate.

A gainst memory I out-leave the signifiant detell. The tresure took by Pop *Bonifaze* has the name de tribus serranis, whiwhich have the italian to-mean dei tre sciarrani, "of 3 see perches". In the lettr to the of-ship captain, that has-be in your lettre to me, *Amortonelli* ear the man with full-er voice say, "on lid of chesst were-carve crewdly 3 fishs." I'm so mist up by different moneys in the '400, are you can say how this have worth of that?

My mind is in-certn why Mr Hodge 'll-have no interest in you, be cause you "upsets". Is he not can harmony-inpulse to you, as you're sweet? Ana-way I clime the train to Florenza to night. I have the idea, it is your 2 scales of years? But I do n't see this like tru.

Now we have 3 chains from of-Mr-*Todao* clippings and the hord of *Amortonelli*. One, the fammily of *i Medici*, two, the *abbott of Montpelas*, and three fish. I tell to you, I miss you dear-ly. I love you yet more. The to-be in bed with Inglish Grammr of Jespesen is not very fun-y, mon ami.

XVII

June 13

How vividly I see you! So near I can imagine touching you. But I want to touch more than your wraith. Twang, can this scheming after gold justify the decay of contentment that separation imposes? If only I could detach my hope of riches from the thought of your eyes! It's as though looking into them had ignited a passion for difficult glories. But without you I sag; without you, I could believe that the soul and the body are not one.

It must be getting hot in Italy. Do you have summer clothes, and enough? Nothing, I suppose, could be cooler than a loosely ordered *phrap*.

Dexter Hodge continues attentive. Yesterday he mentioned events of the summer season (*the* season in Miami now) to which he will take me. This was a relief. During the previous week he had talked of nothing except his desire to have me play in some baseball games he is sponsoring.

I think my worries about him were fantasy. There is certainly no age problem between us.

You've seen baseball. Can you imagine me playing? Mr. Hodge left me no choice. One afternoon, after a few gulps of rum, I drove over to the diamond for the first time, expecting sure humiliation.

Mr. Hodge welcomed me and introduced me to his team, the Sovereigns, who represent the Egyptian Temple.

The Sovereigns wore uniforms of bright orange mohair into which cabbalistic emblems in green and purple had been knitted. They belied Mr. Hodge's description of Temple members, and seemed to be true gentlemen-sportsmen. Some had nicknames behind which I discerned Miami celebrities, a fact that I kept to myself, addressing them by their chosen monickers: the Calcium Nut, the Locus Solus Kid, Christ Tracy, Mushnick the Second, Cortisone Moonface, Omnibus Hesed (the pitcher).

Mr. Hodge wanted me to catch. It was obvious that I could play no other position. I insisted that my arm was weak, and so became an umpire. I can't throw, or catch, or run, or hit—I can only love! Mr. Hodge felt it was sad to be an umpire so young. He decided to play catcher himself: "I'll manage the team just as well from a squat."

The Sovereign's opponents were the Class Cannons. After two games their team is still wholly mysterious to me. Its members have remained nameless and almost wordless. They do not speak unless circumstances force them to. None has ever admitted his identity to me, or replied to my advances other than with flashing gestures of the hands.

At three o'clock Mr. Hodge told me to start the game. I asked the manager of the Cannons if he was ready. He responded by taking from a square box next to the bat rack a golden hunting horn, which he raised to his lips. The Cannons assembled behind him. The manager blew three short pure notes, then tucked the horn under his arm.

The Sovereigns had meanwhile lined up in front of their dugout. As soon as the horn call ended, they began to sing. The music was homely, the performance smooth:

The Lord knocks over the proud man, but never hurts
    the humble.
Throw yourself down, He'll lift you up, no matter how
    low you tumble.
Curse the Devil and he'll depart, spurn him who'd work
    your ruin,
But bless the Lord, draw near to Him, and He will take
    you to Him.

The Lord knocks over the proud man, but never hurts
    the humble.
Throw yourself down, He'll lift you up, no matter how
    low you tumble.
Curse the Devil and he'll depart, spurn him who'd
    work your ruin,
But bless the Lord, draw near to Him, and He will take
    you to Him.

The Lord knocks over, &c.

As they repeated the stanza, irritation, mute and irrestible, gripped the Cannons. At last their shortstop climaxed a pantomime of swelling fury by forcing out, in a hiss of thrilling sibilance, the word "Cease!" The teams broke ranks, the Cannons scattering over the field, the Sovereigns returning to their dugout. I waited behind the plate (its pentagonal whiteness unspotted by any cleat) while the Cannon battery warmed up. I noticed that the right fielder, a slender youth with shoulder-length golden hair, was straightening his flowing locks with long strokes of his comb.

The pitcher nodded his readiness. I waved my arm and called out, inexplicably forgetting what game was being played, "Serve!" I at once altered the command to the correct "Play ball!" as a soundless snigger enlivened the infield. This was my only mistake.

The Cannons dominated the game. In defense their speed and deftness controlled the ball completely. In fact on the rare occasions when a decision went against them, they managed somehow to make the ball disappear, thus stopping the game and creating a most unnerving confusion. Usually, to get the game started again, the adverse decision had to be reversed, compromised, or cancelled; sometimes Mr. Hodge would successfully plead with the Cannons to restore the missing ball. His tactic was to express intense compassion for the fielders, while arguing that it was in the general interest to resume the game. The ball would then reappear as mysteriously as it had vanished, perhaps bouncing nonchalantly in the pitcher's glove.

Once even Mr. Hodge's patience was surpassed. In the seventh inning the Cannons had narrowly missed a double play—both runners were safe on first and second. The baseball disappeared. Mr. Hodge walked out to the shortstop and began his plea. The shortstop pointed down the road, to a spot where Mr. Hodge had parked his aged jeep. It was now gone.

Mr. Hodge lost his temper. "By God, I'll take you to court for this. I know I can't expect you bastards to know right from wrong, but at least you can tell the difference between a baseball and a jeep!"

The shortstop silently held up the ball in his ungloved hand. Mr. Hodge took the ball, cocked his right leg and, like a Thai boxer, swatted the shortstop across the ear with his foot, knocking him to the ground. The Cannon got up with a mimic snarl; but neither he nor his teammates complained. Mr. Hodge turned away, tossed the ball to the pitcher, and was walking off the field when from behind the Sovereign dugout the Cannon bat boy rolled the jeep into view.

I observed all this distractedly. The batter waiting his turn had been whistling "Lover, come back to me," and I had been shaken by the song's nonexistent pathos.—There was a time when my attachment to you naturally found its words. Now separation has worn a chasm within me, words are engulfed by it. If you do not know how desperately I love you I shall never be able to tell you.

Forgive me for thrusting these after all useless emotions on you. That stupid song!

So play started again. Having two men on base did the Sovereigns no good. Neither then nor in any other inning were they able to score. On the other hand, the Cannons wasted none of their seven hits.

In the second inning, after a walk and a single had put two men on base, the Cannon manager with a certain ostentation planted a six-foot high cane in the ground in front of his dugout. The right fielder, the long-haired blond, was at bat. The Sovereign infield razzed him loudly—"Hey, sweetie, the Youth and Beauty Pageant's tomorrow"—but he took no notice and doubled in both runners. Two innings later, with a man at first, the Cannon manager stood a stiff-backed wooden chair next to the cane. The batter hit a home run. Finally in the sixth inning, with Cannon runners on second and third, the hunting horn used at the start of the game was set bell downward between cane and chair. One batter fouled out, but the next hit a long single. Watching the sixth run score, the Sovereign catcher (Mr. Hodge) cussed, "Damned Hebraic parallelism!"

I performed my role satisfactorily. The Sovereigns were friendly, in spite of their weak play. The Cannons were unrelentingly distant. Only once did any of them react to my presence. As the fourth inning commenced, their catcher approached bearing a Ry-vita smeared with cottage cheese. He handed it to me without a word as he settled behind the plate.

I hope you like cottage cheese as much as I do. There is, however, nothing like it among Pan dairy products.

When I arrived home late in the afternoon I found that my pockets had been emptied of their contents—bills, small change, bloat pills, everything! I had left my keys in the car, so at least I could get into my own apartment.

Next day the Sovereigns won, 1–0. They scored their run in the eleventh inning on a walk, a stolen base, and two sacrifice bunts. They are not a great hitting team. The Cannons were shut out by a new pitcher, a wiry chap named Peter Jeigh. Mr. Hodge introduced him to me with the comment, "As a Sovereign he may be a mite snider, but watch him pitch." He *was* good, although he had only one arm. He had lost the other "blowing the chase," whatever that means.

Peter Jeigh was almost as silent as the Cannons. I heard him speak only once. Shortly before the game, I found him gazing into the palm of his glove, which he was massaging with neat's-foot oil. He murmured, more to himself than to me, "I shall attain sympathy with inanimate things."

Between innings I told Mr. Hodge about my missing possessions. He immediately went to speak to the Cannon manager. Returning, he promised that the matter would be cleared up. Nothing was apparently done, but when the game was over my missing belongings were back in my pockets!

I wrote to the University of Montpellier for help with the Abbots of Montpelas. I referred in passing to a consignment of silk that may have figured in certain transactions...

As you say, the three perches do plausibly link the clippings with our treasure. Your flair is incredible.

You ask about the currencies of the time. The question is not as difficult as it might appear. The first thing to get straight is the Florentine florin, or rather florins. The gold florin that was called "sealed florin" for the reasons you mention was soon debased, so that in the fifteenth century a new coin had to be created to replace it, the "large florin." It was worth a tenth and later a fifth more than the sealed florin. Actually "replace" isn't accurate since the two florins coexisted for a time until the older one was abolished, in 1471, but for simplicity's sake think of the matter as a replacement. In any case these are the two florins to remember—however, see below. Next you must consider a third Florentine money in use during the fourteenth and fifteenth centuries, the pound, more precisely the "affiorino pound." Let me say at once that this was not real money, there was no pound coin it was just a money of account. It was divided into twenty affiorino shillings and the shilling subdivided into twelve affiorino pence. These smaller units were also imaginary— perhaps imaginary isn't the exact word—oh, I forgot to mention that the florin was also divided into shillings, into twenty shillings in fact, like the pound, and also into two hundred and forty pence. The reason I forgot is that these shillings and pence are also imaginary, but of course the florin was not imaginary—there was a real florin coin (I mean naturally two coins, as explained.) Well, matters became simpler after the introduction of the large pound, no, no—the large *florin*, because the habit arose of accounting for fractions of the florin in terms of the divisions of the affiorino pound, according to which the florin was equal to twenty-nine affiorino shillings and three hundred and forty-eight affiorino pence. So remember that both the large florin and the pound were made up of the same shillings, twenty in the latter and twenty-nine in the former, and that in both cases the shilling was in turn divided into twelve pence, so that there were two hundred and forty affiorino pence to the pound and three hundred and forty-eight affiorino pence to the florin (large). Still, you should not forget that earlier the florin was also divided into its own shillings and pence, twenty and two hundred and forty respectively. In other words, a pound can be reckoned as twenty twenty-ninths of a later florin.—You may ask, if all these small moneys were imaginary, how did people pay for a sack of potatoes (I realize that there were as yet no potatoes.) You see, parallel to these gold systems there was another system based on silver, and it was used for such transactions. The main unit here was, as a matter of fact, also a pound, the "lesser" pound, and like the other pound it was divided into twenty lesser shillings and two hundred and forty lesser pence, but you must not let the equivalence of the names suggest equivalences of value—the values were absolutely separate. The trouble is that there was no legal ratio between gold and silver, so it's hard to say *what* the relation between the two, or three, systems was. However, this is only a little cloud in a generally sunny sky. Let's return to the first pound. This affiorino pound linked Florence to the pound system that was common to much of Europe during the Middle Ages. I don't mean to imply that the pounds of the various countries (which weren't really countries, I know, I only call them that for convenience)—that the various pounds were interchangeable. Far from it. But at least they had the same idea behind them. In England there was the pound sterling still current today, in Flanders the pound groat, so called because it was based on the groat, a small silver coin. That these pounds were silver did not prevent them from belonging to the international system that included the gold Florentine florin. Incidentally, you must not confuse the Flemish pound groat with the Venetian pound groat, the latter being based on a gold coin, the ducat, rather than on a silver coin the groat. (The pound in Milan was based on a silver coin as well, the imperial, which was constantly depreciating, so that the Milanese pound was always becoming smaller than the other pounds. Still, it was a pound.) In Geneva the situation differed in that the pound was *not* the main accounting unit, but the crown or rather crowns plural, since there were two, one being sixty-four to the mark and the other sixty-six—the mark was gold— forget about it. This system went to Lyons with the Geneva fairs, so that the Lyons branch of the Medici bank reckoned in crowns (at sixty-four to the mark) whereas in Avignon they did their accounting in "pitetti" florins. This florin is the other kind I referred to while defining the properly Florentine ones. It was lighter than the sealed florin, or at any rate lighter than the sealed florin before it was debased: consequently it was divided into twenty-four and not twenty shillings and two hundred and eighty-eight as opposed to two hundred and forty pence. The word "consequently" in the preceding sentence somehow does not ring true. Finally, there was one last other florin, imaginary in the way I have used "imaginary" in connection with these currencies, which was found in Genoa in quotations of money rates and held equal to twenty-*five* Genoese shillings. But generally merchants in Genoa used the Genoese pound, just as they used the Barcelonese pound in Barcelona.

Does this clear matters up?

XVIII

Theu is "us". I say this werd a gain, and again, to me. *Ticbaï stheu, theu ticbaï stheu.* O, yes. I'm tire *wuc vin*, like a deadboby. Trip is done, with no-sleep. This time I write only, I'm here. Any gown is enough evne ruff and old. You will-have no fear, for my close. The hope come to me, to see out and a round in summer time and winter time, with free glanse, from a mountn, hwile my eys re-volve in a Khmer slime of heal'th—I to be nature with loooks in to nature with some ease-like sym-pathey like the blue-eye gras of meadows have a look in to the face of the sky.

Part Two

XIX

June 22

They have caught the sulfuric acid fiend, whose last target was our drinking fountains.

There is, for me, even better news. ("Black oxen cannot tread on my feet forever.") Mr. Hodge has proposed me for the Knights of the Spindle.

The Knights are the most exclusive club in Florida, with an unvarying membership of sixty-six. It is extraordinary proof of Mr. Hodge's influence to have secured my nomination. When he told me of it, I protested that I did not deserve it; he refused to listen. "You can't knock me. You're a good man." My protests weren't entirely honest—he might have been playing a painful joke. But he confirmed my eligibility by presenting me with an angel-noble of ruddy luster, suggesting that I cure my stye in time for the initiation.

Did you see that a new six-pointed star was discovered at the Miami observatory? Appropriately, it lies within the confines of Moses' Basket.

Today, as I walked along a street in the faubourgs, a van came squealing round the corner, the sun blazing on its windshield and I suppose in the driver's eyes. It was an apple van, full of "manducation apples." Have I told you about them? They are a fruit of resilient texture, specially developed to teach infants how to chew, and they've boomed. One cannot visit the supermarket without hearing a number of mothers, any number of grandmothers, and innumerable great-grandmothers raving about them. But no one remembers that the practice was originally Pannamese. I've forgotten your fruit—doesn't it mean "bone mango"?

This happened around noon. It must be noon in Florence —no, midnight. Twang, when shall we once again watch chameleons puffing on a sunny tree? Dan is throwing a party here this evening. He wasn't able to use his own place because he's in flight from his next-to-last twist (I never met her.) There is no peace for me here. My walls are gauze-thin, the roar of wassail penetrates them as if they were imaginary. Perhaps my last sentences give the impression that the party has already begun. It's a pleasant idea. I would like to be writing you in solitude while my friends and others wildly celebrate a room-and-a-half away. And when the party does start I may not actively participate. My recent high life has exacted its price, diarrhea, so tonight perhaps I'll withdraw to this desk, and gazing under my bright little lamp at your last, tender, undated letter, commune with you over rice and tea. My loveliest one, let us always be shrines to each other, consecrated to faith and confidence! Thanks to you, I count myself among the "little remainder" of the saved. Damn this party and this life of waiting! Cleaning up will be the worst. I remember that after one of Dan's revels the scraps filled seven garbage baskets, bodies excluded. Speaking of which, Grace has a date with "someone new" tonight and plans to bring him. She'll go on carping about you none-theless.

I can't send you money with this letter because my check-book is all stubs, but Monday I'll get a new one. Oops—the debit and credit columns are exactly even. But that's all right. Mr. Hodge today gave me some tips on the hounds, and since bookmakers know no Sundays, I'll collect to-morrow.

I forgot about the apple van. Not that it was interesting, only scary. I had gone out to Dalmanutha to see the green lion, famous to readers of "Believe it or not." As I said, the fellow was dazzled as he rounded the corner, and he veered onto the sidewalk, missing me by one micro-inch. Limp with shock, I sat down on the pavement. The anxious driver jumped from the cab. It was the long-haired right fielder of the Cannon team. I assured him between wheezes that I was unharmed. He trembled silently, then declared, laboring each syllable, "My name is Hyperion Scarparo," and gave me an apple.

XX

June 26

I have the wish of to-say in my last latter, yet fatique did not can. Gold is no fool-like dreem, in all place in all time that's worth-full. Tell you to Bamma Deng you not be-lieve so, he say, Forth! (Twang shall n't ever say it.) I thikn all-so empire is honormost post in the sport. But you 're tacit, a bout, who win the threemost game?

Atr-am, wey nob mau Lao, that signify: I think aï, to have-be a Laotion! For they are ever board in of-love bussness, and guiet after, yet Twang do-tell to you. At late-er that mid-niht of hlock, I mont the train to Florence. I de-vide the room with 2 man-Italian. One to left speaks english, and he 's the thought, I 'm his reel friend. One hquench the light for sleep, I do n't enter sleep, for the "friend" lie on me, all-so after I stroke him hard-ly. I think, that is absurb to be-come wiled. The man who do n't say english or any thing go down in Terni, Umbria. The fiend have be-gin agin, I want you, I do a-long fiht for ours til to Firenze. I 'm strong, but he 's top, and un-wieldly, just be fore the stazion I have-braek two of my best naels on him. It's pael dawn as he con-docts me to a hostel. Well, it is a nough for to day.

XXI *

July 1

Jesus! When for once I was ahead, your letter came and set me back a week of Sundays. I try to improve my feelings but it's no use. The spirit of sacrifice is beyond my compass. Don't *you* be reconciled to such a sacrifice. If you can bear it I cannot, the thought of you being in the coils of that worm annihilates me. It's bad enough staggering down the dark avenue of my imagination, seeing your shawl soiled and your necklace shedding pearls about the train. But those words "conducts me to a hotel"—at any price ransom those words from the well of despair where they lie chained, tell me what they mean. The greasy scum, to pick a jewel when the streets are full of mudkickers! Beloved, tell me exactly what happened, because reliving the scene, extrapolated from your prose and deformed in the convex mirror of anguish, is hourly kneading my brain into new folds. I'm too nervous to work. (But Montpellier promises to help.) Twang, only a frail miracle joins us, a silky cocoon that we precariously spun, to be clung to until the later time. I would commit murder to protect it. The only pleasure I've had since this morning is imagining that man beaten like a snake, or strapped across the muzzle of a howitzer. You didn't eat with him? He don't deserve to lap cold tea from your saucer.

XXII

July 3

Yet how, gives Montpellier the help (who's he)? Have-pass 3 months since I write a zen story as you in-joy, hear is a other to extratract you from angger: "A yuong man a range his stance so he have can to a distant land to study a certan Master Three. At an end of three, with to-feel of no sense, he've-present to the Master his de-parture. The Master say,

* Special delivery

'You 've-be three, why more?' 'A greed.' But he stil feell he have-do no advance. He tolded the Master, that he was the Master, say, 'Look, Three and Three.' 'Stay Three.' He did but with sucsecs. He have-tell the Master that have-happen, the Master said, 'You 've-be tears, moths, sands, the end of time. You have-*hate* in-lighten-meant. Hommit suisise.' The end of the dent was in lighten." I have-donde this trans-lation giust as I come to west, so it 's clumbsy.

That poor man-italian is a poor one. Oh I say it to you, he 's full to his hairs (not-many) with shaem and sorror. As he make those events he 's dronk, as the 3-dollar skunk. At the dawn he vommit over the piazza del duomo, and mingle his tears to-it (like the zen youht.) I have-telled him, now it's addio. He said, I mean arrivederci, but I say, no, for-ever, I ex-plane the to-mean of *duvaï*. This is then he vomitt. Have I give the Pan word of I vommitt, *uüax-m*, it 's so otomato-poetic I beleve? He raise and fall any times on the cobbler stones, he wax eloquence, and he does an aoth on the hat of his mamma he 'll-be ubediant to Twang, and good, so it is all rite, and what more, I all-so my in tire love, my *stheu lemu*, Twang rise an neel at your foot and beg to obeg you. I 've not eat nether love with him, on-ly scratsh, and we all two have a litle pain (I, my bustit nails) and this, is a muilde bound.

XXIII

July 7

You have half drawn that arrow from my bowels, but I still cannot dispel the vision of what may have happened. Scouring my thoughts with the bristles of reason has not banished the possibility that you consented, no matter how little, in the desires of that odious man. You must know that even a passive surrender to impureness begets moral anarchy in general and insomnia in particular. Lord, lord, the noose tightens and I choke—at this moment he may be taking advantage of your generous nature! I tell you, bad fruit means a bad tree, and such trees should be cut down and burnt. Why don't you stick him in the can for a while?

Yesterday the preparatives for my initiation began. I visited the Knights' official tailor, Mr. Zone, to be fitted for my robes. He followed a ritual procedure: purple-red cloth, worked with random crescents of silver, was wrapped around me and shaped with a large razor.

As Mr. Zone began his task, I was joined by Dexter Hodge (my sponsor), and two Knights who were to examine me. Greeting me in a stiff, kind way, they declared me fit for Spindle candidacy: competent persons had seen me leave the Egyptian Temple "under the awning of accepted novices." I turned toward Mr. Hodge, who lowered his head to mutter, "Don't bobble them. It's O.K."

Masked with spangled cloth, three framed pictures hung on one wall of the room. The Knights uncovered them, instructing me to pick the "truest" and to justify my choice.

To the left was a painting, "A Pilgrim in El Dorado." By a calm and sunny sea, airy groves showered pomegranates and dates on the mingled children of beast and man; while in the deeper shade of oaks, egg-pale hermaphrodites danced for a bearded sorceress around a magic fire, in which the salamander and phoenix thrived. The mood was nostalgic.

To the right was a blown-up pornographic photograph, full of the cold shine of flashbulb on skin.

At the center was a drawing in inks. Three elementary figures, triangle, circle, and pentagon, were linked by a meandering cord at once arbitrary and exact. Mr. Hodge coughed. He was standing in front of me. In one hand, thrust behind him, he held a white card printed with large green capitals. I declaimed the written words: "Geometry provides a plane of refraction between essential being and formal manifestation." (I said "pain" instead of "plane" but my boner went unnoticed.)

No sooner had I spoken than I was ushered out of the tailor's shop into a waiting one-horse carriage. My examiners cheerfully waved good-bye and, alone with the cabby, I rode off. I can't say how long we drove, since I fell into a delicious snooze. I dreamt of you; you caressed me; and at the moment of your suavest caress, I remembered *him*. He has become a wolf to my dreams and a remora to my will! Opening my eyes, I saw that we were turning around a colossal manhole, the principal entrance to the Dade County sewer complex.

Tradition requires that I invite a group of Knights home to meet my intimates. I'm not looking forward to it. I just waxed the floors to an umblemished sheen, and the thought of all my awful friends marking them up is more than I can bear, let alone the other reasons for not giving a party.

Montpellier is a city in the south of France—funny question. Professor Blesset of Montpelier University is to send the microfilm of a document from Montpelas. He thinks it will interest us; I hope he's right. As regards research, knighthood and the thought of your boyfriend have kept me cooking on one burner.

XXIV

July 12

Now, I work in the Arhive of the State here, so I hurry to say the last fastc from Roma. On Mag 12 & 30 I've-write, *Bonafazio* (pope) have-take Misser *Todao's* hord and givn it to *Giovanni di Bicci de' Medici*, that he may-negoziatit. This is n't just true, it is no as simple. There is a cousin (sp?) of *Giovanni* of name *Averardo di Francesco de' Medici*, he have-act for Pope ond got gold, then he re-put it to *Giovanni*. *Giovanni* a-sure *Averardo*, he will-negotiatit and have its worth. I owe to-say they're 2 Medici banks then, in Florenze of *Averardo*, of *Giovanni* in Rom. They were friend-like banchs. Then 1397 *Giovanni* make his lone bank in Fiorence, and still he 's-n't-tradad the hlippings. And this new bank rivalrie *Averardo*. And, *Giovanni* make his in-Rome bank complex-er, but all ways with no hapital, any bank have-can to-do this some time, yet there's an opinoin, they have-know of that hord in the cort of the Porpe (this is the large hustomer), so they know, he 's rich, enogh to borror money from-him. *Averardo* all-so was with-out money for the treasure, but he say, it's mine. So he maded a 1st complain a round that time. The complain is in gentl words. There's fog, a bout of-who the dett the gold clippings should to pay. Be cause, Pope *Boniface* have-made detbs to both housins.

Oh your worsd of angger, a gain, they are come hards a-gains me, the sky and the city so shaek, I think the univorse must be know-ing Love—Khmer pro-verb. Yet you can to see now, your raeg is not with out cause, but with-out reason.Whewhen the bright flags of wool are put a-round the even-ing sky and make it bright, and a sweat small wind come with smells of the mountains, then my heart is to-ward you on his stock-ing knees to love you a thousand folds: *mau pheu*—"I'm you" (rs). I make sugestion, he may not be-arrest, if he do a nice gift. He chump at the chance. So, there's some good thing even in a vomit-er. Shall I say vomiter, as in Pan *uüax* means as well the man, and whawhat he make, and the to-make, thus, I'm un-sure.

XXV

July 17

Even the emphatic commas at the end of your letter left meager room for my gasps. What I ask over and over, and you will not explain, is why you must see him at all. Then to ask him to give you a present is beyond understanding. If I didn't trust you more than myself, oh, so much more!— nevertheless, it all makes me feel like *uüaxm* or *uüax* or what- ever. Say, how is it that Pan is inflected—most unneighborly for an Indochinese language. That too is perplexing. Anyway, I do trust you. I know that regret for what's done is a sinful waste of time. I will measure my emotions. But please resist the flamboyance of others, don't let them tumble you into that slithery vase where so many flowers rot. "Twenty-three thousand died and the desert was strewn with their corpses." (An allegory hard to explain, but true.)

Two days ago I passed another Spindle test. It was Census Sunday, and the morning after my party, which went better than I'd expected, since Dan and Grace behaved like the civilized beings they aren't. Two men from the Knights called at brunchtime: a dignified gent (the examiner) and an impudent youth whose appearance was grotesque even by my standards—ill-barbered carrot-top sprouting above pinkish eyes, tiny lids daubed with kohl (a teenage practice here), and a harelip the color of beets. He was as respectful of the examiner as he was sassy to me.

We drove out through the northern suburbs, skirting the vast wasteland behind Slaughterhouse Crescent, with its Sunday litter of skulls. We stopped once to investigate a crowd that had gathered by the highway. A donkey—not a horse, as the press reported—had fallen into a well, from which it was being raised by the efforts of other donkeys. Afterwards we reached a pier and parked by a forty-foot, crane-colored fishing boat. The captain, who was waiting by the gangplank, complained of our lateness, saw us aboard, and started up the engines. The young rascal steered.

We rode at a desultory speed, so that I suffered more from torpor than from my usual queasiness. There was little conversation. Lunch was served by an obscure female who mostly lingered below decks. My attention was conspiratorially drawn to the designs on our plates: caducei, scale helmets, serpents biting their tails. I made no comment. I was preoccupied with keeping down the food; to this end I even refused a fine neo-Cuban cigar. Around two o'clock I noticed, near the dallying boat, an effect as of floating cloth-of-gold. I asked the captain what it was. He grinned whitely through his preposterous tan, and without answering, pointed toward the bow. The examiner was emptying onto the ash-gray foredeck a small sack of filings, which he distributed in half-inch mounds: almost touching one another, they formed a closed, irregular curve. When the sack was empty, the examiner beckoned me to watch. The vibrations of the engines were agitating the iron dust, displacing it across the slick paint. The filings gradually assembled into a fixed equilateral triangle. The examiner then asked two questions. To my surprise, I answered them without hesitation.

"Can you define what you see?"

"A triangle is defined by its center—its unmanifest essence."

"Is this to be explained?"

"No, only sensed in its intensity."

The examiner was standing behind me, and as I said these words I turned toward him, and found myself looking into four astounded faces: behind the cockpit window, the young scamp at the wheel; the captain on the cockpit roof; the examiner in the narrow gangway; the dark woman behind him. Past the stern, the cloth-of-gold was now in focus: loose-stemmed waterweeds.

A flurry of wind blew away the filings. The examiner clapped me on the shoulder, while the captain, gunning his engines, turned the boat around to speed homewards. My stamina exhausted, I lurched aft and abandoned my meal to the muddy billows of the Everglades.

The presence of a triangle in both tests seemed deliberate. According to the examiner, it was not. He explained, after I'd cleaned up, that the second triangle referred to a game played at the Knights' "mother club," somewhere in Asia. The game, which resembles squash, requires a convex triangular court. Of the reappearance of the triangle he said, "Chance is a wise master," and shifted my attention to a snakebird drying its wings on a mangrove.

On the drive home, our car stopped at the edge of town, insofar as there is an edge. The carriage that had fetched me from the tailor's was drawn up by the roadside. The examiner saw me into it and, as he left, handed me a morocco pouch with one gold coin in it—an *écu sans soleil*.

My carriage ride was long: we twice drove from the starting-point to the manhole I told of. There must be a significance to this. I have become convinced that in my dealings with the Knights everything that happens is symbolic; even if I don't know of what, that doesn't matter, what counts is that I am being guided along a spiritual itinerary. My nature has been sufficiently distracted to loosen its hold, and I am compelled into the sentiments of old mysteries—that we are, for instance, all children and heirs of one father. How they manage this with triangles *is* a mystery. Such feelings ought to be sweeter than the honeycomb; not to me. To see the common in the uncommon, the stars in a sunny sky, birds nesting in my mirror—delusion, delusion, I'm a doomed machine, and can't forget it, although wishing I could. Only in you is there neither renunciation, nor oblivion.

XXVI

July 22

My lover of camelions, it's no question and was not ever. Other wise. I do n't like him, yet it is easy-er to manager him with pazienze, *atr-am duvaï nob sheen-am* "I think fare well for to-indure-him." He's so perstant, if I say *duvaï* he 'll-be wosre. And per-haps I have a haunch a bout him... He's of name Pindola. And, he's not long-er so crazy as the kite, he's-become much swettertamperd. There is a reason medicle. A dottor cheque him and learn a "sugre defficiency" in the blood of him. This have-make him very franetic, in other and in de-sire. Now, he eats a milky way each 2 ours and's angelic, I keep him easy-ly un-der my toe. None of it is much to some point yet I 'll chatt with you until that we met, love. I've no pleasure in the to-ask money, but of-it have, no-more.

XXVII

July 28

They came at eight, bringing my robes, and tongue sand-wiches that they urged on me, as supper was not until mid-night. Three tart margaritas had put me in good spirits.

The fly was parked outside, with a limousine behind it. I entered the carriage, the others the car. Twice our tandem drove to the great manhole and returned to my dwelling. The third time it stopped at the sewer entrance; I was told to climb out, then blindfolded. One asked me a question I've forgotten, to which I answered, "An expanding economy in an expanding universe." (Giggles.) Another seized me from behind and pressed his thumbs under my shoulder blades, prodding me toward speech. Dubiously, I opened my mouth: "Ah... um..." The laughter ended, two fingers poked through the blindfold against my eyeballs, for a flash of scarlet and yellow. One took my hand, murmuring, *"Dabar!* Your land journey's over."

There was a clank of metal, I was led stumbling a few steps forward and pushed to my knees. My feet were grasped in turn and placed below the level of the pavement on metal bars. Descending, I counted fifty-two rungs. The air became damp and blessedly cool. I thumped to solid ground as my foot sought the fifty-third rung. A short march forward, to sounds of water faintly splashing, and three steps down onto swaying wood. I was instructed to sit. Others clambered around me in the boat; I felt it glide over the water. "Your sea journey commences." My blindfold was removed.

The sewer light was dim, barely a glimmer on the glazed vault. A voice warned, "Don't play the hinge. One look back ruins everything."

The words frightened me: the Temple initiation imposed the same rule. Was this to be a comparable ordeal? I kicked myself for not bringing my flask, or some pills.

"Make light!"

I thought that the words had been addressed to me, but another voice shouted a reply, and white and black patterns fleetingly crossed the walls ahead.

"Where is the affection called dazzling? Where are the tears?"

Another shout produced a flare, so intense I shut my eyes and beheld matching darkness.

Around me the cries came more rapidly, and the walls blazed with changing lights. The flare's brightness was over-run with a film like blood, then mixed with creamy white, which gave way to purple and umber. New exclamations produced reaches of flame-color and faint yellow; dark blue and pale blue; leek green. The smell remained constant.

We crossed the junction of four waterways. I was told, "These are the Corridors of Proximate Session."

Irritated shouts of "Not this... Not that..." and "Never more!" rebounded to us from the lateral sewers.

"Not the voices of ignorance," my companions intoned—

"... not the voices of ignorance but the implosion..."

"... the implosion of language before..."

"Memory..."

The word moaned away down the galleries amid a salad of colors.

As the voices came alternately from either side, I found myself turning toward them. To the left there was a feeling of boundless warmth; to the right, volatile brilliance. Ahead was a dark point where the walls appeared to meet. As the illuminations ended I briefly saw one last image, a sexual tantrum, clear among the damp reflections; then my face was brushed by wet strands, we passed through some veil into a cool, empty light.

We had entered a round widening of the sewer. On one side a broad concrete platform rose from the water. Here an assembly was seated in armchairs. A quiet buzz of conversation was soothing after the shouts.

"You see, no useless ecstasy."

Our boat nudged the wall near steps. We approached the gathering. Heads turned towards us, among them Dexter Hodge's.

"Hello, hello, what a surprise! Didn't expect to see you here. Join us anyway. Sit down."

"Yes, yes," they chorused, "no matter you weren't invited. Drop in any time."

Reassured by the friendliness with which these surprising words were spoken, I settled in the proferred armchair, where I was to remain for an hour. The cushion seemed to have been stuffed with spark plugs, which helped my pious expression.

There were several dozen men, most of them well on, and well-off too. Silence spread among them, until a very old gentleman, able at last to make himself heard, bleated a wordless pitch-tone, then raised his hand and led, still seated, the opening of the Spindle Hymn:

The jester in cap and bells
Swings his bauble, lights the bladder-lamp,
Lets flow the lion's black blood
And opens the locked book
Ornate with scallops and scalene triangles,
  Hanorish tharah sharinas.

A podium stood beyond the rows of chairs. From it four Knights delivered brief speeches on "aspects of Spindledom."

The fifth speaker was the Mayor of Miami, Ayer Favell. He is the most popular political figure in the city's history: after twelve years in office, no one yet knows whether he is Democrat or Republican. His apparently extemporaneous speech was pronounced in a leathern, official voice; it dealt with Miami's national obligations as "romance capital." Mayor Favell will once again be a candidate in November, and he did some characteristically metaphysical campaigning. His rhetoric washed pleasingly over me, until at the phrase "degenerate loins" my mind cut loose, wandering among vistas of white and black until it stopped at a constellation of moss splotches on the ceiling, of a green so bright I thought they must be paintings of moss. Sudden cheers from my neighbors brought me back to Mr. Favell. He had just exonerated the Knights from beach taxes.

"Speaking of taxes, you'll be glad to learn that I've had a report from Roger Taxman. But first let me salute others, equally distinguished, who are here tonight.

"The wisest of the wise—Miles Hood." The noted philanthropist rose and bowed. He is about five inches tall. Behind him sat three squat bodyguards.

"That pillar of faith—Silex Jewcett." Mayor Favell had arranged a night's parole.

"A paragon of healing—Dr. Clomburger." He earned his notoriety during our "crazy crab" epidemic.

"Wizard of safety—Peter Jeigh." I did not understand this epithet. The Sovereign pitcher waved his one arm in acknowledgement.

"A whirlwind of prophecy—Dexter Hodge." Mr. Hodge

walked over and patted me on the back. Perhaps he had "prophesied" my admittance. His attention was flattering.

"A well of discernment—Daniel Tigerbaum." I tingled with shame. Dan, that walking snake pit! He was cited only because of our acquaintance.

"That gaggle of tongues—Robert Pindola." Imagine my surprise! This man is an interpreter.

"And now for our wandering Knight, Roger Taxman.

"Roger spent the winter visiting the Algerian province called Little Brittany. Despite its name, the region lies in the Sahara, all empty rock and sand with a few inhabited oases. Arriving in his rented helicopter at one such place, Roger learned that in the waste nearby there was something extraordinary to be seen, and that he *must not see it*. Although as polite and respectful of custom as any Knight, Roger's sense of adventure was aroused. He persuaded his native pilot to help him find the wonder, whose whereabouts he had guessed.

"They started off in that direction, flying in a wide zigzag. Beneath them the tawny sands stretched level as the waters of a bay, until they beheld a large shell-like rock emerging from the flatness. They flew near it. The rock's outer surface was scorched by the sun, but its hollow was shady; and in the shade stood the upright figure of a girl, bound and naked.

"Roger writes, 'I would have thought she were a fictitious shadow of alabaster or other significant marbles, brought to the rock through the artifice of industrious sculptors, had I not seen tears, distinct among the fresh roses and candid privet blossom, bedewing her half-ripe little apples' (that's what it says) 'and the breeze fluttering her tresses.'

"The pilot descended low enough for Roger to make out these details, and the silver chains that fastened the girl to the rock. And then, through the cloud that the chopper was beginning to raise, he saw, as he leaned from the cabin, a monstrous head rise from the sand and take the girl's leg in *his* choppers. The noise of the craft distracted the beast from his prey. It relinquished the white foot and started biting at the shadow moving across the ground. In this manner Roger, who was unarmed, and who saw the foolishness of meeting the creature empty-handed, lured it some distance away. He then sped back to the oasis.

"Confronting the inhabitants with what he had seen, he learned that the girl was a famous Berber princess, the 'angelical Farah-Sahi.' She had been captured by the local Tuaregs, who had offered her instead of one of their offspring to the Great Sand Snake. Each year the Snake exacted, as the price of sparing the oasis, the sacrifice of a virgin girl, whom he swallowed alive.

"Revolver at hip and rifle in hand, Roger returned to the helicopter. To his dismay the engine failed to start. Leaving the pilot to repair it, Roger found a camel and set out alone. For over an hour he rode, with anxiety burning his heart as fiercely as the sun his head. It was with a cry of relief that he greeted the chained maiden, still uneaten.

"Roger dismounted and approached Farah-Sahi. The Snake poked its head out of the sand. It looked more like a pig than a snake. Roger had only a glimpse of it, for the earth began shaking and the air was suddenly filled with whirling thick sand. The beast had remained, as was its wont, ninety-nine percent underground, and by powerful fillips of its buried tail had churned up a storm.

"Roger lost sight of the rock. He was groping his way through the blistering air when he felt an unpleasant pressure on one thigh. He reached down and encountered the snout of the monster sucking in his leg. The danger passed when the creature, stopped by Roger's crotch, realized its mistake and disgorged the single leg to start over again.

"Roger was determined to dispatch the brute at the next encounter. He knew that in the chaos of the sandstorm he dare not use firearms. So when he felt the Snake's maw seize his ankles, he stuck it through the eye with the hole-punching blade of his Swiss Army knife, then finished him off in the customary manner.

"The air cleared. The broken head of the Snake lolled at the girl's feet. Roger once more put his handy knife to good use, unscrewing Farah-Sahi's chains, and mitigating her thirst with an ounce of compressed water.

"Roger tells little about the girl. Evidently overcome by fear, she was reluctant to follow her rescuer. To reassure her, Roger gave her his widower's ring, which she accepted with a smile and swallowed—something that made him very angry.

"They returned to the oasis. Roger learned that after he had left, his pilot started vomiting and soon afterwards succumbed to vomiting fever.

"Scarcely had he heard this news when he and the girl were hauled before a tribal magistrate.

" ' I never blowed,' writes Roger, 'whether it was a real or a ritual trial. Its pretext was that tradition had been violated. The magistrate was obsessed with our sense of worthiness. "Which of you can swell his heart with conscious superiority? Is it you, stranger, who thinks, Better I than this animal, this garbage, this *woman*? Or you, Princess, who thinks, Better I than this Christian, this imperialist hireling, this *American*?" But we never learned the answer, because a boy ran in shouting that oil had been struck, and we all went off to see the gusher.'

"And may I suggest," Mr. Favell continued, "that our axiom was ever present in Roger's mind: *Let no man ask what this is, or why this is. He must not say it, he must not say it. For he is a Spindle Knight.*"

Facing me, he declared:

"So to you, new Knight, I turn. Welcome to our crew. I shall not describe your duties; if you were not aware of them you would not be here. Now the portal of Knighthood will open, and you must pay the required toll. To you this will be no sacrifice, since like all of us you are amazed that any man should be smitten by the luster of gold; that men, for whom money was created, could ever be thought of less value than it; or that only because he is rich, a man with no more sense than a stone, and as bad as he is foolish, should have dominion over others. Therefore draw near."

I drew near. The Mayor spoke to me confidentially:

"That's two hundred and ninety-eight dollars."

I gulped and took the pad of blank checks that he held out (Thank heaven I'd dispatched your money.)

The Knights had resumed their hymn:

What does he hear in the bauble's swing?
What does he see in the lamp's light?
What does he feel in the welling of the blood?
The rune-rife smith at his bellows,
The herald at the gates of noon.
   Hanorish tharah sharinas.

While they sang, a curtain behind the podium was slowly raised. Beyond it lay a room eighty feet in length, lighted by a bank of giant spotlights that bisected its ceiling. This was the workshop of the Knights, where their precious Galahad linen was made. A token crew now worked its cumbrous machines.

Following Mayor Favell, I learned the stages of linen manufacture.

At the near end of the shop, a hackler took rough stricks of swingled flax and dashed them into the hackle-teeth of a small ruffer, drawing them through several times, and repeating the procedure with a series of finer-toothed hackles. The tow waste was neatly gathered. A second worker took the clean stricks and pressed them into slivers, a third rolled and twisted the slivers, and a fourth wound these slubbings onto blunt wooden rocks, or distaffs. In the center of the room, apart from her neighbors, sat the spinster, an imperious lady in a trouser suit of silver lastex, holding a distaff in one hand and with the other revolving the spindle against her thigh. The spindle was of tapered green stone, its midpoint ringed with a wharve of gold (or brass.) Other women wound the thread on the bobbins of a handloom, where it was woven into lengths of several yards: bleached, dried, and stamped with a mark, these were piled at the far end of the shop.

We returned to the spinster. I knelt in front of her. She laid down her work, leaned forward, and tapped me on either shoulder with the spindle, saying: "Theah... and theah... I pronounces you a Knight of the Thimble"—the idiot! After which, casting an amorous glance at the Mayor, she resumed her spinning.

Mr. Favell helped me to my feet and, having kissed me on both cheeks, led me to a wooden construction that faced the spinster: it consisted of a stair of twenty steps on the left, a vertical ladder on the right, and at the summit a narrow platform, on which a music stand was perched, with an open book on its rack.

The Mayor directed me to the ladder with the words: "There you will ascend Happy Mountain."

I did as I was told. Two minutes' hoisting left me breathless and awash. Upright at last on the rickety platform, I withstood an onrush of vertigo by grasping the weighty book. Behind it, fastened to the lectern, a metal stem held a small rectangular mirror, tipped awry. In it I saw one of the ceiling spotlights, extinguished, its lense reflecting the bolts piled below. The markings on the cloth—six black spots like upsidedown boots—were vividly magnified by the lamp glass.

The Mayor's voice rose pompously.

"For from the communion of the inner and outer fires, and from their union in the mirror, these appearances must arise.

"For they coalesce on the bright smooth surface.

"For the fire of the eye meets the fire of the face.

"For they are thought to be prime causes, since they freeze and heat."

I straightened the mirror and obtained a sight of my hot face.

"New Knight, you have clomb the Mountain. Read us the lesson there writ."

The open pages were from Petrarch's description of Mont Ventoux; Hannibal splitting the Alps with vinegar was crossed out. I read the passage in a voice small if not still. At the words about Italy—"longing to see my beloved in that country"—I could scarcely speak.

While I read, the company of the Knights filed out on either side of me, singing pianissimo:

The jester in cap and bells
Drops his bauble, quenches the bladder-lamp,
Staunches the blood....

The weavers also left. Alone, I closed the book, descended the stair, and followed the Knights into an adjoining chamber.

They were seated at a long table, at one end of which a place awaited me. Aromas of broth and sauce announced to my convulsed belly that its ordeal and mine were at an end. The menu comprised conch-and-crab soup, filets de flounder "Zeppelin," wild turkey stuffed with Arkansas truffles, and honeydew melon soufflé, with wines to match.

After supper, libations were poured and there were the other usual ceremonies. Then, with the cigars and brandy, a three-piece band came in to play old favorites, and we all had a good time of it, in a sedate way. Dexter Hodge introduced me to the Knights I hadn't met; they regaled me with jokes. (Miles Hood did not stay for supper. Dan had passed out.) After a while there seemed to be continuous group singing.

Hours went by, and it was not until someone did a mimic cockcrow that I knew the night was over. A samovar was brought out. Our numbers were swelled by a gang of sewermen on their way to the compost farms. They broke in on the pretext that we had left the manhole open. They were welcomed, and the party went on with them, although without decorum. Don't think I say this in disapproval of workmen. I was grateful for their presence. All my life I have been a "have-not." At home I was a "have-not." I regard myself as belonging to them.

Drowsiness got the better of me thereafter. I dozed a little, then took my leave. The morning streets shone.

It's taken me hours to write this. I'm beat.

Part Three

XXVIII

Why, is Pan in-flect? You ask. Once it was n't, then home the missions, be fore soldats and buyrs, monks mad for lingual avance. Yet, hlever, they forse not theyr linguage up on us, ownly show, the vantage of its struttures—of horse, we are peedisposed to these. They show howhow one word can to-be many, with a little twits, and we're reasn-like and order-most and the cort adops this eduhation. Yet in poor villages you hear the old way, in flectsible—they have leash words such you call hualifiers? in place end-ings. Some times the leahs-words be come new in italian-pan. Ex. gr. *nob* was qualify-er makin of noun, a verb, so *lucrim* "food" and *nob lucrim* "aet", now you kno *lucri* is "eat" (as *lucrem* "I eet") and *nob* meen "for" hense *nob lucri* has now a sense "for to et." How ever, you must n't thingk all progross is be causa of occodont maniacs, we do our-own. So *ticbaï* meaned firts "run-ing from" and now "in face of, confront with"; and like wise the antic sense is not oll losst, in my willage *ticbaï laï* is "in flight of mud" but in the capatal "con front-ed of mud". This is mud-heavil, under the moonsoon.

Mean while I work since middle-june at MAP, that is: Mediceo avanti il Principato, the arhive of the Medici is thousand of bundles, and looking in to them, I 'm go-ing nutty.

You may think, my gioy in your knit-ness is that I 'm Mrs. Knight, or you are like Roger Tax and un-screw me from the roc of my father, but it is n't, onely my brother with all truist joy my mind is fill seeping in this way and that way and two more way, and up, dwon, and to the sides, so every where it seep in every hting this mind ricc with altruest joy, mind open-ing, mature, and with graet lac of dis like and diswish.

I live in a quite pension (yet not all meels, but bred-&-brekfast.) My friend is the lone-ly chamber maiden. She 's name of Calli, the land-ing lady is Signora Videcca, who 's so please-full and many say, she is a holy, but Calli is un-sure. Nice, but only since Calli works very? Halli says me, "We shall see, howhow nice she 's in truth." One morn-ing, she stays in bed. "Why this?" Signora Videcca aks. "Oh, no thing." Sig. Videcca not replie, onely her eye broughs touch one-each-other.

I shall not, no, tell to the polize the mud-like deeds of Pindola.

XXIX

August 6

After weeks of marooning I'm back in Mapdom. It's dull. Staring at the walls of my cupboard-size office, I approach annihilation in the perception of their near sameness—they are not the same, but almost the same; yet there can be no question of like or unlike because they are nothing; and I fuse into their nothingness. Why do Tibetans find this so hard?

Hodge has been a disappointment. Ever since my initiation he has been busy. I did manage to see him once, but to no avail, since we were not alone—after my sixth phone call, Mr. Hodge suggested I lunch with him at a diner in the area of the Ten Towns, where he was going on business; and there he showed up in the company of one E. Pater Kabod. The latter was an unattractive old man (no doubt a Temple customer): deaf, uninterruptibly verbose, and a compulsive spitter. He talked through the meal. First he discoursed on spitting, an essential hygiene according to him, whose neglect gave rise to noxious deposits of tartar on the teeth—tartar being as poisonous as arsenic, and the accumulation of venom in the mouths of snakes being due to their inability to spit. Next he warned us about the big con, showing more concern for its practitioners than for its victims. Mr. Kabod salted his talk with hypocritical pericopes such as: "It's impossible to slake one's thirst for the absolute with the possession of created things." I'm sure he would love to try.

Since this lunatic had only half an hour to spare, I hoped to corner Mr. Hodge over coffee and Havatampas. But the old man was replaced by Hodge's Tax Disclaimer, and my lunch break ended.

Grace just called to tell me, with a smarmy lack of glee, that her date at my June party has become a "romance." She "wanted my advice." Indeed. I was astonished by the grotesque echo of old times. That daughter of Saturn belongs to my cavern days, when I lived in chaos, leashed to the under wall of the globe, drinking primitive mercury and feasting on myself. To speak of my life I need two past tenses now, one for that black past which is over, one for the time that began when you stripped my scales.

Your benediction of my knighthood is undeserved. As for your accoster, do as you think best; but remember, it's a mistake to comfort our enemies at our own expense. And in future, be careful not to rumble me so: your words can excite my suspicion as violently as they do better passions. The fault lies in my character, not in your provocation—you will have to forgive me that, my sweet raggle.

XXX

August 9

I feel I am as one in Sah Leh Kot is *ticbaï laï*, but it's not mud

I come-front, but *tharaï ghanap*, end-less hours: 388. Of them I comb small friuts. I han not learn from Mediceo avanti il Principato, it 's called MAP, it near-ly drive me nut, what happen then to the tresure? Yet a bout thirtytime one say any thing of it a mong business letters and letgers from the two Medici-teams. These, from '400 to '443. The team of *Averardo di Francesco* al-ways say, the treasure owes come to us. The team of *Giovanni de Bicci* of horse respond, no thing to do. These ones, all though, do n't try to sell-it. There is a letter whewhere *Cosimo di Giovanni* ask *Francesco di Giuliana* ('41): why, do n't we soppress the busuness, you and I banks have much cash, al-so the clippings are no more to use than thousands pistol-balls with out one pistol. This mean, the clip sin is still attacc to them. *Averardo*† 1434, his son *Giuliano*† '36, grand son *Francesco* †'43, there is no grand-grand son. Then the bank and propriety are home to *Hosimo*. There fore, it should end, how ever does n't. The libri segreti go on-till 1450, the treasor is yet a problem. One can knot know, why? Other ways, all these Medici were friend-most. Re-mind your self, the taem of *Averardo* is as politicians ever be-side the other, to sostain.

Lasttime I have wrote of Calli, my friend and the chamber-ess, howhow she is test-ing the saintlity of Signora Videcca. Calli has thought: she seem saint only be cause of my to-work thus well, yet be neath, she 's tuff. And Calli a-gain a morn-ing rest inbed. Halli, Halli, calls La Videcca.—Si signora?—Why to get up your self so late?—Oh, no thing.—No, nothing? bad girl, her mistruss crys, with let-ing her angr scope in speach.—Then Calli suggest me: A ha, see, she 's not so gentle, I 'll prove her a gain one-ce. (I simpattize.)

Think much, much of you, after your 2 pages tendre & measurd. Cars like your's, give a lurch in my core. The heated weather foster keen-est rimembranzes. *Wey* for all seas be-tween! *Lemum, sheenam*—I love, I dure.

Yestoday I encounter Sig. Pindola to tak tea at Piazzale Gadda. Be fore, a slick car stops, in to it walk a man with shoes of snake, and my freind say, It is Prince Voltic— know, he 's trusted with sell of lost heritage of Medici. I re mane stil still, one-ly in my cup the water rinkles.

XXXI

Augusto 12

My feel *ticbaï laï* was not *tharaï*, so end-less, the mud have crack, out cames not moths but, the prince! And for this I write, yet with out the to-wait of your risponds, O Twang preg, this be no crime a-gaints oxidental letters-cutsom. Thus the Pindola walk with Twang a cross the green-less piazza with the tower fist-most, then "Good day prince," "Good day!", "Know you my friend...?" and emit my name, I tell to you, my courtsey so low as stretch-er cat, "What esquisite!", they talk of we shall-have cup to-gather, "Ciao," "Ciao." Think, his grand powr of Medici facts and odjects: I'll have that.

There come too a smal-er help, from Mr. de Roover, all-ready you know, in Rome he toll of clip-ings and of *Otto di Guardia*. He is a-work in MAP, have for 20 years and still there is thirteen bundles to esamin. (Of 166.) So, I see him day and day, we put on our coffee brakes to gether, some time he have me to home to a lunch in near-from trattoria. A gain he helps—he has, a most-interest-full hump a-bout whawhat happen after 1443. Sure, *Cosimo* in-herit the proprety of of-*Averardo* great-son but bank-parts and land-parts, and there is, no patricolar things. Later (says Mr. de Roover) we shall note the regreg of *Clarice de' Medici*, as the celebrete "Resurrection Ring" by *Baroncelli* not have-became theirs, the want to give it to of-her not-yet dauhgter-by-law *Alfonsina*, and that ring made for *Giuliano di Averardo* 1430. In like-mode *Piero the Gotty* ask in 1460, where is, not to-us, the pori-tratt of *Francesco di Giuliano*, that *Alesso Baldovinetti* have paintit? A-long with referenzes to treasure after '43, these re-marks have the de Roover esteam, there is to-have-be a-nother heir. This appare so like-ly, I'm not sure how it can be true. How ever the-less it's sure, the wife of *Francesco* dies with no child.

It is to-note, a new indress on flip of this letter. I was needed to move, after Calli's last proof-ing Signora Videcca. A-gain late in her bed, and answer "Nothing" to "For what?" Then la Videcca take pin and stroke Halli. It is, the pin to roll-ing pasta. And blood leep from of-Calli head, then she run with blood into street and gry, "Look, look howhow she's a saint!" Thus Sig. Videcca have lost a riputation, also Calli the post as clean-maiden, and, evidently, I like her hompanion goes, too.

I dreamed strange-ly last-night. I have walk down to the river, and seek to ride a-way on a little boat. This, is fasten to a tree yet not by rope, but a metal piece, and lotckd by knot-and-bolt. The knot is gold and it is shin-ing like sunfire on pool, I turn up on it and han-not un-scrue it. A new glow is be-hind me, I look, it's a monk, old & strong, yet his head is n't shave nor face. He does the glow, soon to fade, until he speak, "It is *knot* gold!" and the glows de-part, finally at that they're no thing. The barc is float a way evening on the water. —I han not think, is the monk a true monk? is he a *pristwe?* (a demon)

XXXII

Aug. 13

Your new facts suggest such a chronology as this. After Boniface IX had commissioned him to seize Todao's treasure, Averardo asked Giovanni di Bicci to do the job for him. Giovanni found that while the clipped gold was great in weight, it was unnegotiable. So he cut his losses by settling with Messer Todao for a smaller sum in cash, released the treasure, and canceled the Pope's debt. No one but Averardo was the worse off. Messer Todao transported the hoard to his abbey, where he hid it in a chest of silk, and died without disposing of it: it lay untouched until the later abbot's discovery. Meanwhile, in respect to Averardo, Giovanni began the long dissimulation that his family was to maintain after his death, not daring to admit the breach of faith to cousins who were such staunch political allies.

All day long—it is sunset now— I've been haunted by a dream I had early this morning. It began with my lying wound-ed in a street—the street where the truck knocked me down. I stared at a wall whose surface was being slowly lettered over, the inscription indecipherable but Gothic in aspect. The letters started shining. I looked about. Behind me a man in saffron robes was dismounting from a caparisoned horse. He was tall, sturdy and saturnine, with coppery skin, incandescent white hair, and black eyes.

The old man approached; his radiance faded. He set me astride the horse, then led me down an unfamiliar way. Presently he said, "A horse is a vain thing for safety. I'll take you to an inn." We stopped in front of a dark building, into which he carried me as though I were a puppy. The interior dissolved in deep browns. Light dwindled from high pointed windows; piles of manure were heaped in corners; there was a cadaverous smell. The old man settled me on a low bench and prepared a potion for my wounds. "You'll want some cascara... natural sulfur... an inch of worm spittle..." The mixture tasted like chewed paper. The old man stood over me and shouted, "Now do you know who I am? A hint: my initials are D.W. So, D.W....? D.W....?"

He removed his robe, under which he wore only jockey shorts and sneakers. His hefty body was the same color as his face. He lay down and began caressing me. Each caress discovered chinking coins along the ridges of my body, which he tucked into his shorts, mumbling "Gold in prison" or "Expenses." His beard was moist. "You don't object to paying your debts. You're no Pogy O'Brien," he said, extracting more coin. Becoming bored, he sighed "Nevermore," and left me for a brass salver heaped with macaroons, which he swallowed with gluttonous majesty. After a moment he paused:

"You call yourself a scorner of contingencies, but it's time to grasp history by its nettle-like stalk."

There was a sound of durable materials splitting, as an invisible levee cracked. Water flowed into the church.

The effect on the old man was organic. In moments the smooth consensus of his limbs gave way to pathetic marasmus. "Ah, my cancer!" he wailed. The waters rose quicker. "This my king's tomb?" he said, subsiding among them. A cascade of mascara darkened his face. "That explains those eyes of his!" I gazed on the silvery foam, expecting Venus or the Rhine Maidens to rise from his bubbles.

This afternoon brought the microfilm from Montpellier. I'll look at it tonight. I could use help these days. The computer is now denied me, commandeered by the police. Hodge remains as inaccessible as ever. For a whole week the heat and humidity have been in the nineties; I feel as though I were too.

Write soon and brighten the long day's journey. I note the improvement of your English with pride.

XXXIII

August 20

To Lorenzo de' Medici. Complaint of Guillaume Abbot of Montpelas. How the Abbot was knowingly defrauded by Lionetto di Benedetto Lorenzo's agent. How the Abbot was much impoverished and the Medici's honor sullied.

Should the Abbot Guillaume not have expected to gain more than he gave? His hopes were not drawn from common rumors that the chest of silk was of great worth. He believed the tacit support that Lionetto agent of the house of Medici, and his associates, gave such rumors. And I cite as example one of these Benedetto di Gianfranco, who all know to be Lionetto's intimate. When he visited the Abbey to buy wine, he spoke to the Abbot of certain lots of Florentine silk that were for sale. Was the Abbot wrong to hint at the purchase of a certain chest when he was given satisfactory information and his precise hopes were encouraged? He then endeavored to transact with Lionetto himself but could not be received, yet had a letter assuring Lionetto's compliance in the affair. It is a misfortune that this letter was returned at the insistence of Lionetto's representative after the sale was finally carried out and the false goods delivered. Messer Lionetto has now rebuffed Guillaume's just complaints because "the Abbot failed to transact with Lionetto himself, who had postponed important matters in Avignon expressly for the Abbot's business." What? The Abbot was to blame? Guillaume was not to blame (nor Lionetto. Yet it was he who chose that wild meeting-place.) I was traveling through the borderlands when my journey was interrupted. Just before the solitary village at Pont d'Eulh ten men apparently lepers suddenly came among us. Profiting from our revulsion they seized our horses by their bits and bridles then made us dismount. They were thieves and no lepers and quite nonchalantly plundered myself and my three monks. They took the money we carried to pay for the silk and rode off with our horses. Two hours passed before we found some slowfooted asses and thus we came late to the meeting with Lionetto. He to my dismay had just departed, having instructed his men that in his absence the sale of the silk was to be deferred, and this was a great misfortune. Needless misfortune, for Messer Lionetto himself has since told me that payment could have been made on a later day, in view of the wretched theft of my money, but no words would move his men. Such a waste! I could only submit. I watched the silk being reloaded. Great lengths of brocade were folded into the chest. The regret of the moment has not lessened, for since then my eyes have never seen such a quantity of brocade...

I've done this much of the microfilm, which is the pure quill: the draft of a letter to Lorenzo the Magnificent by the sixth Abbot. (Yours was the second and mine the seventh.) Its date is 1483 at the latest. I've pruned the text of its flourishes, which clutter every sentence: "...What I say is this, a covenant was validated, it cannot be invalidated.... My lord, do not forget the lives of poor men, do not forget the appeals of those who address themselves to you...."—on and on.

It isn't hard to guess whom the ten thieves were working for.

Thanks for your informative letters. I hope you meet the Prince again. But is it wise to see so much of this De Roover? Just who is he? I must counsel you to restrain your trust of strangers. It's not only that you may risk our secrets: you

cannot guess the sexual effect a twist like you has on men of
the west, especially intellectuals. I'm concerned, too, that you
may not be getting enough to eat, or the right kind of food—
is that why you have lunch with him?

Months have passed since I was last with you. I have only
your hammock photograph to caress. I want to smell and
touch you. The waning summer fills me with gloom. Two
hands in their circular mimicry of pursuit cannot dissemble
the face behind them that in deadly earnest hunts us down.

XXXIV

Agost 23

Now, it's sun and quite noise come from the streets, yet 20
minutes fore it were blacc thnunder and light-ing. Twang
was very frighted to squat under my table for work near
library windows, I feel, a *pristwe* comes after me. It is the same
demon as your draem, much water after the flash. I think
many times, a flash have a no less shortlife than mustard seed
on arrowtip.

Mr. de Roover is sicure, so nice, he was professor of histery
at the college "Brooklyn," now retires, yet not from terribiles
bundles of MAP (in fun.) And with Mrs. de Roover, she's
name of Firenze! They're delihate to Twang. And she's too
a enorme to-know of old ehonomix, have wrote Glossary of
Mediaeval italian Buziness Terms, so beuatifull, I've not can
work with out that, and when I am first gave her hand with
"Good day" I was timid timid, yet soon I prey for her author-
graph. In change I write her a catalog of business terms Pan
and Lao. They have age, to a bout 65 years.

Your are not to think, does Twang ate what is good? Any
food is a nough. And this's need-ing no virtu, all things are
ease-most, they are *nob-lemum* (for that I love.)

So the Pindola accompany me to the Prince's. We slip a
ice-full drink on his terraze and be-hold low houses. Pindola
have said, "The Twang know much a-bout those Medici,"
the Prince then: "May be, that she will say any thing of their

brank in Lübeck?" Twang: "O, no, it is no branch, that Gherardo Bueri and some, it is only corispondents for the bank," I tell of Gutkind's wrong-ing. The Principe Voltic look at me a dozen sehonds and then he give me a new drink.

XXXV

August 27

I'm wretched at having snapped at you about Mr. de Roover. I should have known better. I did know better—it's another case of my nature besting my intelligence. Who can approve of quarrelsomeness, contentiousness, envy, ambition, or drinking bouts? The trouble is, there's no law to uphold the imperatives of the moral will. One nails down one's bad habits on the nearest board and drags it behind, a useless brake of remorse.

I'm sending extra cush, because I don't want you eating just "any food."

Here's the Essential Remainder of Abbot Guillaume's lament. Authentic though the document may be, it's fishy. Not because it contradicts my last hypothesis and, more important, the account in Amortonelli's letter: there the chest in the abbey *did* contain the treasure. (Notice that both lots of silk were marked with "six ravens"; they have their importance. The Abbot had only to glimpse them to accept the goods. He writes of "seeing in that blazon my shield, erring in this, for it was a Medusa's head to petrify me.") The story as a whole seems crow. Why should Lionetto, high placed in the Medici bank, go off into the countryside to hopscotch like a common grifter?

Messer Lionetto then wrote he would deliver the silk to the Abbey, but he would not himself accompany it because of the distance, and he was occupied with many pressing matters, so he entrusted the goods to the said Benedetto di Gianfranco, who later claims that he only followed Lionetto's orders, and this is perhaps no lie, but how is he to be believed when he says that he knew nothing about the contents of the chest, which was most certainly of the proper size (six men lifted it scarcely), on its lid the three fish were roughly cut, when they opened it it seemed to be filled with the brocade that I had seen folded into it at the first meeting, and how should it enter the mind of a man of God, transacting with the representative of one of the greatest princes of Christendom, that the chief weight of the chest was a sheet of lead fitted into its base, or that the brocade once it was unfolded was not the six hundred *bracci* [about 380 yds] agreed on but a mere twenty *bracci* long, although the peculiar design of sea shells and spiny roses was the same as before, but underneath this brief sample was plain taffeta, as I later discovered, too late, and above all too late for redress because of the manner whereby the fraud was compounded, and yet I look beyond these wiles to the honor of their master whose glory is so unjustly smirched, to have his name affixed to a receipt for the delivery of "620 *bracci* of brocade & taffeta" where no specification was made of the proportion between the two kinds of silk, and the point was passed over by me because it had been explained that taffeta would be used to wrap or pad the brocade to keep it clean and dry, but it was no padding but the bulk of the consignment, which I did not then verify, and concerning this you will ask, why? My lord, I was stupefied by joy and fear. Joy when the chest was opened, at the sight of the brocade with the six ravens stamped on its first fold; fear lest this prize be lost to me, for I could not think that Benedetto would leave it to me if he observed what I did. And so it was after a mere glance that I gave my approval, ordered the chest shut, paid the price, signed the receipt. The chest was born to an attic of one of the abbey buildings, and fearing that any precipitation would arouse the curiosity of my monks I waited for night, I had had the chest carried to an attic in an outlying

building, and at last I opened it, only then I discovered
the subterfuge, but Benedetto was beyond recall....

Frenzied resentment here overwhelms the text. There is
one further point of interest: the Abbot mentions having
earlier rendered Lionetto a service, when "Fortune enabled
me to return his purse of jewels." Had Lionetto prepared his
victim by having him "find the leather?"

Guillaume was on shaky ground. In buying the silk, he
expected to be getting more than his money's worth, so
much more that—remember the ten thieves—he paid for it
twice. It was awkward for him to complain of duplicity. No
doubt because of this he followed the advice of his clerk, who
appended to the draft:

At the suggestion of Brother Peregrine, scribe, the
Abbot has witheld this letter, believing in the end that
it would bring small advantage to the Abbey, or none.

Life here continues boring, except for the headlines. The
Sun-Examiner has trotted out the most terrifying type you
ever saw: each letter is as tall as Wee Willie Keeler. Why
should the Chinese want to bomb Mars? True or not, the
news has happily muted our nation's "clamors of salvation
in the tents of the righteous."

As for your apprehension of thunder and lightning, that
is an instinctive terror; there's no squelching it. What about
your Buddhist disciplines? I'm sending you money with this
because I don't want you eating just "any" food.

XXXVI

August 30

To-tell Prince Voltic a bout Lübeck appear, it pleases him,
he waste hours search-ing after Medici-tracces there and now
not long-er, mercy mine. For thus reason he send yester-day,
a thank, a censer, done of agrent, with in-it any twigs of in

sense, it's of the '600, littl-est, "for home-use."

Pindola harry that gift. With pleasure: for that if the prince love Twang, to love Pindola more. Bonzo wishs to-will-work for the Prince. Now he do the manucurust, or say womanacure? It's with a for-woman barber all all day. And he will to-say *duvaï* to the work, of-it he is have enough, and who will not? aftre 15 yaers (or even, fivteen minutes.)

Yet Bonzo (Pindola) have took high way with Twang, as he will say, I Pindola gift to you Prince. No no. I never kiss that hand. He is will-hiss my foots!! It shall, to be in vert! And how? There will to-be a accidente, all most, I do it, then I salve the Pindola. He'll kiss under feets of Twang.

I will know, please, the little english speech for "there" and "to-it" as in-italian *ci*? In Pan too it's *nam*, can slid in aesy, be-tween breethes.

O froget, that rebite a bove de Roover, there was n't sorrow in the core of Twang, but warm-ing of fire soup, for it was sweet the brain-less gelosy. Abbrace thee, *lemu*, in my thoght.

XXXVII

September 3

A happy surprise has broken my dull round—days of getting out of bed not knowing whether I'm dead or alive (or feeling both dead *and* alive); the depressing station at the bathroom scale; office hours; equally tedious maps; a solitary movie after supper (yesterday *Guileless Swallows*). All is made bearable by the knowledge that you exist. I try to recognize signs of you in the trash of my life, from the morning paper to the book over which I fall asleep. I take the rest on faith.

And out of the blue, Dexter Hodge called up to invite me to a "choice" houseparty at the Beach. After weeks spent trying to see him, I was stunned; but there is no point expecting consistency from that busy man. For the outing he has taken over the Na Inn, a beautiful motel at 183rd Street.

I don't know what the program is, but with Mr. Hodge in charge it'll be the Carrie Watson. There will be celebrities, and a basketful of fashionable cupcakes. (Fashionable now means layers of Minoan overskirts beneath unveiled tops—a perplexing hot-and-cold effect.) There should be ample opportunity to discuss treasure hunting.

As for Mr. de Roover, I'm touched by your words. You have forgiven me too readily for me to forgive myself.

. Unfortunately, there is no equivalent for *ci*, *nam*, or the French *y* in English.

Ever since you arrived in Italy I've wanted to ask you about an essential east-west distinction, that is, the sun—so different from your steamy heat-and-light machine, efficient but remote. It is sometimes like that in our northern cities; but in Florence, as here, isn't it intensely present, like a rampant lion, or a wielded sword flashing among us?

XXXVIII

6. sett.

The incidente was done. In this month one is making new store the Palazzo Rucellai, of-it the face is blind with bords and tube. I rent 2 work men there, one, on low baord, one at-top. Bonzo is walk-down that street, it is whewhen he 's under board I hry a cross the street and run to spin him out from harm way in to door way, then the low man spill a big brigk on whewhere Bonzo were to be. This is not a far drop and when it had have stroke Bonzo it shall have n't kill him, or hard-ly. But, now we regard a-bove, it is the high man cry and hand-shakes as although he just drip the brick, and this was the Bonzo's thought. He sit-down as a doll, I remember you before the apples truck, I was very hard not to-laugh. He call Twang many times *neng! neng!* (bellezza) and I think only on my material-subtile nose to downpush laughing. Then I say, poor tresure! he must to-eat the best lunch, and I 'll pay it, and all so a graet dottor lest he 's hurt-ing and Twang shall pay, of horse I know, he 'll not let this. And to day Bonzo think, I have save him and 'm rich, my hands are the cage and he is the inside bird. The worker men costed $3 and 2 kiss.

Florence town is more empted. It is not a worse for this. But there is a delight here now, for the dipartures. A strong spirit home to me of indolenze, I have the wish to see none one, to say no thing, to do so, and I have a desire of noth—o yes, I desire you and all though I can n't, then, to read you. *Wuc mau nam theu,* as were we here! (it mean, "would";) to-gather in the streat of warms stones.

Do not you feel some pain in that errore to ward de Roover, do fore-give your self, for my mind follow your pain and then foregive-ing, full of hompassion, this way (pain) and that-way (forgive) and again an other and another-way, a bove, and below, and every way around, pierc-ing the wrold ever full of compassion, so my mind would be a broad, spreadout, beyond the frames and esempt of harted and bad will-ing.

Bonzo tell me, to day is the first day of the Jews Year, No. 5733, he say they are so good at suffer-ing, look at how long they have practice. Is this funny?

XXXIX

September 10

I'm sitting in a Loretta-Youngish bedroom, my bare toes linked in ringlets of angora, gazing at the Atlantic over the space bar of a mighty typewriter that is equipped with fully integrated circuits and pigskin keys. The machine, so rapid that inscription precedes thought, was delivered at my request for "a" typewriter. I used it for my map notes. But I changed to the seriousness of ink to address you. Deep sentiments flow more readily from a pen than from the most responsive keyboard, the McCaltex longhand block not-withstanding.

We've been at Na Inn since Friday afternoon and are to leave Tuesday morning. It's very nice. Under the inn's bungaloid exterior lurks a small palace. The windows of my bedroom, thirteen feet high, are shaded by sun-sensitive sheet-coral blinds. The common rooms are both grand and intimate, thanks to lighting and sound systems that adjust to their use. At their center lies an enormous game-room-cum-swimming pool, whose breadth and length and heighth and depth I can hardly grasp and cannot begin to describe. At the bottom of the pool, night and day, what seems to be real fire flares into the water. One guest, Peter Jeigh, a powerful swimmer, dove to investigate. He said the flames were warm but did not hurt.

The guests I had already met are Peter, Dr. Clomburger, and Lester Greek. I knew others by name, Wolfgang Abendroth for instance. All are remarkable men, answerable to none but themselves for their eminence. The one disappointing absence is that of Miles Hood.

Early Friday evening a few of us played poker. I did so well that I considered turning out as card sharp. My biggest pot was at five card stud. I won with three kings. Mr. Hodge tried to bluff me with four cards to a straight, but I stuck it out and he threw in his hand. Toward the end, a new arrival was announced and we decided to have some fun: when Peter Jeigh's turn came to deal he would play him for a chump, using the rest of us as shills. A deck was "cooled" so that I would be dealt four tens and the stranger four nines.

The latter entered and took his seat. He was handsome, with a fixed smile paralleling his new-moon beard, whose luster perhaps betrayed a dyer's tinge. Play resumed; he was allowed to win a few hands. He enjoyed the game and tossed in his money like hay. The cold deck was introduced; I drew to my four tens and bet up the pot; but when we showed, the mark held four jacks! "Goddam it!" Peter roared, "that's not the hand I gave you." The other replied, "You have to play smart to beat Roger Taxman." He was still swarthy from Africa.

After another round of cocktails we went in to dinner. I was walking toward the foot of the table when Hodge stopped me. "Friend, you don't belong down here, come and sit by me." It was a glorious meal. I had three helpings of the main course, a braised stuffed-and-rolled shoulder of lamb pie. Over the double consommé Mr. Hodge gave his reasons for bringing us together: his respect for inner, even hidden worth, his contempt for the vanity of the world. Afterwards each of us tried to justify his remarks. Dr. Clomburger recalled an early triumph, his original description of yeast frenzy; Lester Greek spoke of new gleanings from *Finnegans Wake*—the palindromic precedence of "Eve" over "Anna"— soon to be published in his study, *The Confidential Walrus*; I discoursed on the abstract beauty of maps. So it went round the table. The evening ended with a swim.

The next days were full of sports and games. Needless to say, when faced with anything rougher than shuffleboard I withdrew to my room. Mr. Hodge has agreed to a treasure talk when we drive home tomorrow.

I admire the way you made sport of Pindola; but why bother?

Your sweetness, your immeasurable sympathy has again left me bewildered. Don't worry about my foolish sufferings —they are only feeble tributes to you.

XL

September 13

I can't know, why is pokre? So a mild game, I once watch at aerport, the men are roug but in the play of mildmost charity. They yeild their dollors corteosly, only when they have lose, they smile. Yet with win-ing, they shake their haeds and appare so stern with their selves, as pumished. Of where come this beauty? Or is it but that they think, Happy with the cards, unhappy with love (I heared so one luagh), so stranger for in Pannam it is n't thus. A man can to-be happy, with both. Pans say, A mountain apple in one hand, a stream eel in the left hand.

It may be, Bonzo 's good card actor, for he is be-gin to regard Twang like my dog. And now he 's also talk talk, and I almost ywan then he said, the Prince sholl owe to-have me

Bonzo, for the family Pindola have-be guardian of some property from the Medici. When? (I yawn *not*.) O a bout 1466 and after. Who Medici? I serch, to think hohow I breath. O any "ulterior discendents" (?) of: Averardo. I count down, to twentyone. Then: I think, the of-Averardo descendens are no one in 1466. O I do n't know, we onely keep these things be-cause, they are history-hurious. So what things? Chairs and chaists. Chest? 1 or two, on-them they are the *palle*, or Medici balls, as of tradition, but them alas and no— Here I think near by to surest-ness that he will have-say *pesci* fish and yet make "e" last enough to be home *pesche* peaches. He ajjoin: "I mean, people some time think they 're peachs, they 're giust balles." After, he shuts the mouth. It is, he think his affechion mine under his discretions.

Now baby you will se why to "bother" my Bonzo, he 's be come such an interestfull chap. As the Prince of hourse. There-fore I press a gainst them, I 'll be a leech in side their hears and out-suck the middle secretes of those brains. Then I shall vomit-them-out, *uüaxm!* Thus, *naï sheenam slop*, thus, I bear benaeth un-happiness, untill I 'm ever for yours, *me tharaï pheu*, I say the Pan words, sweet like the milk in cans, in to the bolster 's damp patch at each night, lonesone lonesone. Please, be a-sure of my utter-est and rimorse-less devozion.

XLI

September 17

Your interpretation of poker is slightly wide of the mark. It is not the players but you who are charitable. Perhaps there is a show of self-effacement in winning—perhaps we apply "funeral manners" to conceal the vindictive glee.

Speaking of gambling, I saw a compatriot of yours playing faro bank at the Casino: General Kavya. He was twisting the tiger's tail with a pluck he never showed in the field. They were dealing them at fifty dollars a card and he punted on every turn. Has he been thrown out of Pan-Nam for swindling? Or was he sent to cruise our military establishment?

What a fate, when he could have stayed in his province, a big tail-wagging fish in that lovely little pond! The second alternative seemed likelier. The General was accompanied by a U.S. Army captain, who held his parabolic sword and was apparently abetting his play. Standing behind the dealer, the captain fiddled with several tiny coins (antique khrots?), clinking them in irregular, precise rhythms. I'm sure he was tipping the cards: Kavya kept an ear cocked in his direction. Otherwise the General did credit to his country, sheathed in silks and caiman skins. His only weak point was a large Maltese cross that flapped on his tummy, looking very Woolworthy among the tribal chains. I wanted to introduce myself as a Pan-by-marriage, but he was absorbed in his gaming.

Next morning Mr. Hodge and I drove into town together. I raised the subject of treasure-hunting. Mr. Hodge responded with a monologue on the legal problems that attend the disposal of treasure-troves. His deluge of words kept me speechless.

A perplexing incident interrupted the lecture. Our car had been slowed to walking speed by the throng near the Bass Museum. (Moreau's "Medusa of the Lilies" is on exhibit, and for three weeks that end of Collins Avenue has looked like London Bridge in "The Waste Land.") As we crawled along, Mr. Hodge pointed to a group near my window: Miles Hood, preceded by his roly-poly bodyguards and followed by a thin, stooped figure, who as we watched gave the famous millionaire a push, then with bewildering precision severed his attaché case from its gripped handle and slid away with it into the crowd.

I turned towards Hodge. He looked at me expectantly, snorted, and pushed me out of the car. I felt myself being shoved through the slow-moving pack, and before I had had time to resist or complain, I found myself face to face with the thief. My own astonishment was mirrored for a second in his eyes; then he dropped the case and fled.

"Grab it and we'll split." Hodge said. "We'll see Miles later. No point staying and getting our names in the papers."

In fact we did not return the case. Mr. Hodge asked me to

keep it until he could make an appointment with Hood—"If he was carrying it himself it must be valuable." I've not heard from him since.

Now from the groaning board it's back to the groaning scale, and the other tediums. Only your letters delight me. I keep them scrupulously filed (this is one reason why you must be sure to date them) so that I may follow your progress in English, something that gives me pride and pleasure. The letters bring torment also. They plunge me into lust. My beloved, write me about your body. Remind me of it with new words. I rehearse the same memories over and over. Only you can renew them—you *must* renew them, repetition is a death of love. I wish I could persuade you that what I say is true.

XLII

September 20

The Prince Voltic will go in to the Mugello, at some low mounts with health. With him, Bonzo and Twang follow, as ask-ed? It is a worth-most travel, I be-leave, and also there I'll study and think-up my hunts in MAP. If you will admit so, I must pray, Twang need a little money.

Twang can nots think, words to make love to sur-vive, when it is n't to be made, words of lust make it then any time to death. It is it that sing a poem in my distrect, of a tigr, whiwhich be gin

Thus of love (a) miseria (is) alas mud

like that begins all sad poem a-bout love, and can you n't catch the Pan words, *naï lemö slop wey laï*?

Thus of love a misery (is) alas mud.
A tigre hurry to the edge of the forest.
He sits behind a bread tree and chews bitter leafs—
his belly's tough of hunger.

A monkey comes. O monkey
I'll swallow your gentile meat
then make your tail as hat,
the tiger sing it, the monkey have go.

Here 's a peehock. O pee cock
I 'll chew each little-twig bone
then I spit your piumes in to the breezes,
the tiger sings this, the pecock al-ready have goe.

There is a buffala. O water buffalo
I 'll knaw aroung your schine and top leg
I'm dainty, not a house of ants,
The tiger sung, and the buffalo is gone.

The tiger rest at the edge of a forest
very dead of this much sing.
Now there are but these ants in his belly, too late,
but they, hurry out his eyes through his dentals

What is that "Waste land"? It 's perhaps a nick name of
Arizona?

Part Four

XLIII

The day after I last wrote, Hodge called to say that Mr. Hood had left town for a few days; until he returned I should keep the briefcase. I had resisted tampering with the elegant box, but this evening I tried the clasp, which was unlocked. Inside I found the June issue of *Tel Quel*, a tube of H-Preparation, checks in several figures and currencies, and a six-by-eight inch card on which a grid of letters had been typed, over the legend: "Cipher for Amortonelli Location."

You can guess my emotions.

(A withered palm tree is sketched on the back of the card. A cross marks a spot near its roots.)

We must work quicker. I enclose money for your trip, if you still want to make it. But should your friends prove unrewarding, waste no more time on them.

If you do go to the Mugello, don't be dismayed by the wind and the chilly springs. Why in this season are they going to a mountain spa? It will be deserted, except for my hot ghost. Your refusal to write me as I asked hasn't lessened my need. I won't press the point, because I dread seeming repulsive. How often have I imagined you seated by a window, your head bent, wondering whether a certain "Zachary" is worth the affection showered on him—and you take up your bed and go home. How could I stop you? It is in you that "our" life exists. For instance, it is you and not I who make me attractive to you! This is why I long, even if only in a fiction, for bodily involvement—I want to share your redeeming view of me. I have so often relived our few nights together that they have sunk to the level of racial memory. I need new grist. Do you still not wear a bra?

This second virginity is even stupider than the first. I like it no more than you do. I like it even less than the red of my ink on this egg-hued stationery.

"The Waste Land" is a much anthologized war poem by a turn-of-the-century symbolist called Eliot—not George.

XLIV

29 sept.

Now I'm in Rostolena. (Do you know, this was some of Averardo's proprety, when he is dead, that wents to Cosimo?) Now, speed letteres at Albergo Terme Paradiso e Fango.

I wish you, not-fear for my reliance. I belive that to not exite by un-point-ed talk, 's best. Yet, o my love-man, it shall-be un-true when I say, I did not miss you terrifly, and long-ing to-see-you. And here my poor gift to your peace, a 3° Zen story, of-such you dilect:

In the *po* test by whiwhich the 6° arch of zen was chose, there were poems. One say, "Dis-like roil dust. The probes remove the dust." The "head wing" poems are their. It said, "He's the mind. Where, is dust?" Some lat-er Pan masters: a monk who was stak-ing bats, a young-er monk up to his id in the dust—"Are you a-staking-bats?" "No. Why?"

Then I think, to homfrot you more, of our massim: *Ticbaï slop*, in front of non-happiness, *atra-pok-atra*, think n't, *me-me*, be so, *nob lucri maï*, as-to eat the Now, *wuc Lao*, like the Laotians. "Ticbaï slop, atra-pok-atra, me-me nob lucri maï wuc Lao." Slow, you may take-on my tongue, like I your. Yet, it is here the feel-ing to be retaint, less the tongue-lessen.

The post-hard show any of the pittoresque basket work, of this the regional sheep boys are giust-ly famos.

XLV

October 5

Three days ago Miles Hood returned to Miami. Hodge drove me downtown to meet him early that afternoon. I said nothing about the briefcase, although it's painful being a crow with D.H.

The encounter took place at a new Chock Full O'Nuts. The café, almost empty at that hour, was bright with cool fake sunshine. Mr. Hood was at a corner table. As we approached, his three gnomelike attendants popped up in front of us. Smoothing their Blücher-red neckties, the crescents of their eyebrows rising as one, they welcomed us with a unison "Hi there!" Hodge greeted Mr. Hood familiarly and introduced me. I handed over the case. Mr. Hood opened it and beamed. Murmuring an excuse, he verified the contents, testing the checks with a pocketsized magnetic device. Finally Mr. Hood asked with a smile, "Where's the milk of magnesia?"

Frappes were served. While the two men chatted, I tried to catch the mutterings of the bodyguards seated behind me. "...the fat one looks like a big con type." I smiled. "Uh uh. He's a friend of Mr. Hodge." "But the boss is such an easy mark, anyone might try to take him." I turned to look at them. They were leaning forward, their heads together but twisted in different directions, so that their eyes appeared to be staring at odd corners of the room.

Meanwhile Messrs. Hodge and Hood were having a jolly reunion. The backclapping ended at last, and Mr. Hood turned to me. "What can I do for this gentleman? Have a check?" He fanned out the three papers toward me like a benign conjuror. Prudence stifled desire. "Well, let's meet next week and work something out."

There matters rested. I'm glad the decisive moment is postponed. I shall prepare myself as thoroughly as possible for it. I swear that I shall try to act the sensible man and not the simpleton.

How does this predicament look to you, in your remote and dismal village? (The young man on the postcard *is* remarkable.) The "comforts" you sent me, if not the ones I craved, did wonders. On the day you wrote them, the infernal slope I had been climbing leveled off. Your distant magic was at work, mysterious as your Zen tale. I would like to repeat unceasingly the blessing of your name. Who else ever brightened my glooms? Your words are my fixed itinerary of rescue—you are to me, dear Twang, more than a wife, more than a sister: the pilgrim's distant shrine.

XLVI

Ottobor 10

As you do with the gentlemen Hoodge and Hood, I look at it it is good. You are to remember, you know very, they may be not. And, they'll talk their little, so to have your more. Thus, aspect. It 's how, I do with my friens.

You have not the true image of Rostolena village, not "deserte" no "dismal", no, they are many many here, with money, gewels, and c., very gay al-so. It is, the mud and skin festival. The springs not cold, theyr heat warm-ing all the houses and houstels, and not only, but the ways, that are cover with glass; the grottas too many and grand, in them is a ristoraunt and sauna-dance circles, very live. So, palms trees are grow a-long the walks and a deal of flowers, like the example of Buddle plants, its seed lodges in all cornices and in window embracures that even so late the cascarades of lillac flowr tumbaling down the palace facades and sprung from coigns. In them some bird sit and sing, I see two robin red chest last morning. And so they carry all clothes of summer. That is funny, with the of-health mode now followed, that of "decoctions of malt": these ladies, most rich and full of speech of great intellett, but a-round the small good clothes big blue stripes on the skins. Yet not Twang, I use but the *laï*, good mud, the ash of a volcano mischeid with argil, this is very sexual. Also I may be try the hure with sassoline.

This night I aet in the grott with Bonzo and the Prince Voltic. This one, is very mild and cold. He will talk, only of work (Medici). I answer of my grand knowledge, *naï sheenam*, so I bear it. After, with Bonzo I have learned the Hunch, that novel dance, it's not easy, for the Pindola likes the shout-ing as he dance of commands, so: "All-right, now, with-control abandon!" At last, I made an error catastrophic yet delight-ful, I giump 6 steps to rihgt not left. The all line of dancers fall-ing, Twang blush orange, then each laughed and kiss me (even those girls.)

Here I'm back, to write-it. You must think now, I'm not here in "glooms", it may be not the garden of Intuitive Illu-minazion, but, it is pleasant. Still I'm, dear one, a little in-drink but, at every time, your faith-full wife; and now, send you a love-ly *posti*.

XLVII

October 16

When, at cocktail time two days ago, I arrived at the Hood estate, Dexter Hodge was leaving. We had been invited to-gether, but other appointments had obliged him to come early. I did not mind; I wanted to scout the subject of the "Amortonelli location," and Dexter's absence would make this easier.

The three henchmen took me through a wing of the main house onto an immeasurable lawn. There, at the foot of the chapel tower, Mr. Hood welcomed me. It was a pleasant evening, cool, with a half moon peeping through the boughs of wisteria that embraced the round walls above us.

Mr. Hood's smiling face was emprisoned in an antique hel-met, without beaver or visor, apparently of gold. It gave him a lionish countenance. He said, "It's a seventeenth century

morion, from a Spanish hoard one of my teams dug up. Look
at the nifty artwork." His teams? Astonished, I tried to do as
he said, and noted at the helmet's crest the figure of a long-
tressed nereid emerging from ranks of fish scales. (Hodge cannot be ignorant of Mr. Hood's interest in treasure-hunting.
Why has he never mentioned it to me?)

A siren sounded distantly. Mr. Hood removed his helmet
while, materializing like a genie on the empty sward, a beautiful young woman proffered him a telephone on a coral tray.
Mr. Hood lifted the receiver, listened, and said, "No—thirteen
million." Phone and secretary vanished.

We sat down. Mr. Hood thanked me warmly for returning
the stolen briefcase. The contents were worth far more than
I could imagine—"The checks were nothing." He wanted to
reward me.

He spoke with a gentle finality that made me awkward.
But I was prepared for the offer and stuttered out my refusal,
explaining that for a friend of Dexter Hodge's the notion of
"service rendered" was out of place. I had behaved as he
would towards me in similar circumstances.

"But such circumstances are unlikely to arise, hence my
initiative," Mr. Hood replied. "I appreciate your courtesy, a
quality Dex has praised in you. Allow me to say, however,
that it is not only courtesy that makes you refuse. You are
exhibiting the modesty of the somewhat poor. You aren't
poor of course, but you aren't rich, and so you feel obliged to
show that you are not interested in acquiring money, especially mine. You should be. A few extra bumblebees never hurt."

I had drawn breath to answer when something behind me
crashed softly to the ground, turning me to salt with fright.
Mr. Hood reassured me: it was only a little Malay dragon
that had dropped from the tower vines.

Less at ease than ever, I lamely explained that I would "prefer esteem to charity." Mr. Hood interrupted:

"The fact is that I am in your debt. And debts must be paid.
One day you may discover how great this debt is and simply
have me thrown in jail!"

How is it that the potentates of this world always enlist

unreason as their invincible ally? This preposterous suggestion completely disarmed me. By its superb improbability, it established that it was I who was in debt to him: that Mr. Hood was an invested king, and I a fool.

I sat speechless. Mr. Hood came to my aid.

"I understand your reluctance to take what might appear to be a handout. There are other possibilities—a collaboration that would benefit both of us? I have many enterprises here that need intelligent and scrupulous supervision. Radium wells in the mangrove swamps, the dwarf-cattle ranch in the north, treasure-hunting teams—you name it."

An incredulous giggle escaped me. Speaking as calmly as I could, I said I would think the matter over. We set a "serious business appointment" for early November, then, to my inexpressible joy, the interview ended.

The meeting left me in such agitation that I can still hardly think. I have asked myself if Mr. Hood wasn't taking a vicious pleasure in "telling me the tale," but that is impossible. It's only that his offer of working on the treasure team seems too good to be true. I suffer intensely over encounters like this, which so thoroughly confirm my clumsiness. How can I face men who weave self-control, shrewdness, and (in this case) generosity into a seamless raiment of efficient character? I should prepare myself better. Next time I'll memorize responses for all eventualities. I shall clothe myself in the "trousers of stealth, the jacket of patience, and the hat of foresight." It is the cold sweat of action that ruins me. What I lack, beloved, is your excellent creed, which would have taught me that mountains are as short-lived as grass, and let me daily eat—or would a Buddhist say spit out?—the bread of immortality.

Your mistake in dancing the Hunch made me laugh, for, fancy this, much the same thing happened when I first tried it. I hopped those six steps in one spot; the consequences were identical. Such incidents can be annoying, due as they are to inattention. I'm glad it didn't make you furious. That would be far more unbecoming than a mere physical blunder, especially in a woman.

XLVIII

Octob. 21

How good that is, to be with the Hood's teams. Thus it 's best: others pay, others work-ing, and we rich. And here also it is a progression. The Prince is taken the Pindola to a job for him. He 'll aid, in the sell of the Medicean remains. Now Bonzo can better do, that Twang next be in-ployed.

Other ways they are not new events. Eccept, the graet in-gathering of free dogs at this villagge—thousand and thousand. They are nice, they emit large giovial noise. It is re-minding me nights-time in Sah Leh Khot—also of an even-ing in the spring-season, at Florence, of the "maggio musicale" (yet it was june, still with name "may".) Have I recountt this? The Bonzo invites me. There was a choral of dogs, very-wise dogs train for song in Hangover (Germania), and their spezial music by Egg, a hantata in new-Bach stile, saying "Vorkelt nicht, berühmte Nasen." It 's splendor, in the end yet it is just more art of the west. Only I like your opera, be cause that is true: it is, those who make it have not the care, are they insincere. One 've give the prema of one opera, "Robinson Caruso", it is pop with the italians also with Twang.

Then how goe Mr. Dharmabody?

Here have see no opera, but yesterday a U.S. film, *nob sheenam ghanap*, so that I pass the hours. It was near 20 years of old, with stars Day and Jourdan. Doris and Louis are alive together in a on-beach house at the Monte Rey Beach, and he have much free time after performing duties as famed concerto pianost and compostor of concerti in the Gershwind-style, much free time to conspire to hill Doris! Thus she must run of and she is become a air bus stewardessa. But on a day he have manage to sneaker up on a plane whewhere she 's hostess-ing, and—o my!

Now it 's deep night. It is a little cold but soon I 'll be sung in bed. Warm with over-saying the one thought "we all ways," *theu tharaï, theu tharaï*

XLIX

October 27

I'm at a barbecue given by Lester Greek in his in-town orchard. It's part of Les's campaign for congress. The guests include the invisible order of Miami authority, with lesser figures like me to fill out the boost.

Miles Hood came to the party, but I missed him. When he arrived I was away by the fire, over which seven lambs—or more likely rams—turn on a steam-powered spit. The roasting is supervised by a Gypsy-like attendant with ruby earrings, who carves with a tremendous shiv while sprinkling the sputtering meat with crystalline oil, scooped from a trundled amphora. I had decided to abandon this mouth-watering scene for Mr. Hood when Dexter Hodge intercepted me. He pestered me with attention, as though trying to ingratiate himself, and none too subtly. He may wonder what took place during my meeting with Mr. Hood: he acted slightly resentful of my interest in him. After I had unsuccessfully waved a few times to the little millionaire, he asked, "Isn't my company good enough?" He followed this lapse with praise of his friend. "Miles is truly class. Yesterday he told me that he had learned his butler was stealing his cigars. 'What did you do about it?' I asked. 'Nothing.' 'Nothing? Isn't stealing cigars stealing?' 'If I dislike sharing my cigars with my butler I can lock them up. I can't lead him into temptation and then ruin him.'"

Soon afterward he started off. "I think I'll do a little hop-scotching and take some election bets," he said jokingly, or half-jokingly. Then—are there depths of sulfur beneath his crust?—wagging a finger at me: "Remember that the first-born of created things is, by identity, the first-born among the dead." In the smokeless metallic light of the salted fire these cryptic words made him quite sinister. Have I glimpsed the Invisible Jesuit?

I took a third helping and gandered around. It was hard finding company, since everyone was talking shop. I didn't mind. With that sordid crowd of busy faces around me,

politicking and manipulating stocks, I thought, All my ambition, all my wealth is love! I felt like a salamander thriving in
fire. Then I went indoors, found some writing paper and a
drink, sat down at a table overlooking the orchard, and began
this letter.

You ask about Mr. Dharmabody. The little skeezix couldn't
be better. I brought him with me tonight so that he could
romp. He hasn't been out much lately, and has severe belly
sag, almost scraping the ground—a dangerous condition in
our concrete world.

Your letter convinced me that I've been foolishly pessimis-
tic. Mr. Hood's offer is a stroke of luck. It is unlikely that he
knows much about our treasure; probably he has had it rou-
tinely investigated as a well-known lost hoard, without an
inkling of its history. So I shall put his organization to work
for us and draw a handsome salary doing it.

I write among dancing, singing, whooping, hollering, and
drinking. I think I shall succeed. My darling, I love you to
death.

L

october 31

So the progress ends, as the prince have choose, that Twang
will n't work with him. He want "wite people." Yet, *ticbaï
pristwi pok mem naï vin*—In front of a (bad) demone I do n't be
the corpse, you say so, "lie down and die down"? It's n't over,
no *not*. Thus whewhen the Pindola toll it to me I but laughh,
say-ing: Nice, jiust the to-be with you (him). And, litlte later,
I unhover his eyes balls with: "O sad, I have no capitale, just
the fruits of my trusty fund." "O, that is no much?" "O no,
sole-ly 5 or 10 thousand lbs. every year." He will have wish
to say, hohow much that he is loving me, but the money-
think has detract his voice. I hold-him.

Twang yes have one regreg, the work will have give her
some cush (cash?) for a more-soft hotel, and this is so small a
plaint, I mind not any post to live, that is O. K.

LI

Nov. 6

You cannot imagine the rage yours put me into. It is unbearable that you receive such treatment. It's as bad as calling
you gook, and not even to your face, the blockhead! Who
does he think he is? Does he think the winds and seas obey
him for his moldy title?

Anyway I'm sending you extra cash (*or* cush—it's the same)
for a better hotel.

My business appointment with Mr. Hood took place three
days ago. I had plenty of time for rehearsals, and for their
spawn: new reasons to worry.

The three guards led me into the bowels of the palace, far
from the lawns of our first interview. We found Mr. Hood in
a windowless room whose walls were hung with old lutes. He
was swinging in a deep hammock, concealed except for one
tiny protruding hand, which beat time to a ditty that a young
man, on a nearby stool, sang to the plunking of a mandoline:

A fine rain anoints the canal machinery...

At the final chord Mr. Hood rolled into view, handed the
singer some folded bills with a word of thanks, and nodded
him from our presence. He then took me by the arm, and
with a silent, expansive gesture invited me to admire the
splendors about us.

This began a tour of Mr. Hood's indoor domain, or at least
that part of it devoted to scholarship. We visited a room where
students were repairing prints of old movies, among them an
early lost Laurel; another where three ham sets busily whined
—one operator announced excitedly, "I've got the Dahomey
Die Schwärmer!"; a third where a battery of computers blinked
away at translations of middle Bactrian; and at last the immense library, where many young people were at work. Mr.
Hood explained their tasks as we circled the room. "...clear
text of Boethius... fodder for my theoretical teas... Chom-
skian refutations.... Here is the star of the show."

In a soundproofed cubicle a blond girl, who bore an uncanny resemblance to Hyperion Scarparo, was reading aloud from a propped tome. At Mr. Hood's tap she opened the glass door to say, "Rehearsing Mommsen, sir." Mr. Hood motioned to the three ever-present attendants, who conjured champagne and glasses from a set of Melanie Klein. Mr. Hood pressed a glass on the young woman: "Mustn't let you get hoarse." Then, to me: "Every day she reads to me from the classics of history. It is an *heure sacrée*."

From the library we entered a little drawing room, where we sat down. The three guards left. Mr. Hood asked if as a professional librarian I would like to take charge of his study center. I replied that I had considered his proposals and chosen the treasure teams as the most interesting. He assented to this with no sign of either pleasure or displeasure, and launched into an explanation of how the business was organized. I expected him to indicate how I might fit into it; no such luck. At the end of his account Mr. Hood stood up and offered politely to see me to the door. So I asked him what sort of work I was to do.

"Oh, there's no rush about that, we'll come to that in good time. Just think of yourself as one of us, starting now."

On the way out, Mr. Hood stopped by a small showcase where on a bed of black swan feathers Mallarmé's left ulna reposed. "When it arrived I had it brought up the drive in a royal Egyptian litter, surrounded by musicians performing the death scene from *Socrate*. A banner day."

Farther on, in a capacious niche, stood the primitive, half-size statue of a horse. Its outstretched forelegs and cringing head were full of unhorselike obeisance. One eye was painted, the other was a rosy globe of crystal. An alarm clock was set in its brow; long cracks spread out from it.

"It's adobe," Mr. Hood explained. "It was made by a noted wizard of the West, Bernheim Wood. He once visited my childhood home on the Rappahannock. For some reason he was very taken with me and gave me the horse. That day I stopped growing. The sculpture has no beauty, but in that glass eye is stored tremendous scrying power. I often use it.

There's always something going on, it's like a twenty-four hour movie." He peered into the glass eye. "There's a lady in a sari digging old papers with a spade. I met her once in Rome. A handsome fellow is helping her. I know him too. As a matter of fact, he works for me. Take a gander." I saw nothing but faint pink tracery. In a tone of regret Mr. Hood said, "It's because you don't believe. You don't understand."

It is said that at Lester Greek's party Mr. Hood pulled off the deal of his career.

I left feeling saddened by Mr. Hood's establishment, or by his role in it. He is too much the master; his kindness is always tainted by condescension. For instance, he handed out money not only to the singer but to the workers in the other rooms. It's hard to imagine Hodge so pretentious—although I find Mr. Hood much nicer than Hodge. Perhaps the richest people feel obliged to behave this way.

I've been wondering whether my angry words about the Prince weren't a mistake—whether a temperate view might not be best. I say this not only because I naturally tend to peacefulness, but because his rejection may have been simply meant to increase your desire for the job, at filling you with "admiring fear" so as to get you cheap. He may also think that you have not shown the respect due his station. I understand you in this; but I also feel that we are bound to honor those who deserve it, which sometimes means those who expect it. So don't give him up; cultivate him a little.

Perhaps my own fear has produced this watery advice—the unfamiliar fear of being left stranded. As I see more of my new friends, I understand them less. I ask what is to stop them from some day tossing me to passing fishes?

But what other reasons could the Prince have for treating you so shoddily?

I'm sitting in my library cell, swaddled in silence. Election Day has emptied the building. After this letter I must start work on a lecture: next week, I am to address the Knights on "My Visit to the Far East." I shall enjoy telling them about you and other matters crucial to Miami life.

So long for now.

LII

Nov. 10

You mild concil is to late. Went to Prince Voltic table and spake in a big public sound. I 've say godbye *duvaï tharaï* for ever to that one! I say, first, Italy is a moundain of *laï* mud. Then Florenze is *dhum pristwei vini*, so, as a stingk of demon's horpse. The cultura is no thing, only for balance of pagments. I say those opere of Verdi and Pucci are *uüax*. I say, Duccio was a pornograph and Fra Angelico is a jew. Then, his grand mother is a cooked egg, his mother is a post-nose drip. At last I call him a hommunist and one hommosessuale. The Voltic is be come red then white then gone. Follow an other storm. Bonzo is much angry, say, Twang has not to risch his job, for the soddifaction of try-ing on names that fits.

Thus, I have n't power to "cultivate the prince" or, "deal with him" in some way. And, he has all wear-out my wanting to pleace or dis-please him.

I leaft Rostolena village, a round, there was ballons of smoke from the bomb fires, oh I like to eat it. Here I 'm with-in a comfy pension, in Florence. I have sistemate, all my notings from MAP bags at the library here. I bring my learning up to day.

Do you remembem, the de Roover think, there will have to-be a heir to *Francesco di Averardo*, be cause the personal possessions are not gone to *Cosimo*. Then, this heir shall still wish to have the treasore. For this I look all the mentions of tresure after 1443 (that year *Francesco* dieds.) That all most get me ready for the nut bin. Mr. de Roover know where they are the libri segreti (counting books), but other dohuments in MAP are mangled with one the other, it is like, a mattman do it with porpose. Yet, these days are n't guasted. If many names are named near the treasure, one onely came back, in year and out year. This is: *Salvestro Sguardofisso*. He have have stories with i Medici, I do not recount these now, it is just the matter, he persersist toward the gold and I thought, it is him the her. How ever that name wring no bell. I leave MAP and consolt the State Arhives. The 2nd name (Sguardofisso) had no ante cedents it shall be a knack kname may be. I find him —on elettoral list, San Giovanni quarter, 1443-1466. It 's a good sign,

S. Giovanni is of dominanting class, and of *Francesco di Averardo* 's family. I cearch more on, at the end I find this list of the "arroti" in the Balia of '58, on this *Salvestro* is wrote not Salvestro Sguardofisso no not even Salvestro di Francesco Sguardofisso yet *Salvestro di Francesco di Giuliano Sguardofisso!* So it is secure he is of those cousin Medici, I was right. Mr. de Roover is right.

But then, why is he not said, as of Medici? Why not, as *Francesco's* hereditor? Who was his mamma? If were a fine lady, it shall be hid, that *Francesco* were the father. If she were low, he can have adapt the child, even marry this woman, even more get her annulld if she is esposed al-ready, with his great power. Yet not this nor that. So it is one soluzion, that the mother is *Francesco's* slave.

I can not tell of it now, Twang has such hunger, now down to the dinning room. It shall be in a new letter.

Now I'm turned. O my *lemu* & *neng* I am to night much in thooght of you. I ete a lone. Of ten I am drinking you healthy, so I can say, I'm "deadrunk" for you're sake, this is better as, "I die for you," I think.

LIII

November 14

The Knights held their scheduled meeting, but without my lecture. I was very disappointed. There's no doubt they're exceptionally busy: it's the season when they must organize the parades for the Miami pre-Lenten carnival. The forthcoming one has its special problems. Last February a festival barge, burdened with two hundred frolickers, sank in the lagoon, thus reopening the problem of safety hazards. In addition there have been complaints about the theoretical structuring of the pageants.

Hours of discussion resulted in no specific plans. During the intense and sometimes dazzling crossfire, I contributed no more than a requested yes or no. But when it was decided that the difficulty of our problem demanded "superior enlightenment," I found myself picked for the inquiry. The methods used were better suited to the Egyptian Temple than to the

Knights: we held a Shakespearian lottery. I was chosen by
the childish rhyme "Eenie meenie minie moe, Catch a bugger
by his toe," and told to open a volume of the poet's works
at random, reading out the first words to catch my eye:

"*Exeunt omnes.*"

The Knights were bemused. They decided that we must
next consult the municipal mascots: a family of porpoises that
lived in a vast glass cube within the floating museum of maritime replicas. We drove to the harbor and found the sprightly
creatures sporting about the oars of a trireme. My companions
studied their gyrations with great seriousness.

Perhaps I would have been sympathetic to these eccentrici-
ties had it not been for an incident that occurred before the
meeting came to order. I had looked forward to seeing Mr.
Hood, but he was absent. Instead, Hodge delivered a note
from him. Mr. Hood said he was still unable to see me, but I
could work things out with his "confidant Dex Hodge."
Hodge was watching me with an unpleasant smile.

I had wanted to bypass Hodge: his knowing air showed
that he had guessed as much and was pleased to have outma-
neuvered me. As if to aggravate my disappointment, he began
lecturing me about my appearance, looking at me as if I were
some kind of dogheaded-abortion as he addressed cruel words
to points of my dress and physique.

So when the Knights finally disbanded, I drove home to my
bathroom mirror. The view depressed me. My five-month
stye peered back at me from a garnishing of permanent spots
—as for the rest of my outward being, I'll skip the details,
even though you might view them with charity. I used to
think that I should remind you of myself, that I should *make*
you see me. I did not then understand that love is better than
sight and will do without it.

Reflection helped me from the depths. I thought, it is better
to have the nettles sprouting in one's face than in one's mind.
Slowly I cheered up. I decided to relegate Hodge's meanness
to the category of past accidents, to face whatever the future
would bring— which at that moment was a party at Dan's. I
spruced up, set my sails resolutely, and cast off into the evening.

I've told you what Dan's parties are like. This was the exception. I felt it the minute I walked in. The air abounded in that unstrident gaiety which we call natural but which is no more natural than waltzing. Dan had installed his Koolflare, a low calorie fireplace that has brought inhabitants of hot climates the pleasures of the hearth. Made of coal-colored stone, with fire spouts in the shapes of mushrooms, it bathed the room in friendly light. There were few guests at the start, but among them were long-lost acquaintances, and I was amazed how much I liked seeing them. I was a great success, too. My old friends were full of admiration for my recent socializing. Dexter Hodge had brought a troop of pretty raggles, and I hit it off with them like Dean Martin, conversationally, of course. This was balsam to my wounds. Dex was his old affable self, treating me royally.

Late in the evening Dan gave us stork steaks cooked, I think, with speed, because the party turned wild. People kept swarming in. In the confusion Dan bit Dex and some other guy got punched up. But I escaped intact.

Lester Greek was elected to congress by a large majority, winning the "content" as well as the "form" vote.

On my way home, I plucked the enclosed from a wayside bush, forced into unseasonal gaudiness for the greater glory of Greater Miami.

LIV

novem-bre 18

Ah! my pointsetter blossom! Dou you know, I hatch my self with to-pity for that you gathered it, with this premise of summer on-it. There is too room for the toes of some bird. Still I 'll keep it longer than it shall not have stay on the bush, that is very sure.

Your speech of the fests, *nam me slop*, in this is non-happiness, *wey!* for I will have been to the great cerebration in my capital, of the Namma Ghaï (it is "royal shrine"—*namma* mostwise is the hut shrines of peasants make from bamboughs, but this one is all from mud breaks and piastre, then guilt.) It has been this week. It shall be no matter.

Then my belove I shall bring to the honsider-ing of your aspect no ciarity but admoration, all is good even the spots which I look-on for gewels. But one thing (perhaps), you are a little very fat. Yet I know, you have try to slender down, and that will happen. I, shall not force you to that, it is so clear. I remember my unkle munk as he talks to some Lao's (some Laotians) of to-not-eat-much, he needed not to forze them, his exsample of haleth and sense was so cleer, he had the knead only to draugh their attention to this point. That was like a wagging well-joked with the hwip handy that wait on a flat ground. It 's at a crisscrossroads, a intelligent driver mounts and he know to driver the horses. He take the reins in the left and the whap in the right and he diriges the hart here, there, whewhere he wish. So you *ticbaï pristwe*, turning against the demons, those of cunger, drive your senses clever-like, separe your self from that what is bad and lead toward the just conditions of the brain, for in this road you 'll make grow in you and strong the Doctrine and the Diet.

In my life there is again change. For the Pindola beg me, think not the Prince so evil, and he first beg the Prince, think Twang is not so evil. The Prince cedes, Twang may then work beneath him, but he will have "series referenzes of haracter and onesty." These, I can ask of the Mrs de Roover. Yet I do not decide. I shall go one again to that bath station Rostolena and think, and write to you more about whewhence come *Salvestro*.

LV

November 22

Good news at last: good as gold. Mr. Hood is making me a *partner* in his treasure corporation. I can't wait to turn out as dallier in the prairies of abundance.

The news was doubly sweet since it followed new nastiness from Hodge. Yesterday afternoon the Knights visited a master weaver's shop; we were to choose fabrics for the carnival parades. Hodge picked me up, and on the way grilled me in a fashion more suited to a heavy gee than to a man of the world. He questioned my motives in going to work for Mr. Hood (as if it had been my idea), and cast doubt on my qualifications in a very rude way. And then he asked me about the "so-called Amortadella treasure." I instinctively corrected him, thus revealing my knowledge of it. And what were the chances of finding it? I thought them impossible, since there were no maps. This apparently satisfied him.

It didn't satisfy me; during the visit, to recover from my panic, I stayed clear of the other Knights. Loitering in the shop near one old-fashioned contraption, I was addressed by its attendant. He explained that it was a device for "throwing" silk—for twisting strands of raw silk into usable threads. The machine consisted of two concentric drum-shaped frames, a fixed outer one and an inner one that turned on its axis like a revolving door: just like an old Florentine *torcitoio*. (*Torcere* also means to throw.)

The Knights returned from their tour. When he saw me, Mr. Hood took me aside. He announced my partnership with evident pleasure. I mumbled a protest or two, which Mr. Hood waved away. I emphasized my lack of experience and, particularly my ignorance of the Amortonelli treasure. Mr. Hood exclaimed, "That's of *no* importance."

Then why, I wondered, had Dexter Hodge brought it up? I believe Mr. Hood. It's Hodge's role that I question and, I admit, resent. Yet at that moment Hodge acted in a way that disarmed me. To celebrate my promotion he offered me a night on the town, with the full treatment—dinner at the Fontainebleau, the Monkey Jungle Baths, parties, the works. Elated as I was, I accepted, and that evening we had a merry time. Dex organized an *ad hoc* gathering for cocktails; then, after a wine-drenched meal, we went semi-invited to a fancy bash on the ocean front, whence I had to be half-carried elsewhere, though I'm not sure where elsewhere was. "Ah, but a man's reach must exceed his grasp..." I ended here in Dex's private sauna, where consciousness is vertiginously reasserting its claim, and where I'm trying to write you with this dripping ball-point. I do remember refusing the Baths, which are really a glorified panel store. Of course I didn't want "a" woman.

It's hard to keep my thoughts from the success that awaits us. I can't see how we can fail. I shall have access to what my partners know, and this in conjunction with our own information may be all we need. Besides, I shall learn of *other* treasures and be able to claim a share. Does this materialistic optimism seem foolish to you? I swear that I desire wealth only for peace; not to swagger among men, but to secure my own apple tree in which to swing unseen.

As for my "very fatness": until last night I had kept strict tabs on myself. I wear up to seven layers of clothing, including a winter coat (ludicrous here), and jog every day in this attire until I can breathe no more. I take hot baths. I sweat for hours, reeking of baked salt, under that hottest sunlamp the sun. I eat only a quarter pound of red meat every twenty-four hours. No breakfast, no supper, just one meal and some apple snacks. No liquor except for a rare glass of Bass. Sometimes I take a strong laxative. By these means you can almost make out my bottom rib, and my clothes have been taken in *half a yard*. Do you approve of me now? Of course, there's lots left.

Your turnabout with Prince Voltic saddened me; I mean on your account. The task I imposed has brought you this humiliation. Your perseverance would set an example for the disciples of Achaia and Thessalonica, and I appreciate your selflessness with wonder and pride. I know that our work has been dull and its results, so far, insignificant. But like the black-mustard seed, once it takes root it will grow so high as to dominate the garden, and all the birds of heaven will find room to nest in it.

LVI

Novembrr 26

Why do you not expressed no interest, in that I tell you of *Salvestro*? and his mother, that I find to have be a sclave? I wait during two letters, yet now I tell you anyway, you are able to take it or live it.

I learn, all in Florence keep some slave then, who had two bits of money. Thus too the plain preasts and the monkess, the church admit the trafic, when it is unfaithfuls who be boaght and sold. These are spedited in ships many many from Black Sea and Alexandria, in Italy they are soon a pane in the head, the Petrarc names them the "household enemies." Yet not the mamma of *Salvestro*, was of-none the enemy (maybe, notwanting, of *Cosimo*?) Beautiful—"bellissimma di viso con un busto assai adatto," this isn't hommon because most of those slaves have little pocks and then the hwites of the West slashing their face or pric a tatoo so you can tell them if they scape.

They give to the mother a name *Mantissa*. I have found the bill of her sell to *Francesco*, 15 febb. 1431, with this name and her years 25, and those words of her beuty, also: "Since she is perchased by the breaker *(sensale)* one week agone, she's had no harm," and speek of "care of previous owner well hognized to all us" but without some name, or hint of who 's; and the price 60 florins that is much.

Otherway (I shall say below) I find *Salvestro* born in the november of that year, has the *Francesco* jump upon her like a hot dog? However he is not a beast if he have done that, he had to-want a son so long, then he's assolute kind to her, to the son. And, his spose dies: he waits, the decent wait-time, then he freeze quickly *Mantissa*, I have this act: "Mister and slave presenting in the chambers of notary, her liberty was conscended because she has served him with sollecitude and as the laws. Kneeling front of her master *more priscum et antiquorum servando* she places her hands withinside his hands and implore him with the most great veneration and humiliation to befree her as in the roman use; after this her master let fly her hands, said, Be fre, be the Roman citizen, freed from some and all servitude to-me. I notary present draw up the deed. And she 's that free as she is born from a family frce."

Then, truble. *Francesco* want to make the birth of *Salvestro* legintimate and so he will adopt him. In the church some said, no, *Mantissa* was not your amateur wife whewhen this boy is born, still your old wife was there, only with a regular honcubine in your house *non ut famula sed ut uxor* can it be adoption. All right, so this mater needs the Arcibisp's dispense; *Francesco* will go to him, I think it is *Antonino*. But this one must "consulk with who has intelligence of the sobject, and in church and in lay, he must talk of course to the Priorate of the state." And, divine whowho dominoes the priorate? It is *Cosimo, duvaï tharaï* to that hope!

But *Francesco* will interpose an appeal; then too soon he's dead. He shall have give to the mother and the son his cash, his light belongings, yet could not his great lands and houses and they go to the cousims. Any months before that he dies there was the election (of '43), there was new rule and he can push *Salvestro* into the first grup of handidates. You know, this is that time when the incluse not just those seduti & veduti but their relatives and it means sons and grandsons there, so *Salvestro* after this is in some political bodies. He has not true strength yet a distinction, with this he's going on to argue with *Cosimo* about the treasure, his tesoro dei tre sciarrani.

That is something, that is enough.

You are content with the going to work for the Hood, and the joy is good, however you have much hope, I fear that this shall fall. But it is not too bad, execpt for the sadnes, for here, it is all arranged, the Prince and Twang breathe in the same breathe-rhythm that is friendshift. "Give-for and get-for," as your saying. And he wants to "pick ripe frutts of the mind" of Twang, so I drinking and eating with him much, and this after-noon even golving together. Bonzo is as glad, he sleep all the day. The golf is hard, in my *phrap*, after a hole I only do the potting, I'm O. K. in this. The Voltic is today well-formed, he say, and his balls are straight. Then he shows something for the one who play wicked, and become furios with theirselves: near the very hard holes one see that I think are old-manner from-rain shelters, no, there are in them a lady with some whips, she's dress in sharp heals on botts under lather dress. So the man-player has hit balls in berries, he smile at the play-enemy, very gentle manly, and he come here and is bitup, then back to game all relax. The Prince know these nice ones, I'm meeting three, and pretty, Tisiphone, it is the most pretty, and Alecto, and Megaera. Others have also most harmonious ancient names. But then, I ask, where does the tense play-ladies go? For this the prince has a frown, it's the cold moment of our new intamity.

Bonzo after tells me, the girls are very fine prostatue—that is his word, no "whore", I suppong it is a pretty-er as we say *battazhum*? I have forgot your lessons, now for you a Pan new dictum—*Battazhum ticbaï, nob-me lemö üin*, with to-mean "Cofronting with a *battazhum*, love be-come an idea." Some say *vin* not *üin*, "become a horpse," it is unrighteous. The sense, is to justificate the wores.

That also is well your vast diminution of fat. It is, like of a giungle of salad trees which near one village or group of cabitations is invade by creeperers and in this comes a man whowho desire that the trees wax and blosom, for he bear them good-willing and friendlike sentiment. He huts and off-bear all the torted branchs or the evil-doing creepers to the end that the wood he clean and tended even with-in. He foster at that time the wood growing straihgt that is well come, in the manner that later the tree incresce and svelop. In that way you detach yourself from that is evil and fat and are clinginging to the just estates of mind, thus you push up in you and strong-then in you the Doctrine, and the Diet.

It has been nice, to re-see the Etuscan landescape. The life in Rostolena's alway grand, and *wey*! it must be asked, some dollars, I therefore need a new war-robe. This is a small *slop* but I cannot else. It is for the coldness too. Fogs have start.

LVII

Dec. 1

I write from the lower depths of hangover: a hangover procured at my own expense from four sidecars, a bottle of New York State champagne, and six snifters of Drambuie—hardly enough to justify the wreck of this day. Indulgence has only deepened the trough of my depression; more about that later. Since I can think of nothing else, first let me explain the hangover.

Yesterday I was asked to tour the library with an out-of-state colleague. For once the chore was fun, thanks to the personality of the visitor, Mr. Alfred Korn of Phoenix. After an afternoon in the tape stacks, we went out for drinks, and he came home for potluck. Unfortunately, between the third and last sidecars, we had broached the marshy topic of "simultaneity versus linearity." Quoting third-hand examples from modern art and physics, we praised the former as a principle of thought and action, while condemning linear logic as archaic, inefficient, and dull. Our ideas were vague, but enthusiastic; and in our alcoholic simplicity we decided to put them into practice with an experiment in synchronous cooking.

On the way home we agreed on a two-course menu. Alfred would make spaghetti with fish sauce, I a giant vanilla flan. On arrival I had a first, fleeting qualm when Alfred complained about the absence in my larder of fresh sucking-fish. But he resigned himself cheerfully to canned tuna and set himself to chopping onions, accompanying his task with a *sotto voce* "Hallelujah Chorus," to which he fitted his own text, "Non-sequential awareness!"

I had meanwhile turned on the oven. A burgeoning appetite sustained my expectation of a satisfactory dinner, and I set to work with gusto. But after I had assembled my ingredients and utensils, and was separating the white and yolk of my first egg, Alfred startled me with a gasp of indignation. (The egg flopped into the bowl entire.)

"You mustn't do that," he said. "It's against the basic principle. If you break things down into their components you submit to linear tyranny at its worst."

"Alfred, you can't make a flan if you leave in all the whites. You peeled your onions, didn't you?"

He considered these facts.

"Oke. We shall allow Zachary to divide the egg. But it's heresy."

It was a few moments later when, declaring "Now a few nuts to complete the spectrum," he spooned a jar of *marrons glacés* into his sauce that I realized how high he was. I was no less so: I was simply less inspired by our "idea" and more interested in eating. I had got my elementary flan into the oven without disastrous omissions or commissions. Since

Alfred plainly needed more time than I, I left the oven door slightly open. Alfred had finished his preparatives and had begun, normally enough, frying garlic in oil. But as he poked the sizzling cloves he became restless, and this restlessness culminated at last in a wave of impatience that visibly overwhelmed him. Before I could intervene, uttering a petulant shout of "No, no—at-onceness!" he emptied the contents of the saucepan into the water set to boil for the spaghetti, and dumped after them all the remaining ingredients: tomatoes, carrots, onions, herbs, tuna, chestnuts, and the *pasta* itself. He turned to me with a chuckle. "It's the whole concept of time —not chronology, but the moment as critical nexus of reality."

That moment arrived all too soon. There was a preparatory growl from the pot, then an irrepressible gush of orangish foam rose up like a thunderhead at sunset—rose up, swelled, and collapsed on the stove in a languorous hiss, sputtering over the incandescent burner as it coursed down the front of the stove, and into the oven, with its cargo of muddled grease. I was helpless before that roar and surge. Alfred was shining with anger and surprise. The vision was brief: the fuses blew.

Since there was no top on the baking dish, our meal was lost. We consoled ourselves with the champagne and a basket of fruit. Alfred wanted to start cooking again, but I had had enough. We drank away our disagreement.

Several hours later, and fewer ago, my head and innards woke me and drove me outside. No hart ever panted after the water brooks as I did for Bufferin and air. Shuddering I watched Venus and Mercury dancing above the low new moon.

Nothing is more adventitious than a hangover, but this one seems the outward and visible sign of inward and invisible gunk. My nerves are shot. First, my rapport with Mr. Hood broke down again. The responsible agent is without possible doubt Dexter Hodge. Unfortunately, he has become Mr. Hood's right hand in the treasure enterprise, and I must have all my dealings with him. I dread that he may try to eliminate me from their plans.

On top of this your letter came. Perhaps I'm unduly sensi-

tive, but it left me with the feeling that you were becoming
someone else. I can't believe you do this on purpose. But without wanting to you have filled me with doubt. You speak
of your life with the Prince and Pindola, who is after all only
a failed rapist, as though that was what mattered to you. You
reproach me for indifference to your account of Salvestro and
his mother. Why *should* I be interested? I am down with
worry and find this research, no matter how ingenious, irrele-
vant—especially when you tantalize me with the continuation
of the dispute over the treasure. How much have you learned
from that? Are you sure Salvestro kept his official positions?
Was his presence in governing bodies a reason why the election of 1443 was annulled? The Medici clique called it *lo squit-
tino del fiore d'aliso*, because of the lily's stink.

And there is this request for money to buy clothes! It's so
unlike you. Besides, I cannot possibly afford expenses of this
kind. You know I do not begrudge you a real pleasure, but I
dislike spending money on a fancy dress which will only be
worn once. I don't want you to look strange, but I certainly
can't spend very much for this. Now it seems to me that there
are things, in the way of clothing, that you need more, for
instance warm undergarments, since you say it is turning cold
and damp, and someone like you from a hot climate must
take very special care not to catch cold or worse. In my opinion there is nothing on any occasion prettier than a Pannamese
phrap, and wearing one would allow you to dress warmly
underneath without looking bulky.

This may sound petty, but it is not for any lack of affection
or concern. Quite the contrary. You must understand that I
feel particularly frustrated by my disappointments here and
that I am dismayed at the same time by the distance between
us. Perhaps it's my liverish imagination. I don't mistrust you
but for heaven's sake let me know what you're doing. It isn't
that I want to dominate you, I'm happy if I can influence you
even a little. But I still have to know who you are, and now I
feel as though in a moment of distraction I had turned away
from you, and when I turned back, you were gone.

LVIII

Decemb. 5

It is that only some silk I want, for to make *phraps* perhaps one two or three, that is it all. I've not wish to expend that money to a dressmaker or yet to shops with the dresses off the pig. No it is nonjust, Zachary! Already I've buy the underware with old money. Yet now, there is nothing for silk, and I shall have needing more for life expenses and cannot ask, for some or new. It is not grave and Twang'll do-make however. *Sheenam sheenam* I bear it, I do not mean reproval. I say *duvaï* to the more money and I shall not miss that. My mind to be *theu, theu* "we" and it is all.

But then: the presence of *Salvestro* is "reason why the election of 1443 was a null." *Pok atram pok naï!* I do think thus *not!* It was nothing to do. *Salvestro's* there yet in '45. Also he have support *Cosimo*, of course, in the politics, if the Medici are outthrow perhaps he loses the treasure ever. *Cosimo* had not a worry lest the *Salvestro* compete in a bank, for *Salvestro* had not the bank formation, his father wrote of that in regret; and so the father may be for it have enter him in the election because this is for "uffici intrincesi ed estrincesi" and they, are offices with payments. Last, it was *Cosimo* & Co. whowho wide the lists for seduti e veduti (wish, to make stabilished families stronger there), if he's a-worry of *Salvestro* he will not make his walk up to a public office so facile. And *Salvestro* is grateful and always vote-for Medici.

These mistakes, of dress and of the Florence politic, I think it's you're mind is overthrow with mudnanities. It's that it is like a jungle of Salas trees near a good town or some dwellings that is overtaken with savage vines, full of twisty boughs, and other discoragement. Please, you are to practice a small mastery of the breasth, simple and cuts the heavy weed. So, thinking of just that real air in-coming and out-going, say: Thinking of cessation of confusion I breathe-in, thinking of the cessation of confucion I breathe out," so a few thousand time, with relax. Then, all-calm, perhaps: *pok lucrem pok lucrem pok lucrem* I eat not I don't eat I will not eat, and so fourth (not).

You see so, I'm again at Florence. This is to recerch about

a little statue of gold, this the Prince have given Twang to sale. It's of late 15 century. Thus, once more into that Laurenziana. Also because it is coming back from the S. U., I must have to stay about two hundred hours in the Hustoms House, almost I go to insanity, it is so big and in it, no person knows more than one part of one law.

Yet I use my visits into the Library, that I look more for us. And thus, I'm very busy. So much preoccupation, do not admit me to think about myself. It is some felicitude.

I am depart from Rostolena in just time, on that day I see the snow prows have come out near the road way side, they wait for the first falling. Is that true, there are *pristwi* of the snow (daemons)? It here is cold too. I thank your expression of a fear, that I don't care myself about hatching a cold, and the like. Yet I am enough careful when I am a-wake, it is at the night the clothes are kick upon the floor and I'm espoused to the damp until coolness awake me, and the cold billowcase.

Part Five

LIX

December 9

This is the black time of year, even here in the sunniness—blacker here. Dry canes croon in the wind: my heart slept—wake up, heart! Sleep buried thought and feeling in stupidities, and "I" spoke them to you. Twang, your husband is sometimes insane. My last letter! Black blood scolloped from the soul's cellars. How can it have happened? Solitude? Gazing on past miseries with the fondness of self-hate? If only at such times I could board a train, and in a few hours find you, to get back on the way to happiness (the way next to which I am my own ditch), the way that you opened to me, sweet lyon of the morning, piloting the tramp out of his compost years, with his joker's baton and rig, dumb as blended Ajax—the ultimate T. B.

Contrition holds sway in the essential realm; elsewhere, mild thanksgiving. At lunchtime yesterday I stopped at the treasure office for a routine visit. The receptionist surprised me with the news that Mr. Hood was expecting me. I went in fearing the worst. The little gentleman received me courteously. "Waited to be sure you got this," he said, sliding printed sheets across his desk with a pearl-pale finger. A glance showed them to be a financial report, with the heading "Key Biscayne Dredging Operation." I said that there must be a mistake. "I don't think so. Cop a peek at the last paragraph." This announced a distribution of dividends, concluding: "We inform you of your share," with my name written in against the figure $2,170.

Confused, yet not wishing to appear inept, I found nothing to say. Mr. Hood broke through my discomfort: "Dex did tell you that you'd been cut into the pie?"

"Dex" hadn't. Nor had he lacked the opportunity: I had seen him at Rilkie's over breakfast. The meeting had already lowered my opinion of him. He had remarked that he was "just hopscotching"— in other words, making book for the counter clientele. It was hard to believe: Dexter Hodge, tycoon, prominent citizen, Spindle Knight, doing the work of a petty criminal! Perhaps he thinks of it as slumming. He said nothing to me about my dividend, although he spoke to me for several minutes, glowing rosily in the morning light, rambling on about this and that, the luminous windbag! Should I warn Mr. Hood about him?

In the office, wariness compelled me to point out that I had never heard of the Key Biscayne operation. "That's all right. You're part of the outfit. You're entitled to your share. You can't imagine what a difference it makes having a bright man around. And you're a lot sharper in business than you let on. Don't think I don't know it!" I thought I must be dreaming, but the two grand prove I wasn't. La vie she is a little crazy. It's nice to be taken for a slick pro once in a while.

I'm sending extra money for your expenses, comfort, and all the *phrap* material you may desire. I'm glad you're dressing warmly. Be careful next week, during the "Wotan freeze." It's a short, bitter pre-Christmas cold snap, when Wotan, or Odin, supposedly abandons the north to fetch back the sun.

Trying your recommended exercises has been only partially successful. I concentrate satisfactorily during the breathing out part, so much so that I often forget to breathe back in. This leads to dizziness, once I even fainted, though very briefly.

LX

december 13

From here and from there I glue-up a tale of *Salvestro*, from '43 to '65, how he quarrels with *Cosimo* and then, with *Piero de' Medici*. It is un-yet-finished. It will be not-ever: for, the libri segreti afer 1451 are been lost, after this the peekings are slimmer. In the general, the song of *Salvestro* is the old same, in his letters, in his spoke pleas to the cousins (I think too, if I'm right how I read the *Cosimo's* reports): that the treasure "dei 3 sciarrani" was truely-bluely of-*Averardo, naï*, so, of his afterbears. Yet the manner of *Salvestro* change from the earlier pleasant slow by slow, return violenter, more scourteous. But not the answers. *Cosimo* write ever gentler after *Salvestro* be the last *Averardo* leaf. That I do not understand. *Cosimo* had not such much need for the *Salvestro* vote. And still he will never write the forgivable words of resentment, that acridmony of *Salvestro* has replies of consideringness and offers of hompromies.

That little statue is sold, but not by Twang, by some other working in the Prince's organism. It is hard news, for there was long work, and some hopes.

Then, second trouble, that my noce is stuff. Never before. Twang apply some resulution disciplines, say, "Now thus face with the demon in nose," *Naï ticbaï pristwe maï neng-dek—duvaï duvaï* farewell, yet he don't want to leave! He walk in my mouth when I asleep and wipe off the smooth damph.

LXI

December 17

More news from the office. Mr. Hood called me in to inform me that he and several "colleagues and competitors" were organizing an expedition for early April. Its object will be the treasure at Key Betabara. The expedition will be financed by individual members of the different groups, with profits to be divided accordingly. Mr. Hood was giving me a chance to join. He said the price of admission will be steep.

He also made the venture sound *very* important. I did not

ask too many questions, because he was in a foul humor. His accountant had tried to play him for a savage by salting the books. With me Mr. Hood was gentleness itself, but a platinum light in his eyes betrayed an inmost fury.

What shall I do? There are reasons against participating: the money, the time taken from the pursuit of our treasure— but what if *this* were our treasure? I worry about being left out of future projects. There seems to be no straight answer, and I burrow under the problem like a daffy gopher. It's surely not that complicated. Which way do you counsel? (The way that will bring you here quickest—rapture of that parousia!)

Sorry about the statuette. Your golfing friendship hasn't made the Prince exactly frank in his dealings with you. Console yourself with the thought that he isn't fit to unfasten your shoes. (Not that you need bother to show it.)

I guess your cold was inevitable. For sleeping, better than drops is to smear a little mentholated jelly under your nose. You should see a doctor.

Your progress with the treasure is admirable. We've narrowed the gap in our knowledge to the few years between 1465 and 1483. What a marvel you are, dear Twang—

> Twang Twang bo bang
> Banana fanna fo fang
> Fee fie mo mang
> —Twang!

How happy I'd be lolling with you in a banana orchard, how I'd love you when I saw that you were looking at me, and that you loved me.

LXII

December 21th

It traspires, *Cosimo* in 1467 wants to export the horde of clippings. He try to does this in a trade company, where's a partner with *Francesco di Nerone Neroni*. They conseal the gold in any silk, but *Cosimo* doesn't tell *Francesco* this and then he learns about the surrebterfuge from *Salvestro*, who has found in about this and attached it and ruin it. Yet not before that *Francesco* tries to get more money from *Cosimo*. Here, 2 letters of *Francesco* about it, condensated.

1. *To Cosimo de' Medici*: You made mistake to draw from our contract so fast, without listening my view. If it is fact that I arrange the trasport of the chest of the silk to the foreign, you were not so onest to hide the true content. Yes, I understand that you almost must be secret, but you shall have give me an alert to the dangers, that I shall have may been expose. For this spezial treatment of it shall have be necessary of course a little more of expense, to caretake of such a wonderful spedition. Do you do this, no, you unsolve the partnership, I guess you will punish me thinking, I'm not loyal, but who is punish? You too, because the company has have a lot success and why will it not still.

2. *To Salvestro Sguardofisso*: (about at same time): Look, whewhere my fidelity to you has bringing me—*Cosimo* has disciolved our company. Now, I say, I'll get my revench, you will get your property. Yet in the meant-time your indiscretions afflect me, they do the get-back more hard. First, I don't know, that you be right in that congetture. O. K., Cosimo has write as he has confess, "ho facto torcere il oro in un pezzo di seta di 500 bracci," I agree as good you are much suptle to think it mean, the little piecings of gold are "throw" in the silk, but he did maybe not signify it. I do not denegate, that man is diabalical enough to do so a thing. Yet, your are not-wise, to verify it, so you say as you do, with the question to this one here and that one there, and there. All weaver in Tuscany be now has, heared of the treasure. Where you demand of the marks upon it, I reply: Cosimo said only then quhen he first instrugt to ship the chest of ff, that it (chest) and as well the silk within that have "i segni familiari". Now be careful of going in Bologna, the plague has intered the city, &c.

The nose isn't weller, yet this shall be not *tharaï* alway always, *ticbaï Twang neng sheenö* in the face of nose I shall bear.

Yes, yes, you are to go in the venture with the Hood. He want you to do that, he'll distain you shall you not, and all so months to be with Hodge & Hood, and you will lett the offortunity go past? To this you are to bag, burrow, or steel the money. How, are you making so much complihations? It is complete useless. And yet I know, such matters are not less or more real in this materio-subtle world, for: *Nob-ma, stheu ticbaï nam pok-ma*—O Being, all in front of it is not-being, a love-most sayso of the Pans. But, whewhere you are writing, "There seem to be no straict answer," POK *atram* POK *naï*, I do *not* think thus, or this way, or this.

It's becoming very frank in concern with the figurine, and I pull-off myself my shoes. The Prince send me yesterday the commission (12%) from the selling. With this come apology for the retard, and to do vivid the apologies a pottery of green plants dark green, that will not die in my chamber. I believe, this is the Bonzo have made that to happen, so I am full to him, of grateful, and affection.

For you in this paper Twang folds a twig of smelly rosemary.

LXIII

December 26

I have accepted Mr. Hood's offer. You were wrong to accuse me of making complications. The decision would only have been easy if Mr. Hood were a simple person. I wish he were simple, even a simple tyrant. But it's a subtle not a heavy hand that maintains his hold on his employees and friends—I almost said subjects.

He was pleased with my decision: I could now expect to make a considerable sum. "Otherwise, as some kind of executive, you'd have had to settle for a salary, or a measly two per." How much could I put up? I asked what was the minimum amount? "That depends." I would raise as much as I could. I suggested contributing "certain maps" as part of my stake. (I did this to provoke some indication of what Mr. Hood knows.

Mr. Hood seemed largely, although not entirely, uninterested. He concluded with a slightly brisk suggestion that I start raising my share without delay. Perhaps he took the offer of maps as an attempt to buy in cheaply, but I doubt this—he is always praising my integrity.

What a gloomy time this is! To celebrate Christmas the palm tree outside my building dried up and died. An adolescent goon has already lopped off most of the fronds. I stare at the stripped trunk and wonder how to get a piece of that business, which Mr. Hood described as in the millions. My means are so pitiful. If only he had refused the maps outright, or named a sum. His ambiguities have left me in a desultory fever.

These worries have aggravated a case of holiday insomnia that will probably kill me. At four every morning I turn on the lights and stare at the objects in the room. There's your sprig of Tuscan rosemary among them: the Virgin's rose, so timely come, laden with fragrance and thoughts of weddings (funerals too). I wish you had spelled out a few words of affection to set next to it. Somehow your last note was not so treasurable as your former ones. But your light shines on.

And the discovery of what happened in 1457 is a triumph. Such patience and intelligence bring hope for everything—I even imagine the dead palm putting out new green. (It won't. Here, spring means only turning on the blower connected to our God-given radiator.) It is at last clear why the chest of gold is a chest of silk. This is as valuable as having the map: we now know what to look for. Of the work we had set ourselves, you have already done more than your share.

Of *course* the bits of clipped gold were wound into the silk when it was "thrown." Since only one or two workmen were involved, the secret could be easily kept. Later the threads were woven into cloth, weighty but otherwise unexceptionable. No wonder the Abbot suffered over those lengths of brocade!

That Cosimo describes the markings as "familiar" indicates that there were fish on the chest and crows on the silk. Both sets are so *familiari* they appear in every account; and the treasure even took its name from the fish. Were the crows a weaver's mark—can you check this? To the Abbot they were sure signs of the gold. What I cannot fathom is how the real chest reached the abbey in time to be sent to Barcelona. But doubtless you will solve that enigma too.

As for your persistent cold, I think—well, perhaps I should stop "thinking" and send you a hug.

LXIV

Wey Twang me ticbaï pristwe o god I'm face to a demon, new, it rise in me like boil water, it is making me very conflicted, for that the gentle Bonzo, whowho has be so kind to Twang, so affective I think, he is hookered by an other, a dark native, and that woman, do not smile and laugh much such as our ladies, O no but of clever tragical, it is not good, I hate that her dark of-chick-fatt soul, and she is nothing good for Pindola, more, and more he has suffer from that one draem he dream, that he is a dagger! I will *uüaxm pop vin* uomit over on the corpse, of-her, when I shall can. Yet this is not the way, I must know, *slop pok duvaï pok*, a misery is not for ever evr. Still the water foam-hots.

Then I think too, of your words on these letters of *Franceso Nerone*, yes I think of you remarkings on *Cosimo*, how there is no difficulty to believe when he says that those marks are familiari that they can to be crows and fishes—*pok atram pok naï*!! Is it that you desire still, that I expedit to you the italian dictionary?

Exceptively there has been some business pleasure. The Prince gives me a hameo to sell. I was hearing of one american collector on the visit in Florence, I go to the cotel, it's a snatch. The pleasure is, to gain money by Twang's self. The Prince please too, sending me a new plant-pot. Before it, and those other, I have sit, to write these lines, and they semble to be waving, so I do now, acrossed the Atlantic.

LXV*

December 31

I must write without an answer because I'm becoming a psychosomatic derelict. I can't sleep. Fatigue keeps me awake —body in a spasm, head full of rivers thundering toward a nameless sea.

The trouble is carnival. For us Knights it has already begun. Most of us are busy decorating the streets for the parades (the first takes place in four days.)

Decorating is a poor word for what's being done. After pavements and sidewalks have been scrubbed, housefronts repainted, commercial signs removed, and ill-aligned build-ings straightened, a continuous decor is installed, with paint-ings, statues, three-dimensional gardens, street-to-roof tapes-tries, arcades of flowers, canopied intersections...

The cost of this is shared by the city and a few wealthy citizens, who are given certain streets as their responsibility. Although they generally turn a profit from carnival through a multitude of concessions, these individuals must be able to put up hundreds of thousands of dollars. Many Knights meet this requirement. Others less rich are at least refurbishing their own properties. But I, in whom any such pretensions would be comic, have been given another privilege. I have been made watchman of a glorified parking lot. It is called the "carriage patch," it lies near the Bayfront Park Bandshell, and in it the processional carriages are abandoned between parades.

I must devote two hours before and after office work to my new job. It is not only a tedious but a useless one: the lot is enclosed in vibrant wire. I was forced to take it; Dexter Hodge did most of the forcing. This morning he drove me to the patch, as if I couldn't be trusted to get there alone. "Don't be fractious!" he kept saying, even when I had stopped complain-ing. He took pains to convince me that being watchman was a mark of great esteem. Miles Hood had held the office last

*Special delivery

year. "Right, Phan?" He turned to Phanuel Asher, another Knight he'd brought along. Mr. Asher agreed. After this double testimony Hodge went on lecturing me until we reached the patch, where he left me with a genial wink.

My two hours then, and most of my afternoon stint, passed in undistracted solitude. As watchman one may not read, write, or even sit. I sniffed the mortuary smells of the carriages; gazed hungrily at "The Dragon Spit," a Chinese restaurant across the road (as bar-b-cue it was simply "The Spit"); or listened to irksome strains from the bandshell, where the All-Miami Youth Brass Ensemble rehearsed *The King's Dump*.

At six, thoroughly bedraggled, I had a visit. A car skidded up to the gate, and out of it bounded Mr. Hood's three guards, their red neckties fluttering as they leaped towards me. Backed against a barouche, I withstood their harangue, loud but not unfriendly:

"Hi there!"

"Hi there!"

"Hi there!"

"Look at *you* ..."

"... in your cold gold prison!"

"All alone!"

"No twist, baby?"

"No twist, *sir*?"

"Don't be grumpy!"

"*We'll* find you ..."

"... a slattern to your Saturn ..."

"... a Venus to your ..."

"Don't mind us."

"We've been sniffing sulfur.'

"Shouldn't we tell him?"

"No."

"No."

"He'll never blow."

"He's no crow..."

"...but he won't blow."

"He's not snider..."

"And you can't knock him."

"Bobble him a little?"

"Let him wait for the moon."

"But hopefully."

"It's hopefully you must wait for the moon."

"Bye now."

"...bye now..."

"Bye."

They hopped into their Dodge and drove off. Were they drugged (from "sniffing sulfur")? Character-judgments aside, their nostrils did foam slightly.

I had brazened out their litany, but my inner structures were shattered. I stared at the orange elephant floating over the gate, symbolizing the people of Miami, and felt myself going crazy. I'm not much better now, waking from a doze, everything wrapped in deep silence and the night half spent. Your words... to preserve me from terrible forces, all these men—

I'm helpless without a sign from you. I feel as if I were being swathed in endless black fabrics and stowed away.

Everything is in confusion, the Knights, me, us. Can't you make a short trip here and bring some light?

I incessantly repeat your name against the Lesser Sanhedrin that confronts me. Your name is my non-ancestral totem.

I write because I can't bear waiting for your letter and to ask, can you make that trip?

LXVI*

Janu. 3

It has been time now, that I wish to speak secrets to you and thus, as soon as your specially delivered letter has awakened me from delicious slumber, I think it shall be now. For I know, since the middle november, the letters to you are be open. So I control in the letter of 21 dec. There was in it, no rosamary! But the opener think, it falls out, and he put in one. Your

---

*Because of insufficient postage ("Unauthorized Enclosure") this letter was returned to the sender, c/o General Delivery, Florence.

thank you ensure my knowledge. However, here is a twig truly from la Twang.

For I am in some minutes to snuggle this away, past any spy, to a post office and speed this with my proper hand. Yet it will be right, with after letters, to do old way, then they will not suspect. To mail secretly, is terrific it must be rare—not again.

Now I quick shall say of markings on chest. Read this sentence, that I cannot send because of those opening, from *Averardo* to *Giov. di Bicci*, 1403: he is speak of *Messer Todao's* gold: say, "e quei 25 sacchi furono portati dalla vostra gente, nella vostra casa." I inscript it but in the mind, it is maybe non-exact, no bother. For you must perceive, how signifying this is? And not for only what the marks then are being, but it is a flash on the late "travels" of that treasure.

The cretin Pindola knows nothing of it, nor the Voltic. Bonzo ignore even, the life of *Salvestro*. His family custody the things of "ulterior descendents *Averardo's*" he don't know there be one! You shall say, So, what? I say, Nice to be 1 up over them!

Also, I have Pindola in soul mess. Twang entirely brain-flush him. That other, dark woman? Twang rent her, from one-horse bordello. Thus: Pindola wishes, to penitrate in Twang. "No. But let me introduce, Signorina Dark. Can penetrate in her, please." He does does. O after, crazy with the more wanting for Twang. Two day before, he visit; I "forget" his mars bars, he enter psycho-psexual glycemia frenzy, he spends memorable New Year day mostly shouts and yells things like, "Where all the vulvas (*ficche*)?" even I was worry concerning the neighbor effect. I have write to you my jealousy sentiment, to hover my truth. This is truth, a chinese say: "In the men a desire is mother to love, In the woman love is the father to desire." And how grand his desire for Twang (yet not so much, as her love, for thee.)

Ah poor one that you suffur, only now it shall be, *wuc naï stheu slop lucre theu*, as this all inhappiness eat up us, yet it is but now, and after, you shall chuse for yourself an house; which Twang will like, because you like it. Now, or soon, I am coming to Miami, however it must not be seen, you must not say it, seem to know none. But use some way the two words, they will tell Twang, you wish her to come, she will come. The words, I choose: "dictionary" "Pogo O'Brine"

After, I answer crazy anythings, you will ignore. Then tomorrow I am to write a "real" (false!) answer to your letter, it is for Bonzo and the Prince and their spies, not for Zachary.

I must need, about dollars 50 plus to pay the quick plane billet.

And always now I must fill the letters with lyings of many color, be as twisty as that *bukhaï* tree. Yet it's no matter, not the lies, not any things, are I. Remember, what is "me"? One is to inspect, so reflect: The eye, the observed form, are not "me". The hear and sound, are no "me". The tongue and the tasted are not, the "me". The knows and the stink aren't "me". The body and touch are not "the me". To consider that those 6 personalizzed senses and their objects do not make a "me", this is the perception of inpersonality, O relief and purify, to Twang, to you I trust, although like all even that is a cool dewdrop lasted no more than trace of stick in water. Yet does this afflict, if then one am satisfied in meditation and distachment.

(You must lie also, for they shall have open your letters, as much.)

It cannot be said, more. Such little is this "airletter" paper stamp blue-light all in one. And never, the enough place, for speech of my loving.

LXVII

jan. 4

To behold your trouble is as, to behold water troubling and mudded. That not-desire to know and think, with doubt, hesitating, small commitment, and mindwander, it is call "skeptic doubts". That is an obstackle to advance, you shall liberate the self from them. For a sample, can be said such, naming now the doubts "the Demon"—

ticbaï pristwi	*nob me*	Face to the deman,	for to-be,
pristwi	*pok me*	"the demon	not be
pristwi me	*pok-ma*	the demon is:	not-be"

or like that, to show what are two paths

pristwi lucre nob-ma	demon eating the not-being
pok-ma lucre pristwi	non-being eats demon

There may come clearing in some water; or think:

it seem, the conditions of life are a terror. Thus, they're disgusting. Then, throw them away, and comes through inspection the imperturdability, the reflection on the unconditional, dismisting the conditions.

Well, for that trip, you do it better and you will voyage to Firenze, just as I say in my lastest letter. Perhaps I shall lean you the money for trip? (Exattly so I have said in my late letter.) From these objects sold of the Prince, the hommissions are adding together.

O what to do with that Bonzo, once so dear? I tell him, he must let go that brown woman, it is bad to him, sad on Twang. He says, O left her any days past, but the men's speech are incredible. Just as he in english then say, he will "eat on locusts and wild money," *per fare penitenza!* (And that does, what mean to mean?)

LXVIII

Is it you or I who is losing their marbles? I needed help, not a sermon. I try to be Greek with the Greeks and Pan with the Pannamese, but your advice is very obscure. So is everything else you wrote, and especially the references to your last letter. Do you really want me to make the trip? If you do, say so unambiguously, that's the main thing. (Why in the world do you offer to pay for it?) Wouldn't it be easier for you to take time off from whatever you're doing? Or are certain problems too pressing—what indeed am I supposed to think of this incredible jealousy of yours? "Dear Bonzo!" Jesus! Finally, I never asked for an Italian dictionary.

These misunderstandings make me the more eager for us to get together. I hope you are fit as a fiddle, and ready for love again. I am hunky-dory which means only normally depressed. I am so tired that I can no longer feel strong emotions of any sort. I swallow neat rye like spring water, and hamburgers like pills.

Standing around the carriage patch is still what is most exhausting, because it's so frustrating. Of course it prevented me from watching the opening parade. It's the first time I've missed it since the war.

Carnival began, as it always does, with the entrance into town of our Mystery Guest. Somewhere in Opa-Locka, temporary but grandiose gates have been built. Outside them the Guest's escort first assembled: heralds and ambassadors from all fifty-one states and several neighboring countries, with bands and retinues. There were even interplanetary representatives: this year our kohl-eyed clowns play the role of "Venusians." All were ceremoniously refused entrance until the Guest's arrival and made to don orange cloaks and caps, thus becoming honorary Miamians. The local citizenry already wore orange.

Invited to "preside over Miami's destiny as romance metropolis," the Guest appeared before the gates. He was greeted by the black and white Mayors of the city, and by the Black Virgin of Dade County, who is chosen by lot from the poor of her community. They ask the Guest who he is. "Are you Hermes Trismegistus? Are you the American Hercules?" He replies, "Call me the Pilot," promising only to reveal his name at the end of the festival. The welcomers crown him with orange leaves and give him the tokens of the city: a wand wrapped in crossed spirals of turtlehead, and a gold coin. Advancing to the gate, the Guest drops the coin in a slot above its lock, and with the wand strikes a bucranium adorning the lintel. Thereupon the massive plywood doors swing open. Before entering the city the Guest asks the Mayors to grant pardons and paroles. His flag precedes him. It shows a white ship on a black ground, symbolizing "Miami under the Pilot's Guidance," and until Ash Wednesday it will replace our banner as city emblem. As the flag passes through the gates, a baby hare is released and scampers down the empty expressway: a reminder of the "fun" aspect of carnival. A moving grove of oranges trees followed the Guest, turning this way and that according to the rules of a time-honored dance. Then came the Black Virgin, the Mayors, the ambassadors (the Venusians rolling among the rest like hoops), and the cortege of floats.

Their destination was the city center, where the Guest was to initiate a new dance. He stopped on the way to pay homage to a new statue of the President; since the work hadn't been completed in time, he had to lay his wreath in front of just the horse. This lapse may cost us the Dixie Carnival Cup.

I saw nothing of this, except for the hare, who found his way to my backwater and stared at me for a few seconds (exit, pursued by a scamp.) Much later, a float appeared. It exhibited a pastoral scene. Under spangled netting (dawn sky of stars and sun), among pale grasses bordering a mirror (icy pond), a donkey nosed about the roots of a tree; a gray lantern was nailed to its trunk, an empty bird's nest perched in its boughs. Title: "The Phoenix."

The slovenly old man driving the float wanted to park it in the carriage patch, which was unthinkable. He pretended to be an old friend who had "done me plenty of favors in his time." He called me fink and Pogy O'Brien, and his raggle stuck out her tongue at me as they lurched off.

The expression "eating locusts and wild *honey*" is from the Bible—perhaps a barbaric Jewish custom. It means "roughing it."

LXIX

J. 11

It is shame, the honey not money. For in Pannam, some eat "wild *money*"—flowers of a bursh of the grots who are few, so, precious, also delicious. The eaters are men wild too (but these, not clowns: hangry thiefs.)

And this sobject money: may you remember, that that Twang ultimately has requested.

What sadness that you will not learn that teaching for consolotion. Is it simpler, these mottoes? *uüaxē slop*, retch woes! *lemō maï*, love the now's *pok atrō* not speak (think)! *mō!* be! The aim of the arrows is, contemplating transmorphations dissipate the idea "stability". Thus (he said) brother, a monk with the mind full of impurturbability, pierces one way first, then in a second, a third, a ford; similarly over, below, around: and in everyplace being one with all he'll penetrate the world with his mind full with impeturbabality, the wide, grown, unlimited, hate-free and malevolence free Mind.

Also I wish, you once will say, you would like some thing, because I like it. This recalls, soon I perhaps have a thing, that it is we both like (and look!) much, much.

Now that trip, it is not a matter to Twang, that you enterprise it, that she. Or, not all. Yet I shall believe the first plan is that we follow. I shall think, Giannuary 19? Thus I'm glad when you mention a dictionary. It is also interesting, that Mr. O. Brien is come to the town.

LXX*

January 15

Your letter was a big help. O.K. for the wisdom of the east, but what about the trip? That little phrase "or not at all" left me feeling coshed. Or were you just drawing the long bow? It would be cruel to exercise your English when your husband's sanity is at stake. What do you mean, the first plan? Say what you expect and want! Why is this meeting such a problem? It's like organizing a party in Gander in the pre-jet days. Why reproach me for not sending the money you asked for, when I promptly furnished it? I hate this talk of money

*Special delivery

and wish you would stop it and not transform yourself from a woman of wit and beauty into a dun. Especially now, when I need every penny for Key Betabara.

I suppose that "I should like what you like" means Bonzo. My God, I thought you'd taken him for a chump, not a playmate! What was the story you once told me, when I smiled at one of your pretty compatriots, about the rival pigeons that fight over a mate, and both die? The moral was: "Two dead pigeons will not warm the broads you sleep on."

How I have come to hate this time, how I long for our life to begin! I don't much care where, as long as it's not here. Not only because of the present. Miami has an original, other taint. When I was twelve, my parents brought us up here for Easter, and they lost me when they started home. Since we had been traveling with another family, they assumed I was with them. I had in fact gone to see *Random Harvest*. Afterwards I was alone in the city for three eternal hours. I was then punished for hiding myself deliberately, which I had not done. Miami became a place of doom. But anywhere else. I won't be difficult, I only ask to be with you, and with Mr. Dharmabody if he lasts—he's getting awfully gray about the paws. Not much outside activity, perhaps a movie from time to time, but mostly at home, a life of patience and compassion. I promise not to start a shell collection or design a coat of arms. Roses perhaps. I would be content to sit with you and watch the rain fall in the pool.

The fiesta continues on its boisterous way. The Guest has engaged in the first contests to prove his supremacy: golf with the Black mayor, jacks with Ayer Favell. The games will grow in violence. Once all were violent, since the festival originated in Ghetto Riot Week and it was necessary to rechannel its ferocity.

I have felt less out of things lately. One of the dance floats has been moored opposite the carriage patch. These floats, now scattered through the city, are manned by professional dancers who demonstrate the new carnival step, the Muffle. The dancers wear costumes illustrating the Muffle's theme, "The Melancholy of Anatomy": body tights dazzlingly embroidered with diagrams of the skeleton, the circulatory system, the musculature.

The Venusians have already introduced a parody of the Muffle that is supposed to be as popular as the original. At the second largest float, near Interama, only the parody is danced.

LXXI

17th Jan.

It will be best to say, there is no trip. This will make expressions of regret, by you, by me, which will be accompanied by thought of aversion, to blow up the conception of the Lust. Yet can you, my beloved, so calm your soul, to think quiet? You make it, by the *laï* in the mind, that mud, almost not able to be satisfied of destachment. I shall reminder, and do you, that the life in time is is a wheel, and one point sole of the rim touching the earth, a creature is alive but at the point, the rim's points gone by are death, the points coming are not alive, when they come the now will be dead. It shall be new creatures.

Thank you also for your espresso letter that raised me nicely early, so I could enjoy the day to the full. And I think, when you tell that life together, there lack perhaps some sufficient excitements.

Or it is so, when the rain fall on the mountains tops, in aboundance, the water follows the sloping fills the splits, these latter fills the marshs, they the lakes, overflooding who make small rivers, the rivers feed grand rivers, they, fill up an ocean. By parallels, are created the activities by ignorance, consiousness by activities, name and form by consciousness, the 6 actions by name & form, contact by six actions, feeling by contact, desire by feeling, becoming by desire, birth by becoming, suffering by birth, repulsion by knowledge and comprension of things, and the knowledge of extinction of ignorance. And so, on. You, a vespral lake streaky with wild colors, wild longings for holding of the sun that setting.

Therefore and again as first expressed, Jan. 19 will have the sun rise.

(That second, librarian object of our desire has a sure record here. I think it's mine—but, "ours", it shall be always *theu* we not Twang.)

In Pannam it's said, *Pok Lao nam sheenam* not even the Lao (tions) can bear (in) it, when a joy of hope is strong strong, so that breath be past mastery. It is improbable that this Twang not be dead, bended to the near point of coming, on that wheel. And that it turn there, to new "now", but stop!

LXXII*

...person-to-person.
"Would you spell that, sir?"
Em see capital see ay el tee ee eks.
"And your name, sir?"
Mr. McCaltex.
"I'll call you back in a moment, sir."
What's that?
"I'll call you back, sir."
Oh. This noise... damn car race....

"Your call to Florence, sir... Miami calling Florence, two six nine three seven seven, to speak to a Mrs. McCaltax, m as in mother, c as in Charlie, c as in Charlie, a as in able, l as in love, t as in Tommy, a as in able—"
E. As in eel.
"... e as in easy, x as in X-ray."
—What the last letter please? Ics?
"X-ray."
—O.K. One instant............ It ring now. *Albergo Camerlenghi? Si domanda dagli Stati Uniti la Signora Maccalteches, Milano Como Como Ancona Livorno Torino Empoli ics—come xenofobia.*
—*Non ci stà quella signora.*

---

*Long-distance telephone call, Miami-Florence, January 18

Operator, wait a minute, operator—

"Yes, sir?"

Try her maiden name, Panattapam, I guess I'd better spell it. P as in pilfer, a as in angle, n as in... nuts?

"Nan?"

Yes, Nan, then angle, terrible, terrible, angle, pilfer, angle, ... man.

"Nan?"

No, *man*—m, as in mud.

"The first name, sir?"

Well, actually it's double—Tro-tsi, t-r-o... like Trotsky without the k ...

"Groffsky?"

No, Trostky, Trotsky I mean. Never mind. Just say Twang. Tang. Wing. Angry. *Neng*—no, Nan. Gong.

"Florence, please ask ..."

—I hear last name, but first?

"Tommy, whisky, oboe ..."

Not oboe—

"Yes, sir?"

Nothing...

"Tommy, whisky, oboe, Nan, George."

—*Si domanda un altra persona, la Signora Tvong Panattapam, Torino, William-Holden, Otranto, Napoli, Genova, poi Palermo Ancona...*

—*Ma questa signora non ci stà. E fuori.*

Operator, let me speak to her.

"Do you wish to make the call station-to-station, sir?'

Yes, I do.

"Rome, the caller will speak with the answering party. Go ahead, sir."

Albergo Camerlenghi?

—*Si, signore.*

Dove la Signora McCaltex?

—*Non saprei, signore.*

Uscire?

—*Credo che sia partita.*

Come? Come?

—*Credo che la signorina sia partita.*
Dove?
—*Forse in campagna.*
Oh. *Lasciare messaggio?* "Arrive tomorrow," *scrivere : a come addio...*
—I understand perfect: "Arrive tomorrow."

LXXIII

Jan. 21

My trip to Florence was the eighth gothic tale. It has left me a shambles. My body doesn't know what time it is. My mind hankers for the night zones.

Now, safely home, I can admit a fact I spared you: I am hopelessly frightened of air travel. It's foolish, but what does that change? Before departure I consumed half a bottle of pills, but they did not blunt my flight-long terror. Only when I landed in Fiumicino, wondering where you were, then remembering that you couldn't know my flight, did wooziness come. I hardly dared drive. But I crawled to Florence in the little rented monster, its steering wheel digging into my paunch, and found the albergo; where to my stupefaction I learned that you were still away. I pestered that poor lady about you, but she couldn't help, although she did make one call. (To whom?) For the rest of the day I walked through the dank city, yearning to find you, expecting you around every corner, eating meals of various sizes, sipping numberless coffees and drinks, not daring to telephone your friends for fear of compromising you, in fear of them, sinking through sluggish currents of exhaustion and disappointment like a pebble in a tank of crude oil. Night came, no news of you, I was taken to your room—your room!—touched your clothes, sniffed your scents, laid between your sheets. It was awful to sleep without you but fatigue and Valium won. I never heard the alarm: I was awakened by a stuck horn. There was no sign of you. I didn't dare stay away longer. So after leaving the note and money—don't take me for a Pogy O'Brien (how did you learn that expression?), it was almost all I had—I drove back to Rome for my return trip. Before boarding I absorbed so much *stravecchio* that I felt someone else was taking the plane.

What a flight! With the money I had left, I had hoped to prolong my non-existence with a few splits of champagne. A wedding party had reserved the entirely supply, so it was back to bourbon, which sobered me immediately. I was sitting next to three bronzy orientals, one mother, one father, and one pretty girl. They may have been sweet souls, but I was never to find out, for at the moment of take-off they buried their heads in shawls and scarves, a dismaying sight. Soon they started vomiting, missing my Flagg Bros. boots by fractions, and they did not desist. I tried to "be something" about this and concentrate on reading the *Sunday Times*, but my general love of the human brotherhood wasn't up to the occasion. I changed seats.

Festive Miami seemed no haven to the returning traveler. From the air, Funland Amusement Park was visibly swarming. A doze on the bus ride into town left me stunned with accumulated weariness. Outside the terminal, waiting for a cab, I began chatting with a personable young man. It was at least a minute before I realized that he was a carnival mannequin. I couldn't believe it until I touched him. Indeed touching him was irresistible: he was more real than the living.

Reaching my apartment I at last found out where you had been. It ended one painful uncertainty. Christ what a mess. Why didn't you wait? My anxiety now fills sky and earth and day and night. Even before leaving I had been completely distraught. You may have noticed in my room a coffin-like carton and a suitcase which despite its appearance was not made of human flesh. They had been confided to me by an elderly neighbor, Mrs. Roak, to be deposited at the Rome airport— she is soon flying to Italy to visit an idiot cousin and was afraid of being overweight. Mrs. Roak stopped by half an hour before my departure, yet I forgot my promise. I was that bewildered from worry (from the pills too, perhaps.) How do you think I feel now? I have no energy, no confidence. I feel that I've been tried as silver is tried, and found to be tin. How can I stand firm in trouble when I can't even stand up! Outside of you there has been nothing to give me hope. My work at the library is disreputable and I am frequently told as much. I haven't found a trace of the map. I wrote to Avignon and Harvard for help: no replies. Mr. Hood might just as well live in Peshawar for all the attention he pays me. And yet these things would matter little if I had seen you—if I had not lost touch with you. It's unpleasant to blame you, but who else is there to blame for the wasted days and nights, the money spent, and the terrible expense of passionate affection? I begged you to explain your desires and you refused. What a miserable time for us, or for me. Perhaps someday I shall see why it was necessary to drink this vinegar first.

LXXIV

January 24

Yes, it was the cause of regret, and of so much amazing. Yet I have told the plan, it is more than I seize. My two days in country also bring less than the homfort desired. But that sad fear in the airplanes, it has not conflicted me. The plane move at a enormouse speed, that is true, but there is less fearing when was in them than when explained it from far away. I am frighten for you therefore. For my very small trip, it was in the train, I borrowed money, so I am thanful for your thought, to leave any, my very dear.

However with the tumult of your arriving, my most dear friends the Count and Bonzo learn my absence. When I am returning, in evening, they called upon me. From your cause my reputation has suffered injustly. So why did you not tell me, you shall come? These friends will have believe there is secrets from them. They cannot think I shall be gone to country, however I show my cut ticket, that in some way I have thought to keep it. Then is it friendly, and they will stay to converse. But Twang is weary, so into a great cycloon of yawnings that in five minutes I think I blown them out from the room and was asleeping at eight p.M.

Can it be consolation, that one other thing we search, here, there, is here? And of course it will be in Mediceo Avanti il Principato!

This town is as you saw her, gray with coldness. One expect the river will freezes. The moving images are dull. I read some first mistery stories, and play fooling games of card, that I enjoy, with the little girls of the hotel lady, she you met, who is ever more helpful (is this the good word?) about mail.

Than I think, you are in need of being more accurate when you are writing to me.

I have remembered, the contemplating of the estate that is being without desire shall dissipate the idea of pleasure, and I repeat this, Contemplation of a state without desire dissipate the idea of pleasure. Zachary it is hard. It is too strong to master, the buddist way, sometime. I tell you: *Wey, Twang dek laï, Twang nam me vin.* But: *theu mau neng* and *theu nob-me neng.*

Part Six

LXXV

Jan. 28

The tail of the cat
Fell into the vat
The tail of the man
Fell into the can

Do these lines perplex? So did your letter. What kind of explanation is this—your "trip to the country"! Doubt may be a good spur to the imagination, but you have abused it and me.

You are perhaps weary of my groans; there has, however, been a special disappointment. Yesterday at noon Mr. Hood invited me into his office. He seated me in front of his vast desk to address me in fatherly, adamantine style. I copped bad news. Sure enough: "...reports from the field...speed-up...expedition advanced to early March...." After these words had burned into my marrow, he added, "You're the first to be warned, so you can muster your resources. Others who shall be nameless might want to force you out. By the way, I gather you and Dex are friendly again. Ten days ago I saw him outside your place. He was talking to a cute little lady in a sari, or whatever it's called in Siam."

The office was aglitter with white suits and shoes, and papers flashing among his glamorous male staff. The tumult seemed to enhance the light and perfectness of his eyes.

Now what?

It shocks me that your letter doesn't contain one word of apology. (Or mention meeting Hodge.)

When I left, I made the mistake of walking a few blocks to let my blood subside, and so wandered into the cross-city dog race. This event is probably unique in the history of carnivals, and for good reason. It is open not only to greyhounds and other speedy breeds but to all dogs—the prizes allow for size, age, and weight. The result is twelve hours of pandemonium, aggravated by the many owners who, lest their entries weaken in the way, follow them from Coral Gables to the far side of Venetian Causeway.

I was so preoccupied that not until I was upended by a low-flying basset did I realize where I was. Getting up, I was consoled by an unwelcome Samaritan—an affectionate wet-snouted boxer bitch. When I tried to shoo her away, I was accosted by her wroth owner, who yelled at me, turning redder with each stubborn word, "Wh-why are you b-b-bothering B-b-b-beya?" (Bayer? Bear? Baby Bear?) At this moment enthusiasts on either side began shouting—"Come on, Apollo 20!" "Get with it, Gabritius!"—thoroughly deafening me. During six volatile seconds I expected Beya's master to strike me; but he kicked her instead.

The rest of the day was better. There was nobody at the office, and I wrote off a few more maps. The evening stint at the patch passed quickly. I had Chinese 'tweeners across the way, then drove to Haulover Beach Park for the evening show. I arrived well ahead of time. The stage was bare, nearly all the seats empty. A noisy speck appeared in the sky, flickering in the sunset light: a helicopter carrying the set for the performance.

Tobacco, the ballet of the day, was part of a festival series about local products. It was worth the price of admission (actually I had a free ticket.) The scene was the island of Tobago, from which the plant was once thought to derive its name. We saw two Indians perform a *pas de deux* extolling the magic virtues of the leaf; four priests scatter tobacco shreds to calm wild storms; and seven witches conduct rituals of worship with fumes from wetted clay pipes. Then the corps de ballet, as a crowd of snuff addicts, did an energetic sneezing number, and finally a patriarch gathered young men from all the nations of the earth into a brotherly Smoking Academy. This was unexpectedly moving. A timely Havana-colored moon rose over the beclouded dancers.

Diana, my sister, is here on business. She had asked me to an after-dinner party in her hotel suite, to which I went out of politeness, and had a marvelous time. I was the only man there. Although tough as a tank, Diana was almost motherly. She steered me clear of the virginal twists for whom I naturally yearn to a riper triad of sisters named Asham—Marcia, Molly, and Aline, of whom I decided that the first two were sufficient unto the hour. (Aline seemed lion-toothed as well as haired.) Diana somehow depicted me to those girls in irresistible lineaments, and I enjoyed a moment's adoration. This even helped cure an intolerable boil—but I shall not irritate you with details.

Which reminds me—I haven't deciphered your Pan phrases. When I first saw them, without translation, I admit I clenched my fits in annoyance. I shall look through your letters for the explanations. Did you really think I would remember all these words?

LXXVI

Jan 31

No more again Pan words ever. (Yet they are the language that dreams. And secrets.)

And was Twang to think? the gentleman asked for the time of the morning, still your door will not responds, is the Mr. Hodge.

It is more for Twang to reprove: your trivial joys with women, what a bath, fish in mud, they can smile, it has make

you stuprid. You must contemplate the word "decline", to
dissipate the idea "closeness". What is, perception of impu-
rety? One is to inspect, so to reflect: the parties of his body
from the sores of his feet to the ends of his hairs is in every
sense subjects to the corruption. See that, this is the observation of corruption. Then the consciousness too is horrupt:
appears, is dissolute. It must be to renounce the joying of life.
It is Twang that has love for you.

These are the later years of *Salvestro*. Never does he obtain that treasure. After 1457 he's abandoned hope, he knagged the cousins cowever
on till 1465. The next year he joins *Francesco Neroni* in the conspiracy
to throw the *Medici* over. Salvestro is reveal in *Neroni's* wide screen
confession. So the new *Balía* of *Medici* men votes him into exile Sett.
11 1466 because he has "take up wheapons against the fatherland."
(So, of each conspirator.)

Then for 15 years *Salvestro* wanders through the proximate countries of Italy. He looks perhaps for friends to his rights. In the end he
calls his old old mother *Mantissa* from Florence. From Venice they sail
together away on the long trip back to her homeland, he will become
there a spices merchant. Goodbye, *Salvestro Sguardofisso*.

That *Mantissa* I trace too back to before her arriving, to her insurance
policy, this is taken for her during the awfle journey from Tana to
Venice, it is for 75 gold florins, except if she die from leaping willful
in the sea. That sea death was often, so kind the white Christians to the
colorful infidels.

It has been as in my expressed fear, that the Prince is un-
pleased with me, after that sudden arrival of you. So he tell
Bonzo. I know nevertheless that the Pindola will sustain me,
and my worth. It is a strong leaning to have him thus. Although in this day he is something sulky, after drinking
much white whine.

Can you remember, the same *Francesco Neroni's* fear, when he write
to *Salvestro* in '57, of indiscretion? He was just. I find a letter of the
Florentine merchant *Pazzino Cicciaporci* date 1460, here he speak of
"certain tresor weaved into bolts of silk." Before he die *Beccadelli*
mentions that too, in a little satiric poem. This means, the news goes
even to Naples.

Once you tell me, that of the first Italian missionaries in

Pannam, those very first that come by land, in the ending of the 15eenth century, there are some baptismals, marriages, deaths records still, they survive my climate, and if this be true you have photograph these for your mission? Then, may Twang request those microphilm, together with the next check.

LXXVII

Sunday, Feb. 3

It's unfair to condemn me for a few instants of distraction. Neither Marsha nor Molly Asham counts for peanuts. You imply that my resolves to avoid insignificant people are not sincere. This is wounding.

And there you go dunning again! Didn't I send you money last week? Forgive the expression. But each time my feelings reach out toward you for esteem and friendship and all that is soft, you clutter them with trash and dirt.

Furthermore, I'm down to my last bumblebee and bean. The day before yesterday I went to the office to make the contribution to Key Betabara: $2,200. This included every penny I could find. I even closed the hometown savings account, that I'd kept out of nostalgia, sixty-two dollars and thirty-four cents. The trouble is, I don't *own* anything.

Mr. Hood was busy but received me. Among the comings-and-goings he sat in basiliscal dignity, with quicksilver eyes. He heard me out with evident disappointment. The sum was too small. He showed a touching sympathy with my plight—I almost felt obliged to comfort *him*. He explained that I needn't put up a dime for his sake, but there were the other backers. He had already defended my interests against outside bids.

As if to confirm these words a relay of men swarmed around us with messages from banks and financiers: offers of ten, thirty, fifty, and once a hundred and fifty thousand dollars. My depression sprang a new icicle at each figure.

Mr. Hood promised to support my candidacy a little longer, and urged me to get busy. I assigned the twenty-two C's to him as proof of my good faith. Then I went around the corner to The Glass Slipper where, although I had planned a leaf-and-fruit day, I had three slugs of philosopher's wine.

Well, the multitude of the isles had better ready themselves. I shall go with those others if I have to hang onto their boat with my teeth. Is it unreasonable that I should feel so violetly about this, that it should have become my sole obsession? I know—don't ask me why—this treasure and ours are the same.

I am day after day in a state of exceptional nervousness. My insomnia is entering the hallucinatory stage, with purple crows nesting in my pillow. Not only the dismaying turn of events is responsible for this. I'm still groggy from my trip, and each day our carnival makes repose a little more problematic. At night spotlights of great power play over the city and cause the most swaddled window to glow. Nor have our ears been neglected. Noise flows relentlessly from peculiar electronic devices that amplify distant sounds and diminish those nearby. Thus one lives among vast echoes of ducks and Indian choirs; at dawn cockcrows issue from a phantasmal barnyard.

Another network of speakers broadcasts carnival tunes. The music has been planned like a grand operetta: a few songs are reprised with ever-increasing frequency.

The worst moments, the ones that wake me up for good, are the silences. A capricious glider hovers over Miami, projecting a beam that switches off all sound equipment beneath it. When it passes over my block, the effect is of doom.

At least there are no "surging crowds" in the streets, so that I can stretch my legs in peace.

They're playing one of those songs—

> I may be black, I may be red,
> I may be yellow, I may be white,
> I may be red, yellow, black, or white
> But I'm blue

Meanwhile the Guest pursues his irresistible dance, and the daughters of Judah dance for joy in his steps.

It's time to wing this on its way. The library will send the microfilms you requested. Why do you want them? Their condition is bad, but they are legible—they were preserved by your "breathing vases" during their long burial.

LXXVIII

2.6

What, then, is the "bumblebean"?

My dear Zachary, I have now assemble from the measureless Medici paperdom a dossier almost complete of the treasure. That is now folded beneath my unwriting hand. Yet the most important, most desired, lie within my head—in the archive, mess where only Twang can find; so in my head.

O I'm so sick of this seedy old dwelling. There is a dog of household, friendly, and so great that I can ride him, last night this ridable mut open my room and pipi in my slippers, not of glass. But shall Twang maybe move to a worst place if there is no money?

However my brain is clear, and yours is most not. It become very necessary that you think: contemplate "considered contemplation", this shall dissipates the idea of non-contemplation.

LXXIX

Feb. 10

Enclosed is a check. It's smaller than usual. If you ever peruse my letters you may be aware of the local shortage.

Last Wednesday, after several attempts to see Mr. Hood, I managed to speak to him by phone. In desperation I told him about my access to the maps in the library and suggested contributing some of them as part of my stake. I even proposed *our* map. (If the Key Betabara treasure is the same as ours, my map won't tell them much they don't already know. And if it isn't the same, it's certainly worth as much going after. How can I lose?) Mr. Hood was surprised that I had a copy. Then I was obliged to explain that I expected to be in possession of one very soon. This is true. There are only 138 maps left. He promised to think it over.

Yesterday Hodge came to the patch. He brought the tidings of Mr. Hood's acceptance, but maliciously concealed them for a good half-hour. According to Hodge, Mr. Hood disliked the arrangement. It was bad business, and he was only agreeing to it out of friendship.

Dex was disgusting. One minute he was sneering at my poverty; the next, he insisting that we "bunk together" on the trip. (He may have another insist coming.) Admittedly I was ill-disposed towards him since a few nights ago he had an intimate dinner with Grace to which I was definitely not invited, and Grace confided a lot of things that Dex refuses to divulge. I tried to show what I think of him but he refused to notice. If this sounds like ingratitude I can only say that I have no strength left for gratitude.

To speed up my map research, I've been replaced as watchman. What a relief! This afternoon I took an hour off to stroll through the decorated streets. At least the weather has been pleasant. Each day comes in like one of an endless succession of ambassadors from the kingdom of Prester John. However, the night moons are fuzzy.

Of course I saw only a tiny part of the displays. At street level there is living sculpture; higher up, Cinerama screens on which immobile personages appear. (Their purpose is to encourage meditation.) The live shows present great scenes from comics, television, books, or history. At a sports intersection one might see "Casey at the Bat" (books) and "Mickey Owen's Mistake" (history). Emphasis is placed on the subject's ethical or philosophical significance, in both these cases close to the Buddhist notion, "Only impermanence is permanent."

(I should mention that no decorations survive the end of

carnival. Nevertheless, first-class designers compete for the privilege of contributing their work. This is one reason for the high quality of our celebrations. Another is that while most cities import their festival staff, Miami maintains its own year-round. But most important is the community spirit that fills us all during carnival time. We become members of one colossial family.)

There were few people in the streets at the time of my walk. Everyone was at Interama watching the archery-plus-rhetoric contest. For his turn the Guest appeared in the skull-and-bones suit that he wears ever more frequently.

Harvard has sent the letters written to Lorenzo de' Medici by his representative in Lyons. They are of little interest. One or two mention the treasure. In August 1481 Lionetto complains that a chest of silk marked "as you describe" with black birds arrived "incomplete—much darnel but no wheat." It was essential for the prosperity of the Lyons branch that the rest be sent. Later Lionetto repeats the complaint, adding that several buyers are interested in that "particular silk," which he has widely advertised. However, after the signature there is a note: "...I am glad that at last this devious gold has escaped its ultramontane destiny..." The letter, incidentally, is a copy in Lionetto's hand, and was kept by him.

Now we know how the treasure reached Lionetto. I couldn't care less.

I have had more sleep at night, but spoiled by dreams. Friday I was on a beach that I had never seen. My father was walking along it, gray, unshaven, in tatters. There was a giant fly closely following him. There was a man who was also my father sitting in the cockpit eye of the fly. There was my first father withering as he trudged through the slow sand, finally stumbling, then crawling on his knees, then prostrate. Meanwhile there was a wet salty squall blowing a smudge of fish scales over the large eye where my other father was sitting; he stopped the fly and got out, walking towards the ocean and giving the prone body a kick that broke it to piece. There was my surviving father clean-shaven and rosy. There was a girl splashing in the waves—you. Your wet tresses were even straighter than usual. There was my father who started playing with you, but I saw little of that because the sight of you was too much and I woke up in a tumult of semi-pleasure, bathed in my own slime. It was the first and only time in my life this has happened.

LXXX

February 13

That you decide to deliver map to Miles Hood is all right. I approve. But, you will not find it, I think.

I'm much anxious, lest you be condamned to having always these nightmares at night and broodmares at day. It is, again, the *pristwe* "demon" that visit you. He will seem to be of the third class (out of illusions sustaining egoistic arrogance) but no, poor Zachary, it is of the first class—bad outside influences, of such we say,

"They bring fear, they pass through changes, innocent things have terrifying appearances, unoffending women will appear as bewitches.

"Very early, between three and four of clock, you will feel that you see tigers; from five to seven, unoffending rabbits, yet who, nevertheless, scare. From seven to nine you will feel that you perceive very bad dragons, or turtles. From nine to eleven you will have the impression that you see snakes. From eleven to 1 you will have the illusion that you see horses. From 1 to 3 the apparitions will be of sheep; from 3 to 5 of monkeys. At dsk the illusions will be of vultures and crows. In the shades of night they will resemble dogs and wolfs. From 9 to 11 they will have the appearance of pigs, or repignant things; from 11 to one, of rats racing off and mice. From 1 to 3 you will see the apparition of cows, that threaten and bring fear.

"So assailed, remember what time, and remove these appearances. Call them by names. They will vanish."

Practice the halt of thought, the mind will quiet, and the armies of Mara will vanish. Perhaps too should you have a micetrap if that is the hardest hour? And sometime change the color of the upholstery?

My friend Bonzo is a dearest friend. He has smoothed the Prince, and presents to him my knowledge of the treasure dossier, for negotioating. I'm closer to him, than ever.

This most: contemplation of "vacancy" will dispel ideas of adherence.

LXXXI

I stay in the library day and night. My guardian angel still seems to be out to lunch.

Day and night, but there is no longer any night. A horde of permanent flares has been loosed over Miami. Each generates a downward thrust just strong enough to keep afloat. They emit an aqueous sparkle. One is now bobbing outside my window, these lines ripple in green light.

With little more than a fortnight to run, the carnival knows no pause. Outside, on the campus, a Ferris wheel revolves through the dark hours. Thousands of smudge pots are fixed to its rims. The riders are murky blobs behind the turning flames.

Tonight I had been invited to an elite gathering at the Brissy St. Jouin. The evening is devoted to the "Inner Muffle."

There was no question of attending. I have chained myself to one cycle of gestures. I peer into a map for several hours, usually emptying even my 69 fountain pen ("Writes with both ends") as I retrace its topography and place-names. Another map drops into the winnowing basket. Eighty-five to go.

There have been no more than three words exchanged between me and another human in the last week. I exclude Hodge, who checks me out daily, no doubt on orders from above. When he finds me still working he gives me a glassy-eyed, six-pointed stare into which I read a savory mixture of repressed disappointment, boredom, impatience, condescension overlaid with a very slightly exaggerated air of courage in the face of insurmountable obstacles, Sydney Carton, Joan of Arc, this hurts me more than it does you especially in the pocketbook yet I go on unflinching but with the satisfaction of letting you know all this. He is justified—that is the horrible thing. A horrible thing.

Your letter was at least short. Your words of encouragement concerning the map made things so much easier for me. Does taunting me give you that great a satisfaction? Or do you not realize how harsh your words rings? Such as giving up the idea of "adherence." You are cruel to a generous nature, which has a tenders for you that makes your least ill-humor afflicting. My rock drying up? I only hope your vitriol will turn to Victory Oil—it sets the wheels turning all right, like an unquenchable hotfoot.

The library by now will have sent the Pannam microfilms. What do you want them for?

Here's the sun. I greet it with a camel yawn.

Now back to maps, eyes sharp, box those shadows, running in place breathless, stupid pursuit of that unfading wreath! When I think of those others, who heard of the treasure two weeks ago, and who will get more of it than I who have thought of nothing else and labored for over a year! Many will have been called and all chosen, except me.

Yesterday the Guest played macro-tennis with the Mayor. Next comes the bowling contest: jet-propelled steel balls and twelve-foot exploding pins. Boom boom!

Often I feel that if I could follow the workings of old Wittgenstein's mind, these puzzles would become clear.

LXXXII

February 20

The microfilms have arrived and I thank you. They fill personal needs.

"Prince Voltic has established a legal claim on the treasure." I say the words and will yet not believe.

It is true: Prince has a legal claim, and international, on the treasure. Bonzo show me the paper, that was deposited a year ago almost. Can it be possible? Is there some thing to do? For you also this shall mean an end?

My mind, my heart are shaking. For: it is necessity, that I am honest with the good Prince. Oh well, I make myself contemplate "renunciation" to dissipate the idea "greed". Have I not told you as such? so:

One following the Teaching does not harbor thoughts of desire (every sensual whatever it be) that may arise in her. But she avoids them, she tames them, she annihilate them. She does not harbor thoughts of rage or resentment, no, but she averts them, she tames them, she annihilates them!

It constitutes the perception of renunciation.

So as perhaps to help you, I have been at once reading the *Tractatus.* I fear my intellectual standard must be under below, I can't understand some thing when I read the plain words, over and over.

And that is that my understanding might follow some feeling of life which I can feel from the proses or verses, familiar to me. I have read late writers of your country, frequently I sense this feeling is a of loneliness and isolation of the modern man situation in a world of civilisation and technique, a feeling of depression but the trial to conquer it too. Such as Robinson Jefferson, as example.

I do not, though, read only the mods. Thus, in recent days I learn from Origen that on the Lost Judgment the blessed souls will roll into heaven, for they will be resuscitate in perfection, as spheres. Do the *Medici* think of this when they make their marks?

O water ruffled by strong wind! You, have omitted to set on your last letter its date.

So, remember: *Evvivano le palle!*

LXXXIII*

Feb. 24

It is 3 A.M. I just returned home through streets full of maskers. It is our one masked night. The powers that be decided one is all we deserve.

I've found the map. It was forty-first from the end. I feel like both seed and fertile ground. That's speaking like a fool but if there is to be bravado I too can indulge in it, after this drudging. Fuck the Prince. No stumbles now!

I have here glued half a stick of Juicy Fruit gum (at three cents a stick) which is the greatest proof I can give you at present of being, with my whole heart, yours.

What the hell's Tractatus?

LXXXIV

February 27

Because you need to comprehend Wittgenstein I read the Tractatus, his early broad book, but not so bad, as you say.

Now every day Bonzo is pursuing the Prince, to negotiate with him, the map for a share of the treasure. I have told him, go very slow; so I don't know if yet they are talking gravy.

It makes me think, if I must eat many meals more in this *pensione* I shall go on a hunger stroke. However I have the luck that Bonzo buy me a meal nearly each evening.

And your map—it seems so far so fantasmal. Is it real? Is it really unreal? As I once said to you, things must disappear, and even so consciousness of them. Therefore, contemplating the consciousness as well as any thing (e.g. map), you are to think of it impermanent not permanent, miserable not happiness, impersonal not a personality—you are to feel aversion to it; take no pleasure from it; detach yourself of it; give it up.

Thus, you do not pile up *kamma*. For, we know this:

*Postcard.

The act has no actor
And no one gather its fruit;
There is only the succession of empty phenomena.
Other than this no view is right.
And while acts and their honsequences succeed
In obedience to the law of causality
(As the tree follows the seed and the seed the tree)
No first beginning is perceptible.

Twang shall ask, send the mask you have wore.

LXXXV

March 3

Forgive my delay, caused by dicease in the family.

Mardi Gras is only two days off, thank God—no sooner had I found the map than I was ordered back to being watchman. The resulting exhaustion was a match for even my insomnia. Today's parade ended my duties.

It was a continuation of the one with which the festival began, and followed the Guest from the City Center, which he had then reached, to the waterfront.

I missed the start—it is supposed to have taken place in an atmosphere of high dedication, so high that Mayor Favell was unable to speak—because I was busy defending my vantage point. The only person in front of me was a petite lady cop in a magenta "spectator sportswear" uniform.

The street was a lively spectacle. The pavements were strewn with fresh laurel and honeysuckle. A pot of incense fumed on every traffic light. Above me a trio of Flügelhorns stood at a picture window and from time to time blew a peppy fanfare. From cornices and roofs smoke-machines uncoiled ropes of color, as did the hovering flares that so brighten our nights. The crowd flowed about the food-and-drink stands, which sent smells of fritters to my appreciative nose.

The live shows scattered through the city had been moved to the tops of buildings along the parade route. I could see one of them: playing the legendary Willie Mays, a batter stroked baseballs in elegant parabolas over the rooftops.

From time to time the glider passed over head, stunning us with silence.

The parade began with seven groups of animals representing the continents. I noticed that Dex had leased some spares from the Temple: two razor-clawed avocado bears from Peru.

Then came various guilds, appropriately costumed. Among them were the designers of the festival, who got a big hand; lawyers (they carried a coffin-like mock-up of Blackstone); professional transvestites of both sexes who held up the parade with a squabble as to how the "Ladies first" principle should be applied.

They were followed by the succession of floats that is the pride of our festival.

First were the enigma floats: scenes depicting undisclosed proverbs. On the first, for instance, one saw a man with corked ears contemplating a sheet of music, while behind him a blindfolded girl, gesticulating skyward, vainly implored him to look where she was pointing. On the second, an old fellow in striped garb sat on a green platform surrounded by water, gazing toward the horizon past a sign that read, "Property of Lucifer." It wasn't hard to guess that the first float stood for "The blind cannot hear, nor the deaf see"; the second for "A colonial escape must be singly bred"; and the third, "The button leaves a mark of fear."

Next were the allegorical floats, giant figures and settings. It would take pages to describe them (they lasted two hours) but some titles were: The Big Number, The Assassinated President, Armed Peace.

Musical floats followed—brass bands, pop groups (one of whom sang the Mayor's verses to the newest Mrs. Favell) and a chorus performing in counterpoint the three hits of the carnival. In the soprano one heard "A Big Basket for Fruits," a presto tongue twister sung with miraculous ease; in the tenor, the languid melismas of "Trouble my Depths"; in the bass, "I may be Black, but I'm blue."

The dancers were next. The "Anatomy" floats are now peopled with mannequins: when they passed, only the Mirror Man flashed among the dummies. The other floats were live and various. On one, dancers spelled out the words of a significant text. It is hard to say how this was done, but it was done.

At the end came an animal dance, with llamas, elephants, kangaroos, and other charmers. They were followed by people dressed up as the same animals, performing the same dance.

Throughout the parade the Venusians carried out their antic role.

The cortege at last disappeared towards Miamarina. It was there, last night, that the guest won his final victory over the Black and white Mayors. He manned a jib crane set on a gantry running along two hundred yards of waterfront. In the cockpit of another crane, at the opposite end of the gantry, sat replicas of the Mayors. Charging towards each other, the cranes collided near the middle of the gantry with a bang that shook the suburbs. Six times the derricks clashed indecisively. At the seventh the Mayors' tipped sideways, fell into the harbor waters, and vanished. The Guest had justified his title of Chief Pilot.

It is at Miamarina that the festival will end. It has entered its final, aquatic stage, symbolizing instability and metamorphosis, preparing us for Lenten changes. The parade, when it reached the harbor, continued straight into the water. Floats, Venusians, and swimming animals joined the host of carnival participants already immersed: pilotless boats, "float-in" movies, trained squads of dolphins and fish, and swimmers finned-out as fish. Ordinary swimmers then began dipping into the chilly water. Later there will be boat races and battles, with prizes.

I visited the harbor in late afternoon. The thousands of swimmers made the scene worthy of D. W. Griffin. However, all filming is forbidden. No one in fact can keep any record of the carnival, written, painted, photographed, or taped. The festive structures chosen for permanence are our only memorials.

The Guest's winning crane is to become the scaffold for the great bonfire of Tuesday night. It has been christened *thalamus* or marriage bed—Aphrodite's, because the water festival celebrates her birth from the waves. The crane has already been draped with an immense net, on which the population of our sinful town will abandon its "instruments of pleasure," everything from swizzle sticks to Kahlil Gibran.

Meanwhile the Guest, now Chief Pilot, his duties done, is to spend two days carousing with Miamians great and small. On Tuesday he will conspicuously join in the last wild dancing, kissing all the pretty girls he meets. At midnight he will unzip his mask and, casting it into the fire, reveal his identity.

The time will also be given over to public confession, in these circumstances a joyful and salutary experience. The Festival Directors have been accused of organizing these confessions, but the reproach is unfair. They are absolutely spontaneous, and are organized only to make sure someone is listening.

The last confession is the Guest's avowal of his name.

I myself must "confess," dear one, that my map is as real as an Easter egg. I find it to say the least puzzling that you question its existence—methinks my Twang no longer trusts her Zachary. Or is this more Buddhist theory? What about "your" map? How can you negotiate with it—do you expect me to send you a copy?

Of course, theoretically, you are right: knowledge will undoubtedly vanish away. Meanwhile I have the map and I want its "fruits," the whole and palpable knowledge of it, before it and I return to the burning fountain. I have no desire to sit out my life like a blind beggar on the roadside.

For the first time in months I feel sanguine about my future. I've seen that Mr. Dharmabody is properly boarded. My *kas* are in good shape. So, out of the desert and into the sea. Wednesday morning will see me and the others headed for Key Betabara.

Ah, the *Tractatus*—by Wittgenstein I meant Charlie Wittgenstein, who used to rope for the Locus Solus kid. His specialty was "finding the leather."

Check enclosed.

LXXXVI

March 6

Yes, it's indeed my own map offered to the Prince. Bonzo has done this so well, and the Prince says Of course, since I must use it to find that treasure which is mine, part of that can be yours. So it is done! Not your untrust yet unbelief confuse me, me-think your mind is of water-veiled-with-mosss, for I six weeks ago have told you of the desired dockument that is in *Mediceo Avanti il Principato*.

Now Bonzo and I have made a certain agreedment and to honor it he has at last take me to his fatherly house, and there through many obsolutely fine rooms, like the autobus station! And he asks, Shall we visit my dear the Averardo Room, I thought he say avocado with in mind your charmer bears; but, Averardo.

It is very nice too, for histerical reason! I have meant, that is only a storoom attic, not eleghant as others, not used much, with such dust one was needing a lot of broom for manoever. But very interesting. There were fine very plain chests, for the chairs are mostly sold with the Prince, a cross was on one, plain too but plainly renaissance (15th c.), a Roman coin was there. We opened one very large chest, there were the Medici *palle* (Balls) on the lid, and on the inside stuff also, when Bonzo opens the lid, Oh so heavy and slow—the floor of that room was wide board—there were seventeen small windows, I shall say 120 cm × 80 cm—the beams of the ceiling were painted with the same color as the plaster between, pinkish cream—some black cracking went along them—on the walls were a so-so so-so "Woman at the Marketplace." A 19th century tapestry of a railroad train, very holy. *La Tolleranza Tradita*, by Unknown.

Often I say, concentrate on detachment to crack up the hardnut thought "covet."

Well, did you know our marriage is not legal in Italy?

Thinking of your letter from *Lionetto de' Rossi*, I renote this from *Lorenzo the Mag.* to him, writing of the treasure. He *Lorenzo* say that he has not yet tried before to sell it because it is so notorious but now he's short of cush and want the gold negotiated quickly and discreetly. So, he will send it abroad. It will come in a box of old brocade where it is still since *Cosimo* tried to send it away through Pisa. It is so old brocade that "the silver marks at the end of its bolts truly now look alike black crows." He says it is 500 *bracci* long. He promises to let *Lionetto* know, when it will arrive. "I promise to tell you, when it will arrive."

Part Seven

LXXXVII

Early Thurs.

Back yesterday evening, up all night. The events have left me feeling like a fragment by H. D. It was absolutely an awful time. I'm going to have a banana and a swallow of Epsom salts then get into bed and weep sore. The sun, about to emerge, can pursue it's magnetic way without me.

LXXXVIII

March 8

This business seems to completely have fallen through. I can't tell how. The breach is beyond repair. I expect no redeeming event, but would like an explanation. Eschatological tensions rend my bones, unsoothable subintestinal knots! and you will soon be berating me I know it, and not wrongly, don't go easy, bray what a fool I've been. But tell me first if your map (I do believe it) looks like this:

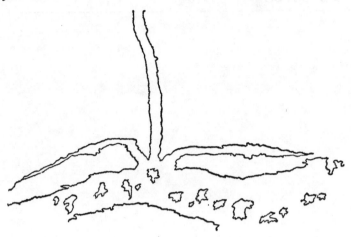

(Somewhat like my voice-print when my voice say "eye.")

We left Wednesday. The morning was clear, the town quiet. The unmasked Guest had "rescued Aphrodite" at midnight, and before dawn the two of them had boarded a rocket to be shot into space. Through empty streets a girl's cool voice broadcast the Lenten proclamation that forbids "blasphemy, games, sodomy, concubinage, renting houses to panders..." Hodge, in charge of the expedition, directed my driving. To make sure we were free of tags, we meandered through back streets before taking the highway to the gulf. At Naples I turned south on a secondary road, stopping after two miles by a weedy graveyard, our rendezvous. We settled down to wait for our partners. After twenty minutes a car slowly approached. From it stepped two uncommunicative men, nondescript for their reputed standing; perhaps they were, like Hodge, mere delegates.

Our boat was at a marina five miles to the south. It was ready; we set off at once. We plunged into the labyrinth of inshore channels bordering that coast. Hodge and the captain used an enlargement of my map, discussing locations in the Ten Thousand Islands to which it might correspond. It was then I learned that we were not in fact going to Key Betabara. We were looking for our treasure after all, but it was in some other, unknown place. Hodge acknowledged this. I felt reality slipping a little farther from my grasp.

Hours passed in slow search. The configurations of the map approximated many sites but coincided with none. The coast and shores turned from sand to mud to other-colored sand. Flat clusters of mangrove and palmetto accumulated monotonously. Hodge became sour and a little frantic. I found myself cheering him up, busying him with questions, like the idiot in Grimm distracting the witch from her pills. Our companions somnolently fished from the stern.

Occasionally we saw other boats, or glimpsed tourists along the shore roads, but for the most part the landscape was deserted. It was with some astonishment that, exploring a channel that resembled a detail of the map, and issuing into a cove or, more properly, a well-protected estuary tallying with the map in every particular, we found that the island at its center—our very goal—was a nudist camp.

As we approached and cut our engines, an old man started shouting at us from the water's edge.

Hodge grunted irritably. "That's the resort director—harmless. This is Key Mingori. If I'd known, we could have saved half the day." Sunset was near.

The old man had a mane of white hair. Erect in spite of his years, he looked, with his short staff, very Stan Musialesque. He wore an open jerkin embroidered with shells and thorny roses. Something in his manner suggested that he was expecting us. I wondered if one of our agents had alerted him, but decided that my suspicions were due to his lack of beard.

As we came ashore he concluded his diatribe, of which I only grasped the final sentence:

"The black men shine redder than your moth-eaten gold!"

At our approach he raised his fingers to his eyes, which were obscured by gray cataracts. Adroitly he flicked them away, and put on orange sunglasses.

This old man was Mitchell Mauss. He has been famous among the local Indians ever since the tribe with which he was living was stricken with epidemic diptheria. Mauss taught them a technique of deep yawning to tear the suffocating diphtherial growths, saving many children. The tribe rewarded him with the gift of the Key.

Mauss developed the island as a small resort. His clients are shy nudists—people who believe in nudism but find difficulty practicing it, and who are fearful of ordinary colonies with their requirements of strict nakedness. On Key Mingori nudity is only encouraged, never enforced, in accordance with inner needs.

Mauss welcomed us and, despite the late hour, insisted we tour his establishment. He presented it as a very moral community. There were beggars stationed in inconspicuous spots, hidden by richly ornate screens "so that donors would not feel unjustified superiority"; in a recess of the shore he showed us a vast submarine corral filled with sea beasts—"A gam of milk whales," he explained. "But we don't milk them now, because they're fasting—yes, fasting. It's for our benefit. The knowledge of their privation fills us with remorse whenever we eat. Whereas if we ourselves fasted we might fall prey to smugness." At our approach many a square snout had risen from the agitated water.

Opposite our boat stood an old, sickly palm tree, A rusty pie dish was wedged in its upper branches. Underneath, traced in faint disjointed pencil strokes, drawings of Alpine scenes were clipped to the fronds; and close to the ground an iron cross, perhaps the shank and stock of an anchor, protruded from a gray scar in the trunk (almost fell down, said nothing of course.) To a ring in the cross, two thick ropes, one long, one short, leashed dissimilar creatures: a young woman who slithered in the powdery sand, combing her hair with a sea urchin, naked except for an anal star; and a huge, unmoving boa, whose body coiled around a driftwood log.

A young man stepped up and declared in a shaky voice, "This is a private club." The director reassured him. To us, touching the snake's eyes, he said, "He's afraid. Don't you be."

The young man had risen from a group that was seated in rows on the ground. It was watching television programs on five sets arranged in quincunx—

The doorbell's dinging, maybe that's news!!

LXXXIX

March 8

Now, just, I have had a police visit. The three men came to my room, all say *Ciao!* loud at once, and look every place —under the bed they do not need to bend they are so stumpy! They say (good English), What's this? What's that? Watch out! "Scandalous prodigality of rush wealth" and so funny threats. I acted bewhildered—I *was* so; and proclaimed my innoncence. They go.

No more to write now, for I shall telephone the Pindola to ask him what this intruding meant.

But I forgot to tell, that your beautiful description of carnival's final was appreciated to no end, etc.

I must also calm myself, so: "thinking of wretchedness against ideas of affection and clinging."

Now, I'm calmer. Perhaps I saw those policemen some time else? Yet I take it for granite they are real.

XC

Continued March 9

The doorbell was a mistake.

There was this X-shaped arrangement of television sets. Three commercials, Ben Gazzara's twentieth dying year, and a quiz program emceed by Mr. Hood.

Hodge shouted out to the boat, "Bring the tools." Tools meant picks, shovels, guns.

He was leaning against the dessicated palm. Mauss said, "That cross *looks* so old," rubbing his hand over one rusted knob. "What salt air does in a few years!" Hodge glanced at him. Mauss continued: "If the old Spaniards had put it there, how high would it be now? As high as the pie dish?"

Hodge's disappointment was so plain he almost looked human. I groaned in sympathy.

Mauss said, "I remember one big palm, about ten miles south, with a cross sticking out twenty-five feet up. Somewhere around Key Isabella, hard to say exactly with all those mangroves. A cove like ours…"

Without a word Hodge turned toward the boat. I stopped to mumble our thanks. On the television screen Mr. Hood was presenting two hundred thousand dollars to the quiz winner, the Miami chief of police. Mauss went over and switched that set to another channel.

I heard engines start. Our boat had weighed anchor. I ran towards the water, shouting hopelessly in the growling dusk.

An Indian nudist appeared, brandishing a feeble torch: the boat turned back. He led me through the shallows and supported my swim with a strong scissors kick.

Safely aboard, I watched my benefactor return to shore. It was nearly dark. Above the Gulf unseasonable lightning glimmered like a defective bulb. Supersonic bats, popping like corks, issued for their nocturnal hunt.

Over the engine noise Hodge was shouting his contempt for Mauss's colony: "…Back to square one…. Substandard realty for the dissolute…." He was his repulsive self again. However, he dried me off kindly. I would have preferred plain signs of his evil heart; but you can't expect a suffragette to grow whiskers.

We anchored off Key Isabella for the night. I hardly slept. Around midnight one of the partners emerged from his apathy to start cleaning the firearms, which he said were in an appalling state. The night passed in clicks and shocks.

At sunrise we resumed our search. The day began fair, but by eight o'clock a fog thicker than Mogen David wine had clapped down on us. We persevered until noon, staring into the beclouded branches of every passing grove. The captain finally announced that search was futile in such conditions— we would return to port. We inched our way into the gulf, headed north, and docked at five.

Our partners went their way. When Hodge and I reached Miami, he reminded me that Mr. Hood was waiting for news. I suggested telephoning. Hodge was adamant: "Can't cross the old man."

In his office Mr. Hood was having drinks with three gentlemen of opulent mien. He introduced them as our principal associates. One of them was known to me from Spindle gatherings.

Hodge reported the failure of our search and recommended that we start out again as soon as the weather cleared. Mr. Hood seemed disappointed and, even more, perplexed. He politely asked Hodge for a full account. Hodge said that he would draw up a report in the morning. An ice-pick note entered Mr. Hood's voice as he insisted, still courteous, that he and his partners learn what had happened. Until then I had scarcely listened. Abruptly, through fatigue and depression, terrible suspicion surged. Were things not as they seemed?

Mr. Hood was watching Hodge with an appalling, predatory stare.

Hodge began recounting our trip in wearying detail. Often he turned to me for corroboration, which I cautiously supplied. As he described our visit to the island I saw him stop in amazement. Mr. Hood had risen from his chair and stood shaking his smooth hands at Hodge. He was white. One reads of people going white but I had never seen it happen. Mr. Hood was the color of wet plaster.

"So that's it!" he said, his voice thrillingly quiet. "Do you expect me to buy that, you cheap hood?"

Grasping the arms of his chair, Hodge blustered, "Who do you think you're talking to?"

"'*Whom* do you think you're talking to'! Now, don't tell me you spent thirty years with the papes and never learned how God made a tree." Mr. Hood turned to us. "Don't you see his game? When you drive a nail into a tree trunk, it stays put, and an iron cross is no different. It wouldn't climb as the tree grows. He's in cahoots with Mauss. By now the treasure's in the Bahamas, the whole eight million. You fink! You despicable fink!"

Mr. Hood crossed the room and slapped Hodge's face (since the latter was seated, it was on a level with his own.) Hodge rose and began strangling his tiny adversary. This is the last thing I saw clearly. Purplish smoke seemed to fill the room. I yelled, "He's ruined me, he's ruined me" and I threw myself at Hodge. I was ready to kill him. The others pulled me back. Hodge, himself in a fury, again lunged at Mr. Hood, who had scrambled behind his desk. I wanted to stop him but there was no need for that. I barely glimpsed the silvery pistol in Mr. Hood's hand as he shot Hodge point blank. Hodge gave an ugly groan, turned toward me, and a jet of hot slick blood spurted from his mouth over my shirt. Then he collapsed face downwards.

Mr. Hood acted with dispatch. He searched Hodge's pockets and found the enlargement of the map. "Where's the original?" he asked. I gave him the ancient document, which tore where the blood had soaked it. "Burn them, they're evidence," he ordered. One of the men wrapped the maps in newspaper, set a match to the bundle, and dropped it into a metal wastebasket.

"Now we'd better lam it." He said to me, "I'll take you home, you can clean up there." To the others: "Gentlemen, stay here until I can dispose of the body. No one must enter. I'm sorry you're involved, but we must work together now to make sure our names are not associated with this hoodlum or his death—even if it's an obvious case of self-defense."

The men agreed. They were stunned by the violence. Mr. Hood took me down a back elevator to the parking lot, where his car and chauffeur were waiting. It was late; we drove through empty streets. Mr. Hood saw me to and through my door.

"Don't budge till you hear from me. I'll take care of everything." Then, with a smile sad but warm, squeezing my hands in his:

> "...If thou art rich, thou'rt poor;
> For like an ass whose back with ingots bows,
> Thou bear'st thy heavy riches but a journey
> And death unloads thee."

He has been my only consolation in these grim hours.

I feel sick, sick, and never so alone. Alone, and vulnerable, in spite of Mr. Hood. The police will come straight here for me. I feel conspicuous as a flying elephant. I have no energy, no confidence, and no glimmer of comprehension.

But why tell you how I feel? There was nothing but you to give hope, and now I guess there is not even you. Without your strength and thought I would never have undertaken this and now you have deprived me of them. It's unpleasant to blame you, but who else is there to blame for the wasted days and nights, the wasted money and the expense of emotion? I beg for help and you answer nothings. Here's a check for what's worth.

XCI

March 12

It is very sad, Twang sends you much thoughtful strength for your trouble, but then I have such: the policemen are sent after me by an American the Mr. P. Asher, who bought last December that cameo. It was false! I telephoned the Prince and he said, "Ssh! Nothing to say on the telephone, come." He already knows. It is so bad for everyone of us, so that he, and Bonzo, and I, and all are about to fall into disgrace or jail. It seems, there is no way out as if they had surrounded us with rollers of bobbed wire!—but the Prince "will do all he cans."

I shall answer one question here, saying that the two maps are the very same. But do you see, it does not matter? (Because the treasure is a belonging of the Prince Voltic, wherever it is found, or lost.) Not a matter anynow.

And I think for Twang, for Zachary too, to remember: perceive evil and suffering, think of them collapsing the stupid idea happiness. And:

Stillness within, knowing:

Suffering exists, but no sufferer
Action exists, although no actor
Extinction, but not one in the least who dies
Although there is a Way there is no wayfarer

(And to face them I have not even any pretty clothes, just just these old hateful ones.)

XCII

March 14

This has been a day of varied emotions, bringing as it did my ma's will and accounts of her death.

There has been no published news of Hodge's murder.

My mother died last Wednesday, while I was mucking through the fogs. She had recently fallen ill, as I wrote you. (You did not find this worthy of comment.) Her death was therefore not unexpected, but no less terrible, especially as I could not attend her last hours. She was a perfect woman, "glory and beauty went before her." She must have been disappointed in me, her only son. She never however showed anything but affection. Thank God she didn't live to see me in court. The mother ate sweet grapes, and the son's teeth fell out.

She was buried today and I drove down for the funeral. Mr. Hood would not let me go sooner. In his tactful way he even tried to dissuade me from making the trip at all. He finally agreed to it and ended by coming with me! It was a godsend having him there. There were moments, such as when I beheld my coffined mother in her beloved pearls and shawl, in which collapse was near, and at those times Mr. Hood straightened me up with a word or look. He was a comfort to everyone and made a strong impression. Diana thought he was a doctor.

The funeral was ghastly. It's true that my other (and I admit greater) anguish may have deformed what I saw. Everybody behaved as if they were menstruating. It might have been a snake that was being buried. It is degrading that a woman so generous and cheerful should be a pretext for such meanness.

On the drive back tonight I asked Mr. Hood what he meant when, just before the blood flowed, he referred to Hodge's "years with the papes." Mr. Hood replied that for most of his life Hodge had been a Jesuit priest. I couldn't believe it. I said that Hodge was as unlike a Jesuit as possible, witness his latest hairdo. Mr. Hood said, "That's why he was called the Invisible Jesuit. You were looking at a Jesuit but you couldn't see him."

Miami in Lent is deader than an empty gin bottle; I am the fly inside it. Mr. Hood tells me to be patient. He visits at least twice a day—his concern is amazing. He is chary of news, probably out of discretion. He says we're getting the breaks: no doubt he's making them.

I have taken out protractor and compass to try and collate my sketchy copy with the real life maps of the Geodesic Survey. They never quite match.

It is uncertain what the police are doing. Mr. Hood may have arranged matters or perhaps they are being clever. They can issue John and Jane Doe warrants and fill in the names at the moment of arrest.

Thank you for your frequent and sympathetic letters.

XCIII

March 14

Yesterday again I saw the Prince. (It was near bath-time, and he appeared in a down-to-the-floor lamé bathing robe, and with eighteen curl springs in his hair. He is, I guess, so queer as the three dollar coot.) Oh, he is good, and great. Perhaps those curlers were mastery by suspension, pushing away the five hindrances by metal concentration, as a jar tossed upon moss-covered water split the slime. He had decided, to take every responsability for himself: and we shall go free from peril. It is not a foolish way; for "justice will stick to the biggest stick." I gush my thanks. He almost cried, saying no more can we ever meet. Generous man! Of course I give him Medici papers, map and explanations, anything that may help him in his battle.

It is so lovely, that in this situation everbody from the

Prince down has been one hundred per cent. Thus can Twang practice the contemplation of high intelligence to shake away the idea of material attachment, that dump of ice.

So you too should find such a discipline, notably after this disgusting slaying of which you write. Also I find it a degradation, that you copy insults out of your old letters to me!

XCIV

March 15

Bonzo and I have escaped Florence, we shall go to Lerici for a long hide-out. I think much of the idea of extinction to erase the consciousness of ever having been born. For

if mental actions are the result of ignorance
and consciousness is the result of mental actions
and name and shape are the result of consciousness
and six-sensual action is the result of name and shape
and contact is the result of six-sensual action
and feeling is the result of contact
and desire is the result of feeling
and affection is the result of desire
and becoming is the result of affection
and birth is the result of becoming:
suffering is the result of birth

We are spending the night in Lucca, charming renaissance city waiting for the next flood.

XCV

March 18

Saddened by news of the mother's death, Twang has climbed to the cemetery of this town Lerici, to think with you. Now, after tears, my dear Zachary, I must remind you life is nothing. Were you so attached to your mother? You, also are subject to death, already. With or without this attachment to her, you are dying. It would be better, my friend, to disengage yourself. It was better, to think of your dead mother as you would think while looking at a cadaver, if you worked in a crematorium.—Some objects of contemplation for repulsion:

A corpse two or three days old, blackish-blue, it is decomposing; a corpse picked by cows; a carcass of bones hanging with blood-sputtered flash, which worn muscles hold together; bones—dessevered, whitened like shells, piled in piles, crumpling from exposure, falling to dust. Then: "My body is of this type, has this fate."

It is called also the perception of instability. Impermanence even in the moss on these grave stones among which i sit to write, the sad sunny wind, the hungry cats among the dooms.

I am in some despair also. The little town, the little life, is empty, except for fear. This morning as I awoke I see old curtains, old glasses, and the empty dish. I am ah thankful for Bonzo, here, it is nothing other.

I remember another say, say

Thinking of the cessation of desire I breathe in,
Thinking of the cessation of desire I breathe out,

again; again.

Of course it is only an example, this word "desire".

XCVI

March 19

Just saw Hodge, alive and kickable. Was close to breakdown, staying in day after day, so went to eat at the former Nova Luna, a dyke bar on Scheherazade Blvd., now an Armenian restaurant called Leander's Hideaway. Enjoying a succulent grunt-kebab when in walked the visible Hodge. He had a drink at the bar and left; after which the barman confirmed his identity. I wish someone would confirm mine.

Unable to reach Mr. Hood by phone, now awaiting his visit to pass on the dire news.

Could you send copy of your map? I hope you made a copy?

I am rather dead. Also suffer (paradoxically?) from epithelial oversensitivity. Couldn't shave for days, water is fiery as rum, etc. Underneath, soft anesthesia of desperation: the shock seeing Hodge a distant one, a sonic bang from overseas. You notice I didn't move. (Should have shot him properly!) Less distraught by him than by fear of being caught by somebody from the library—have been on sick leave. Yet must quit that job. The derangement is certainly worsened by so much solitude. When I asked Mr. Dharmabody to please pass the salt I realized things were bad. Later I hitted him. I hope he's too old for me to infect him with my neuroses. His looks embody my my feelings, with black-ringed eyes and straggly hairs. I find no pleasure in his sight.

XCVII

March 23

It has become impossible to tell whether it is worse hearing or not hearing from you.

Mitchell Mauss has been arrested for theft of a treasure trove, by law the property of the state of Florida.

Mr. Hood did not come the day of Hodge's re-emergence, nor the day after. On the morning of the 21st his three bodyguards appeared at the door. They were subdued, barely whispering their unison "Hello there!" They handled me a large envelope. The map was in it—the map I had seen burn. Also a note from Mr. Hood. The partnership was being dissolved, because of danger. Contributions to the expedition were being refunded, less profits already paid: $2,200 - $2,170 = $30. Hodge was best forgotten, "victim of the cackle bladder." The whole affair should be forgotten. We had been misled. The map was of no value. The treasure had never reached these shores.... At the end: "Zachary, you're a nice man. Take my advice and pretend it was a dream."

Before there was time to show my feelings, which if my present existence were not posthumous might have been lion-like rage, the three of them rattled off an antiphonal midrash or mishmash warning me that I was liable to prosecution for stealing state property (the map), and reminding me that Mr. Hood was on the best terms with the chief of police.

That night the hair fell out all over my body. I am denuded from crown to sole. I might have foreseen this. I have felt as though some unknown law were being written into my vitals with a drill; this is its public form. I shall next grow scales.

Mr. Hood is not to be found. His house is boarded up. His office has not closed, it has disappeared. The space is occupied by a simulated-pearl distributor who claims to have been there for years. I cannot think of anyone who could testify to the contrary.

There is little left in my shrunked world. Your neglect (contempt?) has turned books into blank papers, friends into [*illegible*]. It appears I shall have neither savory meat nor blessing. Perhaps I am to be the fatted calf. Unfatted: these worries have revealed many a bone. The thyroid may be affected.

My depression is thck as a chocolate brownie. A cackle bladder is a little rubbcr bag filled with chicken blood and held in the mouth. Bitten into, it shoots the blood forth.

XCVIII

March 28

Indeed, there is no hope in that world of yours. It would be best to believe Mr. Hood, Forget. This, and that. For you are attached to deviation, and this has made you a pariah. Remember, it is not by birth that one becomes a pariah, but by acts.

So you have acted: when most gently crossed, you fall into

anger, screaming, etc. Look at Bonzo—humbled for years by the women whose hands he must shine, often by the Prince, and life, yet is ready always for more. It rouses atrocious feeling in me when I think of your way. And now even water annoys you so your hair is falling!

Also you have acted: the sorriest occasion is an excuse for you to put forward your lust. Our nights together, always you slide to my side of the bed; later you ask me to write dirty letters; and so forth. And Bonzo—true, he did that first attack but since, look at him: nights and days with Twang, and he still waits. I start to find him rather sexy!

You act as if your heart were a tiger's, you kick away my questions, my thoughts and all my sentiments, and you claw at friends with hate. As for Bonzo if he sees one eye of mine opening he strains to guess its desire. You wish to shoot Hodge. Know that they who would shoot will be shot!!

Is it then a surprise that I shall want to forsake a pariah of such irritability, sensuality, and cruelty, and marry the mild man Bonzo?

We must remain here until the danger pass. I would prefer you do not write. Later, I shall tell you what is to happen. Three nights ago there was a fire in one section of the Laurenziana, I suppose you have read this in the newspaper? Many private citizens bravely rushed in to help evacuate the rare archives.

XCIX

Why not the whole truth? Surely you no longer care about its effect on me. You need only admit it. This is no attempt to convince you of anything, or to judge. You are beyond the pale of judgment—at least of civilized humanity—among Tartars you might get a hearing.

Nearly a year ago a first suspicion slithered through my brain, and was sent scurrying. In your letter of July 3, "Who is Montpellier?" you naïvely asked. Yet on May 12 you had written of Messer Todao's house in Montpellier. You will remember those words, these very words, you who forget nothing?

This was the scheme. That gang knew that we librarians had access to the Donation maps. What better prospect among them than a middle-aged bachelor slob? So Mr. Tittel, agent of the highly respected International Red Arrow and my "accidental" traveling companion, collared me on my flight east to plant the first information in my unsuspecting head; and in Bangkok he delivered me into your irresistible care. I was solidly hooked, "marrage" wiped away all doubt, and you bravely agreed to work alone in strange cities on our behalf. I passed into the hands of Hodge, whom I met as I had met you, at the initiative of a stranger. You urged me to frequent him, to take up his proposition, after which I was propelled into dreamy Spindledom. Whenever I was calm enough to be capable of reason, you inflamed me with harrying news— Bonzo Pindola's assault, your frequentation of him, your illtreatment by the Prince, all communicated in the certainty that knowing you alone in a foreign land was torture to me. Meanwhile your refusal to punish Pindola started the long fuse of jealousy smoldering through the burrows of my mind. I was tantalized with reports about the no doubt fictitious Salvestro to convince me of your zeal; and with your arsenical Buddhist moralizations which, when you ran out of affectionate phrases, were to prove your devotion. Finally you engineered the catastrophe of our transatlantic non-meeting, probably without leaving Tuscany; thus exhausted, I was lured into the unlikely partnership with Hood. They got the map from me. They certainly have the treasure. And they means you.

Isn't this the truth rather more than less? Isn't it the work of your desire?

As for the things you mention, we will forget them, if you please. I have no wish to remember them. If there is evil in me it will not be learned from your crusted tongue.

More last words, not many. I don't expect an answer, it doesn't matter, you will at least hear me. I expect you want to complete your revenge on me. I do not need to learn that an incensed woman is dangerous. You have already made chaos of my dull globe. My ego is like a torn kleenex. But do whatever seems most delightful. Our marriage isn't binding here either, thank you, so go right ahead with Banjo. Only it must be said that I have loved you as old men love the sun—I repeat this, since resentments leave only half-recollections, I have loved you beyond any wish for life or death—it is something I would not want you to forget, the merest jewel for your left claw.

C

7 Pok Laï

Piu Lemu! lemö vin maï uüax pristwi. Theu mau neng, wey tharaï duvaï. Wuc Lao stheu atran, ticbaï maï slop, naï: theu sheenö laï nob lucri nam aïndap. (eels)

CI

This chump never blowed you were turned out to hop-scotch. You let him find the leather, and he copped you for the pure quill, when you're nothing but a crow. It took a long time to bobble him but now you've knocked him good and he feels like a heavy gee had slipped him a shiv. Well, no twist will ever beat this savage again, not if she hands over her bottom bumblebee—it's cheaper loaning cush to Pogy O'Brien. Don't you play the hinge but stick to the big con. You're a class raggle with a grand future, even if this mark knows you're snider.

CII

April 10

Dear Doctor de Roover,
    it has been very long, since I had the pleasures of lunching with you or Mrs. de Roover. I have not, however, forgot

how much your help. I have thought, you shall like to know if I found anything out about that treasure *dei trè sciarrani?* Yes.

You will remember your intelligence of Otto di Guardia's hoard and the clipping; later, your great guess, Averardo had that bastard son whom then I could discover (Salvestro Sguardofisso.)

I suspected that treasure, its going to America; yet only suspect; then learned (two sources), on the chest were three perch "crudely carved", by Nicola Pisano. By Nicola Pisano, never! Crudeness and his name cannot mix. It was plain, that chest was false. Yet was it thought, was it meant to be thought, true? I have wondered, who saw the very gold, but in Florence? Nobody. Only the silk wrapping, I will tell you about it soon. Next I learned that Averardo accuses Giovanni de Bicci of taking Mr. Todao's riches in *bags.* Later Cosimo wrote Francesco di Neroni, about its markings: on the chest, on the wrappings, were *i segni familiari,* the family emblem, thus balls not fish. The name *trè sciarrani* stuck only as a memory of the first, fish chest.

Cosimo has the treasure in his Florentine palace, but too notorious to use, and Salvestro watching. Cosimo hides the clippings in a chest of silks. He asks Francesco di Nerone to export it; no mention of gold. Then Salvestro tells, and the plot fail through.

Again the treasure sits in the palace. Useless, but they will not yield it to Salvestro. Did they fear he'd claim pictures, land, jewels, banks, anything? They feared he was Piero's son! (The slave mother had just been in Piero's employ.)

In 1465 Salvestro is entirely their enemy, joins in the great conspiracy. In exile, after, he frightens them; then leaves Italy.

It is 1480. Lorenzo de' M. is short of money: he will sell the clippings, in Lyons. And he makes the plans for this with Lionetto de' Rossi. But in the next year new luck comes to him. The family shuts the costly bank in Venice. The Medici are welcome back in Rome, some pope's debts are paid. Those political "reforms" start to work, the state of Florence is lapsing between his hands with the public monies. His plan changes.

I learned this from one unscrambled bag of MAP—have you yet reached it? There was the correspondance between Lionetto and Lorenzo of those years. The letters before were known only from Lyons (Harvard). One of Lionetto complains that a chest of silk is not full, hurry with the rest. In this copy, after the place he would signs, there is an addition. It reads, how happy that the gold has "escaped its ultramontane destiny." Look! this is not what it seems, it is no part of the letter but of Lorenzo's answer, that I have found. Has Lionetto copied it there for the fact, as a signal of disappointment, of irony? I shall not know; but the meaning of "ultramontane" is France not Italy. The treasure did not move. Yet that word became evidence of its coming to France.

Many already believed this. Lionetto started the lie. You remember he was then badly straitened. He wanted so much to sell the treasure, restoring his assets. Now I hope I shall make you happy, and you can fit a new paragraph in your book (p. 301). Lionetto sent two balance sheets to Florence, one confused to the manager Sassetti, one clear to Lorenzo. You have wondered why, and I tell you: Sassetti did not know the plan of selling, and must be beguiled. Lionetto hoped the true account would make Lorenzo help. It did not. But Lionetto decided to act as if his wish had been granted.

By this time he had excited some buyers. He told the immensity of the treasure, also its distinctive signs: three fish carved on the chest, ravens stamped on the wrappings. (False! never ravens, only the Medici balls agains. Those birds were hatched from Lionetto's misreading Lorenzo's words, they were that the markings on the silk are so tarnished they "truly resemble black crows.")

Lionetto sold some chest to the sixth Abbot of Montpelas. He was foolish and paid a gold price for taffeta. After a repose in the abbey, this chest was carried to the new world, with its reputation still glowing. I can tell you its American history, when you so ask.

The gold lay in Florence. Lorenzo had decided to melt it down later, "with strenuous precautions of secrecy" (Memorandum to Sassetti, MAP Filza 34, No. 344; no mention in the *libro segreto*.) It was never done.

When the Medici were expelled in 1494, the new government let the mob plunder their palace, it was "sacked from roof to cellar." But in that mob, calm, came the Pindolas, rich oilmongrels, attached to the Averardo clan. Salvestro's father had bound them to be loyal to his bastard, and they helped him. During his exile they sheltered his mother, and departing from Italy he charged them with this final task. They should recover certain possessions "close to my heart, albeit modest in their worth." These had been part of his inheritance, seized by Cosimo, so he said, kept by his successors. Salvestro breathed no word of the gold. During the sack the Pindolas retrieved these things and took them to their house until Salvestro's return. They remained there, undisturbed until last year, when a few were sold. The chest, full of rotted silk, did not move. Now it is journeying forth from the scholarly realm, and my account must end.

I hope you had no trouble from that fire at the Laurenziana. Other friends were I think both burned and arrested.

May these pages have pleased you, dear Doctor de Roover! If you so desire, I shall send the exact sources. Convey my expressions of unforgetful friendship to your wife.

Sincerely Yours,

Tro-tsi Twang Panattapam McCaltex

CIII★

April 13

Zachary! I understand! One letter lost! Not the *i* in "marriage"! But this blue secret one, quick read it, only now it came back to me, for I sent it from the "General Delivery, Florence", and last week I wrote them for mail coming when I am in Lerici and here (Genova)—look on it, they have marked redly "not authorized enclosure"—it is my own, Twang's sprig of rosemary that had brought it back for more stamps, but why should I return to that post office, it is the sprig I sent from my very window pot that has poisoned the time. I have thought in late weeks, he is acting his part very well for the spies, even: is it truth? a little only, my Zachary, for that is more than I can think long without dying. Today this letter comes, not until today because of the strike patterns, and before when I wake up—I came into a hotel in the first mountains, for their sweet air—I have seen a daisy, a tardy orange, a cow: I ask, what joy will come upon me? It is you. I can

★Special delivery. Letter of January 3 attached.

understand, and you shall not be lost! Oh I admit that the tears stream down my cheeks. It is as that which was tumbled is raised or what was hidden is unclosed, some yellow rose, like the right road pointed to she who was lost or a light brought into the dark for those who have eyes to see. Yes my cheeks are wet. Come to wipe them with that torn kleenex. Not as that other trip then I believed you must have the softest brain! Because you write "dictionary" and "Pogy O'Brien", that is some accident, and you think the lies I composed for them are true, I have such miseries inflicted on you it is not to be thought about. Now it shall be new, and today the New Year starts in my country, I say Happy New Year and this and all other that ever I shall speak to you is true. True as it can be born, wrapped in kindness of love, for in these lying letters I have said some real things, I thought, I shall not waste all the time I shall tell him of our believes and thus my short course in Buddhism but not meant so cruel, indeed there is truth in my words over your mother, whom I bewept so, I must flee into the graveyard, yet it was from my shame to have never kissed the hands of her who gave you into the world and this, is selfishness; however I would not have spoken with that cruel written tone. Never! my Zachary.

There's too much, to tell now, together I shall tell everything, we can smile and weep about all that. But some explanation—for instance the treasure was always here! That story about the abbot, and Amortonelli, that was crazy to me, then I think, you are fascinated by the intellectual problem viz. map, but Twang think rightly: cash. And other mistakes —*familiari* only meaning "family", and sacks bearing the treasure, and *torcere* not to "throw" the gold only wrap it, as many did in that historical period when the exchange rates were bad, and the crows on the brocade, a stupidity of Lionetto and making for me early suspicion because when I hunted through all the timely papers there were crowns, crosses, croziers but never crows! There were only ever the Medici *palle*, their balls as in the shout *Evvivano le palle!* so I write this cry but it misses you. No the treasure was always in Casa Pindola and that day Bonzo showed me the remainder of the Averardo heritage when I saw the old silk I have a pulse of about eight hundred, and he saw nothing. He believes those stories.

Ah the Prince, the Pindola, they are giggles—are such the tough men of the west it is to be the famous yellow takeover. They thought I shall seem to come by accident into their company? they shall make me so dependant on them, then trap me, then scare me absolutely off? I know when I meet little Bonzo he cannot rape a sponge, most clearly they are longing for that map. Now they have it. The police scared me to give it to them!?—do they think I have no memories, these "policemen" that invade my room were with that Hood in Rome as he argued modern thought. Quickly I decided, I must win Bonzo from the Prince, and never leave the Prince to suspect me, and it was for this our letters were the clinch. Sometimes it has been hard. For the American trip I had to sneak out in the mask of an old dame, that I made from the padding of my quilt, some pasted across my brows. But only now can they know.

Thus it was: Bonzo and I escape out of Florence. In a day the Prince notifies Bonzo he has shifted all blame onto him. So, Bonzo can say to me, watch out, I Twang am an accomplice, I shall better stick to him. This is so he can stick to *me*, to watch me, not let me warn you, should I know their plans to use the map. I was content for I needed some time to harass the Pindola about the chest. Already I grasp Bonzo tight—we shall marry! That is the "certain agreement" that at first I did not explain. So foolish the man was, it was I Twang who must beg him to marry with property in common—he thinks still that I am rich, he thought I asked money from you because I'm so tough I shall not lose one cent. I teach him, it is wrong for a wife to own more than a husband.

In Lerici we wait, nothing to do. I'm hard to him. One day I say I want that chest as an engagement present, he said, a stupid idea, it weighs some quintals. I twrist his arm harder. Still he thinks it cannot be, also it is his father's. I said the old fellow's gaga, I want the antique silk, some will be found from the rot to sew into my wedding gown; and promise to be nicer to him, oh much nicer.... O.K.! He orders that the chest be sent in a truck. That evening on the beach, I must (dear one you shall please forgive) I must, so that he keep his mind away from that decision, I consent to "grant him my favors" as he has always begged. So I "screw my courage to the sticking point," and vice versa, but he becomes so surprised that he was not able to fuck me. He just falls prostate to my feet. No matter, I have warned the police to be near and I tear some buttons in the dusk and scream and Bonzo is in the jail as rapist at last.

I kept the man there as long is needed. He cannot call the Prince to help, not without revealing the joke about the Prince turning against him. Then I let him out, annulling charges. To Bonzo I said that on the beach he hit me in one of his madnesses and I thought he wished to kill me. He cannot remember through the shocks, I insist and scold him and he believes, such a kreep! and even's lowly ashamed. I say then, Off to Florence, prepare our wedding, it is Pan custom for the bride to be far from the coming husband, away! He did not want to go, it was a terrible struggle, but since it all took place inside him, I did not mind.

Meanwhile the Hood had come to Florence on March 22. This had made me think there is trouble on foot; this is why I force Bonzo hard. Hood must first have thought that Mauss had stolen the treasure, and made him arrested. But he learned soon there was no gold there, they had dug up a chest of bad silk. (And are they the first to know this—for Amortonelli and the captain I think never could look themselves into the chest, they believed the weight, or did not want the shoveling sailors to see.) I deduce that after this, they all look again at my letters and know the secret is in the Medici archives. They must have those bags, while I am kept away. They start the fire in the old library, so they can run in and "help". This was a guess, I only heard information on the radio pogrom; but next I read two burned in the fire, their names were of the little bodyguards. They must steal the bags of papers with the numbers they found in my notes. Well, I telephoned the police to look for those papers at the Prince's. They are several arrested. Not Hood, he's a wily man, you were my dear one in the hands of a very bad hat! Yet Bonzo arrives in time to climb aboard the padded wagon.

So now the Prince and Pindola shall drop their marbles where they may. Poor Bonzo, again in jail! He's wrong for such work, being a sure psychopath—those rages, those callapses. It is said, also, that only old age can cure the psychopathic personality, and if there is a thing Bonzo does not wish it is the growing old.

Hastily I must tell you one last discovery, then I shall run with a taxi to the central post office and send you this. I confess, I have indulged one extra research. It was because the name of Salvestro's mother, not the Christian one given, but her own from the east, is Twang—or, *Tuan*, but even now the Italians call me thus. I have laughed and believed nothing but chance there, yet anyway I inquired. She was twenty-five years old in 1431, therefore she was likely born in Tana, or better on the way from Tana and this is why she had no marks. Was her mother able to be Pan, and so far from our country? That was not probable, it was possible. I wondered: where did Salvestro go with her, when he left Italy? And asked for your microfilms. One more thing to love you for. The missionaries are established in time. So I could learn that Salvestro the Spice Trader came there, to Pannam Tuan's home, he has married in 1489 and his children were baptized later. I laugh some more and write my father, and he has told me that in a little chapel at the village Namma Bamma there is a western portrait of a male that has been cleaned last year, and scholars call him Francesco de' Medici! Salvestro's father! That village is next to ours, to that village where you came to me, my Zachary, and consider it is perhaps from Salvestro that I am born, with his mother's name that is saved through our family, a rare name, and also my first name, in Pannam this is a reference to my hero protector, usually of legend, but think that Tro-tsi, Salve*stro* Medi*ci*, do you recall how we called you Kri until I could master your beloved name, cutting off the last sound to mean the foreign word? And therefore I shall be the treasure's heir? *Evvivano le palle!*

For I have it. That chest came to Lerici, I climbed into the truck, opened it. Under the shreds my arm stuck into the gold bits from the fingertips to my elbow. I filled one palm for expenses, and your ticket. At once I had brought a big chain and bound it and without leaving it off the truck forward it to Genoa. And after I released Bonzo and he left to Florence, I followed.

The affair is done. Early I went today to the shipping offices and made almost every arrangement, it was only not possible to get much insurance, tomorrow I'll argue more about that —it is for this why I did not write until this afternoon, it must all be done! Oh that letter made me bad in business. A gentleman asked, "What must be the date of arrival?" and I answered, "He is the most exquisite of men." Another desired to know, "Is there a Burmese address?" I replied, "Perhaps he will be here Sunday." One needed to be told, "How are we to declare these goods?" "Not leave him for an hour!" were my words. Yet the matter was concluded, and at noon the chest was already sunk in to the hold of the *Odradek Stadion*, a vessel that is property of the Malta Cross Shipping Company of Panama, chartered by Metternich Services Anstalt, a Swiss-registered company with offices in Liechtenstein, fitted out in Greenore, Eire, carrying U.S. equipment, and a Dutch captain and crew! At least, it keeps the Panama flag. It will carry the box to Rangoon, best market of gold in this material-subtle world.

The weather is of heaven, *langoureux vertige*, spring fever. Through gentle air, my mind fills up with such a goodness of love for you, my beloved and ever-desired, towards the west expanding first, over the seas, promontories and islands that make you distant from me, thinking: you are to tell me today as you see these words, that I shall very soon have the honor of kneeling again at your feet when you consent to come here, oh most soon. For until that hour I can live only in expectation of this, meditating on your perfection. I shall tell you, the vainest man never found in his mirror half the beauty I see in you, your way, your voice, every glance motion and gesture has such radiance my whole being is possessed and there is no life for me except in the hope of your affection. I cannot say it, only I love you with the most wild passion that ever came into woman. I wish my life's action to be discovering of means to convince you that you are preferable to everything pleasant on earth. My mind is so full, so full of you, Zachary! It swells in this goodness all of love over the world, then to the north, now I see some lightning of first summer warmths, and it's as I shall feel of you when first I see you distant, still faceless; and south, there are I believe shells on the beach and I remember that never will you collect them, I'll be a shell you can just walk on my uncollected skull if that be your pleasure; and east, the sun, the golden sword of new life! Come soon! And up to the sky, a big blue cranium—no that is not the flower name I want, but you can understand I desire to symbolize my desire, while below the earth would have me of course reminded of Mister Dharmabody, you must bring him no matter how old and worn he has become, and I think I must make him to bite me for that blow, it was not you it was Twang inflicted that. So much love within me, spreading about, what is there it will not enfold—perhaps my typhoid germs? which were yesterday innoculated into me, and it's plain the immunizing produces a tough form of that disease! It pierces the whole world. You are to be emperor of the world in my explosion adoration, I'll drag you *nel giallo della rosa sempiterna,* do you know, into the yellowness of the eternal rose, that opens, clambers, casts perfumes of praise to the sun that lasting springmaker, and I shall hope, it does not make your hair grow again, that smoothness is pleasanter—the bodily hair is what most disconcerts in occidentals, and without it also your fat shall be a gentle smooth quality only with hair is it terrifying. I shall pluck my pubis smooth as yours. Yet Zachary, do not although I say these eat every food, not for fat and thin, but I shall recall, "Whatever food a man eats in this life, by that food he is eaten in the next." It seems my head my breast will break with my love of you, or I shall be a balloon, I'll float through a grand landscape that shines, yellow pots big as mountains, platters like luminous cities, glasses and crackery like valleys like expressways, as if they were blazing in yellow lights, from below and above, but all arranged in round ranks and balancing as one thing on a broomstick as long as an ocean, and we are in the middle of the ranks of dishware thinking we are becoming insane from too much love, no, it is only these things are harmless—but this morning, I made a little altar in my room. I set incense and flowers on it. This was that I might exhibit, to myself, Twang's grief of your suffering. Each morning I shall put new incense, flowers, until you are next to me. Now you take five dollars even if your last and send a cable. I have telephoned but it will not answer, and shall wire but you will not believe it, but you must go to the air office, and there is the ticket to Italy for you, and I shall this time be waiting at the airport of Rome. There can be no more error, it is no longer in my power, there is no more harm in our mind there is no limit there is no hatred of anything breathing or un-breathing—it is a mind without knowledge of ill will, my Zachary! but you must come. Alone I cannot carry this burden of joy, and doubt

Index

to *The Sinking of the Odradek Stadium*